ALONE TOGETHER

Mattie glanced at the clock. Midnight, straight up. The witching hour.

During the past ten days, she'd probably spent more time with Collier in this kitchen than she'd spent with him all total during all the years he'd been married to her sister. And she couldn't remember ever being alone with him before. Or if she had, she hadn't noticed. But she *must* have noticed. Collier wasn't the kind of man a woman could be alone with and forget.

Unless the woman was determined not to remember.

KAREN CRANE

THE
GOOD
SISTER

ZEBRA BOOKS
Kensington Publishing Corp.
www.kensingtonbooks.com

ZEBRA BOOKS are published by

Kensington Publishing Corp.
850 Third Avenue
New York, NY 10022

All Kensington titles, imprints, and distributed lines are available at special quantity discounts for bulk purchases for sales promotion, premiums, fund-raising, educational, or institutional use.

Special book excerpts or customized printings can also be created to fit specific needs. For details, write or phone the office of the Kensington Special Sales Manager: Attn: Special Sales Department. Kensington Publishing Corp., 850 Third Avenue, New York, NY 10022. Phone: 1-800-221-2647.

Zebra and the Z logo Reg. U.S. Pat. & TM Off.

ISBN 0-8217-7695-9

First Printing: March 2006
10 9 8 7 6 5 4 3 2 1

Printed in the United States of America

*This book is dedicated to Jane Toller and Shirley Johnson,
for showing me what it means to be good sisters.*

*And in memory of Lois Gideon and Effie Jackson,
who showed them what it meant.*

*And for DeAnn Tracy,
the best gift my aunt ever gave me—
a little sister of my own!*

Grateful acknowledgment to:

Maureen Scoggins and her son, Chad, for sharing their knowledge of Holt-Oram Syndrome.

The staff of Cherry Street Dance Studio, for answering my many questions.

Roberta Montgomery, for support and understanding and friendship.

Jodie Larsen Nida, for helping with the details.

Debbie Widuch, for the massages that got me through the pain.

Laura Peterson, for being smart, supportive, and the best agent in the world.

Genell Dellin, for help along the way.

Paula Hamilton, for being a better friend than I deserved.

And last, but not by any means least, my husband, Don, and daughter, Jill, who always wind up being the encouraging voices that say, "Yes, you can."

Thank you, in every language.

CHAPTER ONE

The first time Mattie disappeared, it took two hours to find her.

Not because she chose a great hiding place—she was, after all, only five years old—but because it took that long for her mother to miss her.

The next time she disappeared, she hid on purpose because she didn't want to go to her sister's stupid piano recital. Her mother found her in less than thirty minutes that time and she got grounded for a week because she'd made them late.

By her ninth birthday, Mattie had perfected her disappearing act. That day, her birthday, she made it all the way to Wichita—a hundred and fifty miles from home—on a Trailways bus. She promptly phoned her dad, who promptly called her mother, who promptly told him that no way was she driving clear to Kansas to pick up their daughter and, since Mattie had finally made good on her threats to find him, she could just

stay there from now on and he would have to deal
with her.

But the new Mrs. Joseph Owens didn't care for that
idea and convinced her husband that his incorrigible
daughter would have a detrimental effect on their two
young sons. So Joe, born to live between the prover-
bial rock and a hard place, caved in to the pressure
and reluctantly—or so he said—returned Mattie to
Reyes City and her mother. With tears in his eyes he
explained that he couldn't take care of her and that
she needed to stay with her mother and sister and not
show up at his house again without an invitation.

Mattie knew what that meant.

She wouldn't be going to live with her dad. She
wouldn't, in fact, be seeing him again.

And if she had to stay home, disappearing looked
like the only way she would ever get her mother's
attention.

From then on she put a lot less planning into her
disappearances, leaving whenever the mood hit her
and returning when she was good and ready. She
never stayed away long, only for short unaccounted-
for interludes when she deemed her absence would
cause the most inconvenience for her mother and
Meredith. An afternoon here. Most of the night there.
Long enough to get noticed. Long enough to get into
trouble.

"You're grounded until further notice" became the
most frequent words her mother said to her. "Like I
care" was her standard reply. It was only when Meredith said, "What's wrong with you, Mattie?" that she
actually felt she'd done anything wrong.

But then, next to Meredith, how could she ever do anything right?

For a while, in the throes of adolescence, Mattie ran wild. If she couldn't do anything right, she decided she might as well make a religious effort to do everything wrong.

Except, as it turned out, she wasn't very good at that, either.

While rebellion had its pleasures, she discovered it took considerable effort and held the prospect of a lifetime of regret. Vanishing for a few hours here and there was one thing. Plunging all-out into the netherworld of mutiny was another. The new friends she had cultivated pierced and polluted their bodies with foreign objects and illegal substances and, while Mattie wanted to be as careless with herself as they were, as oblivious to the cost and consequences of their actions, she couldn't bring herself to destroy the one gift she had, the one gift she'd been granted at birth.

Through some magical alchemy of genetics, she'd inherited a lithe and supple body. The body of a dancer. And with it a deep, satisfying joy in the one thing she could do well, the one thing she was confident she did even better than Meredith.

Dance class was Mattie's oasis, her serenity, her bliss. Dancing was her release. Dancing thrilled her, took her spirit and flung it out of the shadows and into a light that was all her own. Dancing made her fearless, gave her hope, set her apart. Dancing offered her knowledge of herself, of the abilities locked inside her graceful, adolescent body, of the possibilities hidden inside her awkward heart. When she danced, it didn't matter whose sister she was or if her mother approved.

It only mattered that she could dance.

But the only reason Mattie was allowed to take classes was because Meredith did. At Miss Victoria's Academy, Meredith shone like a star. Her barre work won accolades from the teacher. Her technique always elicited praise. She won competitions and was encouraged to apply for further training. Miss Victoria couldn't say enough about Meredith's talent, Meredith's dedication, Meredith's gift. But Meredith didn't care about dance. She didn't hate it, but she didn't love it either. Being good at something without having a passion for it—Meredith excelled in that, too. She didn't even have to pretend she loved ballet to be good at it. Better than good.

But in this one thing, Mattie knew she was better.

Meredith dazzled people. Mattie didn't. And so no one saw her talent or noticed her passion.

Except Meredith.

Meredith, who took classes long after she might otherwise have stopped because she knew that if she quit, Mattie would have to as well.

Meredith, who found her little sister's fierce desire to dance a curiosity and who enjoyed the role of benevolent older sister, of making a sacrifice—albeit not much of one—to purchase Mattie's loyalty and devotion.

Meredith, who liked knowing that Mattie envied her the attention she so effortlessly received from the teachers.

Meredith, who found pleasure in having the power

to bestow this gift on Mattie or snatch it away on a whim.

But as long as she got to dance, Mattie didn't care. She'd do anything to feel the way she felt when she danced.

So her time as a hellion was short-lived and would have passed without a major incident if she hadn't done a couple of incredibly stupid things.

Even though she'd mostly avoided the temptation to use drugs, she hadn't had the sense to avoid the pals who used them or the parties where they were plentiful. And she got busted for possession. Not once, but twice.

The dust had barely settled on those offenses before she committed another. On a dare from one of her new buddies, she stole a purse and some jewelry, shoplifted it practically right in front of her mother, who was at the time chatting with a friend, who also happened to be the store manager.

Alice, already horrified and humiliated by Mattie's other mix-ups with the law, determined this time her troublesome daughter needed a good, hard lesson she would long remember. The long and the short of that decision was that Mattie had to spend two weeks at a juvenile detention center and six months doing community service work afterward. A harsh sentence, instigated by her mother, who was good friends with the judge's wife, but one Mattie weathered without breaking.

Her spirit bucked, though, when Alice told her she was no longer allowed to take ballet.

Like she was going to give *that* up.

This time, she meant to disappear for good and

would have spent the rest of her teen years as a runaway if not for Meredith.

*"You can't leave me, Mattie. You don't know what it's like
for me when you run away. I know you don't think she worries about you, but she does. And she's hateful and mean to
me when you're not here. If you're going, I'm going with you."*

And if Meredith went, they'd be found in an hour.

*"Don't you dare go without me, Mat. I'll tell her everything
I know. Where you go. Whom you stay with. I'll tell her and
she'll find you. And she'll lock you up and you'll never ever
get to take lessons ever again."*

And Meredith knew all of Mattie's secrets. Over the
years, she'd wheedled the information a piece at a
time. After every disappearance, Meredith had to
know the details and Mattie, ever the sucker for her
sister's flattery, had revealed her every resource.

*"I'll help you. She'll listen to me. And if she doesn't, I'll
cover for you. Just don't disappear again, okay? I'll hate you
forever if you leave me. I swear, Mattie. I will."*

In the end, Mattie had stayed. She lied about her
age and got a job stocking groceries in a local convenience store. Miss Victoria, forewarned and
informed by Alice, wouldn't continue Mattie's lessons, but there were other teachers. Mattie burned
through every one in town and managed, with Meredith's help, to stay one step ahead of her mother. For
every door Alice slammed shut, Mattie scrambled to
open another and through high school, she never
once stopped dancing.

She graduated without honors and set her sights on
the big city. Alice's lack of support had cost her the opportunity to train with a professional company, but
Mattie meant to discover what else she could do with

her gift. And when she drove away from Reyes City with her mother's predictions of failure ringing in her ears, she saw a world of opportunity spooling out before her like the highway under her wheels.

Thirteen years later, she'd learned a lot about opportunities lost and gained and she'd come to uneasy terms with the idea that her relationship with her mother would most likely always be a thousand shades of gray.

Not one of them as pretty as the winter dusk that shifted and settled around her as she stood at the gate outside the old Trummell House, her right hand curled over a curlicue of iron fencing.

The big house rose like a crown on its crest of hill, two-storied and multi-windowed, a gem of 1920s architecture, a sturdy white candle in a dark, dark night. Wrapped by a swath of southern-style veranda, the house seemed impervious to the intrusion of streetlights and the soft, electric glow from neighboring houses on Dewey Street. Of course, Meredith's house would be a leftover mansion, majestic and grand and lit from within. Even the darkened windows reflected an intangible energy, as if each person who had ever sought shelter inside had left behind a whisper of life force that couldn't be entirely contained and so spilled outward across the lawn, toward the city, into the fathomless sky and the universe beyond. As a child, Mattie had loved this house from a distance. She'd imagined it as belonging to a big, boisterous family where parents smiled approval at each other and upon each child. She'd imagined it as the house in which her childhood could have passed in a happy haze. She'd imagined it as the house where someone who loved her would be waiting for her to come home.

She'd never imagined it as a house that would belong to her sister.

A brisk wind whipped by in a flurry of winter angst and the January chill crept into Mattie's consciousness like a memory. Indistinct and uncomfortably cold. A wisp of conversation that floated away and then returned as a shape, a smoky sound that became her sister's voice in some far-distant past, some long-gone moment.

Stop running away, Mattie. What do you expect Mom to do when you disappear like that? Call out the cops?

Behind her now, on the street, two black-and-white cruisers sat by the curb like fat cats ready to pounce on some unsuspecting prey. Mattie didn't have to turn around to know they were empty, that the policemen who manned them were inside, talking to Collier, to her mother, to anyone in the house who might provide the slightest clue to her sister's disappearance.

Meredith is missing.

If ever there were two words that didn't belong in the same breath, it had to be those. *Meredith missing.* In all her life, Meredith had never made a misstep. So how could she be missing?

Inhaling a sharp breath of frigid air, Mattie jerked her gloved hand off the gate, leaving a few desolate blue threads frozen on the iron bar. If she stayed outside much longer, she'd freeze into an icicle, numb to the core, and still she'd have to face the people and the situation on the other side of those ornate double doors.

Meredith didn't come home last night. No one's seen her since yesterday around noon. The police are looking, but . . .

It didn't take a rocket scientist to know Collier had called Mattie only as a last resort, that he had to have been desperate to ask her to come here and care for her mother until Meredith's return. The first few times they met, Mattie had thought he actually liked her and she'd liked him in return, thought she might enjoy having a brother-in-law. But then, practically overnight, his warmth toward her cooled and, taking her cue from him, she'd pretended there had never been any warmth to begin with.

She could readily imagine what had happened, figured her mother had felt it was her duty to inform him of Mattie's checkered past and her run-in with the law. Probably on the premise that Collier was planning a career in politics and needed to know any potential problem that might arise in future campaigns. Alice would have done a great job of painting the portrait of a problem child, too, described the difficulties she'd faced as Mattie's parent, emphasized the stark contrast between Mattie and Meredith.

As if Collier wasn't smart enough to see that for himself.

The wind returned, slivered through her like a sharp reprimand and she let it flail her cheeks and lips with its bitter cold until her whole face stung. Yet she couldn't get her feet to take the final steps of her day's long journey. Just being in Reyes City diminished her in ways she'd couldn't name. Just standing outside the door of her sister's life brought back an embarrassed yearning to belong inside. And she would never belong. Not really. She knew that. She accepted it . . .

until she found herself back here, in the place where she would always be treated as something less than she was, where she could never be anything more than Meredith's sister.

Stop running away, Mattie.

Meredith's voice resurfaced, a memory stuck in her head like the cashmere threads from her gloves stuck to the icy condensation on the gate. Any attempt to remove the traces of blue from the metal would only result in more casualties, further loss to the glove. And the gate wouldn't feel a thing.

A fine mist saturated the air and she inhaled the cold dampness as well as the come-hither scent of firewood and warmth. One more deep breath, then she picked up her suitcase, pushed open the gate, and walked briskly up the paved pathway to the house. She took the stairs nimbly, avoiding the slick patches that shone like silvered mirrors on the thick concrete steps, moved with purpose across the wide veranda, and jabbed the doorbell with a gloved finger tingling from the cold. Inside the house, Big Ben chimes tolled a deep, mellow summons and, a moment later, she heard footsteps, hurried and urgent. Her mother flung open the door, expectant, hopeful, fearful—and disappointed.

Always the disappointment. Mattie wondered why that still caught her by surprise.

"Hello, Mother."

Alice sighed. "Mattie."

Another mother, another daughter in the same uncertain circumstances and they might have fallen into each other's embrace, sharing a fear they couldn't speak aloud, finding solace in the solid presence of the other. But Alice simply turned away, back into the golden-toned interior of Meredith's house, leaving Mattie to follow. Or not.

Her place in the doorway was quickly taken by a large dog, a clipped and coiffured black poodle, who regarded Mattie with suspicion and a disappointment even greater than her mother's.

"Hello, André."

The dog stepped back, wary, a growl of warning curled on his lips.

So much for being welcome.

And out of the blue an ache of loss swept over her. A longing for the sister of her childhood. A yearning for the one person who, however indifferently, had always been there to welcome her.

Meredith would have welcomed her now, if only because her sister was an immaculate hostess and honored protocol above personal preference. But then, if Meredith were here to welcome her, Mattie wouldn't have come. There would have been no call in the early morning hours, no request to make the journey from Texas to Oklahoma, no need for Mattie at all.

She stepped across the threshold, out of the cold night and into the sunny beauty of the house. Beneath her feet, the polished sheen of the aged oak floor reflected the golden light of the chandelier that hung from the foyer's high ceiling. The walls held close to a century's worth of welcome, laughter, and greetings, the hellos and good-byes of other generations, the ringing echoes of visitors past. And yet, the moment Mattie closed the door, her sister's shadow enveloped her.

Meredith's presence was everywhere. In every fleck of paint, in the artful scattering of mail on a low credenza, in the fresh flowers—Meredith's favorite yellow gladiolas arranged with leatherleaf and baby ferns held in the blue Baccarat vase. She was present in the satin luster of the banister railing and in the evenly spaced fringe surrounding the large oval, antique Turkish rug. Her perfect touch and perfect style branded the room as undeniably as fingerprints. Her presence filled every breath Mattie took in. Even her favorite perfume—Paloma Picasso—lingered in the air like the final line of a poem.

"Don't you understand, Mat? I wanted to be the Sugarplum Fairy. I was supposed to get cast as the Sugarplum Fairy! Not as dumb old Clara."

Meredith's voice again rose unbidden from Mattie's memory album.

"But it's *Clara*," Mattie had answered, starstruck by her sister's coup in landing a role she herself craved with all of her ten-year-old heart. "You get to dance the part of Clara in the Nutcracker Ballet. I'd give anything to dance in your place."

"So take my place. Be Clara. I'll just sit in the audience and watch."

But in the end, of course, there had never been any doubt as to which sister would dance as Clara in the production and which sister would sit in the audience and applaud.

Dropping her suitcase where she stood, Mattie stripped off her gloves as she walked briskly, purposefully toward the room where her mother had gone, the room that after their first visit together to this house, Mattie's fiancé, Jack, had begun privately referring to with great amusement as "Miss Scarlett in the Library with the Chandelier."

Suddenly that didn't seem so funny.

Behind her, the dog followed at a cautious distance, his nails clicking a manicured tattoo on the floor. She paused in the doorway, unsure what her role would be in this unfathomable drama, uncertain if she'd be included in the search or treated as the outsider her brother-in-law considered her to be.

There were no policemen in sight, so Mattie concluded they must be elsewhere in the house or out in the night, canvassing the neighborhood for information about Meredith.

Collier, standing to one side of his desk, glanced up, but his eyes met hers for only an instant before he looked away and continued with a low conversation on the telephone. Handsome, composed, controlled. All of those adjectives and more could describe her brother-in-law and still not do justice to his inherent charisma. He was invariably polite to Mattie, seldom saying more than common courtesy demanded, but never saying less either. She was slightly in awe of him and, while she hadn't been around him that much over the eight years of his marriage to her sister, she could tell that the last twenty-four hours had taken a toll. She'd never seen his hair disheveled, wouldn't have guessed he raked his hands through it when he had something on his mind. She'd never seen him wear anything but a suit and certainly never with his shirt open at the throat, minus a tie and its pristine Windsor knot. She could never have imagined him in any state as casual as now, with his white shirt wrinkled, untucked, and blousing on the right side, the sleeves rolled haphazardly to his elbows. She'd never for a moment suspected he could look like a man who didn't know exactly what to do.

If she'd been casting an actor to play the role of the husband whose wife has suddenly, mysteriously disappeared, Mattie would have cast him in a heartbeat. He looked that distraught. And that controlled.

A woman, youngish, pencil thin and attractive, with an aura of good education and teeming ambition, leaned against a corner of the desk, talking on a cell phone, far enough from Collier so that her conversation needn't intrude on his. She dismissed Mattie in a glance, turning her pretty, well-coifed head away, lowering her voice even further, as if wary of an eavesdropper.

There was a deadly quiet inside this room. A raging stream of unspoken thoughts and unvoiced concerns roared in silence beneath the woman's clipped alto and Collier's deep baritone. Where her presence dominated the foyer, Meredith's absence occupied this room like thunder, far off and startlingly near at the same time. And every breath taken seemed to count the seconds between the boom of recognition and the lightning strike of reality.

Mattie looked for her mother and found her seated, almost hidden, in the alcove of the bay window. With a drink in her hand, Alice stared out at the darkening sky, toward Dewey Street and the lights of the city beyond. Waiting for Meredith. Watching for her safe return. The yearning for her beloved daughter in every line of the straight-backed posture which, Alice was, at seventy-four, still so proud to possess. She looked as she always did. Careful. Hair carefully combed and meticulously sprayed in place. Clothes carefully selected for style and season, carefully creased, carefully casual. Makeup carefully applied to skin that had been carefully cared for and looked fifteen years younger than it was.

Mattie had often studied her mother's appearance, trying to see herself in the shape of Alice's eyes, in the straight lines of her nose, the full curve of her lips, the set of her chin. If there was any resemblance, it had long since been overshadowed by Mattie's wild chestnut curls and the trapped-cat slant of her eyes. She looked like neither mother nor sister and not much like her father. As best she could remember him, at any rate. She'd once seen a picture of his mother, her grandmother, and thought there might have been some similarity there. But it was an old picture, and it had vanished from her life with her father's departure.

Not that it mattered since the only resemblance that might have made a difference had eluded her genetic makeup. She wasn't like her mother and she was nothing like Meredith. In their mother and daughter circle of two, she'd always been the odd one. The redhead. The plain one. The daughter who didn't belong. The second child her mother hadn't wanted in the first place.

She's not the mother you knew, Mattie. She's not herself, anymore.

Meredith had said that the last time she and Mattie had spoken on the phone. But looking at Alice now, Mattie could perceive no change, no hint of alteration, and so found it difficult to believe that her mother was any different than she'd ever been.

"Mattie." Collier cradled the phone receiver and came toward her, stopping far short of her personal space, staying well within the comfort zone of his own. "Thank you for coming."

It was his politician's voice, his campaign manners. Mattie watched television. She was an informed voter. She could spot a facade whether it came in the form of a handshake or a kiss on a baby's head. And she thought less of him for using it now, for maintaining a pointless caution at a moment when they had something so important in common. His aloofness etched the scars of indifference a little deeper into her heart. "Any word on Meredith?"

He shook his head, worry clamped like a vise in the tight line of his jaw, in the threads of a frown that crossed his forehead, a steady, studied, unreadable calm on his face. "The police are looking, of course. All we know at this point is that she stopped by the florist's at ten-thirty, bought wine at Grady's, and picked up the dry cleaning at a quarter to twelve. She was going to attend a benefit luncheon at the country club, but she didn't show. There's a state-wide alert. That's it. Not much more than when I spoke to you on the phone this morning."

Meredith is missing.

And Mattie's brain stuck stupidly on the thought that Meredith's absence had him rattled. He'd probably repeated that litany of events dozens of times already and still it sounded rushed, uneven, and improbable. Because how could it be real? How could life have shifted so suddenly from perfect order into such uncertainty? "I had the radio on during the trip up," she said, wanting him to know, somehow, that she felt just as out of place in this moment as he did. "But I didn't hear anything about it."

He paled slightly and one hand clenched and unclenched at his side. "The local stations ran a brief clip at five and I'll be making a statement for the six and ten o'clock broadcasts. After that, well, you never know what will happen with a story like this one."

Headlines from other similar stories flipped like flash cards through her thoughts. Names and events that snagged the public's attention. Stories that captivated strangers with the lurid details of a formerly ordinary life. Reports, investigations, trials that aired daily, then weekly, then gradually faded into the collective subconscious. Meredith would be disappointed if her story didn't make it onto prime time. She was a former Miss Oklahoma, a top ten finalist in the Miss America Pageant, and the current first lady of Reyes City. She'd expect nothing less than national attention. The thought shamed Mattie, although she knew it was no less than the truth.

But the sandy grit of guilt returned just the same, and Mattie transferred it where it rightfully belonged. With Alice. Still in the alcove. Oblivious to everything except the drink in her hand and the darkness outside the window. "Mother's taking this better than I expected."

Collier glanced over his shoulder at his mother-in-law. "You're seeing her after half a bottle of my best Scotch. At this point, I'm not sure she remembers why she started drinking."

"Were the police able to question her? Did her answers make any sense?"

"I don't know. It upset her a lot when they searched the house."

"The police searched your house?"

He sighed heavily, his breath rich with the smell of good Scotch. Alice, obviously, wasn't the only one looking for comfort in a bottle. "Standard procedure when something like this happens."

"What were they looking for?"

He shrugged, either not knowing the answer or unwilling to discuss it with her. "You'll need to keep a close eye on her," he said instead. "She's been unpredictable since her stroke."

Mattie had made the trip up to visit Alice in the hospital then. And been told—by a mother who seemed entirely rational—not to waste time coming back. Meredith would care for her. Meredith knew what to do. Meredith could handle the doctors, the insurance, and whatever else needed to be done. Mattie had tried talking to her sister, had made an honest if unenthusiastic effort to help make the decisions they faced. But Meredith had been pregnant at the time, wrapped up in the glamour of impending motherhood, and disinclined to discuss their mother's health care, present or future.

Their few brief phone calls after Mattie's visit evolved into a spat, which migrated into Meredith announcing—as she always did whenever they had a difference of opinion—that she would handle everything and there was no need for Mattie to give the matter another thought. Which meant there'd be no communication from Meredith at all until she decided to forgive Mattie for being obstinate. In the past the silence usually lasted only a few weeks, but on at least two occasions Meredith had held her grudge for nearly a year. Eventually, though, she'd call Mattie, act as if bygones were bygones and all was forgiven and forgotten. If Mattie had learned nothing else about her sister over the course of thirty-two years, she'd learned that Meredith had to be in charge of the relationship. So when Meredith stepped back, so did Mattie. This time, the silent treatment had lasted through the birth of the baby, and Mattie had broken the rules by phoning the hospital to offer congratulations to the new parents, to try and wrangle an invitation to meet her nephew.

Meredith was having none of that. She told Mattie she'd call when the excitement died down, when the timing was right for a visit. But that call hadn't come. Not until a couple of months later. Then from August into early September, Meredith called every few days, chatting about Alice, thanking Mattie for some little gift she'd sent the baby, talking as if there'd never been a silly spat over their mother's long-term care.

She's not herself, Mattie. She forgets things. She can't remember what she did yesterday, but other days she can repeat, verbatim, what I told her three weeks ago. No, I don't need you to come up here. No, I don't need you to send any money. I don't need anything. I just wanted to let off a little steam, that's all. It's not like I can talk to Collier about this.

It's not like I can talk to Collier. Meredith's words rattled in Mattie's head now with a strange disharmony, then stopped as abruptly as that one month of almost daily phone conversations.

"You can't count on her to think clearly," he continued, drawing Mattie back into the moment, making her wish she had a drink in her hand, too. "One minute, she can be sitting on the sofa and the next minute, she's sitting in the neighbor's car believing she's driving herself around town."

"What does she have against your car?"

Her flippancy bounced off him without leaving a mark. "The Armstrongs next door own a Cadillac very similar to the one your mother used to drive. I don't know what will happen if she's ever able to get her hands on a set of car keys. I can't stress this enough, Mattie. Watch her. She can get away from you like that." He snapped his fingers. Maybe for emphasis. Maybe to be sure she was paying attention.

"I don't think she'll be going anywhere tonight. Not after half a bottle of your Glenfiddich."

His frown summed up his opinion rather neatly. "Watch her," he repeated.

"Collier? Ross wants to go over the statement with you."

The interruption came with a side order of conde-scension, a nudge of there-are-more-important-issues-here, and a cool I-know-what-*I'm*-doing-here toss of dark hair.

Collier's attention made a smooth transition, and in a blink, he was Mayor Montgomery again. "Mattie, this is my assistant, Brooke Brittain. Brooke, this is Meredith's sister."

Mattie nodded, offered a polite smile, and re-assessed the ambition in those pretty almond eyes—eyes she'd be willing to bet hadn't seen the far side of twenty-five yet. It crossed her mind to wonder what Meredith thought of Collier's lovely deputy, and the answer came back like misdirected mail. *Inconsequential.* That would be Meredith's only thought about Brooke Brittain . . . if she'd given the girl any thought at all.

Brooke didn't grant Mattie even a nod of response, focusing all her considerable energy on Collier. "The Tulsa stations are providing network coverage and Ross has to know now if you want to make the statement from here or at the station."

Collier glanced at Mattie, spreading his hands as if facing a difficult choice. "I should take this call," he said, ever the politician, always campaigning for the next vote. "You know your way upstairs. Make yourself comfortable."

Mattie knew a dismissal when she heard one, knew what he expected. "I'll just take my bag upstairs and come right back. We don't want Mother sitting in the window in the newsclips, do we?"

But already he'd turned away from her, moving back toward the desk and back into the command center of his world. The dog shadowed him, a curly cloud of canine gloom.

Mattie watched as he took the phone and raked a steady hand through his thick blond hair. Then she started for the door.

"Miss Owens." The soft injunction stopped her in the doorway and then Brooke came closer. But not too close. "There are two uniformed officers assigned to the house tonight. At present, they're going door-to-door and talking with the neighbors. When they return, they may want to ask you a few questions. I thought you'd want to be prepared."

For a fleeting second, Mattie entertained a suspicion that this snip of an assistant had something to do with her sister's absence. But she knew it for nonsense the moment the idea formed. Brooke, no matter what her ambitions, could only ever dream of being a match for Meredith. "Thanks for the warning," Mattie said. "I'll cooperate in any way I can."

Then she retrieved her bag and trotted up the stairs, pausing when she reached the landing and, only then, because she caught the scent of something out of place. Something familiar, but nothing she could readily name.

Meredith's house always smelled of fresh flowers and citrus cleaners, even though Meredith claimed that on rainy days, it reeked of old pipe tobacco. Mattie hadn't been around cigarette smoke since she stopped working as a bartender, but she had a nose for it and if anyone had ever smoked inside this house, she couldn't find any trace of it. But then, she hadn't stayed in the house very often and never, to her memory, on a rainy day. Still, as her hand grazed the newel post on the turn toward the second floor, a strange new scent, subtle and faint as summer, surrounded her with its strangely seductive charm. Like a child after the Pied Piper, she climbed the remaining stairs, letting her hand drift along the sleek wooden bannister as she chased the aroma of—sifting through memories, she tried to come up with a name for it, define it as a reality she recognized.

Almonds?

No, more like linens dried in the sun. Clover. Dew. Baby.

A smile softened on her lips and Mattie dropped her bag at the top of the stairs, turning not toward the guest rooms but toward the room she knew Meredith had converted into a nursery.

The door was only partially ajar, but Mattie nudged it inward with the palm of her hand, holding her breath, wanting to be quiet so as not to awaken him, yet wanting at the same time to make enough noise so he'd wake and she could see his eyes open, his little cheeks soft and rosy from sleep. A nightlight glowed warmly on the wall behind the crib, casting the room in an artificial moonlight. Soft enough for a sleeping baby, bright enough for a guardian angel. Mattie's eyes adjusted with little more than a blink and she took in the layout of the room in a glance, noted its bright baby colors—muted now in the low light—and its plush baby shapes. The crib, the dresser, even the wooden rocker glowed a warm gold, and thick, cushy rugs formed pools of color and comfort all over the old wood flooring. A jungle mural traveled smoothly across one wall and onto another, shadowed except where the light found and illuminated a smiling giraffe and two mischievous-looking monkeys. The nursery, as perfect and imaginative as only Meredith could make it, was large enough for twins. Or triplets. It had once been two smaller rooms that Meredith had converted into this larger space for her son. A closed door in the east wall opened off the master bath, which opened off the master bedroom. The room where Meredith and Collier could listen for their son's cry.

Blake Benson Montgomery wasn't crying now. He wasn't sleeping, either. Across the room, somewhere on the other side of the multi-colored bumper pads, came low coos and a random throaty gurgle. Mattie's heart lifted at the sound, yearning toward the absolute sweetness of it. She had never considered herself a baby person. She'd never been around children until she opened the dance studio. Even then, they came to her walking and talking, little people, a long way from infancy. But the baby smells and baby sounds in this room felt immediately familiar to her, instantly became a part of her life's treasure. As she watched, two tiny covered feet pummeled the air, and the mobile over the crib bounced shadows and light across the ceiling, where silvery stars reflected it back in dancing pinpricks of white.

Another gurgle and Mattie stepped forward, the floor giving a low creak under her weight. The kicking stopped, the little feet dropping out of sight behind the padding. The baby sounds stopped, too. As if he were listening for her the same way she was listening for him.

Mattie tiptoed closer, afraid she'd startle him if she appeared in his line of vision too fast or moved too quickly. Her hands folded over the top rail of the crib and she looked down at the mound of baby, his fleecy blankets in a tangle beside him, his chubby body covered toe to neck in a downy sleeper. "Hello, Blake," she whispered. "I'm your Aunt Mattie."

His eyes were huge and blue, his little face amazingly familiar, although nothing about him was set. His nose, no bigger than a button. His cupid's bow of a mouth barely over an inch top to bottom and side to side. His cheeks were round and pinked even in the moonlit glow of the nightlight. He was only seven months old, but Mattie saw the stamp of his parentage already. The shape of his eyes was Meredith's. The color a duplicate of Collier's. The oval of his face very much like his father's, his soft swirls of barely there hair the same fairy white his mother's had been as a child. He looked like both Meredith and Collier and yet, not like either of them at all.

He burbled a greeting, kicked and smiled. A big, welcoming smile.

And in that instant, he owned Mattie's heart forever.

Impulsively, she leaned over the railing and reached for his hand. His precious hand, lost somewhere inside the mittened closure of his jammies. But she found it, felt the instant grasp of his fingers closing over hers, and realized something wasn't quite right. She pulled back the cuffed sleeves, thinking there was a wrinkle or fold in the fabric. But when she drew his fingers into the light, she realized there was nothing wrong with his clothes.

There was something wrong with his hands.

Blake's tiny hands, both right and left, looked different, odd, not normal. On closer examination, she could see he had no thumbs, only fingers. Four on the left. Five on the right. A stunted flap of skin low on his left hand might have been the promise of a thumb, but there wasn't even a bump of origination on the right.

The unexpected discovery of his imperfection squeezed Mattie's heart tight, twisted it into a love knot of sorrow, compassion, and empathy. She didn't know what had happened or what had caused the deformity. She had no idea if his lack of thumbs was a minor defect or if it could be easily corrected. She knew next to nothing about babies and nothing at all about the ramifications of this particular problem or how it might affect him now and in the future.

What she did know was that no one, not her mother or her sister or her brother-in-law, had given her so much as a single vague hint that there was anything wrong with her nephew.

In the seven months since the birth, there had been ample occasion for Meredith to have said something, to have at least mentioned this startling fact. But not one word had been said to Mattie about Blake's missing thumbs, not a hint that corrective therapy or surgery could be in his future. Instead Meredith had told Mattie the birth was uneventful, that she was back to her pre-pregnancy weight within a month, that everything was perfect. Absolutely perfect.

And Mattie, falling too easily into the pattern her sister had taught her, accepted the explanations and the idea that Meredith needed to be in control of Mattie's relationship with the baby, too, that she'd mete out visits and access according to whim. Meredith thrived on power. And Mattie had so willingly given it to her.

But suddenly, inexplicably, the picture had shifted and the hurt burned like acid through heart scars so deep Mattie nearly cried out with pain. It hurt to know Meredith had kept this from her, had denied Mattie not just the joy of this beautiful boy, but the tears and the fears for his future as well. How could she have done that? Was that her way of protecting her son?

Mattie pulled back from the crib, not wanting to see the answer, yet knowing in her gut that Meredith hadn't been protecting Blake at all.

She'd been protecting herself.

Meredith, who had always done everything perfectly, wasn't equipped to cope with imperfection, wouldn't understand how to love something—or someone—with an obvious flaw. Two obvious flaws. A right one and a left one.

Tears flooded her throat, misted her vision, and Mattie swallowed them back, not wanting this baby to ever see her with anything but the purest form of acceptance in her eyes.

The baby's fingers still curled around hers and his grip tightened, tugging as he kicked, calling her back. She leaned over the crib again, offered him a tender smile. "Hey, kiddo," she said. "You've got quite a handshake there. Don't ever let anyone tell you otherwise, you hear?"

A bubble of happy spit formed on his lips and burst in a spray of gibberish. Mattie laughed, in love and enthralled. "We're going to be great buddies, Blake Benson. You can take that promise to the bank."

He kicked both legs at once, an easy gallop, and his big eyes turned to watch the distracting stars that bounced across his bed. Releasing Mattie's finger, he reached for the lights, his odd little hands grasping for one pinprick after another after another.

In the hollow of the house below, the doorbell emitted its throaty chimes, and Mattie remembered.

Meredith is missing.

Taking the opportunity he'd offered, Mattie backed quickly out of her nephew's line of vision, tiptoed stealthily backward to the doorway, and then into the hallway. Blake cried once—a sound more of question than demand—and then quieted again to a mumbling contentment.

His easy acceptance of being alone seemed odd to Mattie. But then, she didn't know much about babies.

On the other hand, she knew her nephew had come into the world with an imperfection that in some way shamed his mother. She knew that seven months later her sister had disappeared.

And she hoped—oh, God, she hoped—that one thing had nothing to do with the other.

Because if it did . . .

If it did . . .

Mattie couldn't think past that, couldn't get her mind to close around the possibility.

Meredith is missing.

That was enough to worry about.

For now, that was more than enough.

CHAPTER
TWO

Tucked cross-legged onto the corner of her bed, Mattie pressed the cell phone to her ear while keeping a close watch on her mother's bedroom door across the hall. "She ought to be down for the count, but honest to God, even half-soused, I almost never got her into bed."

"Well, that's where you went wrong. You should have gotten *her* half-soused." Jack's voice, all those thousands of miles away, teased her easily, offered familiarity like a favorite ballad. "Men have been using that method of getting women into bed for centuries."

"Ha, ha. Very funny. I could use a drink about now, but someone needs to stay sober. There's a baby in the house, you know."

"Don't tell me His Honor, the mayor, is hitting the bottle, too."

Jack didn't care much for Collier—or Meredith,

for that matter—and never missed an opportunity to make sure Mattie knew it. She would never ever tell him how long she'd debated about the wisdom of taking him home to meet her family. They'd been living together for nearly a year before she felt secure enough in the relationship to suggest a visit, before she was willing to let him make his own comparisons between her and her sister. Meredith had never taken one of Mattie's boyfriends. None of the boys Mattie dated held the slightest appeal for her sister. Mattie made certain of that, although her caution never kept her dates from falling hard for Meredith just the same.

Meredith was something special. Any male in his right mind would want to be with her if he could.

Jack was something special, too. Movie star looks and a smile that could have women falling like dominoes—when he chose to use it for that purpose. A shock of careless black hair that dipped like a come-on across his forehead. A manly trace of dimples. Eyes like a November sky. A laugh that had everyone around him laughing, too, even if they didn't know what he was laughing about. Three years ago, he'd walked into the Dallas bar where she worked and singled her out for attention within the first ten minutes. She'd been flattered—what woman wouldn't have been? But leery of so much concentrated charm in such a handsome package.

He'd told her later it was her indifference to his obvious interest that reeled him in, that if she'd batted her lashes and waggled her butt, he'd have been in and out of her bed in one night. She'd laughed at him for thinking she'd have ever made it that easy. In the long run, though, she supposed she had been swayed by his obvious appeal. How else to explain why she'd fallen in love with him before her heart and head had a chance to argue? He was perfect. And he loved her. He seemed fascinated by the idea that she was putting herself through college, one class at a time, while working full-time and helping out at a small studio in exchange for lessons from a former prima ballerina. He was equally, if not more, impressed at how hard she was willing to work and scrimp and save so that in the future she could finally open her own dance school. Probably too the idea that he had the means and inclination to grant her wish had held a certain allure for him, although she hadn't recognized that until much later. Jack liked being generous, especially when it didn't cost him any more effort than writing the check. He liked being mysterious too, and she hadn't even known he stood to inherit a substantial fortune until long after her heart had made a commitment.

At the time, that had seemed like the icing on the cake. She was with a man who was handsome, smart, and rich. A man her mother would be unable to find fault with.

That hadn't stopped her from worrying ahead of the visit that somehow Jack would also disappoint Alice. She'd fretted about the possibility that this time Meredith would be intrigued by Mattie's man and that he, in turn, would be intrigued by Meredith. A pointless worry. Stupidly childish even. Meredith was happily married to Collier. They were planning their family. And Jack had been even less interested in Meredith. If anything, Mattie had loved him even more after that.

Even though Alice had made it clear she didn't expect Mattie could hold his interest long enough to get him back to Dallas, much less to the altar.

Mattie toyed now with the thought of telling Jack about the baby, about his oddly shaped hands, about her less-than-generous thoughts about her sister's need for perfection. But then, she didn't. He was in a strange mood. She heard it in his voice, in his effort to sound normal. So she opted for a half-hearted defense of her brother-in-law. "The situation is tense here. It's understandable Collier might have a drink or two."

"Understandable, maybe, but I'll bet you a hundred bucks he's thinking about how this could affect his political career."

"I'll bet you a hundred he's not. He looks like he got sideswiped by a semi."

"She hasn't even been gone two days."

"It's not like she's off on vacation." Mattie felt her irritation rise and blamed it on the anxiety that rode the household like a hobgoblin. "No one has seen or heard from her in nearly thirty-six hours."

"Just a comment, Mat. Not a criticism."

Jack could be very critical when it suited him and, tonight, it bothered her to have his critical eye focused on Collier. From their first handshake, something about Collier had been like a burr in his socks to Jack. Mattie suspected that underneath the comments about *His Honor, the mayor,* Jack envied Collier his position, his purposeful course, and his steady self-confidence. Jack's family could buy and sell Collier's many times over, but Jack had never had to earn an ounce of respect from anyone. Collier had earned every ounce of his. And Jack, for whatever reason, resented him for it.

"Collier's having a rough time," she summed up, determined to be fair, if only to balance Jack's bias. "Right now, he's downstairs preparing a statement for the media. I don't even want to think about how hard that would be."

"She made the news?"

"She's missing, Jack. There's a missing person's report and everything."

"Are the police there? Have you talked to them?"

"Briefly. As I was trying to get Mother to come upstairs."

"What did they ask you?"

"If I'd spoken with Meredith recently. If I had any ideas on where she might have gone. If I thought she could have been having an affair."

"What did you say?"

The effects of the day and the long drive were beginning to form knots of tension across her neck and shoulders. She needed to stretch. She needed to stop talking about this. "I don't remember exactly."

"You don't remember what you told them?"

"No, I told them I don't remember when I talked to her last."

His pause lingered for a moment. "Meredith doesn't seem like the type to have an affair."

"She isn't having an affair. She wouldn't do that. I suspect the police have already ruled that out."

"So is there another theory? Do they think she drove off the road? Got carjacked? Kidnapped? What?"

Sometimes when Mattie imagined the little boy who might one day be theirs, she saw him with Jack's eyes. Jack's good looks. Jack's laugh. Jack's curiosity about all things that caught his interest, however long or short that interest lasted. But somehow, in all her imaginings, she could never see herself in the child. No matter how she focused, he always turned into a miniature Jack. "No one knows what happened," she said. "And if the police do have a theory, I doubt they're going to share it with me."

"They might. If you asked."

The tension drew taut, began to form a headache. "This is my sister we're talking about, you know."

"Curiosity is normal. It's even healthy, and if you had any perspective about Meredith you'd be asking questions instead of waiting around for someone to tell you what's going on."

They'd been living together for a couple of years. They were engaged and planning a wedding. But something had changed once Jack put the ring on her finger. Maybe it was her mother's pessimistic forecast. Maybe the official commitment scared her. Maybe the idea of marriage itself brought the relationship into such sharp focus that Mattie went from pinching herself over her good fortune to worrying that something was missing. Her friend, Andrea, told her she had a classic case of good-luck itis. If life was going this smoothly, something awful was bound to happen. Mattie didn't believe that. Not really. But moments like now, Jack felt lost to her somehow. Distant. As if there was something much more substantial than mere miles between them. As if he was fading from the picture she held of their future.

"Tomorrow is soon enough to ask questions," she said. Then, shifting positions, she pulled a cashmere soft afghan from the end of the bed and wrapped it around her stockinged feet. The feel of the velvety wool almost instantly made her sleepy and she yawned. "How was your flight?"

"Delayed out of LAX. Arrived in Seattle an hour behind schedule. It's foggy. Cold. Rainy. Have I ever told you how much I hate this city?"

"Only every time you go out there." Which was often. Too often to suit Mattie. But when his mother called, Jack went. No questions asked. And sometimes— often during the past year—she called three or four times a month. Jack was the only child of an only child and the only heir to what had once been a vast fortune. His ancestors had blazed a trail to the gold in California, moved north with their stake, and set up a dynasty in the Northwest that amassed money and power for nearly a century. His grandfather had done his best to squander both in an unhealthy obsession to build a one-man submarine and navigate the oceans. He'd died before completely divesting the family of both, but in the process he'd driven his wife to madness and produced a sickly, self-absorbed daughter, who married beneath her and spent most of her life in a chemically induced state of ecstacy or despair. Her only contribution to the world seemed to be the handsome gift of good looks and manipulative charm that belonged to her son. "When will you be back?"

"I don't know. Mother's had another sojourn at the clinic and come home sober enough to piss off the few sane employees who were still willing to work for her. The financial adviser I hired for her last month is already gone, and it won't surprise me if the housekeeper has packed up and left by to-morrow. It's Mother's usual mess and I'll have to stay and clean it up. I'm sorry I can't be there with you, Mat."

She was sorry, too. A little.

"I'm hoping I won't have to stay very long. Meredith's sure to be back home tomorrow, don't you think?"

"I'm probably not the best person to answer that. You and I both know I watch too much television."

Not exactly the reassurance she wanted. "If I need to, I can always pack Mom's suitcase and take her back to Dallas with me."

"If you have trouble getting her into bed when she's half-soused, how are you going to persuade her to set foot inside your car when she's sober?"

"I won't give her a choice. She can't stay alone, and Collier's already got too much to handle without having to deal with her."

"Is he a suspect?"

Mattie blinked. "A what?"

"Do the police think he had anything to do with Meredith's disappearance?"

"What kind of question is that?"

"A legitimate one. The husband's always the first suspect when something happens to the wife. You know that."

"I know my sister didn't come home yesterday, Jack. For now, that's about all the reality I can stand."

"I'm just trying to imagine how a man would cope with losing his wife this way."

"He didn't lose her. For Pete's sake, Jack, show a little understanding. I know you're not crazy about Collier or Meredith, but I'm really scared."

"I'm not crazy about the way Collier and Meredith treat you. Big difference."

It still fell far short of the comfort she'd hoped for when she called him. "I can't talk about this any more right now. I'll call you tomorrow."

"Wait, Mat. I'm a jerk. You have every right to be mad at me. My only excuse is that it's been a hellish day."

And just like that, she wanted to reassure him. "You're not a jerk. Well, most of the time, anyway."

"What do you mean, *most of the time?*" His teasing only vaguely lifted her spirit and only because its familiarity brought a tiny comfort.

Worry and weariness thickened in her thoughts, and she abruptly changed the subject. "I got everything covered at the studio before I left," she said for her own benefit, not because she thought he'd be interested. "Krisinda will manage the office. Summer is teaching the advanced ballet students and the modern dance. Andrea will fold the younger students in with her classes for awhile. Miss Cynthia is a professional. She'll handle anything else that comes up, probably better than I could. Never fear, I left your investment in very good hands."

"On good feet, you mean. Or maybe, on *pointe.*"

She smiled, not feeling better, but not feeling worse, either. "I'll call the minute we hear from Meredith," she promised.

"Call as often as you can. If I don't answer the cell, leave a message. I want you to keep me in the loop, okay? I love you. I hope you know that."

"I know, Jack." But she couldn't bring herself to say she loved him, too. "I'll call."

"Great." And he was gone. No drawn-out goodbye. No hesitation in simply disconnecting. Jack had already turned his attention to whatever something or someone was next in line.

Turning off the phone, she tossed it behind her on the bed. Eyeing the closed door of the bedroom opposite her own, she wondered if she could peek in on her mother without disturbing her. An optimistic thought, although unrealistic. Her very presence disturbed Alice.

Coming home was like wading into an unfriendly ocean. The further into the water she went, the harder she had to fight to keep her balance.

There'd been a lot of times in her life when Mattie had wished she could stop being Meredith's sister. Other times when she'd wished she could just *be* Meredith. And even other times when she'd wished Meredith would simply disappear off the face of the earth. That thought stirred a twist of guilt, which turned and pointed a finger at her.

Meredith is missing.

As if this was somehow her fault.

As if she'd wished Meredith out of existence.

Reaching up, she yanked out the elastic scrunchie that held her willful hair in place. Squiggly curls bounced and settled around her face, fell in a springy sigh to her shoulders. She combed her fingers through the silky mass, lifting it off her neck and letting it fall again, before massaging the back of her head where the weight of hair had rested since she'd caught it up and fastened it there this morning.

Meredith is missing.

What a strange twist in a day that had started out so normal.

In a journey that had taken her only about four hours, she'd traveled from her own life into her sister's. And tonight, once again, she'd sleep in her sister's shadow.

If she hadn't been so tired, the idea would have kept her awake.

Collier cupped the glass in his hand as if it were a bird he'd captured, protective of the spirits it held, the strength he so desperately hoped it could give him. The windows were shuttered now, the drapes closed against any prying camera lens that might be—undoubtedly was—still trained on his house. He was hardly a celebrity. Not yet, anyway. Only the mayor of a small metropolis. Only a man with an eye on loftier goals. A seat in the state legislature. A run for the governor's office. Maybe the Senate after that. On a few private occasions of grandiose ambition, he'd even imagined himself in the Oval Office. Only last month, he'd received a visit from a state party official who'd asked if he had any interest in being the dark horse candidate in next fall's gubernatorial race. They were looking for someone with a political future to run against the incumbent, although in truth, they didn't expect to win.

He knew he'd been one of several who'd received such a visit. The party was looking for a strong candidate, but in lieu of a clear contender, they'd opt for someone young enough to overcome an election loss.

Collier wanted that campaign. Wanted it badly.

But tonight it meant nothing. Tonight he couldn't imagine being a candidate for any office. He couldn't even imagine ever going back to work in his office at City Hall.

Tonight he was simply a man whose wife had vanished. Tonight he was a man—usually known for saying what he thought and sticking to his word—who for the first time in his life hadn't been able to utter a coherent sentence. Tonight he'd put his helplessness and raw emotion on display for the public to see. Tonight he'd begged for his wife's safe return.

Meredith's disappearance had humbled him, shown him how vulnerable he was to pure, rotten chance.

And the cameras had captured it all. The anger. The panic. The helplessness. Like giant leeches, they'd clamped onto his weakness and sucked it up in a mass of pixels, turning his anguish into a feast for the public's consumption. Politics was his chosen vocation, the only career path he'd ever truly considered. His grandfather had tutored him in the art of disciplining his manners and speech, culling out careless words and any undignified display of emotion, thinking before he reacted, thinking again before he spoke, being—at all times—politically correct. One unconsidered word could cost him everything.

Tonight, for the first time, he'd been a man who couldn't remember why that had ever mattered.

Tell us, Mayor Montgomery. How do you feel? Your wife has disappeared. The police are calling this a suspicious absence. Do you suspect foul play? How do you feel?

The questions replayed like a ticker tape through his head. He couldn't seem to shut them out or turn them off.

Has Mrs. Montgomery been unhappy? What's the state of your marriage? There have been rumors that your son has a birth defect. Would you care to comment on that?

Collier thought for a moment about walking out the front door again, letting them hit him with the camera lights, thrust their microphones back in his face, and then blasting them with every curse word he knew, telling them—and who knew how many thousands of people—just how he felt about their lack of compassion, their need to exploit his misfortune into tonight's lead story. For a minute, maybe a little longer, he let the scenario blow across his mind, let himself feel the pleasurable release of saying to hell with political correctness. To hell with the media. To hell with the public's right to spy on his private anguish.

He swallowed more of the scotch, let his head drop back against the top of the sofa, let his body slump—not relaxed, but exhausted—let his eyelids close. And the moment he dropped his guard for a second, she was there. *Meredith.* Beautiful, as always, in face and form. A seductive smile on her lips as she slipped the glass from his hand and slipped her body into the bowl of his lap, pressed her lips hard against his.

How could she be someplace that wasn't here? Somewhere in the world, but out of place, out of reach. How had this happened? Why had it happened? What should he have done to stop it? And how . . . how . . . had he lived thirty-six years, nearly thirty-seven, and never known until now how helplessness felt?

Collier stood, abruptly pushing to his feet. Sober and scared. He moved to the credenza, uncapped the bottle of Glenfiddich, and poured a stout inch into the glass, drinking it down in a single swallow. He drank purely for the burn, for the slow, sweet anesthetic value only liquor could give. Normally, he calculated every drink with the same care with which he weighed every word. He drank socially, but never too much and never enough to dull his senses. And he never drank alone.

At least, he never had until now. Last night. Tonight. Who knew how many nights in the future he would reach for a bottle in an effort to numb the fear that sat like a two ton block of plutonium in his stomach. *Where are you, Meredith? Where did you go? What happened to you? Why haven't you called? When will you be home?*

Questions ricocheted through him with the hollow twang of table tennis balls. Possibilities rose to answer. Where is she? *Ping.* She's been kidnapped, abducted . . . killed. *Pong.* Why didn't she call me? *Ping.* She forgot to charge the phone. The car went off the road. She's hurt. She's unconscious. *Pong.* Why hasn't someone found her? *Ping.* She's a million miles away. She's hurt. She's trapped. She's . . . dead. *Ping-pong. Ping-pong. Ping-pong.*

He poured more scotch, amazed really that his hands were steady. But then, abruptly, he set the glass down. Getting drunk wasn't the answer. There were no answers. Only the questions. The endless, impenetrable questions. How could anyone just vanish? It wasn't like Meredith not to stick to her schedule. She made lists religiously and stuck to them. Hell, she made lists for him—or had until the election. Now he had Brooke and a whole office staffed with people who got paid to keep him on schedule. As if that had ever been a problem for him. As if his grandfather hadn't drilled into him since birth the importance of planning ahead, of scheduling his days, of staying on track.

Collier lifted a slat of wooden shutter and looked outside. Night everywhere, as dark as a city ever got after the sun went down. But clear as day, he could see the media vans and the reporters lounging in and around them, drinking coffee to ward off the cold, talking, laughing, waiting. Waiting for Meredith to come home. Waiting for him to come out. Waiting for whatever might happen. Waiting.

Closing the slat again before one of them noticed him, he sank onto the cushioned window seat and put his head in his hands. He had a headache. A bad one that throbbed at the back of his neck, pounded at his temples, ached behind his eyes. Tension. Panic. A hollow, horrible dread. Where in the hell was she? What in God's name had happened to her?

He wasn't even sure he wanted to know, and yet knowing was the only thing he wanted. The not knowing could kill a person, could strangle the life right out of a heart. He hadn't realized that before. Hadn't understood how uncertainty worked. He'd been certain his whole life. Certain of whom he was. Certain of whom he would become. Certain of the course his life would take. If he'd ever doubted any of that for a second, he didn't remember.

But then, he'd been certain the baby would be perfect, too. Healthy and beautiful and perfect.

Collier pushed up from the window seat, distancing himself from the negative thought. Blake was beautiful. He was healthy. Healthier than most of the children born with his particular birth defect. The doctors—all of them—believed he would lead a normal life. A perfectly normal life.

After the operations. After the problems with his hand and his heart were corrected.

Before he quite knew his intention, Collier had poured more scotch into the glass and swallowed it in a gulp. This had to stop. He had to get control of these desperate thoughts, had to abort this night's destructive bent. To that end, he capped the bottle of Glenfiddich and carried his empty glass across the dark entryway and into the kitchen. Turning on the lights wouldn't be a good idea. The media had already used considerable restraint due to his position, but he knew that protection was merely camouflage. The reporters had a job to do. Position, influence, none of that would buy him a moment's respite once the story broke wide open.

Meredith Owens Montgomery, former Miss Oklahoma and wife of Reyes City's newly elected mayor, disappeared yesterday. She ordered flowers at Ann's Flower Shop. She dropped in at Grady's Good Liquors where she purchased two bottles of wine—a California merlot and a dry white Pinot. She picked up the dry cleaning, and then she vanished. Mrs. Montgomery had planned to attend the Green Country Hospice benefit luncheon at Seven Oaks Country Club, but never arrived. "I wondered when she didn't show up," said her friend, Laurel Hampton, "but I thought the baby might be sick again and she'd stayed home to be with him."

None of that had come out as yet. But Collier knew it was only a matter of time before the whole town knew not only what kind of wine he drank, but the entire nature of Blake's condition and prognosis. Alice's tempestuous mental state wouldn't be far behind. They'd probably bring up that whole mess about Mattie, too. It would be ugly, couched in the gentlest of terms, but his whole life would be fair game. The public's right to know outweighed privacy—especially when the person who wished to be private was a public servant.

Collier stood at the sink, too keyed up to hold on to any outrage, too sick with worry to think about what he would or wouldn't say when the moment came to make another statement. For tonight, it was done. He and Ross had each made a brief statement about Meredith's disappearance for the six o'clock news, and again for the ten o'clock news. Ross had stood with him not just as the chief of police, but as a friend. He knew Meredith and was her friend as well. So Ross had downplayed the many facts they didn't know and emphasized the professionalism and skill of the many officers who were working the case. He'd said the search would continue until Meredith was found and returned home safely. But he was worried. Collier had seen it in his eyes, heard it in all the reassurances he didn't offer.

Winter whistled outside in the dark, tapped cold fingers against the window panes. Collier turned away from the sink, moved through the kitchen, his path outlined by the soft glow of digital time—1:23—recorded on the microwave and the oven—and by the reflection of street lights on the stainless exterior of the refrigerator. In the foyer, a dusky moonlight slanted across the base of the stairwell, directed into sections by the dormer windows high on the landing, and guided his footsteps easily across the entry and up the stairs. At the upstairs landing, he turned left and tiptoed as he came near the baby's room. The door was ajar and, like a thief, he nudged it open and moved like a shadow to the crib.

Blake had kicked off his covers and they lay in a lumpy huddle against the side of the crib. Collier drew the blankets back over the curl of baby that was his son. His son. He felt the pull of love, the fatal attraction of emotion so much bigger and broader than anything else in his life, and as he tucked the blankets around his sleeping child, the numbness left him. Gone like a whisper.

Here was reality.

Here was hope.

He moved his hand up to feel the rise and fall of baby breaths, let his fingertips drift across a downy cheek, linger to catch the puff of air that meant life. Asleep and dreaming, maybe. If babies dreamed. And Collier thought they must. Hazy, sweet dreams of angels. Long, peaceful dreams of heaven.

Blake's little hand had slipped free of its capped sleeve and moved as delicately as a pianist's fingers. Stilling. Then moving again. His little misshapen thumb—the useless flap of skin and sinew the doctors would remove when he was a little older, a little stronger—all but hidden under the folds of his chin. Dr. Gray had assured them the surgical team would be able to fashion useful thumbs for him, that by his second birthday, he'd have two functioning opposable thumbs and hands that looked only slightly dissimilar to the hands of a normal two-year-old. Later, in a year or two or three, they'd do corrective surgery and patch the hole in his heart. He was better off than he might have been. So many other children born with problem hands and hearts fared far worse. Blake's problems were treatable, correctable. Collier knew that. He believed the doctors, believed the scores of articles he'd researched for his own peace of mind. He believed. Even if Meredith couldn't.

Meredith.

Where is she, Blake? He posed the question to his son in the silence, wondering if there remained some connection between this world and the one beyond—if Blake could sleep peacefully because he could hear his mother's thoughts, no matter where she slept tonight. As he stood there, Collier recognized the comforting relief that he still had his son, that Meredith hadn't taken the baby with her when she left.

But, of course, Meredith wouldn't have taken the baby with her. Other than doctor appointments, she never took him with her anywhere. She said she needed some time to herself, an hour or so when she didn't have to be anyone's mother. She said it would be irresponsible to expose him to the germs that waited outside, ready to attack his fragile system. She said that she was looking forward to taking him out, showing him off, when he was older.

Collier knew it for the lie it was.

The baby had two obvious, undeniable defects. So Meredith hid him away in the nursery. She claimed he was sleeping if they had guests, kept his hands bundled out of sight when she couldn't find an excuse not to bring him down. She avoided taking him out in public. She didn't show anyone his picture unless his hands were hidden, concealed.

Collier wasn't sure if she worried about coping with the questions and sympathies of well-meaning friends or if it bothered her more to see Blake's deformed hands herself.

Where are you, Meredith?

Blake sighed in his sleep. A low whimper. A deep exhale of warm breath.

Collier patted the rounded baby belly, loving the pure, boundlessly simple and endlessly complicated emotion that overwhelmed him in just that touch. His hand was large and dark against the pearly baby blankets. He could spend the rest of the night here. With his son. Watching. Listening for the next breath and the next and the next. Was that the true essence of parenthood? Listening. Waiting. Watching.

Where are you, Meredith? Why aren't you here listening to him breathe? Why aren't you in our bed, lying on your side, your face turned toward the baby monitor so you can hear him if he stirs. Why aren't you home where you belong? Why weren't you happy?

He turned abruptly and walked to the doorway, no longer trying to be quiet, opening the door and drawing it nearly closed again, making no attempt to mask the squeak of hinges.

But Blake didn't wake. He slept on. Dreaming his baby dreams.

Unaware that his mother was gone.

Unconcerned that his father had lost his way in the dark.

CHAPTER THREE

Using the kitchen counter as her barre, Mattie dipped, sank lower, and rose back to her starting position, arm folding in front of her to complete the stretch.

And . . . repeat.

Behind her, on the glowing heat of the ceramic cook top, eggs poached. Above the lid of their shiny pot, the microwave hummed, filling the room with the scent of bacon. Steam wisped from the squatty toaster and scrolled upward from the coffeemaker as the coffee dribbled through the filter and into the pot. The aroma of breakfast saturated the morning air.

Hunger formed little dewdrops of saliva on her tongue and her stomach grumbled through the next set of pliés, reminding her why she'd come down to the kitchen so early in the first place. Yesterday's breakfast and a convenience store bagel eaten midafternoon were now barely even a memory, and her body had awakened her just ahead of the sunrise, demanding sustenance.

Eggs with golden yolks that crumbled at the touch of a tine.

Bacon, thoroughly cooked and crunchy.

Toast, brown and lightly glazed with butter.

Coffee, brewed rich and aromatic.

Breakfast. Her favorite meal. Some days her only meal. When Jack wasn't traveling, she sometimes had lunch with him, but even when he was home during the week, which he so seldom was of late, an evening meal was a lost cause. Her classes ran back to back from three-thirty until eight or nine, Monday through Thursday, until six on Friday, and nine to three on Saturdays. She'd opened Miss Mattie's School of Dance and Drama a year ago last summer with Jack's encouragement and financial backing. The first fourteen months had been a bumpy ride, but there were times now—occasionally seven days in a row—when Mattie didn't stop and ask herself what maggot of insanity had made her want to open her own business. She'd contracted with several qualified instructors and didn't technically have to be in the studio every minute the doors were open. But it was her future on the line—and Jack's money—and she felt better when she was there to keep an eye on things.

The microwave dinged and she checked the bacon, replaced the greasy paper towel with a clean one, and set the timer for twenty seconds more. She did another plié and opened the microwave again with one second still on the clock. Peeking under the two-ply paper, she smiled. Perfect. Not too crispy, but not underdone, either. A crunchy little package of fat and protein. And best when eaten as finger food. A bonus in Mattie's normally hurried mornings.

Carefully removing the tray, she laid the crisped bacon on a plate. One strip and then the other. The toast was ready and the egg timer held only a few more grains of sand. The timer itself was an hourglass and gold-plated, obviously more for decoration than actual use. Mattie wondered if it had been a wedding gift and how often, if ever, Meredith had used it. Times like now she realized all the little things she didn't know about her sister's life— things like what she cooked in this beautifully updated and now ultra modern kitchen. Things like what she ate for breakfast.

Cantaloupe. A memory. Meredith, fourteen, sitting at the dining room table, a slice of cantaloupe cut into measured pieces and lined up like soldiers awaiting execution, in front of her. That was it. No other details. Nothing to tie the memory to an event. Or a moment. Just Meredith with the cantaloupe.

Cantaloupe. Ugh.

As Mattie poured the coffee, she heard André pad into the kitchen, his nails click-click-clicking against the tile. And when she turned to set her breakfast—eggs, bacon, and toast prettily arranged on a floral-patterned china plate—on the table, the poodle observed her studiously with his button-black eyes.

"What do you want?" she asked. "Bacon? You smell the bacon?"

The dog licked his chops. Once. Delicately. Requesting a taste with well-mannered anticipation.

"Forget it," Mattie told him. "Just think what your mommy would say."

No doubt in Mattie's mind. Meredith would have a fit. She adored the poodle, treated him as if he'd beaten out all other contenders at Westminster and walked off with Best in Show, and seemed to think that anyone who didn't recognize his superior breeding didn't know dogs from dirt. Meredith had explained to Mattie—at some length on a previous occasion—how she'd chosen this particular puppy from a litter of champion stock and how much trouble it had been to locate a competent and professional groomer. From the get-go, this pampered pooch had a special diet, with recipes designed especially for him by a canine dietician, who'd conducted a long and involved testing process to determine exactly what André needed to eat. The food came in freezer containers marked "André's Special Formula." Mattie had made the unfortunate mistake of pointing out that, no matter what he ate, he was still, "just a dog."

But he was Meredith's dog, and that meant he couldn't be "just" anything. André, like everything else in Meredith's life, had to be something special.

Mattie snapped off a tiny contraband morsel. Special or not, a bite of bacon couldn't hurt him.

"We don't give him table scraps," Collier said, walking in and discerning her intention even before she'd fully extended her hand to make the offering. He looked pale and exhausted, which somehow emphasized how handsome he was. The first time she laid eyes on him, Mattie had thought he was more than a match for her sister in looks. And Meredith was a beautiful woman. No wonder, then, that Collier could elicit a delicate little "oh" response from his sister-in-law on a morning when that made as much sense as anything else.

Mattie popped the bacon into her mouth as if she'd never had a thought of doing anything else with it. "You're up early," she said, observing her brother-in-law with a critical eye and deciding, with some small surge of inane smugness, that Jack was more handsome.

"Blake's a dependable alarm clock."

That perked her interest. "I didn't hear him. Did he cry?"

"He never cries any longer than it takes for me to get to him."

Mattie thought about that, tried to visualize her immaculate brother-in-law changing a diaper or preparing a bottle. Difficult as that was, she found it easier than imagining Meredith in the role. "So, do you just leave him in the nursery all the time?"

"Of course not." He opened the refrigerator and leaned into the flare of cold light. When he closed the door again, he had a Ziplock baggie in one hand, a carafe of orange juice in the other. He dumped the contents of the baggie—mixed berries—into the blender, added the juice, half a banana, a dribble of honey, and covered the top with a lid before he punched the setting.

The mechanical whir created a line of tension between her shoulders, reminding her she didn't belong in this kitchen. To be truthful, it bothered her a little to feel comfortable here, in Meredith's place, and she could tell it bothered Collier to see her at his table, eating food from his refrigerator, making herself at home in her sister's house.

It would bother Mattie to find him in her kitchen if their situations were reversed. But then, she couldn't imagine any reversal of situation which would put Collier in her kitchen. And even if her mind's eye could place him there, her kitchen was considerably smaller, and they'd have a real problem skirting each other in it. Size of room, though, didn't reflect her determination to get a few questions answered.

The moment he shut off the blender she asked, "What's wrong with Blake?"

Collier's hesitation passed in a flash, hardly even noticeable. "Nothing that can't be fixed." He set a glass on the counter and poured the smoothie into it, leaving nothing but a foamy residue in the blender. Leaning against the sink, he lifted the glass and took a long drink.

"That's good to know, but not exactly what I asked."

His jaw flexed and he lowered the glass. "He was born with Holt-Oram syndrome. It's sometimes referred to as hand-heart syndrome since the hands and heart form during the second month of gestation and a complication with one generally means a complication with the other."

She pushed her plate away. "What kind of complications does Blake have?"

"Other than the hands, he has an ASD. Atrial septal defect. A small hole between the upper heart chambers."

"And—?"

"And it can be repaired when he's older. Anywhere between two and five, depending on his development." Collier turned the glass in his hand.

"The hands they'll fix sooner. The first surgery is scheduled for next month."

Her mouth went suddenly dry. "What will they do?"

He took his time draining the rest of his breakfast, holding the glass for a moment and studying the dregs. "They'll fashion thumbs for him. Didn't Meredith explain any of this?"

"Until I saw him in his crib last night, I had no idea anything was wrong."

"He's seven months old, Mattie."

Accusation trickled through the words. *You could have made an effort to see him before now. The only reason you don't know this is because you didn't care. Some aunt you are. Some sister.*

Mattie scooted back from the table, stood to face him. "She told me everything was fine. Meredith *told* me not to come."

He held her gaze for a moment, then turned away to set the dirty glass in the sink. "I'm going down to the community center. Ross set up a command post to serve as a central location for calls and information. You can reach me there if necessary. The phone number is next to the phone on my desk."

"What about the baby?"

"Mrs. Oliver will be here in. . . " He glanced at the clock. "Four minutes. She arrives at ten to seven Monday through Friday, and she's never late."

"Mrs. Oliver?"

"The baby's nurse. Did you think I'd expect you to take care of Blake, too? I asked you to come and keep an eye on Alice. That's it, Mattie. That's all you have to do."

She watched him prepare to fill a thermos with

coffee, watched as he poured, watched him reach for the lid. But the question on her mind wouldn't be contained; it had to go somewhere, and it fell into the silence. "Are Blake's problems the reason Meredith left?"

Collier's temper, already frayed by uncertainty, arched like a feral cat. The thermos thumped on the counter and hot coffee splashed out, hitting his hand, splattering across his starched white shirt. "She disappeared, Mattie. She didn't *leave.*"

That he wanted, *needed,* to believe Meredith, the perfect wife, the perfect mother, wouldn't walk out on her slightly imperfect son was understandable. A blind spot, possibly, but understandable. Mattie didn't want to believe it, either. Although that explanation would be preferable to so many others.

"Meredith wouldn't leave Blake," he said, firmly, as if saying the words made it so. "She wouldn't leave me." He wiped the coffee off his hand, off the counter, glanced angrily at the dark splotches on his shirt, then he capped the thermos and headed for the door, dismissing her and her baseless question. But just as he reached the doorway, he paused, stopped, and looked back. "The police will be in and out of here all day. At some point they'll probably ask you more questions about Meredith. If you can't keep from sabotaging this investigation with some idiot theory, at least be honest and admit your jealousy of Meredith could color your answers."

Mattie reminded herself of the tremendous stress he was under and bit back the drive to defend herself over a statement that, even on a good day, he undoubtedly believed was true. "I can take Mother and leave for Dallas today, if that will make this easier for you."

"Nothing will make this easier," he said tightly. "Least of all the possibility your mother will have another stroke if you insist on moving her. You haven't been around. You don't know how quickly she gets disoriented now. And agitated. You're going to have a great deal of trouble handling her here, in familiar surroundings, much less if you move her to a strange environment."

"I think I can handle my mother."

"I'm sure you think you can handle anything." He didn't wait for a response, just walked out of the kitchen, the thermos in hand.

Mattie looked down at her barely touched breakfast, cold now and unappetizing.

That went well, she thought. That went so well.

"You're Mrs. Montgomery's sister."

The young detective, having first introduced himself as Joe D. Larson, shuffled in the breast pocket of his suit jacket, and Mattie waited for the requisite pen and notebook to emerge. But when his hand reappeared, it held a flimsy packet of Kleenex. He extracted one and swiped it forcefully back and forth under his nose, wadding the tissue in his palm as he looked at her with apologetic and bleary eyes. "Excuse me," he said. "Allergies."

She waited while he stuffed the used tissue into the outside pocket of the overcoat he'd draped across one knee, as if he liked to keep it handy, as if he might need to put it on and be out the door in a second. He seemed young to be a detective, but maybe that was because his hair fuzzed on his head like a ripe peach and with his ruddy cheeks and pale complexion, he looked like . . . well, like a ripe peach in a bad wig. His hair—an indeterminate reddish blond—couldn't have been more than an inch long at any point on his head and it stuck out in every direction. His face had a flushed but healthy glow despite the allergies, and he seemed somewhat embarrassed. As if sitting in the mayor's house, on the mayor's sofa, across from the mayor's sister-in-law, had him wishing he had more hair. Or a bigger packet of Kleenex.

"So, you're Mrs. Montgomery's sister," he repeated, tucking the packet absently back inside his breast pocket and drawing out a small notebook from some other hidden compartment in his jacket. "Maddy Owens."

He seemed to be asking, although Mattie had already noticed he had a habit of ending almost every sentence on a downbeat so that it came out as fact, even when she suspected it was, in fact, a question.

"Mattie," she corrected.

"Short for . . . Madison. Madeline." He dutifully poised the pen to write it down and she dutifully corrected him again.

"No, it's not short for anything. It's Mattie. M-A-T-T-I-E."

"Oh. Like my friend, Matt. Only his is short for Matthew. But we all just call him Matt. M-A-T-T."

Mattie nodded, disinclined to tell him that in a way her name was short for Matthew, too. Matthew Joseph being the name her parents had chosen if Meredith had been a boy. And since Alice hadn't cared if Mattie even had a name, her unimaginative father had christened her Mattie Jo. But that was really more information than Detective Larson needed. "Short happens sometimes," she said with a semi-smile.

He nodded also, apparently glad they understood each other. "Last name . . . Owens."

She nodded. Again. This could get tedious, allergies or no allergies. "Mattie Owens."

He wrote that down, in tiny, precise block letters in the little notebook. "And you've known Mrs. Montgomery since . . ."

". . . . birth. She's eleven months older." She wished Jack could be here for this. He liked to say that if he hadn't been born with a silver spoon wedged down his throat, he could have been a great detective. Just his luck, the standard-issue badge didn't come in platinum.

"Do you know if she had enemies? Anyone who might dislike her? Anyone she might have a conflict with?"

"I don't know that much about her friends or her life here." That, Mattie realized with a wistful sadness, was a fact. "We're not close that way."

"Do you have a close relationship in other ways?"

Question or fact, the answer to that was complicated. Mattie could answer yes or no, and both would be the truth. And yet, not the truth at all. But before she could decide what to say, something caught her attention. "Excuse me. I'll be right back." She jumped up, hurrying after the fast-moving glimpse of powder blue. As she reached the foyer, she strained to hear the back door opening. Or the front door closing. Or any door making any sound at all. Hoping hard that her mother wasn't already halfway to the neighbor's Cadillac.

But Alice was in the kitchen, taking the carafe of orange juice out of the refrigerator. She barely glanced up when Mattie slid to a hurried stop in the doorway. "Oh." The word traveled into the room on a relieved sigh. "Good morning, Mother."

Alice looked at her then frowned. "What are you doing here?" she asked, sounding as if she didn't care one way or another, as if the answer mattered not at all. "Where's Meredith?"

That, of course, was the only question that had ever mattered to Alice.

"She's not in the kitchen."

"I can see that much for myself." Alice set the carafe on the counter. "Run upstairs, Mattie, and tell your sister to get down here and eat her breakfast. She'll be late for school."

"Meredith won't be late for school," Mattie ventured, unsure if inserting reality into her mother's morning was a good idea. "You know that."

Alice's brow furrowed for a hairsbreadth of a moment, then cleared. "Yes, I do. Meredith is never late. She's a ray of sunshine every single day. I do wish you could be more like her, Mattie."

That did seem to be the consensus. "Um . . . what are you going to do this morning, Mom?"

"I'm going to get dressed and go to work."

"You don't work anymore. You're retired. Remember?"

Alice studied her with thirty-one years of accumulated disapproval. "Do you think I've become a senile old woman? I know I retired. Just like I know that on Thursdays, I go to the hospital at noon and spend the afternoon working in the gift shop. As a volunteer."

Mattie opened her mouth to argue. It was doubtful that Alice had volunteered at the hospital since before her stroke. On the other hand, it *was* Thursday. Then again, her mother retained a certain core vanity, which meant the odds were good that no matter where she thought she was going today, she wouldn't leave the house while wearing her bathrobe. "Okay." Mattie backed from the doorway. "Well, enjoy your breakfast. I'll just be in the other room. If you need me."

She turned away. Stopped. Weighed the pros and cons of leaving her mother alone in the kitchen or of taking her into the study where the presence of a sniffling detective would almost certainly remind her that Meredith wasn't just late for school. Mattie turned back. "Stay in the house, Mom. It's cold outside."

"For heaven's sake, Mattie. It's January. Of course, it's cold. I thought you lived in Florida. Or Arizona. One of those places where it's always hot. What are you doing here anyway?"

"Leaving," Mattie said brightly. Then, trying not to second-guess her choice, she went back to the study and the interview.

"You were telling me about your relationship with your sister." The detective checked his notes and picked up where he'd left off.

Obediently, Mattie's thoughts trekked back to the question. *Close relationship. Do you have a close relationship in other ways?* The answer should have been easy. *Of course, Meredith and I are close. We're sisters. We played with the same toys, wished on the same stars, told secrets and swore to be there for each other until the end of time.* But it wasn't that simple, because the true alliance within the Owens home had been solidified before Mattie was even born.

Alice had given birth to two daughters, but she had loved only one.

And so Mattie had grown up in the untenable position of hating the sister she loved and loving the sister she hated. That had never made for an easy relationship.

Or an easy answer.

"I don't see her often," she finally said. "Once or twice a year. Some years more often than that. Some years less."

Joe D. jotted something into the notebook and Mattie wondered how he had summed up what she couldn't even articulate.

"When was the last time you saw your sister?"

"March. My mother had a stroke and I was here then."

He made another note. "And when was the last time you spoke with your sister?"

"A few days before Thanksgiving. My fiancé and I had planned to come for Christmas, but Meredith phoned to tell me that Collier's family would be visiting them over the holidays, and we should make other plans."

"Do you typically spend holidays with your sister and her family?"

Her family. Even this young detective seemed to have concluded that Mattie was an outsider, that she didn't belong inside the parameters of Meredith's life.

"Again, sometimes I do. Sometimes not. We spent Christmas with them the previous year." She and Jack had been the invited guests for an entire week. Christmas through New Year's Day. It had been just the four of them in Meredith's beautiful house—that being the last holiday season before Alice's stroke and loss of independence. When Blake was little more than a heartbeat on the horizon. Of course, Alice had been with them for much of the time, but in the evenings she'd gone home to her own house and Mattie, Jack, Meredith, and Collier had had a spectacularly good time together.

Meredith had absolutely sparkled that whole week, so happy in her life, so beautiful in her early pregnancy glow. She'd gone out of her way to make the holidays something special. Especially for Mattie. It was maybe the first time Mattie could remember feeling she wasn't just an addendum to her sister's life, but a valued part of it. The feeling hadn't lasted long. Within a couple of weeks afterward, Meredith had reverted to her usual, random reward tactic of being Mattie's sister.

Hi, Mat! I'll have to call you back.

Oops, you caught me on my way out the door.

Oh, you have class now, don't you? Call me back.

Can't talk now. Let me call you later.

You're never home. Do you ever do anything but work and go to school? Call me.

But no matter what time Mattie called, Meredith had something more pressing to do, and when Meredith did call back, it seemed she invariably chose a time when no one was at home. From January into March, until Alice's stroke happened, the sisters had exchanged nothing more than the scattered but basic information that it wasn't a good time to talk.

"We." Joe wrote something on the notebook page, then as if that reminded him of his allergies, he fished out another Kleenex and took another swipe across his upper lip. "That would be you and . . ."

"Jack Youngblood. My fiancé. We got engaged last Christmas. A year ago Christmas," she amended. "When we were here."

The detective made a few more block letters, adding Jack's name to his notes. "Is he here with you now?"

"Jack? No, he's in Seattle. On business. I can give you his cell phone number if you want to talk to him, but he knows less about my sister's life than I do. They've only met a couple of times."

"The Christmas before last. When you visited Mayor Montgomery and your sister."

"Yes, and once before that."

"Seattle." He wrote that down, too. "And that number?"

Mattie supplied it. "If it's busy, leave a message. He'll call you back. The cell phone's the best—usually the only way to reach him."

"You've been engaged, let's see, thirteen months."

"Yes. We're getting married in June. No firm date yet. It won't be anything elaborate. Jack's always wanted a Las Vegas wedding. It appeals to his rebellious nature, I think."

A slight smile acknowledged the information, then Joe D. tapped the pen against the paper as he scanned through his notes. "Have you ever had any reason to think your sister might be unhappy in her marriage?"

A laugh puffed past Mattie's lips, a strange mix of nerves, anxiety, and the absurdity of the question.

"I have no reason to believe my sister has ever been unhappy."

The bleary eyes focused on Mattie for a moment, looking for whatever might lie beneath the surface of her remark. Jealousy, maybe. Or mere naiveté. "What about your brother-in-law?"

"I doubt he's ever been unhappy, either. In the marriage." She added the qualifier, remembering how unhappy he'd been with her that morning. The baby's malformed hands flashed through her mind. Maybe Meredith and Collier had shared some unhappiness, even had conflict, over their son's problems. Blake had a hole in his heart. That was reason enough for at least a few moments of unhappiness within the marriage.

The detective dabbed at his nose again, sniffed, and bent his head to the pad. "So you believe their marriage is solid," he stated as if it were fact.

"Yes."

"Did your sister ever talk to you about her son's medical problems?"

A definite question that time. A careful question. Said in such a way as to elicit the least emotional response possible.

And Mattie was surprised to feel a thickening in her throat, a twinge of heartache because this stranger saw Blake's imperfection as a potential problem. For Meredith. For Collier. For their marriage. That was a lot of responsibility for a baby to be born with. "No, I didn't know about that until last night."

He looked up. "You hadn't seen the baby before last night?"

Like it had been preprogrammed and cued up, Meredith's voice began to play in Mattie's head. All

the excuses her sister had offered to keep her away.
All the evasions Mattie had allowed to cheat her of
the first seven months in her nephew's life. *The baby
has another cold, Mattie. He's had about a thousand ear
infections. He doesn't feel well. I want you to see him at
his best. This just isn't a good time. You'll meet him soon,
I promise.*

"No." And that was the easy answer.

Detective Larson clicked away the point of his Bic
and closed the notebook. "If you think of anything
else, no matter how insignificant it might seem,
please call me." He tucked the notebook into yet
another pocket and brought out a business card.

Mattie palmed the card and stood when he did.
She held on to it as she walked with him into the
foyer and to the front door. "Do you have any idea
what has happened to my sister?"

For the first time, he looked at her with genuine
compassion. "We're following every lead," he said.
"And we won't stop until we find her."

When he opened the door, André flew out of the
formal living room and into the foyer, skidding a
little on the polished wood, barking as if he expected Meredith had arrived. But one sniff of the
empty doorway and the brisk winter air, and the
dog retreated into a disappointed silence.

Mattie reached down to pat the poodle's curly
head and he leaned into her hand for just a second.
As if he needed a friend and had found one in her.

The detective drew on his gloves, looking older
here in the light of the entryway. Not just an allergy
sufferer, but weary. As if he'd seen more of the
world and its ways than Mattie had first suspected.

"Thank you," he said. "You've been very helpful."

An exaggeration, of course. She couldn't see how the scanty information she'd been able to provide could be much help at all. She and Meredith weren't close in any way that counted. Like it or not, that was the truth of that.

"Thank you," she said as he stepped across the threshold and into the winter chill. "Drink some orange juice. For your sniffles."

He waved and trotted off down the steps, wiping his nose with a Kleenex as he went.

Orange juice.

Alice.

Mattie wondered what time it was, tried to gauge how long she'd been with the detective and just how long she'd left her mother alone in the kitchen.

Except Alice wasn't alone in the kitchen when Mattie checked. Alice wasn't in the kitchen at all. All trace of her breakfast had been put away, cleaned up, wiped down. Amazing in a way, Mattie thought as she made a quick foray into the breezeway, that a mind unable to efficiently separate the past from the present could retain the knowledge and desire to clean a kitchen. Amazing, too, that Alice could know this was Thursday, yet not remember her daughters were grown women and not schoolgirls.

Mattie wanted to talk to her mother's doctor, discover more about Alice's evolving dementia. She shouldn't have allowed Meredith to carry the whole burden alone all these months. She felt guilty for not taking a more active role before now. Active, being the key word in more ways than one.

There was no one in the breezeway between the kitchen and the garage and no way to know if anyone had gone out the door and across the yard. Mattie couldn't quite believe Alice would have left the house—even if only to sit in the neighbor's car—without first putting on makeup, fixing her hair, and changing out of her bathrobe. Since there hadn't been time for the lengthy routine Alice had always followed, she must still be in the house, Mattie reasoned.

Mattie had kept an eye on the foyer during the interview, but it was possible she'd missed seeing her mother pass by on her way upstairs.

Upstairs. She'd probably just gone upstairs.

But Alice wasn't in her room, either. The bed was made. The curtains opened.

Mattie picked up her pace and checked the nursery.

A tall, gaunt, sliver of a woman—Mrs. Oliver, presumably—was changing the crib linens while Blake rocked back and forth in the automatic swing to the tune of Twinkle, Twinkle Little Star.

"Have you seen my mother?" Mattie asked.

The woman turned, looked Mattie over head to foot, her thin lips pinched tight with irritation. "Who is your mother?"

As if there were people running all over the house looking for their mother. "I'm Meredith's sister and I can't find Alice, my mother. Do you know where she might be?"

"Have you checked her room?"

"Yes, she's not there." The first vestiges of panic thumped against Mattie's ribcage. "Any other ideas?"

Mrs. Oliver cocked a stern eyebrow. Everything about her looked stern, from the toes of her white nurse's shoes to the cap of short white hair on her head. She wore a uniform, Mattie noticed, and wondered if that was standard agency policy or

Meredith's request. "I'm here to tend the baby," Mrs. Oliver said. "Not Mrs. Montgomery's mother."

"No, that would be why I'm here." Mattie turned on her heel and hit the stairs going back down to the entryway. André still sat on his haunches, watching the front door. Maybe he wasn't waiting for Meredith. Maybe Alice had slipped past Mattie's line of vision and gone out on the front porch. The minute Mattie opened the door, though, she could see Alice wasn't on the porch. However, the poodle seized his opportunity and dashed out into the yard.

Mattie went after him, dragged him back inside, then rubbing the cold from her arms, she headed back upstairs. Maybe Alice had gone into Meredith's room. That seemed infinitely more likely than her wandering out of the house in her bathrobe.

At the landing, Mattie heard a beautiful sound. The kick of noise as a tap was turned on and the faint hum of water flowing through old pipes. She sagged a little, then went on to check her mother's room a second time. Pure relief tickled the backs of her knees when she walked far enough into the room to see the closed door of the adjoining bathroom.

Alice was in the shower.

For a few moments, Mattie stood in the doorway, taking deep breaths, bending her body to the floor in a long stretch, pressing her palms and the scary sense of failure hard into the wood. Stupid. She should have checked—thoroughly checked—her mother's room first. But she'd let Collier's cautions about her mother's condition push her panic button. She'd let his doubt about her ability to care for her mother filter past her defenses. She'd been in the house less than twenty-four hours and already she felt the pressure of his judgment. Neither right nor fair. But there as surely as if she could reach out and give it a yank. The idea that she would fail.

Somehow, it all came down to that. In this house, in this town where everyone knew her as *that other Owens girl*, Mattie could feel the weight of failures she had yet to commit. As if the expectation alone was prophetic. As if she couldn't avoid being the born loser everyone had always seemed to believe she would become.

Mattie quietly closed the door so she'd be able to hear when Alice opened it and left her room. A responsible act. Conscientious. The forethought of a good daughter.

As the latch made a soft click, Mattie prayed Meredith would be home soon.

Soon.

Then with a smart lift of her chin, she trotted back down the hall to the nursery to spend a precious few minutes getting to know her nephew.

CHAPTER
FOUR

Collier had known Ross Clark a lot of years. In high school, they'd been members of the State Championship basketball team, although Ross had been a senior on the starting lineup and Collier merely a freshman who substituted as defensive relief. They'd both attended Oklahoma University, where they'd pledged the same fraternity, although in different years. They'd even double-dated a couple of times when Ross returned for alumni functions and Meredith set him up with one of her sorority sisters.

After their marriage, during the in-between years before Ross returned to Reyes City, Meredith and Collier had exchanged Christmas greetings with him and his wife, Claire. *Happy Holidays from the Montgomerys! Merry Christmas from the Clarks!* And when Ross applied for and got the job as police chief, Meredith had put together a welcome home reception that had wowed the movers and shakers of the community. It was the reception that finally put Collier's mind at ease about the wisdom of buying the old Trummell house, despite Meredith's insistence that it was a necessary first step toward launching his political career.

If you want to be taken seriously as a political candidate, you need the accessories of a serious politician.

He had argued that what he needed was a solid foundation in a solid community. He still believed that, but he'd learned that his wife was right in her belief too. The perception of success most often preceded the achievement. The house had been expensive to buy and expensive to renovate and it made their budget so tight it squeaked, but he had to admit Meredith had known what she was doing. Like a connoisseur of fine old homes, she'd made the house look as if the governor of the state already lived there. She'd restored its history, gotten it listed on the county historic register, and opened the doors to the power brokers who, in turn, opened the door of opportunity for Collier. Three years after they bought the house, his law practice had grown into a busy, prosperous firm, and he'd garnered the enthusiastic support of an influential group of local businessmen. Not long after Ross took over as police chief, Collier was sworn in as Reyes City's youngest mayor. The two men were on the same team again.

But Collier wasn't interested in teamwork. He wanted an answer. And he wanted it now. Before the worry inside the walls of Ross's office folded in to suffocate him. "It's been over forty-eight hours. Where is she?"

Ross shifted in his chair.

Not a good sign.

"I wish I knew, Collier."

"You must have some idea."

"I don't. It's been forty-eight hours and every tiny lead we had has dwindled into nothing. Less than nothing. We haven't just hit a few dead ends. We've hit a brick wall."

"What about that woman who said she saw Meredith at the bank? What about Freda Walker? She sounded very sure when she said she'd passed Meredith going into the drugstore late Tuesday afternoon."

"There's not a bank transaction for the time Meredith was supposedly at the bank, and if she was there the security cameras missed her completely. As for Freda, she is always certain she has a lead for us, no matter what case we're working. But again, there's no corroborating evidence. The pharmacy records show Freda picked up a prescription about four-thirty on Monday, not Tuesday. And again, no one else saw Meredith and there's no evidence she was there."

Collier knew this. He knew it because of the sympathy he saw in the faces of the volunteers. He knew it because right now Ross's expression confirmed the lack of any explanation, satisfactory or otherwise. Collier knew. But he couldn't keep from going over what they did know one more time—on the off chance that this time the answer would miraculously appear.

"So that's it? She just becomes another missing person in your file?"

"We're still working the case. It's methodical and slow, but thorough. We've confirmed Meredith's route until she left the dry cleaners on Tuesday. We've checked your phone records. We're watching for activity on any of her credit cards. Other than a physical sighting, there's no way to track the car and there's no evidence she traveled on any of the state turnpikes. We searched your house. We've questioned your friends and neighbors. We're double-checking every interview, making certain we didn't miss anyone who might have interacted with her in the past few weeks." Ross lifted his hands, palms up, to emphasize how empty they were. "I wish I had better news. Hell, I wish I had any news at all."

Frustration pumped like oil in his veins, thick and sluggish, a slick coagulated anger. Collier wanted to put his fist through a wall. Or a window. He wanted to put his head in his hands and cry like a baby. He wanted to yell and gesture wildly and pace like a boxer on an adrenalin rush before a bout. But he simply sat where he was and pushed the fear back, shoving the emotion down deep, trying to remember he was a rational man. "Give me something, Ross. Tell me how someone like Meredith could just vanish into thin air. Tell me how her *mysterious disappearance* goes from front burner to back in a matter of forty-eight hours."

"No one's given up on finding her. This is still top priority for my whole department. You've got volunteers out there searching parking lots and wooded areas, anywhere a car might be hidden." Ross's expression reflected a pained honesty. "But people like Meredith do disappear, Collier. It does happen. Sometimes it's foul play. But in my experience, when the leads dead-end like this, it's because the person doesn't want to be found."

The anger caught fire in his gut, rose like bile to

his tongue. "Is that what you think, Ross? That what we're dealing with here is a runaway wife?"

The chief shifted in his chair again, but he held Collier's steely stare. "Do *you* think that's what we're dealing with?"

"No." But Collier was the first to look away. "I don't believe Meredith would have left voluntarily." And he didn't. Except for those few, random moments when he did.

"Then neither do I."

But they both knew that was Ross, the friend, speaking. Not Chief Clark, the professional cynic.

"Look, you know how this works. I don't have to explain to you that we've got to find something soon. Are you positive you can't remember anything else that might help? A passing remark? Did she seem nervous that morning? Has she been upset about anything lately?"

"I've already told you everything I recall." Collier's throat tightened around the words, and he tasted the sickening despair that coated them. "I've been over it and over it in my head a million times. Anything I said now would be as much speculation as actual fact."

"Speculation may be the best thing we've got going for us. Think about Tuesday morning. Before you left the house. Where was Meredith standing? What was she wearing? What did she say?"

One more time, Collier locked his jaw against distraction and tried to draw the memory into focus, tried to see it in a different light, made a new effort to separate the image into specific compartments in his mind's eye. "She was in the foyer, at the foot of the staircase. She was wearing sweats. A pink set.

It was new, I think. She said . . ." He closed his eyes, tried to see her, capture every impossible nuance of her voice, every tiny, fugitive variance of expression. "She said, 'Have a nice day.'"

"Has she been shopping a lot recently? Maybe wearing clothes you haven't seen her wear before?" Ross interrupted.

"No, not more than normal anyway. Meredith likes nice things, but she's never spent an exorbitant amount of our budget on clothes. You and I both know she didn't need to. Even if she was wearing a second-hand gunny sack, she'd still look like a million bucks."

"I can't see Meredith wearing second-hand clothes."

Collier's earlier anger jumped to attention. Like a kid with a flashlight, he couldn't seem to keep it from turning on and off. On. Off. "What are you getting at?"

Ross sat silent, steady as a rock, putting forth the idea of an illicit affair without having to say the words.

"She wasn't having an affair," Collier stated unequivocally. Because he did need to say it. He needed to hear himself say the words aloud.

"I didn't say she was."

"No, you didn't. And I suppose next you'll be *not* saying you think I had something to do with her disappearance."

"Did you?"

This time Collier didn't say anything. He didn't need to.

They sat like that for a moment or two. Neither speaking. Then Ross propelled himself up from his

chair and walked over to the window, where he
flipped open a slat in the drawn blinds to look outside. "Dadgummed January," he said. "We haven't
seen the sun in a week. Just this gray smudge,
morning to night." He let the slat drop back into
place, lifted a framed photo from one of the book-
shelves. It was of Claire and their two boys. Miles
and Quentin. Ross flicked his finger across the top,
wiped the resulting dust across his shirt sleeve, then
looked intently at the picture again. "Has Meredith
been jumpy lately? A little on edge, maybe?"

"She's been on edge ever since the baby was born.
You know that. I told you about it at the time."

"Yes, you did. And, as your friend, I suggested you
and Meredith get some counseling."

Collier leaned forward and took a pen from Ross's
desk. Not because he wanted to write something
down. Or make a note about the conversation. It was
just there. So he picked it up. Let it flip between his
fingers and patter at the arm of his chair. *Tap-tap.*
Tap. Tap.

"Meredith didn't think we needed counseling,"
he said. "She thought it would be an unnecessary
expense."

That wasn't exactly how she'd put it.

*I'm not spending what little disposable income we have
on a therapist. We have a baby with special needs. What
we have to have, what we cannot do without, is a full-time
nurse. A baby nurse. Someone who knows a hell of a lot
more about taking care of that baby than we do.*

That baby. As if Blake belonged to someone else.
As if he had no connection to them. To her.

"I probably should have pressed the issue," he

said now, knowing it was an admission, knowing it opened the way for other uncomfortable questions.

And Ross lobbed one as if he were returning a tennis serve. "Why didn't you call and report her missing the minute you came home Tuesday and realized she wasn't there? Why did you wait until the next morning?"

Why? Such a normal question. So obvious. So simple. The answer, though, wasn't simple at all. Or obvious. He hadn't immediately assumed Meredith was missing because she'd been out late before.

You're going to kill me, she'd say when she finally remembered to call. *I saw a movie. Can you believe it? I was driving past this theater and the next thing I knew I'd bought a ticket and the credits were rolling. You don't mind, do you? Mrs. Oliver agreed to keep an eye on Mother. She's such a responsible person, I knew she wouldn't leave before you got home. I know you were probably worried, but I just felt like I'd burst today if I didn't get away for awhile.*

And when she got home, she was like the old Meredith, telling him about the movie she'd seen or where she'd had dinner or what her friend, Susan, had said, or what bargain she'd chanced upon at the mall. Episodes like that had happened occasionally since the baby was born. She'd been depressed after the birth. Hell, he'd been depressed, too. It had been such a shock to them both. Blake's hands. The heart defect. The not knowing how bad it was; the buckle-your-knees relief when it turned out his symptoms weren't as devastating as they might have been; that the prognosis was, if not immediately rosy, at least, reasonably confident. They had every reason to expect Blake could grow up like a normal child.

Collier had felt renewed, alive again after a month of crushing worry. He'd believed Meredith felt the same. She'd seemed happier, less anxious, involved in getting to know their son. But, then, out of the blue, he'd get one of those calls. *I'm driving to Tulsa this afternoon. I told Mrs. Oliver you'd be home by six. I know we'll have to pay her for the extra hour and for watching Mother, but I've just got to get out for a little while, Collier. Please say you understand. I won't be late.*

She often was, though. Breezing in an hour, sometimes two, after she'd told him she'd be home. *Susan and I got to talking and the time just flew by. Forgive me.*

But what was there to forgive? Blake's birth defects had thrown her whole life off-course, had blown a hole in the fabric of their mutual illusion that nothing bad could touch them. For the first time, the golden couple had come face to face with reality. In the form of a baby's hands. In the irregular beating of his heart.

Did he think Meredith was having an affair? No.

Did he believe she was coping with their son's imperfection the only way she could? Yes.

So he'd had no reason to imagine on Tuesday night that she wouldn't walk through the door, late but safe.

"How do you get your mind around the possibility that something's happened to someone you love?" he asked, his voice shaky with regret. "At what point do you reasonably jump from the idea that she's been delayed to the conclusion that she's not home because she can't get there?"

Ross held the picture of his family a moment longer, then set it carefully back on the shelf. "That's a question only you can answer, Collier. But if you were anyone else, I'd be asking if she seemed depressed, if anything about her behavior over the past seven months has bothered you, seemed exaggerated or not right in some way. I'd want to know if there's been tension between the two of you and if you've argued more than normal lately. Or less than normal. I'd ask you if she's seemed happier in the week or so before she disappeared. I'd ask if she's been eager to spend more time with you and the baby recently or if she's more interested in spending time away from you. I'd ask you, point-blank, if you have any reason at all to suspect she might have left of her own free will."

"But I'm not anyone else, and I've already been asked those and about a million other questions by about a dozen other people."

"What did you tell them?"

"I told them exactly what I'm telling you now. She wasn't having an affair. She did not leave me."

With a taut nod that could have indicated either agreement or a skeptical acceptance, Ross walked back behind his desk. "You know I've kept my distance as much as possible during the course of this investigation because I didn't want to jeopardize the case or our friendship."

"Or your career." Collier hated the misery that pushed that thought from his head and out his mouth, hated the uncertainty that had him looking for someone—anyone—to blame.

"Or yours," Ross pointed out. "You don't want anyone coming back on you later with the accusation that I covered for you somehow, or cut you any slack on this."

"You're right." *Tap. Tap-tap.* The pen slapped the

chair arm, snapped back to smack across his knuckle and fall to the floor. Collier bent to pick it up, came up with an apology. "I'm sorry, Ross."

"Don't be. It's a hell of a situation to be in."

And that had to be the understatement of the century. "You know Meredith. You and Claire have had dinner at our house. We've had dinner at yours. Do you think it's possible she would walk out on me? Willingly leave our baby?"

There was a weariness in Ross's eyes, a heaviness in the line of his mouth. "Do you want my professional opinion or the answer you'd expect from your friend?"

"Are they different?"

Ross didn't need to answer that. Collier knew.

"I've been doing police work for a lot of years. It's been forty-eight hours. There's been no ransom call. We have no viable leads. My gut tells me she chose to disappear and that she's choosing not to be found. That's the policeman in me talking. As a friend, I've got to tell you, Coll, I'm praying my gut is right. Because if it's wrong, I'm afraid there's not much chance she'll be coming home alive."

CHAPTER
FIVE

Memories spooled through her head like home movies, flicking on at unexpected moments for no apparent reason. Flashes of a past Mattie hadn't thought about in years, didn't even know that she remembered. But out of the blue, the obscure moments flooded her mind, and she couldn't find the switch to turn them off.

Let's play school.

Nooooo, let's play house.

We're playing school. You're the student and I'll be the principal and you've been bad and the teacher sent you to my office.

Play house. Pleeeasse, Meredith? You can be the mommy.

I don't want to be the mommy. I hate babies.

You'll like them when you grow up and get married.

No, I won't. It's bad enough having a sister. I won't ever, ever, ever have a baby. Now, I'm the principal and

I'm gonna give you a swat for sassing your teacher. You should know better.

In this mental movie, she and Meredith must have been about six and seven. Or maybe younger . . . five and six. It could have occurred in one of those summers when, for a month, they were the same age. It had to have happened when they were still young enough to play-act grown-up roles and try on identities with the same ease they tried on their mother's clothes. They didn't play together very often, especially not after they were older and Meredith discovered it was more fun to play with her friends. But whenever she did agree to play with Mattie, she'd drop the big sister card.

I'm the big sister, so I'll be the principal. You'll get a swat for being bad.

Since I'm the big sister, I get to be the lawyer. You'll be in jail.

I'm the big sister. That's why I'm gonna be the rock star and you have to bring me M&Ms.

So why now did Mattie unexpectedly remember the one thing Meredith had never wanted to be?

Maybe because, as she lay on her side on the nursery room floor, propped up on her elbow so she could watch Meredith's baby on the nest of quilted blankets beside her, she was aware of being glad— so very glad—that Meredith had changed her mind.

Sheltered from the mysterious absence of his mother and untroubled by the stir of activity created by her disappearance, Blake seemed perfectly happy. He kicked both feet at once, toes curled under, his chunky legs all pink and powdery smooth, his skin as silky rich as face cream. His awkward fist curled tightly around Mattie's forefinger and on random kicks he smiled. Not particularly at her. Just a smile in general. As if he couldn't think of anything as fun as being on the floor, toys spread around him, a baby gymboree stretched above him, kicking his bare legs, grabbing every now and then for his barefoot toes, waving his chubby arms, and having his aunt enthralled with every move he made and every sound he uttered.

She'd been in love a few times in her life, head over heels crazy in love. But she'd never felt anything like this. Maybe the emotion had struck her so hard and so fast because of the situation. Meredith was missing and that threw everything into sharper focus, brought home how precious every moment actually was. Mattie would never know for certain, but she felt that she'd have fallen in love with this new man in her life just as fast and just as hard regardless of the circumstances. How could anyone not adore him at first sight? His smiles touched the cotton soft center of her heart. The bright blue promise in his eyes rang as pure as a bell, echoing a future she'd never thought much about before. What would his world be like when he was her age? What would he choose to do with his first thirty-two years on earth? Where would he go? What amazing new things would he see? Mattie found it endlessly fascinating that he looked so astonishingly like Collier, and yet that the feathery line of his hair followed the same exact curves as Meredith's. He gurgled and blew bubbles and laughed with glee when they popped on the bow of his mouth.

Mattie laughed, too. How had she lived this long and never known such a pleasing sound existed? She loved her students, loved hearing their laughter, loved watching them point their ballerina toes and dance in all directions for the simple joy of the motion. But babies didn't take ballet. Or tap. Or jazz. Or modern dance. They had to know how to walk first. And talk. And have gained those important first steps toward socialization. Mattie spent a lot of time with children. But she'd spent none with babies.

And she hadn't known all the sweet pleasure she'd been missing.

Or maybe the pleasure came from just this baby. Her nephew. Hers. Their bonding was already underway. It couldn't be undone. Mattie loved Blake. And she was certain, in some cosmic connection way, he loved her, too.

How could Meredith bear to be away from him?

The thought clenched in Mattie's chest, seized the breath in her lungs and twisted it into pain.

Meredith is missing.

With all the subtlety of a Sherman tank and a precise swish-squish of her rubber-soled shoes, Mrs. Oliver came back into the room, her arms full of clean, folded baby clothes. Mattie pulled herself together, forced the awful possibilities back—back into the shadows where she kept trying to hold them at bay. She blinked aside fearful tears and let herself feel the weight of the nurse's displeasure instead.

"The baby should not be on the floor." Mrs. Oliver spoke crisply as she moved like a brisk wind across the room, settling Blake's clothes in all their proper places. "It's winter. He should not be out of his bed. And he should certainly not be exposed like that." She closed a dresser drawer with a snap. "He needs coverage. Head to toe."

He needed his mother, but then there wasn't anything Mattie or Nurse Oliver could do about that.

"Do you need coverage, Blake?" She crooned to the baby, wanting to protect him from every bad thing, wanting to do whatever she could to fill in the gaps in his little world. Wrapping her hands around his feet, she thought he felt rosy warm and not even a touch chilly. "Do you want your snowsuit on?"

Nurse Oliver tossed a fleecy coverall onto the baby. It landed on his head in a startlingly blue wad.

"Oh," Mattie said, drawing the onesie off the baby, turning the moment into a game of peek-a-boo, and deciding she didn't like Blake's baby nurse. Even considering that Mrs. Oliver was probably upset and worried over Meredith's disappearance too. Although she did a good job of concealing her concern. "That wasn't very nice, was it, Blake?"

But what she didn't know about babies would fill a library. And what she did know about her sister was that Meredith would have hired the best baby nurse she could find. So whether Mattie personally liked Nurse Oliver or not, she needed to defer to the woman's training. And since Nurse O. said the baby was exposed and needed coverage, indicating with the toss of a little sleeper that he should have on more than a cotton T-shirt and his diaper, then Mattie decided she really had no business arguing with the woman. Central heating or no.

The last thing she wanted was for her sister to come home to find her baby sick. Especially if the simple act of bundling him in fleece could prevent it.

So Mattie tucked his baby toes into the one-piece sleeper and tugged it into place around him, zipping him into the soft, nubby cover-up. The minute she pulled the mitten sleeves over his fingers, he went still, watching her with those huge eyes, asking what had happened to his freedom.

"Sorry, buddy"—Mattie leaned closer, smelled his sweet milky breath—"she made me do it."

Nurse Oliver snatched him up from the floor and out of Mattie's reach. "It's important he keeps to his schedule. He isn't accustomed to having visitors at this time of the day."

"I'm his aunt." Mattie leveraged up off the floor and began picking up the pad of baby blankets. "I think that qualifies me as family."

"His *family* knows better than to interfere with his schedule. Babies need structure. This baby especially. This sad time, especially." She placed Blake in the crib, despite his sudden fussiness, and kept her back to Mattie, shielding him from view. "He has his therapy now. You need to go."

"Couldn't I watch?" Mattie hastily folded the blankets into thirds and dropped them on the rocking chair. She wanted to know everything about Blake. How he used his fingers, how he managed without thumbs, if the therapy hurt him, if he cried, or if he enjoyed the attention. "I'll just stay over here by the rocker, where he can't see me and—"

"You should check on your mother."

"She's taking an afternoon nap."

"She must be sleepwalking then because she was on her way out the door when I came from the laundry room."

Mattie entertained the suspicion that Nurse Oliver only wanted her out of the nursery, but she couldn't take the chance. She had to make certain Alice was still safely in the house. Meredith was missing and Mattie was here for one reason—to keep her mother from harming herself or anyone else. Her mother, not Blake, was the reason she was here. Her mother was the *only* reason she was here.

Turning on her heel, she hurried through the doorway, shoving back the anxious feeling that she should be doing something more productive with her time; that if she didn't have to babysit Alice, she could work with the volunteers, help find her sister and get her home. Behind her, Mattie heard the nursery room door close with a snap and registered the noise as a little *take that* from Nurse Oliver to her. But about the time she reached the landing, she heard the lock click into place. And that stopped her feet and her panicky thoughts. A nursery door shouldn't be locked. It shouldn't even *have* a lock. What if there was a fire? What if . . . A dozen awful possibilities ricocheted through her thoughts. What if Meredith came home to find something wrong with Blake because his baby nurse had locked the two of them into the nursery? And what possible reason could anyone have for locking that door? Preventing Mattie from interrupting Blake's schedule again wasn't reason enough to take such a chance. Neither was making a brassy statement about who was in charge of the baby, his schedule, and his nursery.

Meredith wouldn't lock that door, and she wouldn't allow Mrs. Oliver to lock it. Mattie was sure of that.

Since Meredith wasn't here, it was up to Mattie to make sure it didn't stay locked. To hell with schedules and therapy and years of nurse's training. Common sense needed to carry the day.

Back at the nursery door, Mattie tapped softly, trying to imagine how her sister would handle this. When she got no response, she tapped again, still quietly so as not to upset Blake, but more insistently so the woman in white would know she had to answer.

When the door eventually opened a crack, Mattie widened the opening with the force of conviction infused into her palm. "If you don't want me in the nursery during the therapy, I won't come in. But do not lock this door again. It's dangerous."

"I'm here," the woman said as if that prevented any possible hazard.

"*Don't*," Mattie repeated, "lock this door."

The white curls seemed to glint blue with resentment. "I won't lock the door, but it will remain closed. Your sister respects the baby's schedule. You need to respect her wishes in this matter as well."

It wasn't an admission of wrongdoing. It wasn't even much of a compromise, but Mattie only cared about Blake's safety. As long as that door wasn't locked, she didn't care if Nurse Oliver believed she'd won. "I'm sure my sister will be pleased to know how cooperative you've been."

Nurse Oliver shut the door on Mattie and further cooperation.

Okay, Meredith, she thought. One possible catastrophe averted. One more still to prevent.

She could only hope her mother hadn't gotten any further than the neighbor's garage.

She'd left Alice tucked under the gold-toned throw on the living room sofa, sleeping off the remainder of a splitting headache she blamed on too much sun. Mattie hadn't corrected her. If something in Alice's brain was intent on producing faulty memories then, for today at least, Mattie intended to consider that the gift it was.

Gifts of more tangible value had been arriving via the front door—and once at the back—since nine-thirty that morning. Casseroles ready for the oven or the freezer. Two cakes, a cobbler, a ham, and a package of cookies. Neighbors had been ringing the doorbell since about ten that morning. They came to the door with hands full of food offerings, their eyes full of sympathy and concern. They were shocked that the mayor's wife could go missing in a nice community like theirs, unsettled by the thought of what might have happened to her, shaken by the suddenness and lingering uncertainty. They wanted to know how they could help.

Mattie had duly directed them, each one, to the community center, suggesting they might help answer phones there, take the casseroles, the cakes and cookies there for the volunteers, and ask there what they could do to help.

And each time they turned away to leave, she squashed her own intense desire to go with them, closed the door, and went in search of her mother who'd drifted away—usually toward the back door, although once she'd gotten as far as the breezeway—while Mattie was otherwise distracted.

On this, what seemed her millionth trip through the foyer already today, she checked the front door to make sure it was firmly closed and locked, then glanced into Collier's study, which was empty, then veered past the formal living room where she'd left Alice sleeping not a half hour ago. Not empty. André was sprawled in doggy slumber across a tapestried chair and ottoman. Mattie's pulse skipped into a faster beat as she picked up the pace and headed for the kitchen. What was wrong with Mrs. Oliver that she hadn't stopped Alice's wandering? Why hadn't she said something about it when she first walked back into the nursery?

But then, no one was thinking clearly. And it was her job to tend the baby. It was Mattie's job to watch after her mother.

Bracing herself to feel the draft of cold air from an open back door, it took a minute for Mattie to realize the kitchen was warm and cozy. Alice sat at the table, a newspaper spread neatly in front of her, an impression of waffled lines still visible on her right cheek, a leftover testament to her recent catnap.

She looked up when Mattie walked in and then tapped a manicured nail on a particular column of newsprint. "Mattie," she said. "There is a mistake in this newspaper."

"What kind of mistake?" Now that she'd found her mother, Mattie felt what was becoming a familiar twinge of irritation at having been worried about her in the first place. Which wasn't fair. Alice was as helpless in this situation as everyone else. More so.

"They've spelled your name wrong. They put Meredith's name here by mistake."

"That's odd."

"It's more than odd," Alice stated. "It's misleading. A newspaper has an obligation to get the story right, you know. I'll have to phone Richard and tell him to print an antidote."

Richard, being someone Alice undoubtedly remembered as having worked in some capacity for the Reyes City Daily Press. Antidote, being as close as Alice's memory could come to the right word.

Mattie was beginning to learn her mother's new language.

"Do you want a cup of tea, Mom? Or a cup of coffee?"

"It says here that your sister has disappeared." Alice tapped the column again and Mattie's heart thumped in her throat. "Do you understand what that means? It means I don't have any way of getting to the beauty shop."

A language that veered off in strange directions. Mattie's heart sat down. "I can take you," she said.

"Don't be ridiculous. You don't know how to drive."

"Yes, I do. Meredith taught me. Remember?" A slight stretch of the truth. Actually, Meredith's boyfriend at the time—a football captain, basketball star, student council president and all around nice guy—had paid his younger brother to teach Mattie the rudiments of driving an automobile. The brother didn't have a license either, but he knew how to drive. He knew how to do a few other things, too. Steal a six-pack. Get a fake ID. Kiss the spot behind her ear until she melted.

Mattie had really enjoyed learning how to drive. "I'm a very careful driver."

Alice looked unconvinced. "I need Meredith to take me to the beauty shop, but I don't know where she is."

"But you know where I am, and I'll take you anywhere you want to go."

"I am not getting into a car with you, Mattie Jo. That would be irresponsible."

However confused, Alice apparently retained some lucidity of memory about Mattie's adolescence. "Okay," she said, wondering how to distract her mother from the newspaper article, how to help her avoid the truth just a little bit longer. "How about some tea and toast? You must be hungry by now. You slept through lunch."

"I never sleep during the day." Alice directed her index finger line by line down through the column about Meredith's disappearance. "Napping causes wrinkles. Remember that."

"I will." Mattie's stomach grumbled, remembering that she, too, had skipped lunch. She'd have to be more careful about that if she had to stay here much longer. Alice probably needed a schedule more than Blake did. But Meredith would be home soon. She was bound to be home soon. "I'm hungry. Would you like something? Toast, maybe, and a cup of tea?"

The repetition seemed to work because Alice smiled. Just slightly. But still a smile. "That would be very nice. Thank you, Meredith."

One step forward, two steps back. "Tea and toast coming right up." Glad to have something to occupy her hands, Mattie popped two slices of bread in the toaster and retrieved a jar of peach preserves from the refrigerator. Homemade, of course. A little something Meredith had probably whipped up after dinner one evening in July when the Arkansas peaches, all rosy and ripe, hit the produce stands. Meredith did things like that. Or, at least, she said she did.

Mattie was struck again by how little she actually knew about her sister and the life she led inside this house. The worried tears threatened again and she turned aside so her mother wouldn't see. As if her mother had ever paid the slightest attention to Mattie's tears.

"It says here that Meredith has a baby. Now why would they print something like that? Why, she's still in high school. You didn't have a baby, did you?"

"No, Mother," Mattie said, still amazed at times how low her mother's expectations for her had always been. "I've never had a baby."

"Good thing. You'd make a terrible mother."

The refrigerator hummed into the quiet. The second hand on the clock ticked off the time. Alice rustled the newspaper. Mattie contemplated how the sins of her youth could have added up to such a roster of disasters in her mother's mind, and why the stroke hadn't wiped away that part of her memory, instead of leaving stray gaps between the present and the past. The toaster coils glowed red hot and then with a click the bread popped up, brown and ready. When she set the plate in front of her mother, Alice pushed it aside. "I can't eat that," she said. "I'm too upset." But she picked up one triangle of the toast and nipped a bite from the crust. "I suppose I'll have to call your father."

Alice hadn't mentioned Joseph Owens in years. Years and years. Not by name. Not by title. Around their house, he'd been a phantom, never acknowledged, never referred to, all evidence of him as good as erased from existence.

Alice bit into her toast. She was a neat eater. No crumbs fell, no peach jam dared smear the corner of her lips or stain the tip of her fingers. She ate as she did everything. Precisely. Carefully. Which made it seem that much stranger her thoughts were so careless and easily scattered. "Meredith sold my car."

A new topic. Maybe connected to what the newspaper had printed. Maybe not. At least not connected to Mattie and all the things she'd done wrong. In her mother's view. "Yes," Mattie said. "She told me."

"Meredith worries about me, you know. All the time. But she's never caused me a moment's worry. She's been a delight to me her whole life. Not like you, Mattie."

If she'd been treated like a delight, or a ray of sunshine, maybe she wouldn't have done things that annoyed her mother. But the time to suggest such an idea to Alice had passed. And likely would never come around again. Mattie bit into her own toast, tasted the cloying sweetness of the preserves and the sugary consistency as the taste dissolved on her tongue. "Did you ever worry about me, Mom?"

Alice set the toast down, reached over, and wrapped her hand around Mattie's. Clinging. Fragile. So thin against Mattie's palm, the skin felt like tissue paper. "I'm your mother, aren't I?"

Maybe it was only the strain of the situation. Maybe in Alice's cross-wired brain, Mattie and Meredith had somehow melded into one. Maybe Mattie was a little needier at the moment than she cared to acknowledge.

But there in her sister's warm kitchen, maybe for the first time in her life, Mattie felt as if her mother might love her, too.

Or maybe that was only what she needed to believe.

* * *

Collier's parents arrived Friday afternoon in a swarm of concern. His mother barreled through the house, sweeping up son, grandson, and dirty laundry into the wide expansive hug of her generous arms and returning them, respectively, to study, crib, and closet or dresser drawer either comforted or thoroughly cleaned. A dynamo of what-needs-to-be-done-next, she took command like a tornado and by Saturday noon when her other children—Collier's two older sisters—and their respective spouses arrived, Meredith's house had been whipped into a super, sterilized version of itself. Not one of Blake's teething rings or any of his rubber toys escaped being boiled. No piece of clothing, no towel or pillowcase was left untouched. Everything had to be washed, folded, or refolded. No nook, cranny, or corner of the house would be granted a reprieve. Every speck of dust had to be discovered, disinfected, and banished to the trash bin in the alley. The floors were mopped and polished. The rugs vacuumed with vigor. The food, so thoughtfully provided by friends and neighbors, was sent to the command center for the volunteers and summarily replaced with Mom Montgomery's special recipes. All of which were oven or microwave-ready and labeled with expiration dates and specific preparation instructions. Not to mention the little handwritten notes from mother to broken-hearted son.

Son, you are strong enough to face any challenge.

Remember: That which doesn't kill us makes us stronger.

Believe that tomorrow will be a better day. Know today that you are loved.

Motherly love on a freezer label. A wealth of

loving support on a two by four inch strip, printed neatly beneath, "Bake for forty-five minutes at 375 degrees. Don't overcook!"

For his part, Harry, Collier's father, seemed to understand that a different form of action was necessary for his son's peace of mind, and immediately upon arriving, he wanted to go to the community center. There father and son stayed, dawn to dark, returning late with solemn faces and weary eyes. Collier's sisters and brothers-in-law, though not as forceful, offered the same solid support. Whatever needed doing, they did. From shuffling volunteers from one place or another to manning phones at the center or at home, to playing with the baby, to picking up pizzas, they did it all as if Meredith's return depended on their whole-hearted assistance.

Mattie spent the weekend observing the entire family's obvious affection for Collier and the simple way they strengthened him. She'd often entertained the belief that Collier had grown up spoiled and pampered, that he and Meredith were a match in that department. But she got a glimpse of a different kind of family during that long weekend. A family who'd never needed to comfort their son and brother, who'd until now only had cause to celebrate the events in his life. Collier had been born golden, like Meredith. Bad things weren't supposed to happen to him, and it so obviously grieved his parents and sisters that something so awful had now happened. Yet they rallied and became a family who stood together in crisis. A family able to unite in the face of an uncertain future. And at their center, Collier held onto the gold, grew visibly stronger, calmer, and more hopeful because, if or when he might need it, they offered him a soft place to fall.

Mattie would have admired them for that alone, but they won additional gratitude with their considerate and gentle patience with Alice—who blossomed like a flower under the light of their attentions. From one moment to the next, she seemed confused as to whom exactly they were, but never appeared to be in any doubt that these familiar strangers were there to help her child. That Meredith remained missing was at once a reality to Alice and a concept she could not master. She said things like, "Mattie, tell your sister it's time to come downstairs for supper." Then in the next breath, she'd ponder what was happening at the community center and wonder aloud and tearfully if her daughter was ever coming home again.

Regardless of which reality she presented, one of the Montgomerys would unfailingly reassure her. "Meredith won't want to miss tonight's supper, Mrs. Owens." Or, "She could be here any minute. Don't worry. She'll be home before you know it."

Mattie watched her mother rise to the occasion, marshal her undependable brain cells as best she could, and—for the most part, anyway—make comments cohesive enough to be considered conversation. Not sparkling conversation. Not entirely understandable conversation. But still she made the effort. And more than once during that weekend, Mattie was surprised by the knot of pride that tightened across her chest. There had been loads of times in her life when she'd despised her mother's affectations, wished Alice were less concerned with appearances and more concerned with what was real. But she learned something that weekend. Alice had courage, because despite the confusion that fought her every step of the way, she still possessed the *will* to strive for dignity, to request—and expect—respect.

Not once during that weekend did she try to slip away from the house. Not once did she head for the Cadillac next door. When Mattie said as much to Linda, Collier's mother, her comment met with a surprised, "Expectation is a powerful force, Mattie. When we were here at Christmas, I suggested to Collier that perhaps your mother would benefit from some outside stimulus. An adult day care program, or an exercise class of some sort. But you know how your sister feels about that."

Mattie didn't know, and she tried hard to remember if the subject of outside help had ever been mentioned in connection with Alice's stroke. But long days and sleepless nights were taking their toll on her memory as well, and all she could do for now was decide the idea had merit and that she wanted to discuss it with Meredith.

When Meredith came home.

That was the question and the answer threaded through every conversation, filtering out from everyone's thoughts. Walk into a room, pass someone on the stairs, and somehow it always began—or ended—with that.

Any idea where Meredith keeps the cotton balls?

Store that in the pantry for now. Meredith can put it away when she gets home.

There. The house will be clean when she gets back.

The doubt, like sand, sifted through the house, settling into the crevices and packing down to wait for the moment when Meredith came home.

Both sisters and their husbands left on Sunday afternoon to return to their own homes and their own distant lives, to Collier's two nieces and three nephews, who were too young to be left with other relatives for longer than a couple of days. The good-byes were tearful promissory notes for whatever support Collier might need, whenever he might need it.

His parents stayed until Tuesday morning, and would have stayed longer if Collier hadn't insisted they go. "We can stay," they offered several times during the good-bye. But each time, he repeated that there was little, if anything else, they could do at the moment and he'd call the second he needed them to come back. Implicit in his assurances to them was his need to return, as much as possible, to the way life had been before. To the way it would be again.

When Meredith came home.

Mattie wondered if he'd prefer that she left, too, and knew that he would. She wanted to return to Dallas, to the *before* of her life, but the thought of what that sudden change would mean for her mother—not to mention her own even-keeled routine—made her reluctant. On a deeper level, she knew the wish to go home was mostly a wish to go back to the moments before Meredith left, to have a do-over opportunity, another chance to be a good sister.

Meredith's absence anchored her in the reality of the life her sister had left on hold. Returning to her own life seemed tantamount to admitting Meredith wouldn't be back, that there'd be no second chances. She felt somehow that Collier understood. That he too recognized Mattie's presence in his home as a necessary buffer between the moment his life had changed and the moment when Meredith would come home and change it back.

He didn't ask Mattie to leave.

And so she stayed on.

Waiting, as they all were waiting, breathless with fear, aching with hope.

Waiting for Meredith to come home.

CHAPTER
SIX

The poodle liked eating Chinese food in the dark.

He'd probably like it just as much in the light, but Mattie didn't feel like getting up to turn on the overheads. The twilight in the kitchen suited her mood, a restless blend of anxiety and anger. The anxiety she could explain. Her sister was still missing. The anger . . . well, that was new, and she wasn't ready to look at it just yet. Which was as good a reason as any to keep sitting in the dark.

As Mattie absently broke off a small piece of egg roll, André snatched it out of her fingers and swallowed it whole.

"Hey, Andy," she said, not caring much for his manners or his pretentious French name at the moment. "Don't get greedy. I'm willing to share, but I don't want you getting sick."

His pom-pom tail waggled with appreciation, its ball of black fluff moving back and forth through the crossbeams of the digital clocks. One green glow spread in a wide swath downward from the microwave. One streaked wide from above the double ovens. One cast a smaller beam from the readout on the coffee maker. Outside lights filtered through the windows and the glass panes of the back door. There was plenty of light to afford a clear view of the dog licking his chops, more than enough to reveal that he was clearly hoping to further expand his culinary tastes.

"You miss her, too, don't ya, fella?" Mattie reached out to scratch his ear, to commiserate with Meredith's dog over Meredith's absence. But the poodle ducked his head and tried to lick her hand, interested only in food—where she kept it and when he would get more of it.

So much for sharing this God-awful apprehension. So much for deriving solace from man's best friend.

Where are you, Meredith? When are we going to know what happened to you? Will this waiting ever be over?

The dog butted her hand, tried again to lick the scent of Chinese egg roll from her fingers.

"No kisses, please." Mattie moved her hand out of range and the poodle sat as if on command, waiting, hopeful. "As a general rule, you know, I prefer cats. But I'm beginning to like you, Andy the poodle. For a dog, you're not a bad dinner date."

Again the waggle. The bright boot-black eyes. The slick swipe of pink tongue.

She was such a sucker for that innocent look.

Miss Mattie, can I have another Hello, Kitty! sticker to take to my sister?

Never mind that Annabeth, the prima ballerina of the preschool class, was an only child. Never

mind that instead of reminding Annabeth of the
facts, Mattie gave an extra sticker to everyone.
Never mind that only last week Mattie had heard
two of the other little girls urging Annabeth to ask
for a second sticker.

They were so quick, her students. So innocently
observant.

And they trusted her implicitly.

If only she could be a sucker for their innocent
faith in her. If only she could do away with all her
self-doubts by trading Annabeth an extra sticker.

She nibbled at the egg roll, and the questions
about Meredith looped back. The possibilities, the
unknowns, the millions of answers she didn't have.
The answers no one had. Her brain had turned
into a rock tumbler, polishing and spinning, spinning and polishing, until she'd obsessed over every
scenario incessantly, until they'd begun to blend
into a single, shiny stone of illogical thought.

*Meredith. Kidnapped. Injured. A victim. A survivor.
Injured. Amnesiac. Alive. Dead.*

Mattie couldn't bear to think about it another
second, so she forced her thoughts to Dallas, to the
school. She closed her eyes and pictured Annabeth
and Eliza, Caroline, Hannah and Chloe, Alexandra
and Kylie, Emma Grace and all the other precious
little ones in the pre-primary classes. She took her
time and let each face come clear in her mind, tried
to remember the cadence of each of their voices,
their little-girl giggles. Then she brought the whole
studio into focus, imagined not just the little ones
twirling uninhibited and freely in front of the bank
of mirrors, but also the advanced students watching
their reflected technique, the adults focusing inward

instead of outward. She thought about the spring recitals and the long summer waiting on the other side. She wondered if this would be the year she could begin repaying the principal on Jack's loan, or if she'd only be able to make the interest. She worried that the last six months had been a fluke, that spring enrollment would drop and she'd be sweating next month's bills.

Would you stop? Jack said whenever she worried aloud to him. *Just stop.*

She lowered her hand and leaned forward, reaching for her glass of water. André, a carpe diem dog, snatched the rest of the egg roll from her fingers, carried it to the rag rug that was exclusively his, and flopped down to enjoy his prize. But he kept an eye on her to make sure she didn't come after it.

"Hey," she said. Then, not knowing how to scold a dog for being a dog, she drank the water. "You want some soy sauce with that, Andy the poodle?"

But he ignored her and crunched quietly in the corner shadows. The kitchen clock ticked off the seconds, keeping track in the dark of the accumulating minutes that Meredith had been gone. Her absence was like another shadow in the room, intangible and intractable. Mattie was only beginning to realize the ways her sister's disappearance had chipped a hole in her own identity. Sisters shared more than blood and DNA and parents. Their memories were intertwined for eternity; their lives, however separate, would always be a reflection of each other, a mirror in which they could see who they were or who they might have been. For better or for worse, they were bound by their common history, by the environment and values that had formed them. Mattie could only imagine how much she would lose of herself if she lost the only other person in the world who knew her history from the ground up, who, though often distant, couldn't avoid being the closest person to her heart.

The thought of that loss surged in a crushing ache across her chest, and she shoved the worry aside, locked it down, and did her best to forget about it for a moment as she studiously lined up the takeout cartons in a red-and-white row across the table. A five-pagoda night. Jack would rate this as a four and a half on his one-to-six Mattie alarm scale. One being her mellow mood after a great workout or great sex and six being her bouncing off the wall crazy after a day spent putting together a financial report on the school or driving home in the horrible Dallas traffic. Anxious. Angry. Edgy. Worried. That seemed to be about the extent of her emotional spectrum lately. If he saw tonight's lineup, each carton open and half eaten, he'd already have the wine uncorked and poured into iced tea glasses. Forget the goblets. Some nights called for tall glasses. And if the wine didn't work, he'd take her to bed and distract her with sex. Rough, blow your mind sex.

Sometimes his remedies worked. Sometimes she pretended they did. Sometimes she needed to be as far away from him as possible, and she'd go to the barre and work her body until she had sweated the craziness out. Tonight, her odd mix of crazy had her missing Jack. Not the Jack of this past year, as much as the Jack who had made her feel adored, made her believe she was something special. Tonight, she missed his crooked smile, the rich sexy sound of his laughter, the giddy way she'd felt in the very beginning of their romance. She wasn't sure when the free fall into love had changed into something less exciting, but more comfortable. Maybe when she'd opened the studio and began spending so much time there. Maybe it had happened when Jack gave her the money to get the business started. Maybe it was the inevitable evolution of a long-term relationship. She didn't have any of those to compare with this. The men in her life had been mostly drive-by romances, lasting a few months at best. Though it hadn't seemed so at the time, now she realized there had been some nice men in that mix, men she might have loved had the timing been better. Probably she'd resisted a stable relationship then because she was trying so hard to be *not* like Meredith, who'd met Collier in her first semester at college and never wavered in her commitment to him.

Mattie wondered if she and Jack would ever reach that level of solid commitment. Sometimes, lately, he said things, little nothings, that touched the back of her neck with the faint chill of unease. Nothing he couldn't, and didn't, explain away when asked. Nothing that didn't sound a bit petty and insignificant when she said it aloud. Nothing that couldn't be dismissed as coming from her own insecurities. Insecurities that rose like specters from the past to tempt her into believing she didn't deserve this. Not Jack. Not a good relationship. Not the future that stretched ahead of her with such possibilities. But that didn't stop her from having moments when it was hard to believe she would ever have the stability, the marriage, the life her sister had.

She reached for the middle carton—Kung Pao Pork—and picked up the chopsticks. Andy got up

from his rug, the egg roll long gone now, and stood
expectantly beside her as she settled again in the
chair. She scooched her back against the back of the
chair, pointed her knees at the ceiling, tucked her
heels in against her hips, curled her toes over the
rounded edge of the wooden chair, and brought the
carton up close below her chin. Chopsticks being one
of those items that still belonged on her things-
to-conquer-before-I'm-forty list. Around her, Meredith's house shifted toward midnight, the shadows
slanting slowly toward the turning point of the night,
the wind whistling at the windows, winter chill tap-
ping on the glass panes.

The overhead light bloomed around her like sunrise and she jumped, startled into a mousey squeak
of surprise.

"We pay our electric bill, Mattie. You don't have
to sit in the dark." Collier walked in as if he'd been
called out of bed to conduct an impromptu press
conference. He was in faded jeans and an old college sweatshirt—two items of clothing he must have
managed to hide from his mother because they
looked like he'd been sleeping in them for weeks.
But even as dressed down as he was, he carried with
him the aura of authority that set him apart from
other men. An air of don't-get-in-my-way purpose.
The reassuring presence of a man who knew what
he wanted and how to get it.

Mattie raised the chopsticks to her mouth, but
somehow all the rice had dribbled out on the way
up. "I am comfortable here," she said. "At least I
was before you blinded me with the light."

His brisk stride carried him across the room and
Mattie half expected the cupboard door to spring

open at his glance. "It's almost midnight. I'd ask what you're doing down here so late, but"—he raised an eyebrow in the direction of the cardboard cartons— "the crime scene speaks for itself."

"I can burp, if that will help you close the case."

He turned away, held a glass under the faucet, and turned on the water.

She used the chopsticks to maneuver a pea from one side of the carton to the other, pretending Meredith's absence wasn't standing between them, screaming to be acknowledged, pretending she didn't know that he had come downstairs for the same reason she had—to distract herself as best she could, to do whatever she had to do to keep from screaming.

He shut off the tap, drank the water in one long swallow, and then turned around, leaned back against the counter, arms crossed at his waist. "You didn't find Happy Panda in this kitchen. You had that delivered."

"Again, guilty as charged. Except for the delivery part. It was a drive-by incident."

"Couldn't you have eaten some of the food my mother left? We're approaching critical mass in that refrigerator."

"I wasn't in the mood for macaroni salad."

"Apparently you couldn't decide what you were in the mood for."

She regarded the cartons fondly. Other than Andy the poodle they'd been her only friends tonight. "Not true. I wanted some of everything."

He came closer, picked up one of the cartons, checked the contents, set it back and picked up another. He said nothing, but she felt his silence deserved some justification. "I wasn't quite as hungry as I thought I was."

"You must have thought you were a starving nation."

"Just a small town in Texas." She tried again with the chopsticks, concentrating so she wouldn't blurt out the reason she was in this kitchen on a Thursday night, eating Chinese takeout at ten minutes to Friday. As if he didn't know. Even if he had any extra reassurances to give out, she couldn't really expect him to offer them to her. In this battle of frayed emotions, it was every man for himself. "I'm only a starving nation when there's a full moon." She managed to get a morsel of pork up and out of the box, and felt suddenly generous with her repast. "Help yourself, if you want anything. The sesame chicken isn't bad. But watch out for the General Tso's beef. It has something red and evil in it."

To her surprise, he pulled out a chair and picked up the closest pagoda. "I could use something red and evil about now."

"You'll be sorry."

"I doubt it." He eyed her iffy progress with the chopsticks. "Wouldn't it be more efficient to use a fork?"

"If I wanted efficiency, I'd get a feeding tube."

"That would be a bit drastic."

"Efficiency often is. You, being a mayor, ought to know that."

"I ought to know a good many things I don't." He chose a plastic fork and began to eat.

Mattie played with her food, practicing with the chopsticks, wondering if, perhaps, he'd wandered downstairs because he wanted to talk. But that presumed he'd known she was there, had heard her go out of the house and come back in. Which he probably had. Sleeplessness lay like deep fog over the house, blanketing all but the dreamers. Blake. Alice. For Collier and Mattie, the night was little different from the days. Darker, maybe, but haunted by the same questions, hampered by the same inability to fix the thing that was broken. To sleep was to dream, and to dream was to search— and find nothing.

Meredith was missing.

No amount of talking would fix that.

No amount of mutual worry would turn brother-in-law and sister-in-law into pals either.

So she tried to ignore him—a complicated process given his personality and the fact that she was sitting at his table, a guest in his kitchen.

At midnight.

She glanced at the clock. Midnight, straight up. The witching hour.

During the past ten days, she'd probably spent more time with Collier in this kitchen than she'd spent with him all total during all the years he'd been married to her sister. And she couldn't remember ever being alone with him before. Or if she had, she hadn't noticed. But she *must* have noticed. Collier wasn't the kind of man a woman could be alone with and forget.

Unless the woman was determined not to remember.

A ripple of warning purled upward from her calf and she felt the tell-tale tingle travel along her thigh. The beginnings of a cramp. She slid her foot forward until the rounded edge of the wooden chair struck her instep, then she pointed her toes at the floor, flexed them up, then down again, doing her best to draw the muscles into a slow stretch and out of the contraction.

Too late.

The cramp caught her, and with a strangled cry she jumped up like a bright child in class, sending the Happy Panda carton straight up out of her hands as she leaned over to grab her leg. She bit into her lip and hopped to the counter where she propped her foot, extended her whole body into a curve of concentration, and slowly stretched the cramp into remission.

"Everything all right?" Collier asked, bringing Mattie back to the reality of her sister's kitchen, of standing awkwardly by the sink, of watching the dog lick droplets of oil and soy sauce—all that now was left of the Kung Pao Pork—off the floor.

"Leg cramp. Did you let him eat the whole carton?"

Collier leaned sideways, checked the poodle's progress. "No. He hasn't made it to the carton yet. There could be something still left inside."

"I can't believe you let him eat all that."

"I thought you were through with it." His fork scraped the bottom of the carton in his hand.

Andy snuffled as he rooted across the tile, hoping for an overlooked morsel of pork or a forgotten sliver of rice.

"Do you think he'll get sick?"

"The veterinarian's name and number are on the message board."

Mattie slid back into the chair and reached down for the upended and empty carton. "You're a wealth of concern, Collier."

Collier chose another takeout carton, glanced at the contents, put it back, and selected one of the others. "I'm fresh out of concern. Especially when it comes to that dog."

Mattie considered the tension wafting toward her like a dare. *Ask me*, it whispered. *Ask me where she is.* If she took the dare, if she opened her mouth and let Meredith's name out, the combination of his frustration and her anxiety would crush the moment's fragile alliance and still provide no answers. Only the questions. The endless loop of questions. She could feel his restlessness humming, knew the anger she felt tonight was only an extension of that same not knowing, the helpless feeling of being unable to do anything but wait. Collier was as aware of his helplessness as she was aware of her own. Only a poodle with a slick of greasy contentment around his mouth could remain oblivious to the tension and the fierce frustration sitting at this table.

"Do not get sick, Andy," she warned the dog. For his own good. Because it was easier than talking about the elephant in the room. "I mean it. Don't you dare get sick."

With a quick tail wag of acknowledgment, André went back to nosing the tile.

Collier dug for a final morsel at the bottom of the box, then set it aside, and reached for another carton. "Tell me about Miss Mattie's School of Dance and Drama."

Mattie blinked, surprised and reasonably impressed that he knew the name of her studio. Knowing he wasn't really interested in her school. Or her. Understanding that, like her, he needed distraction. A flow of information he didn't have to analyze, words he didn't need to angst over. He wanted to eat Chinese takeout in his kitchen and have a casual conversation about things that didn't matter in his life. Any topic would work. Miss Mattie's was as good a subject as any to discuss over General Tso's evil red peppers.

So she told him about her students, the iffy first year and a half of operation, the days she still felt certain she'd made a huge mistake. She described the studio and the special flooring she'd had installed, how a classroom needed a light and airy feel, how she chose the music for her classes, how she tried to make the lessons fun as well as instructive. She told him about the million and one options for marketing and how difficult it was to decide where to allocate her small advertising budget. She talked about Annabeth and the stickers, about one student, a boy, who she believed was already advanced past her level of teaching and should move on, but wouldn't take the risk. She mentioned Summer and Andrea and how much she admired Miss Cynthia. He asked a couple of questions. She answered. But the moment the conversation started to stall he asked something else. So Mattie kept talking, moving on to the Nutcracker production of the past season and the complications of wrangling a group of overly excited little dancers.

For twenty minutes, maybe longer, she and Collier shared their evening in Meredith's kitchen without once mentioning the reason they were there.

Then, as if it had been waiting in the wings for a cue, her name tripped past Mattie's tongue. "Meredith danced as Clara one year. Everyone said she was the best Clara they'd ever seen. For her age, anyway."

Collier sat for a moment, then raked his fingers through his thick gold hair. "Where is she? Where the *hell* is she?"

The food in her stomach clumped into a gluey ball of indigestion, uncertainty, and fear. Mostly fear. "We'll find her. I still feel like she's okay, Collier. Lost, maybe, but okay."

"Lost," he repeated as if the word were foreign and meaningless on his tongue. "How can anyone be *okay* if they get *lost* for over a week."

But it wasn't a question. It was, in itself, an answer.

He stood abruptly, pushed up from the table, and began stacking the cartons to clear the table, clean the mess.

"Go to bed, Collier." Mattie got up and took the empty cartons out of his hands. Her fingers brushed across his and she was surprised, somehow, to feel the heat on his skin, the nip of awareness as it transferred to hers. "I'll clean up. Maybe you can catch a little sleep before your alarm clock goes off."

His bloodshot eyes flicked to meet hers and held. "Don't," he said. "I don't want one more person worrying about me. Especially not you."

He walked brusquely from the room then, snapping off the light and leaving her standing in the dark, holding an armload of Happy Panda pagodas and feeling more anxious than she had before. More alert. More aware.

But no longer angry.

By morning, the anger Collier had taken to bed with him had morphed into an ugly mood. He was tired. Exhausted and edgy. He wanted to open his eyes and find that his life was as it had been before, that Meredith lay beside him, the mask of sleep still on her beautiful face, that Blake cried softly in the room next door coaxing his daddy awake, waiting and ready for a diaper change and his morning bottle. Collier craved the routine he'd taken for granted, the budding noises of a house before the day began. A normal day. Not a day spent out of place, out of sync with the rest of the world.

But this morning began like the past several before it—with Blake's cry and the crushing understanding that nothing would ever be like it was again.

Ten days. Meredith had been gone ten days.

Rising, he pulled on the sweatshirt and jeans he'd worn last night, then went to be with the only person who could have gotten him out of bed.

After Blake had his fill of breakfast, Collier stayed and played with him for awhile. Then leaving his son in Mrs. Oliver's capable hands, he went back to being the anxious, angry husband whose wife had disappeared without a trace and left him hanging by a thread.

By the time he'd showered and dressed, the anger had returned in full measure, disguising itself as action. He grabbed up an empty plate and two used glasses he'd brought to his bedroom during the course of the past couple of nights and headed downstairs to the kitchen. He had a plan. He'd put these dishes in the dishwasher and set it to run. Then he'd mop the floor. Mattie probably hadn't done that. It'd been late when he left her. After midnight. And she'd looked as tired as he felt when he first walked into the kitchen to find her sitting in the chair, feet up, chopsticks in her hand. In his mind's eye, he could so easily recall the way she'd looked. Her reddish hair twisted impromptu on top of her head, her face pale and pixie-freckled, her body an "N" of grace in faded, well-worn sweats.

He wished he hadn't gone to the kitchen last night, hadn't followed the scent of her midnight feast downstairs. But last night, he'd been restless and frustrated and achingly afraid. So he'd sat in the kitchen and begged Mattie to make him feel better, to help him forget.

She probably hadn't realized that's what he was asking of her. He'd never thought of her as particularly deep or thoughtful. And it didn't matter. He'd felt like he'd bust out of his skin if he didn't think about something besides Meredith's disappearance. So he'd asked Mattie to distract him and she had. She didn't deserve the brunt of his frustration. Logically, he knew it was unfair to blame her, understood it was shameful to wish she'd been the one who'd vanished into thin air. But that didn't stop his exasperation from zeroing in on her.

Because there was no way past the fact that her very presence in his kitchen meant he couldn't forget his wife was missing. Had been missing now for ten days. Ten days that stretched toward an eternity.

Today, though, he had a plan to keep from dwelling on that. He'd straighten up around the house. Despite his mother's weekend flurry of cleaning, it hadn't taken long for everything to begin piling up again, needing his attention. Unread newspapers. The mail. Meredith normally took care of any clutter. Swept it aside before it had a chance to accumulate. She was great with details. Newspapers recycled. Bills paid. Mail sorted for him and stacked according to priority. Before this happened, he'd believed he had more tolerance for disorder than she did. He'd believed everything found its own order because she ordered it so, because she found security in the control she exercised over the house and what came into it and what went out of it. If anything, he'd thought she was obsessive in her need to maintain order. Perfect order.

This morning, though, he realized how much he depended on the maintenance of that order, how much discomfort its absence created. Something as minor as a glass he'd left in the study, the plate of crumbs he'd forgotten in the bedroom, the stack of mail thickening in place and then slowly sliding from the console to scatter about the floor as he passed by—it all bothered him. Annoyed him. Set his nerves on edge. Made him angry.

His skin itched with the buildup of tension and he wanted to claw it from his body, rip off the reality that encased him. Without Meredith, everything in the house, in the world, in his life, seemed wrong and unfocused. Even his own body felt as if it belonged to someone else. Someone he didn't know.

Where are you, Meredith? What happened to you?

The questions beat him through the kitchen doorway and the anger peaked when he saw his sister-in-law using the kitchen counter, *his* kitchen counter, as a ballet barre, her body bent in a comma of grace. A comma that straightened into a hasty exclamation point, straight and emphatic, as he walked in. He'd thought she'd have been down for breakfast and back in her own room by now. He'd thought he'd timed his activities to avoid running into her this morning. He'd thought he could pretend—just for a little while—that she wasn't here, that he hadn't asked her to come and take care of her mother.

Because Meredith wasn't here to do it. Because someone had to. Because Collier needed help.

And now Mattie was in his kitchen. Again.

She said nothing as he approached, which annoyed him even more. He'd start the dishwasher and leave without speaking to her at all. It was his house. He didn't have to make polite conversation if he didn't feel like it.

And he damn sure didn't feel like it this morning.

But her eyes followed him, and he caught a glimpse of her body bending into another fluid curve. Jerking open the door of the dishwasher he saw André, a curl of black misery, on his rug. "What's wrong with the dog?"

"Too much Kung Pao." Her arm dipped over the line of her body, bobbed up and then dipped over again. "I've already called Dr. Kristi and made an appointment to take him in."

Collier stacked the plate, moved a couple of items to make room for the glasses. "You're taking the dog to the vet?"

"Yes."

"When?"

"This afternoon. Although he'll probably be feeling much better by the time of his appointment. That's usually the way those things work."

He opened the cabinet, looking for the box of detergent, slapped it shut, and opened another. "I'm certain Dr. Kristi will tell you exactly what I told you. He's a dog. He eats dog food. You shouldn't have been feeding him anything else." It twigged his memory that he'd aided and abetted her in that endeavor just hours before. So he slammed another cabinet door. "And now, on top of everything else, I'll have a damn vet bill to pay."

Silence. Another few dips of that hand, the line from fingertip to shoulder one fluid arch. He didn't want to notice that, didn't want to recognize the lovely, supple grace of her body, didn't want to see the twirl of chestnut hair—neater, this morning and not so haphazard—curling down past her neck, the healthy rose on her cheeks, the dewy sheen of exertion. He'd prefer not to have to see her at all. So he opened yet another cabinet door. Where in God's name did Meredith keep the dish detergent?

"What will you do with Alice?" he asked, not really caring as long as she didn't leave his mother-in-law alone.

"When?"

The discomfort of being in his own skin spread like a fungus, grated on his nerves, itched like a son of a gun. "When you take the dog to the vet's," he said tightly.

"She'll go with me."

"To the vet's?"

Mattie made a sound, almost a sigh, but maybe only a small exhale as she turned and began her limbering exercise from the opposite angle. "Yes," she answered. "Do you think it would be better to keep her caged inside this house day and night? Lock her in her room, the way you keep Blake locked away in his?"

This time the silence hung suspended, breathless, and he stood staring at her. Too angry to speak.

She pulled out of a bend, put her foot back on

the floor, and turned to face him. Aware, apparently, of just how far past too far she'd gone.

He gave her a chance—a full minute, maybe more—to apologize and when she didn't, the anger and frustration crested and spilled out of him, flooding toward her in a string of curse words he hadn't used since he was thirteen and too stupid to know better.

She took it with her chin up, her arms open, one hand still coiled over the rounded counter top. Then, she told him what he needed. *As if she would ever have a clue.*

"You're exhausted. You need some sleep," she said. "And you need to talk to Mrs. Oliver again. She locked the nursery door, Collier. I heard her. I did not imagine it, no matter what she told you afterward. And just now, when she came in, she informed me the baby needs to get back on a proper schedule, that I should stay out of the nursery during the day."

He wanted to light into her, blast her with how wrong she was about him, about the baby, about Mrs. Oliver, about the dog . . . about everything. But having lost control already, he could only make the situation worse. He did not have to defend himself to her. He did not have to defend his son's nurse. He would not . . . would *not* . . . let Mattie annoy him again today. At least not again this morning. He could handle reporters—a dozen at a whack—and he did not have to allow this one small paper cut of a female to bother him. "Have you seen the dishwasher detergent?" he asked in as civil a tone as he could manage.

"It's in the pantry," she said, annoying him just because she sounded so certain. "Top shelf."

"That's a stupid place to keep it. It should be here, under the sink, not clear across the kitchen."

"I'm just telling you where it is. I'm not the one who put it there. Maybe my sister thought it'd be safer there."

"Safer for what? The dishes?"

"For Blake. I imagine he could have a handful of soap almost before you knew he'd toddled into the kitchen."

Of course, she was right. Long before Blake's birth, Meredith had done a baby-proofing exercise—cleaning solvents up high out of reach, electric outlets plugged. The location of the detergent made perfect sense now. And the ache inside him felt like a gaping wound. It would be several months before Blake could be in any danger in this kitchen. He didn't even crawl yet. But Collier didn't say that. He simply lifted down the soap box and returned to the dishwasher.

"Those dishes are clean." Mattie did little pliés, using the counter top for balance. "I ran the dishwasher last night."

"Why didn't you say that before I put the dirty dishes in?"

She shrugged, a move as lithe as the dip and bend of her body. "I wasn't paying attention to what you were doing."

He opened his mouth to tell her to leave. Today. Now. This minute. Take her dancer's body and get the hell out of his house. But just the thought knotted in his stomach like heartburn. And the words wouldn't come out of his mouth, wouldn't budge off his tongue. Because as much as he wanted Mattie to go, he wanted her to stay. If she went, Alice would go too, and he would have to face whatever was coming alone. From what Meredith told him Mattie hadn't been much of a sister, and Alice had had a heck of a time raising her. But she'd come when he asked. And she was doing what he'd asked her to do. And last night, she'd held vigil with him against the nightmare.

If he told her to go, she would.

"Next time I'd appreciate it if you would," he said.

"Would what?"

"Tell me when you run the dishwasher."

"I guess I could stick a note on it."

"That would be helpful. Thank you."

"No problem."

But the *whatever* tone of her voice irritated him again. So he headed for the door, abandoning his plan to mop, to straighten the house, to accomplish anything constructive—at least in any room in which she was present.

"Since we're making demands on each other—" she began, stopping him.

"Suggestion," he corrected, reluctantly turning back. "Only a suggestion."

"Okay, then, a suggestion. Please. Don't discount what I told you about Mrs. Oliver. Something about her isn't right. And she lied to you about locking the nursery door. She did."

He was exhausted. He felt it now in every raw nerve, in the very real headache that throbbed in his temples. He'd been running on adrenalin and hope for well over a week now, using up every available resource. He flat didn't have the energy to spend another minute with Mattie. "Meredith and

I chose Mrs. Oliver for a reason. A good reason.
Blake needs the security of a schedule. It will help
him get through the surgeries and the therapy afterward. I appreciate your concern, Mattie. But I
don't need your help to take care of my son." He
turned again for the doorway.

And again, she stopped him. "We'll hear something today," she said. "We're bound to hear something today."

He knew it was her way of apologizing for being in
his kitchen, for being in his house, for being in his life
at all. He understood she meant it as encouragement
and comfort, but still he couldn't bring himself to
agree and acknowledge the lie neither of them fully
believed. Instead, he headed upstairs again. He'd get
through today because he had no choice. He'd go
back to the center, even though the activity there continued to dwindle into hopelessness. He'd go over
every step Meredith had taken for the last several
weeks. For the past six months. He'd talk to Ross.
He'd check in with Brooke. Tonight, he'd take a
sleeping tablet. Tonight, somehow, he'd sleep. And tomorrow . . . well, all of this could be over tomorrow.

Without conscious intent, he found himself outside the closed nursery door, reaching for the
knob, turning it, opening the door without incident. The door wasn't locked. Mrs. Oliver was an
experienced nurse. She wasn't taking any foolish
chances with Blake. She wouldn't do that. But he'd
allowed Mattie to plant a seed in his mind, so here
he was. Doubting himself. Doubting Meredith. As
if this was the time to re-evaluate every decision.

He said hello to the nurse, who said nothing to
him about schedules, who went out of her way to

tell him how nice it had been to have a couple of unexpected days off at the beginning of the week while the baby's grandparents were here. Collier picked up his son, snuggled into the sweet smell of his neck, and tried to remember how many times he'd actually had a conversation with Mrs. Oliver, how much he actually knew about the woman who cared for his child. After this was all over, he'd make it a point to speak with her more often, to learn the things about her that at the moment he couldn't recall knowing.

Blake gurgled a contented stream of baby sounds as he gnawed on a teething toy and drooled all over his daddy's clean shirt. Collier held his boy close on his shoulder as he walked to the window, where they stood, father and son, looking out at another bleak morning.

They were still at the window when the phone rang.

Collier carried the baby with him into the bedroom and answered it on the second ring.

It was Ross.

They'd found the Mercedes.

CHAPTER SEVEN

Jack's voice, thick with dreaming, answered Mattie's call, came belatedly awake when she told him about Meredith's car. "They found it? Where? How?"

"In Denver," she repeated, figuring he'd heard only half of what she'd just said and processed even less than that. Jack, at his best, went to bed at three in the morning and started his day around noon. "At the Park-It Lot near the airport. It was a fluke, really, that they found it."

"The parking lot?"

"It was a fluke that they found the car in Denver at the Park-It Lot." She heard the sheets rustle, imagined him pushing up on one elbow, the linens sliding off his skin, his hand shoving through his thick, sleep-tousled hair. She knew his forehead was creased with confusion, his thoughts struggling somewhere between a dead sleep and half alert. And she tried to be patient as she went through the brief explanation again. "A night clerk heard about Meredith's disappearance and made the connection with the Oklahoma plates on a Mercedes in the lot."

"They found it." Jack still seemed to be having difficulty getting his mind around that. "In the parking lot."

"The Park-It Lot," she said one more time. "It's one of those long-term parking facilities. Like the one you use whenever you fly out of Dallas."

"Dallas," he repeated around a long yawn. "I didn't think they'd find it there. What time is it?"

Two hours ahead of where he was. Eight. Six. "I don't know," she said. "Does it matter?"

Another yawn. A more purposeful rustle of sheets in the background. "Let me get out of bed, Mat. I'll get a cup of coffee and call you back in a minute. Hang tight, babe." And he hung up on her.

Mattie snapped the cell phone shut and held its trim little body in her palm. Leaning back, she braced her elbows on the stair behind her, kept watch on both upstairs and downstairs from her seat on the landing. Upstairs, Alice was thankfully still in bed, the door to her room still closed. Downstairs, Collier was meeting with Ross, and that door, too, remained closed. Mattie did not feel it was necessary to watch the upstairs door because her mother seldom got up before eight-thirty and it was pointless to watch the downstairs door because once it opened the discussion going on behind it would be over, and she wouldn't know what had been said.

What she wanted was to be downstairs, in the study, with the two men.

"Keep an eye on Alice," Collier had said. "I don't want her walking in on this."

This being what the police knew or suspected or hoped to discover now that the car had been found.

Her mind teemed with possible, improbable reasons for how Meredith's Mercedes had wound up in Denver. She wanted more information, could hardly breathe for wanting to know everything Ross knew, everything he even thought might be true. So how had she wound up sitting on this step, halfway between one place and another, shut out of a conversation she desperately wanted to participate in?

Keep an eye on Alice.

Collier hadn't told her specifically to wait on the stairs. He'd asked her to keep her mother from walking in on what might be a jolting bit of information. She could have taken a stand in the study doorway, where she could hear what was being said and still have heard her mother's footsteps should she come down the stairs. But, no, Mattie had put herself on the stairs. Because the funny thing about being pushed to the outside as a child was that it became ridiculously easy as an adult to believe that's where you still belonged. In this house, it seemed normal, even natural, to step aside before someone had the chance to shove her out of the way. In Meredith's world, Mattie too often avoided giving anyone the opportunity to make her feel unimportant— and wound up being unimportant because of her own actions.

Keep an eye on Alice.

Alice, who had wanted a child so much she'd married a man she didn't love and worked at becoming pregnant as if her life depended on bringing a baby into the world. She'd been far past the prime child-bearing years, but her tenacity had finally paid off and the child she'd dreamed of, prayed for, yearned for, and knew she deserved was hers. A girl. A perfect, special daughter she named Meredith Julia, after her grandmother and a favorite aunt. What could be better?

And that was Meredith's story. Planned, longed for, loved, and adored. A beautiful, bright sparkle of a girl. Alice's gift to herself and the world.

Many women might have viewed a second pregnancy so soon after the first as a bonus, a second blessing on the heels of the first. But Alice didn't like surprises and she especially didn't care for this one. She had the child she wanted, and she wanted to devote herself completely to enjoying mother-hood and Meredith. Joseph's attempts to persuade her that this unexpected second child would be just as special, just as dear, sealed the fate of the marriage and Mattie's future.

No child could ever match Meredith. Alice wouldn't allow it, and she resented Mattie's intrusion from the start. The pregnancy was troublesome, the labor long and difficult, and Mattie arrived on the hottest day of a long, hot summer, screaming her lungs out, red-faced and angry. As if she knew, even before drawing her first breath, that she would have to demand her mother's attention to get it.

That was Mattie's story. The mistake. The trou-blemaker. Alternately, grabbing for the spotlight and conceding it without a whimper. That was what she had learned being Meredith's sister and Alice's other daughter.

She wasn't that person anymore. And yet, here she sat, choosing to interpret her brother-in-law's request as exclusion, accepting her self-designated role in this household as if she had no choice.

Bouncing up from the step, she had reached the foyer when the cell phone trilled an irritating summons and vibrated in her hand. It took a moment to remember she'd called Jack and that he was calling her back. Because he hadn't been awake enough to separate her words from whatever he'd been dreaming. Because he would be alert enough now to want her to repeat everything she had already said. And already repeated. He'd ask a million questions she couldn't answer. He'd offer his own interpretation, which would be no more insightful than her own. Flipping open the phone, she lifted it to her ear and leaned back toward the landing and one last check of her mother's door. Still closed. "Jack?"

"Sorry about that." His voice now held the seeds of caffeine and a jolt of wakefulness. "So . . . I'm ready to hear how some amateur sleuth managed to find Meredith's car in a Denver parking lot."

"I can't talk now. I'll call you back later."

And she ended the connection, cutting him off as easily as he normally ended conversations with her. She didn't want to talk to him now, didn't need what sparse comfort he could offer long distance. She wanted the real story, first hand. Meredith was her sister. She needed to know what Ross had to say and, as she passed the credenza, she was barely aware of dropping the phone on a shifting stack of mail. Already, her mind was tuning in to the conversation going on in the study, already her ears were reaching for the sound of voices inside, already her hand was reaching out to open the door.

" . . . VIN numbers match and the tag. It's Meredith's car." Ross stood in the center of the room while Collier paced from the big desk to the big window and back. Tension nipped Mattie like a static charge, and her breath crackled in her mouth and throat with a sharp, icy tang, as if she'd chased a breath mint with a gulp of cold, cold water.

"But how did it get there? Tell me how you think it got from Reyes City to Denver."

Ross glanced at Mattie, aware that she'd come in even if Collier was too distracted to notice. The chief's demeanor was weary, but calm. A calm born of many years spent behind his badge. He was the professional here. The only one with an ounce of perspective. The only one with any hope of maintaining some perspective. "I don't know. No one knows. Yet."

"Does it mean we're closer to finding her?"

"I don't know, Collier. I've told you everything that was said to me. We just caught a break. Give our guys a little time to work on it before you demand answers."

"I just want to know how it got there, Ross. How does it possibly make sense that it would be in a parking lot in Denver?"

"Let's concentrate on what we do know. Not what we don't."

"We know Meredith wouldn't have driven to Denver."

Ross frowned, obviously trying to balance diplomacy and friendship. "Our guys will be very thorough. When they get through with the car, we'll know if anyone else was with her."

Collier shot him a skeptical look, a mix of challenge and fear.

"We'll know," Ross repeated. "And that's a whole lot more than we know right now."

"So why are you checking airline records? You can't seriously believe she got on a plane."

"Those parking lots are generally used by someone who's traveling by air. We're just covering all the bases. At this point, we've got the car. That's all we've got for certain, but that's more than we had yesterday. A lot more."

The reassurance seemed to bring Collier off the apex of his doubt, seemed to settle him again in the reality of the here and now, in the knowledge of what he could do and what he couldn't. "How long before we hear?"

Ross plunged his hands into his pants pockets and jangled the keys and coins he carried. "Tomorrow, at the earliest. More likely, it'll be next week. Or even longer. This case is top priority for me and my guys. It won't be for the crew in Denver."

"No one there who owes you a favor?" Collier had to be desperate to ask that. Mattie could see the cost to him in the fine lines around his eyes. "Isn't there someone you can ask to give this a bump up the ladder?"

"I've tapped every connection I've got. Now we just have to wait."

"The longer this goes on, the further we are from finding her."

"We're doing our best."

The two men exchanged glances, a brushing of one's gaze across the other, a moment that held both challenge and apology and settled the tension between them into a fragile but mutual understanding.

The breath Mattie hadn't been aware she was holding escaped in a slow, painful sigh. She was tired of the waiting, too. Fearful of the not knowing.

But even more afraid to have it end.

"I could go to Denver," Collier said. "Look at the car. I might notice something everyone else would miss."

"The best help you can give a team of investigators is to let them do their job. Stay here. Take care of your son. Work from home if you can. Occupy yourself however you can. Waiting is hard, I know, but it's the only thing left to do."

Collier's hand shook as he raked his fingers through his already disheveled hair. Mattie could see the tremor from where she stood inside the doorway; she felt the terrible frustration of his helplessness as if she were on the other end of a rubber band stretched to the breaking point, knowing at any moment it would snap.

"I can't stand much more of this," he said, his voice grating and raw with emotion. "If she's not coming home, I'd rather know. Right now. Face it. Deal with it. For all we know, finding the car may mean nothing. For all we know, Meredith is dead."

The words dropped into the tension and set it rippling like a tsunami that would sweep them all into its undertow. It was nothing they hadn't each thought at one time or another, nothing that hadn't permeated the consciousness of the whole community, of everyone involved in the search. But for Collier to say it, to give voice to the unbearable clamped Mattie's heart in a vise of pain so harsh, so crushing, she wanted to scream out a rebuff, make him take back the words. But when she opened her mouth to correct him, to reinstate the denial she needed, the denial they all needed, someone else spoke first.

"Meredith? My Meredith is *dead?*"

Alice's voice, lucid and clear, rose behind Mattie—and the cold fear in the room crested and then shattered like glass around them.

She whirled to see her mother staring at Collier in horror, turning pale, swaying like a tree caught in a winter wind.

"Alice, no." Collier moved quickly to catch her. His eyes flicked past Mattie and skimmed away, leaving a thick guilt behind. *I asked you to watch her,* they said. *I asked you to make sure she didn't hear this.*

But blame had no place to go because Alice's mournful wail filled the room to capacity and ricocheted off every eardrum, growing louder and more distressed as she crumpled in a heap of sorrow to the floor. Her cries spilled out through the screen of her fragile hands, poured from her in agonizing distress.

Mattie sank to her mother's side, sick with regret, whispering repeated denials into her mother's ear, offering a belated, blind comfort. For days she'd kept her mother safe, watched her, entertained her, tried to find a back door into a rational, reasonable corner of her mother's mind.

And failed to protect her just once.

When it mattered most.

CHAPTER EIGHT

Mattie was halfway up the stairs with the tray when the phone rang. She turned around, careful not to spill the hot tea all over the little lace doily that nestled between the cup and saucer. This was the third time she'd made this trip, and she wasn't giving her mother any reason to send the tray back. Again. Mattie had followed instructions to the letter and Alice would drink this cup of tea or go without. Hysterics or no.

"Mattie!" Her mother yelled down from upstairs. "The phone's ringing."

"Thanks, Mom, I didn't notice," she said under her breath, even though Alice was in her bedroom and wouldn't have overheard in any case. The morning's panic had ebbed into a querulous, fretful afternoon. Nothing suited. Nothing was right. Somewhere around noon, Alice had lost the memory of what had upset her, but not the feeling. Mattie had tried everything—except drugs. And if this tea didn't work, Valium was next.

"Mattie! The phone!"

Screw the tea. If she kept screeching, she'd interrupt the baby's afternoon nap and Nurse Stick-to-the-Schedule-or-Else would come bolting out of the nursery to fuss at Mattie. Again.

Reaching the bottom step, Mattie gingerly switched the tray to one hand as she picked up the cordless phone from atop a tottering stack of mail. "Montgomery residence," she said blocking a letter cascade with the tip of her elbow, looking around for a clear spot to set the tray.

"Mattie?"

Her hands went limp and the tray tilted. The teacup tipped into the saucer and the steaming tea sluiced over the side, and Mattie just let it go. "Meredith? *Meredith?*"

Her voice squeaked, a screech of a sound, but even that was overshadowed by the clatter of the tray striking the floor, the china cup striking the china plate, shattering as they broke apart.

She adjusted the phone to her ear, giving it the full pressure of both hands, pressing it hard against her ear. "Meredith?" she repeated in a husky whisper, afraid to hope, certain she had cast some other voice into the tone and cadence of her sister's.

A sigh. Long, lonely, and tremulous. "Mattie. I didn't think about you picking up. I thought I'd get the answering machine."

Mattie sagged like the tea bag, crumpling into a soggy wad of relief. "Meredith. Oh, God. Oh, God! You're all right!" She had to stop for a second and swallow the gummy dryness in her mouth, find the breath that had shortchanged her. "You . . . you *are* all right, aren't you?"

"All right. All. Right." Meredith repeated the words slowly, carefully, her voice mulling them with contradiction. "I guess that would be a matter of perspective."

"Who . . . whose perspective? Your"—she dropped her voice to a breathy, painfully hoarse whisper—"kidnappers?"

The laugh came, startling, short and edgy. "Oh, Mattie, you've always been such a slut for drama. Put Collier on the phone."

Mattie's heartbeat fluttered, fast, faster, as rapidly as a hummingbird's wings, understanding on some level that she'd missed something, but unable to stop thinking: *She's safe, she's safe, she's safe.* "He's not here." The words tumbled out in a rush. "He took the dog to the vet. I . . . I could reach him on his cell phone."

"*I* could reach him on his cell phone. What's wrong with André?"

"Nothing. A stomachache." Mattie couldn't think about the dog. "Where are you? Are you really okay? What happened? Where have you been? Are you . . . what . . . where—"

"I'm okay, Mattie," Meredith interrupted. Firmly. Impatiently. "I'm okay. Really. Nothing's wrong."

"You've been gone ten days. Something must be wrong."

There was a hesitation like a car engine idling, somewhere between the decision to roll through an intersection or come to a complete stop. "Let's not turn this into a melodrama."

Melodrama? she thought, wondering how Meredith could treat her disappearance so lightly.

"It's been very tense here, Meredith. We had no idea where you were or if you were safe."

"I'm safe. That's really all you need to know."

She sounded normal. Perfectly normal. As if she'd just phoned to say hello, to ask a question about the dog, to offer her little sister a piece of advice. For someone they'd thought might be dead only a few hours ago, she sounded insanely normal. "What's going on, Meredith? What happened to you?"

The pause hung there, lasted forever. Maybe longer. "This is something I should discuss with Collier."

"You won't even tell me where you are? We've been frantic here, thinking something horrible had happened to you, thinking you might even be . . . dead." Yet Mattie realized even as she spoke that the words lacked conviction. Some internal barometer had kept her from believing that was the truth. She'd attributed it to denial, a buffer between possibility and reality. But now, connected to Meredith by wires and air and a tenacious history that stretched from childhood to this moment, she felt the twang of their kinship, knew it could not have been severed without some level of awareness on her part. For better or worse, they were sisters. The good sister and the other one. "Even Mother thought you might be dead," she finished, but the indictment fell short of accusation.

Meredith's answer came as a sigh, a remote form of regret. "I'm okay. I'm safe. I'm fine. I'm . . . happy."

Words that should have been reassuring, words that should have filled her with gratitude and thankfulness instead sent a chill through her body, shocked her system with an adrenaline surge of bewilderment. Ten days. And Meredith was okay? All that time, she was safe. She was fine. She was *happy?* "You disappeared for ten days. Okay doesn't quite explain that."

"I don't owe you any explanation, Mattie, and I can't imagine you'd understand it, if I offered one. Suffice it to say, I didn't know this would get blown all out of proportion. Until this morning, I wasn't aware of all that was happening there."

"Oh, come on, Meredith. You disappeared. It's been on the news, in the papers. You had to know we were searching for you. You, of all people, would have expected everyone to search for you."

"What does that mean? *You, of all people?* I didn't expect any of this. I thought things had been handled."

The cool, above-it-all affront in her sister's voice picked up the remnants of Mattie's relief and twisted them into anger. How could Meredith—how could *anyone*—be so self-absorbed, so completely selfish? "How could you think it had been handled?" she asked tightly. "How could you not have picked up the phone and called to say you were all right? How can you justify not doing that?"

"I don't have to justify anything. You used to disappear and no one even blinked an eye. So don't you dare fuss at me over this. I thought it had been handled. Leave it at that."

"Why should I? You've put this family through hell. I was a stupid kid when I ran away. You're an adult. You know better."

"I don't have to listen to this. This isn't about you, Mattie. It's about me. Tell Collier I'll call back."

"*Wait.* Tell me where you are. Tell me how to contact—"

"I'll call back."

"When?"

"I don't know. Tonight, maybe."

Mattie could feel her sister slipping away, distancing herself, leaving behind more questions than she'd answered, snatching back the relief the sound of her voice had so briefly provided. "When, Meredith? *When* will you call?"

"I'll call when I'm sure Collier will be there."

"Tonight. He'll be here tonight."

Another sigh. As if calling back would be an imposition.

"Tonight, then."

"You swear? You *promise?*" It was a request from childhood, from the younger sister to the older, a plea for reassurance, a petition for a binding pledge of trust.

"Mattie." The answer was a command from childhood, from the older sister to the younger, an admonishment to cease and desist, a warning to let sleeping dogs lie. "I'll call when I'm ready."

And a sudden, disconcerting anger flooded Mattie's heart and mind in a red wave. "Tonight," she uttered a command of her own. "You'd damn well better call tonight."

Then, before she was even aware of her intention, Mattie flung the phone across the room, where it struck the wall and broke apart, where a chunk of plaster chipped off and plunged to the floor in a puff of furious dust, where the connection with her sister ended as abruptly and unexpectedly as it had begun.

Shaking from head to toe, awash in emotions that

felt both frightening and invigorating, emotions she couldn't even find words to describe, Mattie looked at the mess in Meredith's foyer. The scrape across the honeyed wood where the tray had gouged a small scar. The stain still spreading on the Turkish rug. The chips of bone china winking in minute fragments all over the floor. The plaster. The phone, its back broken, the battery spilling out.

She'd hung up on her sister. Meredith had called and Mattie had hung up on her. Even if the intensity of her emotions had caused a seizure, she should have held onto the connection, checked the Caller ID, insisted Meredith give a number where she could be reached. Something, anything, other than precipitously ending the call and destroying the phone.

Her hand ached from the hard grip she'd had on the receiver. Her ear stung from the pressure she'd shoved against it. Her mind seethed with the impossible thought that Meredith wasn't dead or kidnapped or murdered or held hostage, but just *away*. By choice.

By her own choice.

And what should have been good news seemed suddenly like the worst news possible.

"Mattie! Did you spill my tea?" Alice's voice was on the move, coming from the upstairs hall to the top of the stairwell. "I certainly hope you haven't broken your sister's good china."

As if a broken cup and saucer mattered. Mattie felt as if she could break them all with impunity, could shatter each delicate piece without regret. Anger wasn't the reaction she'd expected to have. Anger wasn't what she wanted to feel. But she didn't really know what other response would be appropriate under the circumstances. How could Meredith have done this? How could she have abandoned her husband and child? How could she have walked away? How could she have been gone so long without calling? How could she not come back? Now. The very first moment she could.

But then, she could have come back anytime.

While they searched and worried and feared the worst, Meredith could have come back any time she wanted.

"Mattie?" Her mother's voice floated down to her from the landing, the last syllable trailing off as she came in view of the foyer. "I knew you'd broken that cup and saucer. I knew the minute I sent you downstairs that you'd break your sister's good china. And look what you've done to that rug. It was very expensive, you know. Almost priceless, and now you've ruined it."

And Meredith had ruined the life Mattie had envied her. Not exactly an even swap.

"Go back upstairs, please, Mother. When I've cleaned up some of the mess, I'll bring you another cup of tea."

Alice sniffed her disapproval. "I'd rather do without."

How about doing without your precious Meredith? How will you feel about that?

"You should call someone about treating that stain. Before it's too late and the discoloration sets in."

Too late. Too late. Too late.

But Mattie just stood there, too confused to move, teeming with an uncomfortable resentment, an unsettling shock and an old, old envy. Meredith had been born with so much. Such a glorious birthright.

There had been a time when Mattie would have given anything to be allowed to stand for one minute in her place.

She had to phone Collier. Or maybe she should call Ross, let him be the one to inform Collier that Meredith had—had what? Had left him? Had left her baby? Good news, bad news . . .

They'd hoped for this, prayed for this, begged God to let her be okay, pleaded with the universe to have the news be good, to have her phone home and tell them she was all right.

And she had.

"Go upstairs," she repeated, aware of her mother's watchful stare. "I'll be up in a minute." Because she would not tell her mother now. She couldn't. She didn't know how she would ever find the words to tell Collier.

"For heaven's sake, Mattie, get a towel and soak some of that tea out of the rug. It's going to be ruined. Utterly ruined. I don't know how Meredith will ever forgive you."

Meredith had bigger problems.

Mattie looked up at the landing. "Go back upstairs. Please, let me handle this."

Alice lifted her eyebrows, but she said not another word as she turned and ascended the stairs, retreating from Mattie's line of vision. As she watched her go, Mattie's anger began to mutate, took the form of questions pondered during the past week and a half, changed shape in a strange, new context. What if Meredith didn't come back? What would Collier do? What would that do to Blake? What would happen to Alice? How would Mattie manage to be Alice's only daughter instead of just her other daughter? Mattie would have to move her mother to Dallas. Find someone to stay with her. Or somewhere she could stay while Mattie worked. Would that be difficult? And expensive? She couldn't stay here with Collier. He'd have his hands full with the baby. He'd have to keep Nurse Oliver. Or move closer to his parents so they could help. What would this do to his career? Like a pond disturbed by the skip of a stone, the ripples from Meredith's phone call widened out, ruffled the waters, and moved toward the shores of change.

This isn't about you, Mattie.

But it was. It was about her. It was about Alice. And Collier. And Blake. It was about Meredith's whole life, and about the people in it.

For a moment, a dozen heartbeats, Mattie let herself remember everything about Meredith's call. The tone of her voice. The pauses. The words. The sighs. She tried to remove her own interpretation and analyze only the facts, but that proved impossible. Meredith had called. She was all right. She had chosen to leave, to walk out on her marriage, her baby, her life.

Why?

So many questions summed up in that one query. So many unknowns still left. If only she'd told Mattie why. And what was supposed to happen next.

From hoping her sister was alive to hoping she'd have the courtesy to make one more call. From a morning that started with the first break in Meredith's mysterious disappearance to an afternoon when sheer relief gave way to confusion and a bewildering wrath. From an ill-defined fear to a sharp and painful ache. It had been a long day's journey already.

And the worst was still to come.

Collier.

She had to tell Collier.

Gathering in a deep breath, Mattie held it, then let it go and pulled in another until the air flooded her lungs, expanded them, made them hurt. *Relax. Relax. Relax.* She let the breath out. Slowly let it go. Until the air was gone and she had gained enough control to go into the other room and lift the phone.

They sat like lumps in the study.

Collier behind his desk. André on the floor. Ross on the sofa. Mattie in the window seat.

Waiting, as they'd been waiting all evening, for the phone to ring.

Mattie wished Blake was still with them. Collier had brought him down for dinner, fed him pureed squash and strained pears, and let him bang the lid of a pot on the plastic tray of his high chair. When the percussion became rhythmic enough to clench teeth, Mattie had snatched up the baby, cleaned him up, and set him on a blanket in the middle of the study. From there, he'd done his best to provide entertainment for the adults, babbling and batting at his toys, rolling onto his belly and pushing up onto his hands and knees, rocking in that position as if he meant to go somewhere the very minute he figured out how.

But as the evening passed, he grew bored and with his first cranky yawn, Collier had swooped him up, blanket, toys and all, and taken him back to the nursery. Mattie hated that he spent so much time alone in his room, thought he was such a happy baby he deserved to be the center of attention every waking minute. Every sleeping moment, too.

But then, no one had ever told her she'd make a good mother.

And no one would believe Meredith, who was good at everything, had abandoned motherhood and her baby.

Abandoned.

Mattie couldn't think of it in any other terms. Even if Meredith came home tomorrow, she'd done something that couldn't simply be wiped away as if it hadn't happened. Her disappearance was real. The accounts of it would linger. Collier worked as a public servant. He'd be a candidate in future elections, an elected official for years to come. The last ten days would always be out there, information lying in wait, available to any competent reporter, ready to pop up out of nowhere and spit in the Montgomery family eye.

Meredith had disappeared as spectacularly as she did everything else, ensuring these ten days would never be completely forgotten.

Bending her head to her drawn-up knees, Mattie concentrated on finding something other than her sister to think about, focused her thoughts on things that made her glad. Like Blake's gurgling laughter. Like the way he smiled at her. Like the fact that her mother had taken a sleeping pill, gone to bed early, and had been out like a light for the past hour and a half.

Tomorrow would be soon enough to try and explain to Alice that Meredith wasn't coming home.

Although, of course, she would come home.

And be forgiven.

And take up her life where she'd left it. As if she'd never left it.

Mattie couldn't help thinking that was wrong, begrudging Meredith an easy resolution. Losing everything ought to be the consequence for walking out on the people who loved and trusted you. Losing your home, your daily pleasures, the future you took for granted should be the forfeit for leaving a husband who'd been shattered by the possibility of your death. Being kept from your son's first smile of the morning and last yawn at night could be deemed a suitable penalty for abandoning the baby you'd brought into the world and who depended on your presence. Being forgotten seemed a just tradeoff for not saying good-bye to the mother who, even in her state of dementia, mourned your absence.

An eye for an eye, a tooth for a tooth, a life for a life.

But those equaled justice only in theory. In reality, there was seldom a punishment that equaled the crime, rarely a penance that neutralized the harm done. When a trust had been violated, there was no such thing as restitution. In the end, there was only forgiveness or condemnation.

And so Meredith would be forgiven.

Which was probably as it should be. No matter how hard it was to justify at the moment.

Laying her cheek against her knee, Mattie stared out the window, noted the street was dark and largely deserted, heard the north wind rustle the bare tree limbs, watched the shadows move in a skeleton's dance. Behind her, Ross flipped the pages of a magazine. André chased a squirrel in his dreams. Collier read pages of printed material. A city council report, maybe. Or a recommendation for reviving strangled budgets. She doubted his thoughts were anywhere near Reyes City, but then, men seemed to have the ability to close off unpleasantness in one area and concentrate on other matters that were nearer at hand. Maybe he was thinking about budgets and not thinking about Meredith at all. Maybe he was aware only on a superficial level that it was nearly ten o'clock and still she hadn't called.

Pulling her own thoughts away from that worry, Mattie sent them off to Dallas, to the sparkling mirrors and shiny wood floors of Miss Mattie's School of Dance and Drama. The studio would be closed by now. Even the last class of the day was long over. The trash baskets would be empty, the lights out except for a few they kept on for security. The doors were locked, the alarm set. No one danced in the dark tonight.

Mattie longed suddenly to be there. She missed the smell of the studio—a blend of wood soap and sweat and little girl dreams. She missed the quiet creaks of the old building, the way the floor settled after a full day of classes, almost like a sigh. She missed the nights when she was the last one to leave, when she could lock the door and leave on the lights and dance for her own pure pleasure. Just her, the music, the movement, and the place she belonged. It was the dancing that saved her, soothed her, and she missed the—

The phone rang. Like a ringside bell announcing the start of a fight, it shrilled out a take-your-corners challenge and Mattie jumped, startled by the sound she'd been waiting for hours to hear. She jerked upright, shoulders back, eyes wide as she watched Collier reach for the phone receiver, quiet the bell before it rang again. "Meredith?" His voice held hope, a reedy reflection of the hope in his eyes and on his face. Hope that melded with relief as he repeated, "Meredith."

For the next interminable minutes, not a sound dared breach the silence. Mattie hugged her knees tighter. André stopped twitching in his sleep. Ross didn't turn any more pages in the magazine. Collier stared across the room at the opposite wall, at an oil painting of a windjammer on a treacherous sea, and listened to the voice on the other end of the phone. He listened like a statue. Not even a frown marred his concentration.

Mattie wished for a speaker phone, and conversely was glad she couldn't hear the one-sided conversation. Collier's expression stayed carefully blank and unemotional. But his eyes—oh, his eyes—gathered a terrible blue storm, a watershed of disbelief, of pain and anger, an ugly wound that would gouge a terrible scar.

"Where are you?"

His voice fell into the quiet like volcanic ash, soft and deadly.

The moments stretched like hours as he listened and Mattie waited, hardly daring to breathe for fear of setting something horrible in motion, unable still to believe it was Meredith who had done exactly that.

Collier's fist cracked on the table, and he stood abruptly, sending his chair spinning backward out of his way, its wheels rattling as it bounced against the wall, came to a startling stop. "No, Meredith, I don't understand. How could I? I can't even understand how you can think it's all right."

Mattie could only imagine the soothing tone her sister was trying to apply, could only wonder what inner strength kept her brother-in-law calm, prevented him from yelling and cursing into the phone, from reaching across the wire and dragging Meredith home by the sheer force of his will. Mattie could only sympathize with the tremor in his hand, the agonized anger threading through the hoarse tenor of his voice.

Ross shifted on the sofa, watched Collier with a troubled gaze. Waited for his turn.

"Tell me why."

Another minute. Two. The clock in the foyer chimed. Ten resounding bongs. Ten knells. A toll of ten.

"Who is he?" The words, like a pronged fork, punctured the room and Mattie's heart began to bleed.

Oh, God, Meredith. Not that. Not that.

"That's not what I asked you." Collier's voice, somehow, remained steady. His fist, too, stayed clenched and white-knuckled. "I asked who helped you. I asked who you're with. I asked you to tell me who he is."

The silence glowed with tension, hot as lava, red as molten glass.

"Don't insult me with platitudes. You planned this . . . No! At least be honest. You *could* have talked to me. You *could* have told me. You *could* have prevented the search from happening at all. You could have done everything differently. It did *not* have to be this way."

Mattie swallowed hard, shrank further into the cushions and corner of the window seat.

"I don't want to hear any more of this," he said. "Justify your actions to yourself. I want no part of it. And now I have nothing else to say to you. Ross, on the other hand, needs to hear directly from you how and why you duped him and his men. He may be interested in . . ." A pause, and then a tightly voiced, "No, I don't want to hear this."

Collier tossed the phone onto the desk top where it rocked in empty air. Ross moved quickly to pick it up and move away from the desk, where he could conduct his part of the conversation in relative privacy. He did it, Mattie knew, to spare Collier as much further turmoil as possible.

But Collier paid no attention. He sank into his discarded chair, the leather making a soft squawk of protest. He lowered his head into his hands and sat there, a study in bewilderment and grief, a man defeated, gut-shot, betrayed. Mattie couldn't look, so she looked away. But as if she were caught in a train wreck, her gaze drifted back, unable to avoid the drama unfolding around her.

Near the bookcase, Ross spoke softly but firmly into the phone, his words indistinguishable, his intent clear. He had to have answers now. Meredith would have to give an explanation free of emotional blackmail, would be asked to provide just the facts. She had caused a tremendous upheaval in the status quo, had cost the community not just effort and energy, but tax dollars as well. Some reparation might have to be made. She might even be charged, face fines or incarceration. Mattie's familiarity with the legal system had ended with her shoplifting spree. She didn't know how much could be forgiven by the police chief, what constituted a legitimate reason for prosecution or prompted the law to show mercy. She did feel sorry for Ross. Whatever he had to do next would be painful for him because of his friendship with Collier, because he'd put his integrity on the line, because Meredith had betrayed them both.

Mattie realized she was holding her breath and released it in a gush that brought no relief at all.

The questions came back. Where was she? Why had she left? Was she with another man? How had she come to call today? Just as her car was found, just as a hope that had been all but depleted revived?

Questions.

A million questions.

And not ten feet away, the answers waited. All held in Collier's large hands. All ready to be spoken aloud. Not real yet, but no longer mere supposition, either.

When he lifted his head from his hands, he didn't speak. He caught Mattie's gaze and held it. Held it so long, the breath in her lungs froze, her heartbeat thudded painfully in her chest, her fingers turned cold with apprehension.

There was no relief when he released her from that strange look, either. Only fear. A knowledge she couldn't grasp, didn't want to discover.

While Ross continued his quiet conversation, Collier pushed up from the chair just as forcefully as he had earlier, but this time the wheels were already against the wall and the chair had no place else to go.

Mattie watched her brother-in-law walk around the desk, watched the squared, harsh set of his shoulders, the controlled movements he made as he went to the bar and poured two drinks. Two stout drafts of good Scotch. Two glasses. Two inches of liquor each.

One for him. One for Ross.

Except he picked up both glasses and carried them to the window seat. Except he didn't wait for Ross to finish the phone call. Except he kept one glass for himself and offered the other to her.

She looked at it, at the glint of light in the amber whiskey, the viscid swirl of a liquid much heavier than water, the promise of a burn to prove you were alive, then the slow numbing to ease the pain of being awake. She looked up at Collier, a little puzzled. "No, thanks."

"Take it," he said.

So she took the glass from his hand.

"She's with Jack."

The words wouldn't have carried the distance between one heartbeat and the next, but they reached her, splintered off and zigzagged through her brain. She couldn't make sense of them. Not immediately. Yet his name tripped off her tongue as if it had been waiting for the opportunity, as if she'd known it had to be said. "Jack?"

Spoken in a whisper. Spoken as if it were impossible. Spoken aloud, in disbelief. Spoken just ahead of an icy sensation that started in the pit of her stomach and spread outward as quickly as if the sun had exploded and warmth had ceased to exist. Spoken as all the pieces shifted and fit, became part of a larger picture. Jack's interest in the disappearance. His intense curiosity. His inappropriate questions. Her own sense that something wasn't right. Meredith's call this afternoon, not long after the Mercedes had been found, not long after Mattie had relayed the information to Jack. Meredith and Jack. The impact of truth thrust hard through her heart, gave a twist, and knifed in deep.

"Jack," she whispered again. But this time, it echoed with a sad acceptance.

Even had she been ready with a denial, Collier held her gaze, steady as a lighthouse on a black night, making certain she understood. "Meredith and Jack," he said, making it precise and clear. "They're together. She's with Jack. He's with her."

A frantic argument got wrapped up in Mattie's silence. It couldn't be. It could. It couldn't. It could. Meredith. Jack. Not possible. But maybe it was. No. Yes. A thousand times no . . . and one ultimate, yes. And as the idea sank in, was rejected, and returned again, she held onto the clear, cold truth in Collier's eyes. If it weren't true, he wouldn't have said it. He wasn't cruel. He didn't make jokes. He wouldn't hurt her if there was any way to avoid doing so. Meredith and Jack. It had to be true, then. It couldn't be . . . but it was. Because Collier had said it. Because he wouldn't lie. Because she could see in his eyes the same denial, the same bewilderment, the same betrayal.

The grandfather clock chimed softly in the foyer. Once. The quarter hour. After that, all she heard was the ticktock, ticktock of time and the click of the second hand moving down and down and around again.

One second.

Two.

Fifty.
A minute.
A lifetime ended. Another began.
Then she lifted the glass and drained the scotch.

CHAPTER NINE

Meredith woke to strangeness and fog on the other side of long windows that stretched from floor to ceiling. There were no drapes, no shutters inside or out, only the glass, thick-paned and slightly tinted against the sun. Except there was no sun. In ten days, she hadn't caught even a glimpse of sunshine. Only mist, rain, and fog. Lots of fog, from thick cloudy gray to thin wispy white. But always a veil of one sort or another to keep her from seeing the world beyond these windows. On the other side of the fog, she sensed the ocean, felt its rhythm, heard its soothing lullaby. All day it would sing to her if she let it, if she stayed cuddled under the down comforter, between the sleek sheets. She'd awakened in this bed for over a week now and each time she felt the same displacement, the same eerie feeling—as if she had traveled to a city she couldn't remember and taken up residence in a grand but vacant hotel.

Seattle. She was in Seattle. Outside Seattle actually. In Jack's family home. Estate. A huge, elegant old house serenely located in the lap of Pacific Northwest luxury.

She stretched, the cotton so finely woven it slid across her bare skin like cream. As soft as a baby's blanket. As smooth as Blake's perfect baby skin.

Blake.

The sheets wrinkled as she shoved them aside, kicked them back with restless feet, and swung her legs over the side of the bed. A glance showed her the place where her head had crumpled the pillow and the pillow beside it where Jack had slept. He was gone. It must be noon. Or after. She'd stayed in bed every morning since their arrival, sleeping in daylight because she didn't, couldn't, sleep in the dark. Drifting downstairs when she got hungry, wandering upstairs again for a late afternoon nap. The few times she'd come across Jack's mother in her meanderings had been enough for Meredith to know she should avoid Evelyn Ellis Youngblood whenever possible. Evelyn fluttered about like a trapped bird and made the whole house tense with her manic movement.

Which meant that Meredith had spent the majority of each day in the bedroom, either in bed or on one of the settees, sleeping or staring at the fog-bound view. She hadn't known how exhausted she was, how depleted all her reserves were, how good it felt to do nothing for hour upon endless hour. And still, after all these days resting, she had to muster the energy to rise, leave the snug comfort of the bed, think about anything except the magazines she leafed through, the biography of Emily Dickinson she skimmed.

She knew she should be thinking about what she'd done. She knew she ought to consider the problems she'd now created and that, sooner or later, she would have to set aright. She knew pretending this was simply a much-needed vacation from responsibility wouldn't hold up under scrutiny and that she should spend this time examining her heart.

But she did none of that. She wasn't sure where to start.

Did she begin with the question of how she'd allowed this to happen? Did she look first at her marriage? Or did she start with her own discontent? Had it begun when she first met Jack? Or had it been in the works long before that? At what point would she be able to see exactly why she'd left her life without a backward glance? When had that become an option? And how had it turned around until it seemed the only option she had left? What had driven her to act so precipitously and yet with such deliberation? What burden had she left behind, and what freedom had she gained that had her feeling lighter, happier, with every mile that separated her from her previous life and pointed her toward a different, uncertain tomorrow?

Blake's sweet face flashed in her mind's eye and the ache of missing him flooded her. Again. When she'd been home, able to walk into the nursery at will, she'd avoided going there except for a morning visit and again in the afternoon. Before his nap when he was sleepy and sweet. When he curled his fingers down and looked almost normal.

His hands.

She would never be able to look at them without remembering that first time she'd seen him. The immediate horror she'd felt. Something was wrong with her baby. Something was horribly wrong with his hands. His heart, too, as the doctor informed her later. But that first time, it had been only his five-fingered hand, his missing thumbs that terrified her. Later, the test results had singled her out as a carrier of the bad gene that had caused Blake to be deformed. Deformed. The word crackled inside her head, felt weighty and heavy and hard. She had caused her son to be born deformed. How could she bear it? How could she ever learn to live with that knowledge?

That ultimate failure was how she'd come to turn to Jack.

Or, to be truthful, that is how she'd come to leave Collier. Jack had happened before. At Christmas. A year ago Christmas. Or maybe it had started that first time Mattie had brought him for a visit and Meredith had seen the dare in his eyes, the challenge, and the invitation.

That in itself was hardly a novelty. Men came on to her all the time, mistook her friendliness for something more. She'd never been tempted. Not really. The thought crossed her mind now and again. Of course it did. The idea of being faithful to one man for the rest of her life spooked her. She'd met Collier so soon after getting to college, and she'd known so quickly that he was the right match for her. Smart, ambitious, charismatic. That they'd make a great team had been a foregone conclusion. He planned to spend his life in public office, serving his country and his community. She could so readily see herself in the role of First Lady. Together, they would make it happen. Success was all they had known, all they ever expected to know. Everything was possible, because failure was not an option. For either of them.

Neither was an extramarital affair.

That definitely had not been in her plans. Collier was wonderful and wonderfully handsome. Everyone liked him. More importantly, everyone wanted him to like them. Women found him attractive, charming. He could have had any number of affairs, but she knew he hadn't, knew he wouldn't. Not only because he wouldn't risk his political future on an illusion of power, a whim of vanity, but because he would consider unfaithfulness to her a dishonor. And he was an honorable man.

She knew other women coveted her dynamic husband, imagined themselves in her place, fantasized about the man and the life that were hers. She liked being envied, liked knowing she owned the love of a man other women wanted. But after eight years of marriage, she found Collier predictable, unexciting, and focused on the future to the exclusion of everything else. Little wonder then that she indulged in some harmless flirtation. Not surprising that she occasionally trifled with the idea of being with someone else. It was only a thought here and there. She didn't plan to act on it. She believed a bit of uncertainty kept a marriage on its toes, thought Collier was more attentive because he wasn't one hundred percent certain of her. She believed a little coquetry kept her vibrant as a woman, made her more attractive and exciting to the man she married. And was it such a terrible thing to like the attention other men were so eager to pay her?

No.

She enjoyed feeling admired and—yes—lusted after. Nothing ever came of it. She never let anything go too far, never felt she or her marriage was in any danger. Above all else, though, she flourished under the knowledge that she maintained her own source of power. She liked knowing that she could choose, and that she would always choose not to complicate her nearly perfect life. What man would be worth risking what she already had?

Then Mattie had brought Jack home.

Meredith pushed up off the bed and walked across carpet so plush it held footprints in her wake. Her feet sank into the soft fibers, and the silky luxury of fine wool cushioned her steps, warmed her bare soles. With its rich golds and vibrant berries of color, the large room enveloped her in the illusion of coziness and hospitality, offered up a sumptuous comfort and an unstudied opulence. She could see herself living forever in a house like this, could imagine her life inside these huge, old, and graceful walls. There was a peace in having great wealth, she thought, a no-worries kind of isolation from trivial realities, from the daily stresses that could fray a soul from the inside out. Meredith had come here in search of peace.

And somewhat to her own surprise, she'd found it.

Stopping a few inches from the window, she lifted her hands and placed her palms on the glass. It felt cold, but not like at home. Not a wintery, snowy cold so much as simply wet. Somehow, even through the panes, the cold felt wet. The fog wasn't as thick this morning and she could catch a wavery view of the water, whitecaps as frosty white as snowdrifts. It would be cold in Reyes City this morning. But not this wet, humid, watery cold.

What was Collier thinking? Was he stunned by her escape? How long would it take before he could forgive her?

He would forgive her. She knew him too well to believe he would forever begrudge her this lapse. It would be painful, of course. For both of them. Meredith knew her absence would have shaken his faith. In her, in himself, in their marriage, and in the future they planned. But she thought—hoped—it would remind him of the beginning when their union had been all about passion. Ambition and passion conjoined into a singular *we*. It would be that way again. She would cry. He would be angry. Then it would be over, relegated to the past, the things no longer mentioned, but never quite forgotten.

And he wouldn't take her for granted again.

She pulled her hands from the glass, watched the imprint of her palms wither and fade.

She had run away, disappeared. She'd done something Mattie would do. Something Mattie had done. Not since she was a kid, but running away would always in Meredith's mind be the kind of stupid stunt her kid sister would pull. Not a thing she herself would ever be tempted to try.

Except that she had tried it, and now she and Mattie had something in common. They'd both run away from their problems.

And they'd both had Jack.

Meredith hated that she'd taken her sister's fiancé. Even knowing Mattie's romance was destined to fail. Even knowing that some other woman would have come along to steal him from her, sooner rather than later. He'd been ripe for it, appalled by the commitment of engagement and the forever-and-ever vows of looming marriage. She didn't know how he'd let the relationship with Mattie go that far. What did he see in her little sister that had prompted him to take such a serious step? Meredith hadn't yet figured that one out, but it hadn't taken her more than a half hour in his company to understand that Jack would break her sister's heart.

At the time, she hadn't thought she would be his accomplice.

It had been a rotten thing to do. Maybe the first truly rotten thing she'd ever done.

Unless you counted passing on a defective gene to your son.

Hugging her arms tight across her breasts, she felt their lax fullness and unwillingly mapped the changes pregnancy had brought to her body. The silvery stretch marks on her breasts and stomach—the slight curve where those stomach muscles were no longer youthfully tight. The loose, fuller sway of her hips. The heartbeat that had overshadowed a faster, fainter beat for nine months and now would always feel somehow incomplete. She wouldn't get pregnant again, wouldn't put her body through the strain or the pain. There'd be no more children, no second chance for her defective gene to mutate and migrate. No other lives made imperfect by her DNA.

When Jack had first suggested this escape plan, it had seemed harmless. Or harmless enough. A few days with no worry. A few hours of uninterrupted peace. That had been the promise that convinced her. Peace. No worries. She'd done nothing but worry since Blake was born. No, even before that. Since her mother's stroke. That had scared her. Shaken her. She'd been so frightened that Alice might die. And then, when she didn't, when they knew she would survive, it had been a kind of death to watch her mother's struggle to make sense of the world she once had commanded. There were moments when Meredith knew that Alice realized she had said the wrong thing, that her thoughts—as valid as they seemed in her head—were confused and wrong when spoken aloud. Her mother had left her in little ways, inescapable ways already, and Meredith missed the strong, competent woman she had been, missed the lifeline her mother had been for her. Perhaps things would be different if she hadn't had to witness the deterioration first hand, if she hadn't had to live with every mistake Alice made. Meredith hadn't the patience for that. Or the coping skills. Her life wasn't supposed to be filled with worry, scheduled chock full of demands. Blake. Her mother. Collier's career and the socializing that was required of her.

She hadn't wanted anyone to see Blake's hands, hadn't known how to answer when someone asked about him, didn't appreciate the banal assurances of those who were aware of the problem, who believed she and Collier were lucky that the defects were not worse. After all, Blake's problems could be corrected. His hands and his heart. He could be fixed, even if imperfectly, and that was supposed to be comfort enough.

But he was her baby, and his problems were the worst she could imagine. There was no rationalizing his imperfect hands and the hole in his heart with meaningless platitudes and the it-could-be-worse line of reasoning. He had been born flawed. Because of her. And always, forever, there would be scars, ready reminders that it was her fault he hadn't been born perfect.

She turned from the window, thought about going downstairs for a late breakfast, an early lunch.

Her stomach clenched, destroying any appetite that had stirred. As long as she lived, she would remember the look on Collier's face the day the doctor had told them that she, not he, was the carrier of the defective gene. His test had come back negative. Hers, positive. Collier had been relieved. Visibly relieved. Glad it had been her and not him.

Relieved, glad, and . . . absolved.

That knowledge would always be there, always between them in the form of Blake's hands, in the shape of his differences from other children. She knew, no matter what Collier said, that he'd never look at their son's hands without being grateful it had been her, relieved that those scars hadn't been his fault. She, on the other hand, would forever feel an overpowering guilt, a helpless remorse that, untouched by the mutation herself, she had nonetheless managed to ruin her son's life before his life had even begun.

She'd thought about dying then, about what it would mean to stop living, to die of the shame she felt. She thought about what it would be like to simply give up the life she'd made. She wondered if that life hadn't ended already.

That's when she'd turned again to Jack, whom she

hadn't seen since last year's brief affair that began only a week after he'd gotten engaged to Mattie.

She'd end it again. She knew that.

It wouldn't be difficult. Jack cared about the conquest, not about her. But for now, he was what she needed. He was the only reason she could find to get out of bed in the morning or go to bed at night. He made her feel alive again, and hopeful. He turned her guilt around and reminded her that she was important too. That sacrificing herself for her husband's career and expending all of her resources on worry over Blake were both unnecessary and self-destructive. She deserved better. She deserved more out of life. And she believed him. Jack teased her, cajoled her, told her to stay in bed if she felt like it, nurtured the luxury of peace her body and spirit craved. Sex with him was titillating and dangerous and new. Just being with him revitalized her. For now, for the short term, Jack was the only person she trusted. He was the reason she kept breathing.

And when she told him good-bye, he'd regret only that she'd been the first one to say it.

She wasn't ready yet. The thought of going home, of returning to the life that no longer felt like hers, made her shaky and scared, nauseous. She needed more time, more rest, more peace. She needed to regain her strength before she went home to face Collier.

A few more days. Another week. Two at the most. Maybe three.

Then she would go back . . . and patch things up with her husband. Offer her son a lifetime of apologetic kisses.

And, somehow, learn to live with the knowledge that she had failed.

CHAPTER
TEN

Dissecting a relationship turned out to be a little like choosing the perfect paint chip. If it looked good in the store, if you absolutely loved it and bought a whole roomful of accessories to match, it was hard to admit that after two coats of paint had dried what you'd imagined would be a luscious bronze on the walls bore more actual resemblance to river mud. Mattie had, of late, been vaguely conscious of a feeling that she and Jack didn't match up as well as she'd first believed they did, that the accessories of their life together clashed like two different combinations in the color spectrum. His schedule never quite meshed with hers. He liked late nights and champagne brunches that bled into lazy afternoons. She was more lights out by eleven, up, breakfasted, and at the barre by nine. He liked going out. She liked staying in. Opening the school had taken up so much of her time. Traveling at the

beck and call of his mother's many investments occupied so much of his.

She'd told herself those things were minor adjustments, that all couples made little lifestyle
compromises to accommodate the relationship.
Once they were married, once she was finally
through with grad school, once the dance studio
had another year under its belt, she and Jack would
be fine. They'd feel settled again, happy, as they'd
been in the beginning. She'd told herself this so
many times, she'd actually believed it was true.

Until Rachel, a lovely gazelle of young woman-
hood, moved into the condo next door and blinked
her doe eyes at Mattie's man.

Jack had laughed when she mentioned Rachel,
said he'd hardly noticed her, barely knew who she
was. He'd said she had a boyfriend. He'd said Mattie
had no reason at all to be jealous of anyone so young
and inexperienced, so far removed from his life.

He hadn't said she had good cause to be jealous
of someone closer.

Jack and Meredith. Meredith and Jack.

No matter how she turned it over in her head,
how she tried to shake it loose, the puzzle kept
falling uncannily into place. All the random, un-
connected pieces she'd gathered and discarded
came together like hands folding around the
rosary, preparing for prayer. The suspicion she'd
directed at an apparently innocent Rachel. The
feeling that something had changed, and that she
and Jack no longer worked as a committed, caring
couple. The vague sense of unease she'd attributed
to the stress of opening the studio. The way she
worried about paying back the money Jack had

given her to get the business started. The guilt she felt about not doing more to help after her mother's stroke, leaving so much of the burden to her sister. Even though Meredith had insisted on doing it her way, even though she'd cut off Mattie's attempts to be part of the solution, Mattie should have found a way to share that responsibility.

And she should have been suspicious of Meredith's random voice messages on the answering machine.

Where are you, Mat? I thought you'd be home. Call me back.

Those messages suddenly took on an undercurrent of code. A shorthand for "I'm home. If you're there, pick up. Or call me back." And how easily Jack could have heard the message, picked up his cell phone, and called Meredith. Mattie could see the way it would work—the same way he'd kept in touch with her at the start of their romance. By cell phone. He never used anything else. Land lines were obsolete in his life. Worse than useless. Too public. Too limited. He lived with the cell phone on his hip, answered it in his sleep.

He'd given Mattie a phone two weeks into their relationship, told her he wanted to stay connected to her. All the time. No matter where he was. No matter where she was. No matter what time it was.

She'd taken the phone and felt oh so special.

She didn't need the specifics to know that's how he'd conducted the affair with Meredith. He'd have given her a phone too after those August and September messages. Mattie would have bet the studio on it. Jack, who loved mystery and secrets, had foreseen one avenue of discovery and cut it off by giving

Meredith a phone. A phone he'd bought and on which he paid the monthly bill. A small, ordinary cell phone used only as a means of contact. An exclusive connection. A private line between lovers. Easily hidden in plain sight.

Time together?

His travel permitted any number of scenarios. He could have been in or near Reyes City once or twice a week. Meredith could travel to Dallas and back in a day on Jack's credit cards. They could have met in Tulsa or Oklahoma City, in Wichita or Ft. Smith, all only a few hours' drive from Reyes City. Collier worked long hours and many evenings. Meredith had hired a nurse to tend the baby. She had paid extra for that nurse to watch Alice and to stay late. The possibilities, turned on their head, took on multiple disguises, a million ways of hiding the truth from a trusting husband, a gullible fiancée.

Mattie, once again cast in her sister's shadow, hadn't suspected.

You be his girlfriend, Mattie. I'll be his lover.

She should have known . . . and perhaps on one level, she had. She'd had doubts about Jack at the beginning. If she reached into her heart for the truth, she'd have to admit she'd had doubts all along. She'd questioned his commitment even after she'd agreed to marry him. She'd wondered if he was really ready to settle down, ready to be monogamous. She'd felt unsure of him on a number of occasions. She'd worried about taking him home to meet her sister. She'd suspected him of beginning an affair with Rachel. And the last time he'd come back from a spur of the moment

SPECIAL INTRODUCTORY OFFER!
Zebra Contemporary Romance
FREE! Zebra Contemporary Romances!

Zebra Contemporary

FREE BOOK CERTIFICATE

Yes! Please send me FREE Zebra Contemporary romance novels. I only pay $1.99 for shipping and handling. I understand that each month thereafter I will be able to preview 4 brand-new Contemporary Romances FREE for 10 days. Then, if I should decide to keep them, I will pay the money-saving preferred subscriber's price (that's a savings of up to 30% off the retail price), plus shipping and handling. I understand I am under no obligation to purchase any books, as explained on this card.

NAME_____

ADDRESS_____APT._____

CITY_____STATE_____ZIP_____

TELEPHONE (_____)_____

E-MAIL_____

SIGNATURE_____

(If under 18, parent or guardian must sign)

Thank You!

CN036A

To start your membership, simply complete and return the Free Book Certificate. You'll receive your Introductory Shipment of FREE Zebra Contemporary Romances, you only pay $1.99 for shipping and handling. Then, each month you will receive the 4 newest Zebra Contemporary Romances. Each shipment will be yours to examine FREE for 10 days. If you decide to keep the books, you'll pay the preferred subscriber price (a savings of up to 30% off the cover price), plus shipping and handling. If you want us to stop sending books, just say the word... it's that simple.

THE BENEFITS OF BOOK CLUB MEMBERSHIP

• You'll get your books hot off the press, usually before they appear in bookstores.

• You'll ALWAYS save up to 30% off the cover price.

• You'll get our FREE monthly newsletter filled with author interviews, book previews, special offers and MORE!

• There's no obligation —you can cancel at any time and you have no minimum number of books to buy.

• And – if you decide you don't like the books you receive, you can return them. (You always have ten days to decide.)

Ill..l..lll....llll.l.l.l.l.l.l...l.l.l.l.l.l...ll.l..lll...l

Zebra Contemporary Romance Book Club
Zebra Home Subscription Service, Inc.
P.O. Box 5214
Clifton NJ 07015-5214

PLACE
STAMP
HERE

trip to the coast, she'd had a persistent, unsettling feeling that he'd been with another woman.

Doubts. She'd had them and she'd reasoned them away as little nothings, engagement jitters, an over-active imagination, a small dose of possessiveness. Like a rash that itched, the doubts had prickled be-neath her skin, and she'd medicated them by pulling on the gloves of a cottony rationale to keep from scratching too deep.

She should have scratched. She should have trusted her instincts. She should have questioned her own drive to gloss over Jack's faults. She should have poked at the quickness with which she blamed herself for not having enough faith in him. She should have taken a long, hard look at her reluc-tance to put her doubts on the table and invite him to discuss them with her.

She'd suspected she would have to work at trust-ing the man she was going to marry.

But she'd never for a moment suspected he was having an affair with her sister.

Because it had never once crossed her mind to suspect that Meredith would have an affair.

Betrayal was an ugly act. Perhaps the ugliest thing one person could do to another. It uprooted trust, gave faith a vicious tumble, and swagged a jagged path of destruction between two points. The point before and the point after. And in between, lost there, trying to figure out how she hadn't seen this coming, sat Mattie, new victim of an age-old heart attack.

Riding the emotional aftermath of Meredith's disappearance was more difficult than anything

Collier had ever done. He'd had precious little experience with failure. And this was failure. A big one. When a man's wife left him for another man, somewhere inside he knew the problem had to have begun with him. He felt immense relief that she was okay and intense anger that she'd left. The days of uncertainty had made him weary, but the clarity of the answer had him shot through with adrenaline. He needed to do something to fix this. Now. This minute. But what it was he didn't know, couldn't grasp. He was furious with Meredith and anxious about her state of mind. Ross had said he'd seen this kind of thing before. A perfectly sane person, one with no apparent problems, suddenly doing something completely out of character, acting in a way no one could have anticipated.

What Ross hadn't said was that women left their husbands, and husbands left their wives on a daily basis, but they didn't usually disappear without a trace and then call ten hellish days later to say they'd just needed a time-out.

A time-out of the marriage.

A time-out of motherhood.

A time-out.

Collier hadn't had a lot of experience with anger, either. Life had pretty much gone his way until now. Until this. Until he'd found himself at odd angles in an embarrassing triangle. He wasn't accustomed to being embarrassed. He worked hard to avoid situations with the potential for embarrassment. Present or future. But now Ross knew, Claire knew, others in the police department knew, probably even the janitors at City Hall knew that the mayor's wife had run off with another man. They knew she'd had an affair right under his nose. They knew she'd chosen Jack over him. They knew she'd left of her own free will. They had to be thinking—just as he was—that it was his fault, that he had done something to cause her to leave, that he could have done something to stop her. Been a better husband. More attentive. More understanding.

He should have been enough. And he'd failed.

That embarrassment fueled his anger, and the absolute fury roaring in his head a whole sleepless night after the phone call, flashed outward in all directions. Anger at Meredith. Anger at Jack. Anger at Mattie for bringing another man into Meredith's life.

But the root of it all, the rotten core of emotion responsible for his inept rage, was his own helpless embarrassment.

He hated the feeling with every fiber of his being, but no matter which way he turned, its frustration stared him in the face.

He'd felt helpless when he thought Meredith had been kidnapped or murdered or hurt and unable to come home to him. He'd been embarrassed when he'd been questioned about the possibility that she'd walked away of her own free will. He'd felt helpless when he'd heard her voice on the phone but had no way to reach her. He'd felt embarrassed when the future he'd never had any reason to doubt began dissolving beneath his feet and he knew the whole town would soon know his embarrassing failure.

How could she have done this? To him. To Blake.

That's where the anger boiled hottest, where it turned gooey and black as asphalt, as sticky as tar.

He couldn't have imagined either side of this

pounding outrage. Not before the Tuesday she disappeared, not before the fear had eaten away everything except a numb waiting, the expectation that tomorrow the news would come. Meredith would be found.

Tomorrow had come. Meredith had been found.

Her betrayal was wending its way through the phone lines, across town, across the state, astounding family and friends, or maybe confirming suspicions never voiced, secrets never told.

He was helpless to understand how she could have done this.

He was frustrated because he'd never for a moment thought anything like this could happen to him.

He was embarrassed to the ends of the earth because it *had* happened. It had happened to him.

But above everything else, he was ashamed and embarrassed and angry because he'd failed to satisfy his wife and driven her into the arms of another man.

No matter what happened now—whether Meredith came back, if he decided to allow her that option—he knew how it felt to fail.

And that knowledge burrowed like furious little termites into the foundation of his soul.

Over the weekend, a storm brewed. The sun came out with its seductive promise of warmth, its pseudo invitation to go for a walk or a jog, its leave-your-jacket-at-home siren song. But behind the sunshine and blue skies, the temperature dropped, clouds gathered, and winter reconnoitered for another assault. Inside, a different sort of gloom lifted, only to be replaced by an angry tension that dominated the house like an occupying army. The uncertainty which had held sway for ten long days gave way to the knowledge of betrayal and a virulent form of grief.

Collier couldn't bear the thought of his parents' sympathy, the anger and outrage they were certain to voice, and asked them, please, to stay home and allow him to do the same. He'd be fine with the baby, fine on his own. And he wasn't alone. Mattie and Alice were there. It wasn't as if he didn't have someone to talk to. It wasn't as if he had to face Meredith's astonishing choice by himself. Mattie had been betrayed too.

He didn't actually see it that way. He, in fact, felt that Mattie had lost nothing worth having anyway. Jack.

The name alone filled Collier with rage. He'd recognized Jack Youngblood for what he was the first moment they'd shaken hands. "Mattie tells me you're going to be president one day," Jack had said, his smile as cool as all the opponents Collier had faced in debates throughout high school and college put together. "If you'll give me a cabinet seat, I'll not only vote for you, I'll contribute heavily to your campaign."

That was one vote Collier could do without, one campaign supporter he'd rather not have.

But he'd dealt with egotistic pricks before, knew when to use vague replies and specific distractions to avoid getting pinned to the wall on one point of contention or another. Jack wasn't like that. He had the cunning of a hunter, a subtle, manipulative skill beneath layers of casual charm. He was the kind of man who didn't stop to count the cost, the kind of man who could ruin a budding career with a few well-chosen words, the kind of man who could—and would—ruin a life for the challenge. For the power rush it provided. Or simply to prove he could.

Collier had noted all that in the time it took to assess the firm grip of his hand and know that its strength resulted not from confidence but from the desire to out-grip the other man. A handshake, if you knew how to read it, could give as many clues to a man's character as a written treatise of his beliefs.

You can tell a lot about a man by the way he shakes your hand.

His grandfather, Theodore Montgomery, had begun schooling Collier in the art of politics even before he'd been old enough to spell the word.

These are lessons you can steer your life by, Collier. Politics is the art of survival, and survival is dependent as much on the ability to spot a foe as the capacity to make a friend.

Collier had listened to his grandfather. He'd learned. And with that first handshake he'd known Jack would not be a friend.

He'd ignored that feeling in the beginning, wanting—for the sake of harmony—to like the man Mattie had brought home. He'd felt some sympathy for Mattie in the past. It must have been difficult growing up as Meredith's sister, deriving an identity from all the ways she didn't, couldn't, compare, knowing from the start that she wouldn't make the cut. Collier had seen the yearning in her eyes sometimes when she and Meredith were together. Mattie had made some poor choices, a few really bad ones. Meredith had told him about the shoplifting incident, and all the times Mattie had run away from home as a kid, the trouble she'd caused, the worry she'd delivered to her mother.

He didn't normally have much sympathy or patience for bad choices. But when Mattie found Jack, opened the dance school, became less lost in the world, Collier had hoped she'd finally found a way to have the future she wanted. He did believe in second chances, and from what little interaction he'd had with Mattie, he thought she probably deserved one.

Of course, all his factual information about Mattie had come through Meredith. And that information had now become suspect. If Meredith would lie to him about one thing—as she so obviously had—then she'd lie about anything.

Collier should have trusted his gut when it told him Jack Youngblood was a con man. But he'd listened to Meredith instead.

Oh, for heaven's sake, Collier, Jack seems very nice and Mattie's in love with him. I don't know how she did it, but she's lucky to have landed him. A man like that could have any woman he wanted and it makes no difference if you find his tone condescending or think he's not the sort of man to make her happy. My God, we're talking about Mattie. She's a screw-up. That's what she does. She screws up everything. And she'll screw up this relationship too. It's only a matter of time.

But Mattie hadn't been the one to sabotage her new relationship. Jack had seen to that.

Even as the thought surfaced, Collier felt the knife twist of truth. Jack hadn't betrayed Mattie alone. However much he wanted to lay the blame at Jack's door, Collier knew half of it belonged to Meredith. The woman he'd chosen to share his life, the one he'd believed shared his values and ambitions, the one he'd trusted to be mother to his child. The woman he'd moved heaven and earth to find when she went missing. He'd defended Meredith against every single suggestion of an affair, played the fool for her, insisted in every interview and on every occasion that it wasn't in her nature to be unfaithful. She loved him. She loved their son.

And yet, she had left him for another man.

Again the anger shifted and settled on Jack.

Meredith and Jack. Jack and Meredith. Equally guilty. His fault. Her fault. Back and forth, the clouds of outrage scuttled. Until Monday morning, when at last they found a path and became a storm.

The baby's cry brought him out of a dead sleep. The first sleep he'd had in days. The sleep of exhaustion. The sleep of a body drained of energy by a riptide of emotion. His feet were on the floor and moving before he even fully opened his eyes. Like any new parent, he was conditioned to respond to Blake's first cry, moving toward the baby in a haze between dreams and wakefulness, barely processing a glance at the clock on the bedside table, the feel of the plush rug beneath his bare feet, the cooler air as he passed through the connecting bath, the prisms of the decorative doorknob pressing into his palm as he turned it and opened the nursery door.

He was almost to the crib before he realized Blake wasn't in it, before in a montage of images, he saw Mattie in the rocker, holding the baby, patting his back, shushing him in a crooning whisper. Concern, relief, possessiveness, and worry coalesced, and in a split second he ran through all his memories of Meredith and Blake together and not one of them held the sweet joy he saw in Mattie at that moment. And his anger found a new target.

Mattie.

If she hadn't brought Jack here . . .

If she had seen Jack's character for what it was. . . .

If she had never met Jack in the first place. . . .

Why was she still here, anyway? Why hadn't she taken her mother and left immediately after they got the news? What was she doing up at this hour of the morning? Why couldn't it have been Mattie who walked out on her life? No one would have been surprised at that. No one would have called the police. No one would have been much concerned. Why couldn't it have been Mattie who disappeared instead of Meredith?

"Give him to me." He reached for his son, pulling him with unnecessary force from Mattie's arms. Startled, Blake's snuffling cries turned into long, loud protests and Collier patted his stiff little back in apology. "There," he said. "You're all right now. Daddy's got you."

And from the rocker, Mattie watched, her eyes clearly bewildered even in the night-lit nursery. "I heard him crying," she said.

"I'm sorry he woke you."

"I wasn't asleep. I figured since I was already awake, I might as well keep him company and let you rest."

"Not necessary." But he remembered other nights when he'd lain in bed, still as a mouse, hoping Meredith would get up and go to the baby, hoping she would hear and respond before he did. And he was ashamed. Not just of his own selfishness, but because he'd known even as he had the thought that Meredith was waiting for him to get up so she wouldn't have to. Because she knew he would. Because she knew she could outwait him, that he'd never be able to let Blake cry as long as she could. If she had beaten him to the nursery even once, Collier couldn't recall it now. "He's my son. I'll take care of him."

"I can help, you know. I like being with him."

"I said I'd do it. Go back to bed." Blake cried louder and Collier began rubbing his back instead of patting it. "He probably only needs a diaper change."

"I changed him. I'd have gotten him a bottle, too, but wasn't sure if he's allowed to have one this early."

The idea that he'd slept through the baby's cries bothered Collier. Blake was his responsibility. Not Mattie's. She had no business even being in the nursery. "How long have you been in here with him?"

"Ten minutes, maybe. Fifteen."

Blake had cried and Collier hadn't heard him. He'd failed to hear his son cry in time to reach him before Mattie did. He was a lousy father. Blake's mother had deserted him and left only an inept daddy to care for him. Collier had wanted so much more for his son. So very much more.

He jiggled the baby's weight in his arms, jostled him into a more comfortable position, moved in the hope movement alone would quiet the cries. "I've got him, Mattie. He won't bother you again tonight."

"He didn't bother . . ." she began, but stopped. "It's five in the morning and I think he's hungry. I can go down and get his bottle if . . ."

"I *said* I'll take care of him."

She nodded and pushed up from the rocker to

move toward the doorway. It was only then he realized she was wearing her nightclothes—only then he realized he himself was wearing only a pair of cotton knit pajama bottoms. No shirt. No shoes. Only a much-belated modesty. Not that Mattie seemed to notice his bare chest and arms. Not that he didn't pretend to take no notice of the loose flannel pajama bottoms that drooped low on her slim hips, the soft-looking cotton T-shirt that rode above the slope of her navel and did more to emphasize her breasts than conceal them. She had the toned, muscular body of a dancer, the controlled curves of discipline, the soft fluidity of grace. He'd known all of that before, but as she walked away from him now, the relaxed fit of her clothing added a definition he hadn't recognized before. It struck him there in the pre-dawn dark that Mattie was a woman. An attractive woman.

And the awareness stirred in his groin.

As if he didn't already have enough confusing emotions coming at him.

As if he wasn't already sinking into a slough of guilty feelings.

As if he needed the distraction of having improper thoughts about his sister-in-law.

But then, Meredith's actions had blurred the lines of what was improper. In different circumstances, Collier would have dismissed that momentary awareness as the insignificant male-female response it had been. But he wasn't in ordinary circumstances anymore. He was in limbo . . . and he'd noticed.

And that fueled his anger.

He walked around with Blake, who was quieting

in his arms the same way he'd been quieting in Mattie's. Across the room, back and forth, finally going toward the window, where he could feel the snow falling even before he could see it. The whole world nestled in a soft, soundless isolation. That eerie half light of white drifting between sky and ground. The motion of cold, of snow. He sensed it and saw when he drew back the curtains that they were in for one of those rare storms when silence and beauty concealed a killer snow.

For once, the weather completely matched his mood.

CHAPTER
ELEVEN

Mattie huddled in one corner of the window seat, the cashmere throw tucked over and under her feet and legs. Her hands cupped the heat of the ceramic mug and every little while she inhaled the scent of her morning cup of coffee. Outside, the snow was coming down in thick, fat, hurried flakes that jostled and jockeyed their way to the ground. It wasn't quite seven yet and already the ground was covered, the tree limbs were weighted with white, tipped in ice. The streets, too, glistened with the sheen of frozen cold, a slick of transparent gray. She could imagine kids all across town waking up to the excitement of a snow day.

No school. No schedules. No homework. It was an unscheduled holiday, one of those lazy days off that felt like playing hooky, except the superintendent of the school district had said it was okay because the weather made it too dangerous for the buses to run their routes, too risky for parents to drive students to school, too cold for kids to walk. Oklahoma weather could change in a blink, go from blizzard to sunshine, from below freezing to a record high, and back again in the course of a day. But once the call went out and the school cancellations aired on radio and television, the deed was done. Snow day.

Watching it now, Mattie wondered how long this storm would linger. She didn't need a forecaster to tell her it would be a snow day for her too. Although without the fun. Even through the double-panes of the window, she could feel the cold seeping inside. The wind tousled the treetops and whipped the falling snow into a flurry of bad news. She wouldn't be getting her mother out in this. She wouldn't be keeping the appointments she'd made with Green Tree Assisted Living Center, the Gardens Senior Home, Heatherwood Senior Living, or Mary Jane Pinkosky at the local Social Security office, who'd agreed to help her sort out Alice's finances. Already, on the street out front, two cars that had started up the Dewey Street hill had slid backward to the bottom of the incline and were now spinning their tires in a futile attempt at gaining traction on the slick pavement. It was only a matter of time before the snow packed down over the glaze of ice and made driving treacherous. Already the traffic on Dewey—and across town—was slowing to a slippery crawl.

Terrific.

Just when she most needed to get out of Meredith's house. Just when she thought she'd go crazy if she had to spend another minute inside these walls.

Just when the thoughts in her head boomeranged into one tangle of a headache.

What should she do about her mother? How would she go about locating a new doctor, an adult day care provider, a permanent assisted-living arrangement in Dallas? She'd used Collier's computer to search out names and locations, but printed information, while helpful, wasn't a substitute for an on-site visit. And she wasn't putting her mother in a facility in Dallas until she'd researched what was available. But leaving her mother here meant moving her twice, upsetting her twice, going over the same arguments twice. Or more. But what else could she do? Where should she look for another apartment? How good were the senior care facilities in Dallas? Would she do better to look in the suburbs? Where would she find some boxes and how many would she need and how long would it take to get her stuff moved out of Jack's condo and into whatever apartment she found? How long would it take to get a bank loan so she could repay the money Jack had lent her to open the studio? What was happening at the studio? Were things going fine without her? Was enrollment for spring classes up from last year? Or down since last month? How soon could she get back to Dallas?

How? What? When?

The questions buzzed like bees, scurried in and out like ants at a picnic. But there was a storm brewing in her head, a blizzard of cabin fever settling in, and the alternating anger and uncertainty about her future made her jittery, had her longing to be home.

Except she had no home.

At the moment, she had no space at all she could claim as her own. Collier had even tossed her out of the nursery.

A boil of irritation festered at that memory. Over

the course of the weekend, during the two days since
Meredith's astonishing phone call, Mattie had done
her best to stay out of Collier's way. She was wounded
and angry and furious and hurt. She wanted to
scream. She wanted numbing quiet. She wanted conversation and she absolutely did not want to talk at
all. She supposed Collier probably felt the same. But
she didn't want to know. She didn't care. Jack had
betrayed her. Meredith had betrayed her. She didn't
want to share that pain with anyone, least of all her
brother-in-law. The fact that she had to be in his
house maddened her, kept her from running from
the awful truth.

Jack and Meredith. Meredith and Jack.

She didn't want to think about it and yet she
couldn't think about anything else. She was hurt,
she was angry, and somehow those feelings wrapped
around, turned inside out, got jumbled up, and focused in on Collier. Who was no more to blame for
what had happened to her than she was to blame
for what had happened to him. But Jack wasn't here
to yell at, curse at, and receive the full brunt of her
emotions. Meredith, too, was inconveniently absent.

But Collier was here.

He was as tangled up in this double betrayal as
she was. For all she knew, he might be looking at
her and seeing a convenient scapegoat. But bottom
line, this was his house and she was a visitor in it.
She could desperately want to get out of it and lick
her wounds in private, but she couldn't justify
taking her mother to Dallas and plunking her
down in a hotel room where she'd be miserable
and even more confused than she already was. Not
to mention that in the confined arena of a hotel

room, the two of them, mother and daughter, would quickly drive each other completely insane.

The storm meant she had to stay put until it was safe to take Alice out, meant she had no choice but to postpone visiting the senior care facilities in Reyes City. Once the storm blew eastward, once the sun came out, once the streets were passable again, once she got her mother situated, she could head for Dallas and take care of myriad details that Jack's sudden exit from her life had tossed into question.

And with that, the questions buzzed her again and she was back where she'd started.

She didn't want to stay. She couldn't go. She couldn't play with the baby. She was tired of entertaining her mother. She was sick of wearing the same clothes. She was even tired of doing pliés and relevés. She had thought today, Monday, would be her day to get started on sorting out all the things she needed to do to reclaim her life.

Instead, she was sitting in Collier's study, drinking Collier's coffee, and staring out Collier's window, watching the snow fall, watching as winter taunted her with yet another day of trying to stay out of Collier's way.

She heard his footsteps on the stairs, and silently urged him to steer clear of the study as she lifted her mug and took a sip of coffee.

As she was wishing for the super-powered ability to erect her own force field, he walked into her lair, Blake bobbing at his shoulder like a fuzzy-topped Kewpie doll, a portable playpen under his other arm, a floppy, stuffed zebra dangling by its raggedy tail from his fingers. He paused briefly when he saw her—a barely concealed *You again?* reaction—then ignored her presence as he set the collapsible playpen in the middle of the room, squared between the sofa and chair and tried to maneuver it into position with his knee and foot.

It fell.

He stooped and set it aright, jostling the baby at his hip. Blake, helping, grabbed a fistful of Collier's hair and when Collier stopped to disentangle those baby fingers, the playpen flopped over a second time. He retrieved it again and renewed his effort to conquer it in a one-armed, one-sided wrestling match, a frustrating and aggravating failure. Made all the worse, she imagined, because she was there to watch.

She took another leisurely drink of coffee before asking, "Do you need some help?"

He didn't acknowledge her and continued his struggle to get the playpen set up. Blake watched wide-eyed from his perch, his lashes still spiky from tears, his cheeks flushed from an earlier bout of crying.

Mattie could see Collier was determined that the mechanics of a few padded rods and a lot of netting would not get the better of him and when Blake looked over at her, as if to make sure she thought this was as dumb as he did, she winked.

His grin happened in a flash. A gummy, one-toothed grin that turned her into his co-conspirator, his partner in this suddenly funny joke on Daddy.

She grinned back. And that was the moment, Collier glanced up and caught her. His frown turned into a serious scowl and he let the playpen slide out of his grasp. "If you think you can do better," he challenged, "have at it."

Tucking away the grin, she tossed aside the throw, set her coffee cup on the corner of his desk, walked over, and took Blake away from him. She extended her hands and the baby jumped the space to reach her. That took Collier by surprise. But he tried not to let it show. With both hands free, he applied himself to the task, snapped the playpen open, and popped it into position. A little adjustment and he reached for Blake, took him from Mattie and, with a pat on the back and a "there you go," he put the baby in the playpen and dropped the zebra in beside him.

Blake started to cry, an indignant, don't-fence-me-in fussiness.

"I don't think he wants to be in there." Mattie retrieved her coffee cup and brought it back with her to the sofa, where she could sit near the playpen and her nephew. She'd like to pick him up, but Collier was the dad and he was in charge. No matter how out of sorts he was.

"Give him a minute. He'll be fine."

The baby cried harder and Mattie yearned to snatch him out of his kennel. "Are you sure? I could hold him. I'd like to hold him."

"He's fine where he is."

"He doesn't sound fine."

Collier walked over to the desk and began sorting through a stack of *Wall Street Journals* on his desk. "Don't you have exercises to do in the kitchen?"

"Did them earlier. I made a fresh pot of coffee, too, if you want some."

"No, thanks."

Which was probably a good thing since she'd

only made enough for herself with a little left over. But he didn't have to know that.

"Snow's really coming down."

"I can see that."

"I was telling Blake."

"He can see it too."

Mattie was on the verge of pointing out that he didn't have to be so short with her, that she was a little tense herself, when Blake stopped crying, rolled over, pushed himself up, hands and feet down, diapered butt angled toward the ceiling. He rocked in that position, unable to coordinate what should happen next, looking sideways at Mattie, then at his hands and then at his feet. He looked like a turtle trying to figure out what had happened to his shell.

And watching him, Mattie forgot for a moment about the bad things that had happened to her and laughed aloud.

Blake grinned.

Collier, noisily shuffling through the stack of papers, chose two off the top and carried them to the chair where he settled down to read. He crossed one leg over the other, lifted one of the papers, and gave the front page a preparatory snap.

Mattie played peek-a-boo with Blake, raising the coffee mug to shield her eyes and lowering it to surprise him, fascinated by his expressions and the way he rested on his hands and knees and then suddenly thrust his baby butt in the air again. Frustrated because he was confined to the playpen, thinking if he had a little more freedom, he might just figure out how to crawl. "I guess Mrs. Oliver isn't coming today," she said aloud as the thought occurred to her.

"I called and told her not to get out in this weather."

"Good. Maybe she'll decide to move to Florida."

He looked at her over the top of the paper. She didn't see him, but she felt his glower before he gave the paper another tweak and continued reading.

Childishly, she gave him a minute to get started, then spoke to him again. "I'll have to call and cancel my appointments today, which means Mother and I will have to stay a couple of extra days."

He slowly lowered the paper, agitation spilling over the top and onto her. But his tone of voice was perfectly polite. "I imagine a lot of appointments will be cancelled today. There's a travel advisory across most of the state." He waited a moment—in case she decided to say something else—then gave the paper a little shake, signaling that he intended to read.

She thought about going upstairs and getting the novel she'd found in a basket in her bedroom. It wasn't particularly engaging, and she wasn't sure it was worth the effort of walking upstairs to get it. But if she stayed here, her presence alone would bother Collier. His presence certainly bothered her.

The crisp, occasional rustle of pages. Waiting for the rustle when he turned the page. Irritated by the rustle when it finally came. Irritated because she and Collier were here, in this room, in this house, together.

Meredith and Jack. Jack and Meredith. Together. Together. Together.

She didn't want to read. She didn't want to talk, but she didn't want to be quiet either. Maybe she'd just sit on the sofa, drink her coffee, and play more peek-a-boo with her nephew.

She might have been content doing that if Andy hadn't trotted into the study just then, trailing pea-sized snow pellets, bringing a sample of the winter weather with him. His fur was covered in random clumps of dirty white, evidence of a recent trip outdoors through his doggy door, and he looked like he'd rolled through the snow from one end of the yard to the other. Of course, no one actually registered his entrance until he reached the middle of the room, where he stopped to shake, a bit of canine strategy that managed to splatter Collier's newspaper, sprinkle the baby's face, and splash fat, muddy splotches down the legs of Mattie's slacks.

With a startled gasp, she jumped up to brush the particles of ice and snow off her clothes and managed to spill coffee down the front of her blouse.

Blake, startled by the flying drops of cold, lost his precarious balance, dropped flat on his belly, and began to cry.

Collier jumped up, the newspapers scattering to the floor at his feet. He grabbed the dog by his rhine-stone-studded collar and dragged him out of the room, calling back. "Stay put. I'll bring you a towel."

Mattie didn't stay put.

She tugged the hot spot of blouse off her stomach with one hand, set her cup aside with the other, then reached into the playpen and made an attempt to wipe the pinpoints of wet from Blake's red face. But he wanted to be picked up and her gesture made him think that's what she meant to do and her failure to do more than dry him off set him wailing in earnest. Mattie tried to soothe him with her voice while she leaned over the side, awkwardly patting his back and holding the clammy fabric off skin that burned and stung from the dose of hot coffee.

Great.

She'd upset the baby. She'd ruined the only decent outfit she had with her. Not to mention the only clothing that wasn't at this very moment in the washing machine, taking a soapy tumble.

She hoped Collier brought a big towel.

He didn't. When he walked back in with a chastened and miffed poodle at his heels, he didn't have a towel at all. Worse, his mood, thick as a cloud of sand flies, sucked the happiness right out of the air. He was strung so tight, she half expected him to twang when he walked.

Okay, Mattie thought. She'd go upstairs and . . . What? Wrap herself in the blanket on her bed? She might as well just go and sit in front of the washing machine, until the cycle finished. Then she'd sit in front of the dryer, waiting to pull out something clean. And dry. By which time, the stain and the fabric of her blouse would have a committed relationship.

Something she, obviously, knew nothing about.

"I'll get a towel," she said, her tone sharp as a pinprick as she started for the door.

"I forgot to bring a towel."

Of course. He'd forgotten her the minute he stepped out of the room. Just like Jack. All men were just like Jack. A bubble of renewed anger and hurt popped inside her, spread like bad blood. From now on, she'd get her own damned towels.

"You ought to soak that blouse." He said it as if

she tossed blouses into the trash bin at the slightest speck of discoloration.

"Gee, why didn't I think of that?"

His lips tightened into another frown. "I thought you might want to change clothes. I wasn't trying to trample on your right to be a martyr."

It was a nothing, a slight tear in the thick tension. Throwaway anger, that nonetheless piqued her own, had her standing in the doorway ready for a fight, even though he wasn't the adversary she had in mind.

"I'd like to change clothes," she said. "But you may have noticed I didn't bring that many with me and I put all the others in the washing machine before I came in here with my coffee. I don't really have anything to wear until they're clean."

Collier motioned and André sank to the floor, humiliated. "Wear something of Meredith's," he said as he grabbed up some of the scattered newspaper pages on his way to the pen where Blake was red and screaming. "What's wrong with Blake?"

"He wants out of that playpen."

"Well, why didn't you pick him up?" Collier leaned in and lifted the baby out, smooth as silk.

Another bubble of anger popped in her throat, followed by another and another. That wasn't fair. None of this was fair. She stood there, wet cotton sticking to burned skin, dirty splotches all over her good slacks, watching him quiet the baby, as she'd wanted to do.

"It's okay, Buddy," he crooned to Blake. "It's okay."

The baby snuffled, settled his unhappy little

cheek against his daddy's shoulder, looked accusingly at Mattie.

"Go change clothes," Collier ordered when he looked back at her. "Borrow anything you want. *Take* anything you want. Meredith obviously doesn't need her clothes since she left them all behind."

That brought up an uncomfortable, hurtful image. Meredith with Jack. Jack with Meredith. "Why would she need clothes?" The words snapped off Mattie's tongue before she could stop them, before she even wanted to stop them. "She's got Jack."

"And whose fault is that?" Collier snapped back.

Apparently hers. Mattie narrowed her eyes at him, thought of so many ugly things she could say, that she wanted to say. To Jack. To Meredith. And, in their stead, she flung them at Collier. "Yours," she said, unable to intercept the emotions boiling over and out of her. "I think it's your fault."

"I don't think so." Although she could see on his face the fear that she was right. "I think it's your fault."

She tossed her head, pretending she wasn't scared that might be true, too. "I'm going to Dallas as soon as this weather clears up long enough for me to find a suitable assisted living center for Mom. Don't for a minute think I want to stay here."

The tension pulled tight between them, arched and spit like a feral cat. "You can do all that by telephone. Or computer," he said. "Don't let me stop you from getting on the road as soon as possible."

"I can't leave her in a place I haven't even looked at."

"How are you going to look at places until you get to Dallas? Why didn't you leave before the snow set in?"

"I can't take her to Dallas until I've found a place to put her."

"Right. You certainly wouldn't want to put her in *your* apartment."

"*I* don't have an apartment. Jack owns the condo."

His gaze tussled with hers, hers with his, as they each fought the knowledge that arguing with each other was pointless. The jilted fiancee. The duped husband. The betrayed. Angry at each other because they couldn't bear the anger they'd turned on themselves.

They might have stayed like that all morning, if Blake hadn't made a soft cry of protest. A bleat for comfort. A demand that broke the tension. "Hey, there." Collier snuggled Blake closer, patted the small back with his large hand, offered a big dose of reassurance to a pint sized need. "I'm sorry," he murmured to the baby. "It's all right. Everything's all right."

It wasn't. Everything was a long way from all right.

Collier rubbed his smooth-shaven cheek across the top of Blake's downy head and looked back at Mattie. "Go," he said. "Put on some of Meredith's clothes."

It was an order and a request, a temporary suspension of hostilities and simple common sense.

Mattie, still keyed up and drifting aimlessly in a cesspool of anger, wanted to tell him she didn't want anything that belonged to her sister.

But watching him with Blake, she knew that wasn't entirely true.

Turning on her heel, she went upstairs to exchange her ruined clothes for something Meredith had left behind.

The argument wasn't over.

It settled in like the snow outside, cocooning the household in a wary warmth, concealing the slippery ice of frustration with a glistening cover of polite avoidance. Every so often it erupted again, when Mattie and Collier passed on the stairs or if they wound up in the same room at the same moment. There would be a silence of annoyed patience or an exchange of overly careful words, none of them worth the agitation they caused and yet necessary, somehow, to give all the suppressed emotion an outlet.

Mattie alternately hated Jack and felt sorry for herself. She frequently ranted at him—or at Meredith—neither of whom, of course, was there to answer the anger inside her head.

It didn't help that the icy conditions lasted for a couple of days, giving Mattie a severe case of cabin fever. She began taking a perverse pleasure in wearing Meredith's clothes, finding some sense of justice in stripping one set off and putting on another. Her own clothes—the few she'd packed so hurriedly—stayed clean and neat in her bag while she tried on slacks and sweaters, blouses and jeans that were not her style but that she wore anyway. At moments, she imagined that if she tried on enough of Meredith's clothes, experimented with her sister's perfumes, applied a touch of makeup from Meredith's ample supply, she'd eventually figure out why Meredith had started the affair with Jack, why she'd left so many lovely things behind.

At other moments, the house began to feel less like Meredith's, more like her own. She wandered through it, running her hand across the surfaces, imagining her sister investing so much energy in making the house perfect . . . and then walking away from it as if perfect no longer mattered. She imagined herself in Meredith's place, making those decisions, changing the house to suit her own idea of perfect, fitting herself into its present and past . . . and then leaving it all behind.

But she couldn't do it. She didn't fit, for one thing. Not really. And the more she wandered about the house, the more she felt she was slipping again into her sister's shadow, nestling into her sister's life—the life she'd envied so often—and seeing it still through a dusky veil that, when lifted, made everything beyond it shine with a blinding, deceptive brightness.

Restlessness, like rebellion, closed around her, made her want to do something—anything—to stop from feeling as if she was, once again, fading away, as if the only way to find herself was to disappear. She needed to walk around the block. Run. Do something besides play board games with her mother and work jigsaw puzzles until her eyes ached from staring at the tiny pieces of colored cardboard. She thought she'd go crazy if she didn't find some way to occupy her hands, set her stamp on Meredith's house.

And before the snow stopped falling, she'd thought of something.

It had bothered her from the outset that her

nephew seemed consigned to the nursery, that his place in this household was portable. As if he were a child from another era, the son of strict Victorian parents, he was brought out of the nursery for short periods and then all traces of his presence went with him when he was taken back upstairs. He had a portable playpen, a collapsible high chair, a combination carrier and car seat, a pad to go under blankets and keep him off the floor, and a few toys that traveled with him from upstairs to down and back again.

Meredith had left a house, which was wiped clean of baby clutter aside from the nursery. Mattie didn't know if that spic-and-span tidiness had made it easier for her sister to leave, but she meant to make sure Collier didn't get that option. Blake was a member of this family and his Aunt Mattie meant to ensure no one ever forgot that. Even if it meant upsetting Collier all over again. Even if it scared her a little to think about making changes in a home that wasn't hers to change.

But if she didn't do it, who would?

So she started in the kitchen and made a place at the table for Blake. In the pantry, she sorted through the jars of baby food and moved them from the storage room to the cabinet beside the sink. The boxes containing his cereal went from cupboard to counter, the bright baby face on each cover—one shaded red, one shaded green—smiling out, making a statement worth much more than a thousand words. She took a chair away from the table and set Blake's high chair in its place, and at first she didn't even put the plastic mat down beneath it. Although, after some consideration, she changed her mind about that.

Once she'd finished in the kitchen, she decided to bring Blake's swing and his gymboree toy down to the study. Collier would probably just move them back upstairs, but at least for now, Blake's baby thing could take center stage in the room.

Alice, taking a break from the jigsaw, frowned at the clutter. "Meredith isn't going to like this," she said. "She doesn't like clutter."

"Meredith isn't here," Mattie said. "And I like the clutter."

"Your room was always a mess," was Alice's answer. "A regular pigsty."

Mattie didn't remember it being that bad, wished now it had been worse, that she'd cared more about pleasing herself than trying to please her mother. Her chance was gone, but Blake's chances were still ahead of him. This wasn't her house. He wasn't her baby. But she felt she had to do something to make his presence felt, to let him know—even if he was too young to remember—that she thought he belonged at the center of this universe.

"What do you think you're doing?" Collier asked, walking into the room just as she put her hip against the side of his desk and shoved it another half inch toward the window.

"Rearranging the furniture."

"Because?"

"Because I want to make room for Blake's stuff. Because he spends too much time upstairs in his room. Because when you're in here, he needs a place to be. And not just a portable place, either."

"Last time I checked, this was my house."

"It's Meredith's house. But if you'll give me a hand, we can change that."

He stood in the doorway, looking at her, taking in the swing, the gymboree, the spaces she'd cleared, the spaces she'd filled. And when he moved, he moved in her direction. "Where do you want to go with this?" was all he asked.

"Toward the window."

Then she put her hip against the desk and helped him push.

Meredith's disappearance had caused quite a stir, but finding what had been lost was anti-climatic. Perhaps it would have gotten more press if a scandal in the governor's office hadn't occurred and blown other news to a footnote in the midsection of the local newspaper.

Mayor's wife found safe, was the quarter inch lead-in to the story of how Meredith had turned up safe in Washington state.

Post-partum depression was cited as the reason, the label for the madness that had caused her to get in her car and keep driving.

Mental stress the cause of her brief amnesia.

Being treated for exhaustion explained her continued absence.

DA declines to file charges summed up the whole unhappy episode.

Collier knew he was lucky the story had dropped off the front page and been compressed into a two-inch column in the Reyes City *Daily Press*. Other newspapers in the state carried the same column or dropped the story completely in favor of more reports about the discovery of Governor Lucman's unlucky rendevous with his male lover, the state attorney general.

What was a personal misfortune for the governor was manna from heaven for the opposing political party. The race for the highest office in the state had suddenly broken wide open—and Collier's name was in the right place at the right time.

His own scandal turned from a negative into a positive practically overnight, transformed by the power of name recognition. Suddenly, Meredith's defection was open for interpretation and his own team of political friends and advisors believed the opportunity was there to spin the story into PR gold. Buried on the back pages for now, it could emerge in a few weeks as the story of a family in crisis. A child facing open-heart surgery, other difficulties as well. A mother-in-law with Alzheimer's—a more sympathetic diagnosis than dementia from stroke. A father trying to hold his family together. A mayor making positive changes for a town facing job losses and general decline. A woman who fell apart on her way to lunch. All of it true. Not the whole story by any means, but not a false one, either.

Spin.

Collier, who hadn't yet been approached by anyone outside his own small circle, could read between the lines, was savvy enough to know his plans for the future might be about to get a big boot forward.

He felt dirty. Using the scandal in his life to capitalize on the scandal in Tom Lucman's turned his stomach. He hadn't even pulled himself up from Meredith's sucker punch yet. He couldn't think about the possibility of running for the highest office in the state government.

Meredith had stripped away his illusions about

himself, about his marriage, about his commitment to his career. She'd shaken his belief in himself, taken it with her on her journey to another man.

He vacillated now between wondering if the call would come and hating Meredith for putting him in this untenable position. Because if the call came, if the opportunity opened up—and he knew that was a big if—he didn't see how he could do anything other than turn it down.

Because he couldn't swallow enough pride to ask Meredith to come back.

"I'm taking Blake out to discover snow," Mattie said from the doorway, and Collier looked up to see his boy bundled like a caterpillar in a cocoon of fleece with only the rosy oval of his face showing. Mattie had on gloves and several layers of clothing but no hat and her flyaway hair tumbled about her face in a mass of reddish gold curls.

"You're going to need a heavier coat. Use one of Meredith's. In the hall closet."

"I'll be fine." Her smile bloomed as Blake batted his mittened hand against her head. "I've got Hefty Pete here to haul around. He'll keep me warm. We're going to build a snowman, aren't we, Blake? Maybe a snowwoman, too."

The baby grinned as if he understood the fun that awaited him and Collier realized suddenly that if Mattie hadn't been here, Blake wouldn't be discovering snow today. There was no reason he shouldn't. The doctors didn't think he was nearly as fragile as Meredith did, and they'd advised treating him as they'd have treated any child.

A normal child.

But Meredith had been afraid. And so Collier had been afraid, too.

Mattie, remarkably, wasn't.

"Where's Alice?" he asked and felt a little deflated when the question netted him a frown.

"She's still trying to finish that jigsaw puzzle. I told her she could come out with us, but she said she didn't want to get her hair wet." Lifting her shoulder in a shrug, she allowed Blake to distract her again. "We won't be out long," she said. "Just long enough to get acquainted with Frosty. Right, Blake?"

The baby galloped in her arms, raring to go.

The front door had barely closed behind them when Collier got up from his desk, put on his coat, and went out into the bright white day to join them in the snow.

CHAPTER
TWELVE

The key turned in the lock as easily as it always did, the latch gave a smooth click, and the door swung inward.

But Mattie stayed outside in the hall, reluctant to enter this place she'd so recently called home.

Usually she was in a hurry to get inside, kick off her shoes, make some coffee, and nestle into her cocoon for the night. Usually she didn't even notice the cool, impersonal touch of the brass handle against her palm. Usually she paid no attention to all the other identical, impersonal doors that stretched down the hall on either side and in both directions. Today, she'd driven four hours to get here, fretting all the way about her mother and the assisted-living center in Reyes City where she'd left her, stressing over how soon she'd be able to find and move into another apartment, wondering if it would be better to first locate a place for her mother and then look for an apartment nearby. Alice had been very upset this morning, even though Mattie had taken her to the Gardens twice already this week without incident. Of course, she hadn't left her there on either of those visits. She hadn't been the bad daughter then, dumping her mother in an elder-care facility, driving away, and leaving Alice behind. On those earlier visits, she hadn't had to hear her mother's bewildered accusation, *"Meredith would never do this to me!"*

But it couldn't be helped.

Mattie had her hands full for the next several days without adding her mother to the mix. She had to get an apartment for herself, make arrangements for Alice, catch up on paperwork at the studio, and prepare the necessary reports and financial statements so the bank would loan her the money to pay off Jack's investment. She wanted it all done right away. Yesterday, if that were possible. She had way too much on her mind, far too much to accomplish, to be wasting time standing out in the hallway and fighting her own unwillingness to walk into the condo and pack up her stuff.

But she knew the extent of her ability to worry, to fret, to stress over the rightness of her decisions. She didn't know the dimensions of the emotions that waited for her on the other side of this door. She felt them lurking across the threshold, cooling their heels while she peered in at the long entry that led past the kitchen on one side, the laundry room on the other, and opened, finally, into the great room.

Or as great as a room got in a high-rise apartment.

The tenant board called it a unit. The residents

called it The Crest. As in: *We live at The Crest.* A prestigious place in the heart of an expensive, exclusive, artsy part of the city. Two bedrooms, two baths, a large kitchen, a great room with deck and a view of the Dallas skyline with round-the-clock security and a hefty monthly maintenance fee. Jack had owned it when Mattie met him—he'd kidded her that his condo was half the reason she'd fallen in love with him. She'd teased him back that it was the whole reason. Her last apartment would have fit twice over into this one with a couple of rooms to spare. There were more closets than she had clothes, an upscale ambiance attached to the address, and, best of all, it was located near the shopping area which housed her in-my-dreams spot for opening a studio.

But they'd both known Jack had been the attraction. The sum total of it.

Jack with his dark good looks, his cocky, the world's-my-yo-yo attitude, his live-in-the-moment philosophy, his charm, his considerable ability to make a woman feel like the only woman in the world.

Jack—handsome and rich. The kind of guy she could see falling for her sister. The kind of guy she'd never dreamed would fall for her.

Jack—who'd betrayed her and left her on the opposite side of the life she'd believed they were going to share. Like an atoll split off from its island by underground eruptions, she looked back on what had been.

Which was a great waste of time and energy.

She'd been over it all in her mind a thousand times, spent her wad on heartache, hurt feelings, anger, and self-pity. From here on out she was not looking back.

She and Jack were over. Finished. She'd pack her things and be out of here by tomorrow morning. Maybe sooner. She wasn't sure she wanted to spend another night at The Crest. She thought it might leave her feeling dirty by association. Jack was a jerk, and she wasn't sleeping in his bed. Even if he was sleeping half a continent away.

With her sister.

Yuck.

That thought alone provided the impetus she needed to step inside and close the door behind her. It felt immediately strange. No sense of the familiar welcomed her, even though the lamp in the corner beamed out a warm brightness, and the light in the kitchen had been left burning. Even though she could hear Mr. Moore running the vacuum one floor up—a task he performed nightly from nine to nine-thirty, seven days a week, come rain or come shine.

Tossing her keys on the hall table, she checked the counter for mail, realizing that was mere habit, something she did whenever she walked in.

In general, it was all Jack's. The mail. The furnishings. The art on the walls. The *Esquire* and *GQ* magazines on the sofa table. The coffee table books of varying sizes and complementary colors, their topics wine, Italy, and New York City. The bitter British beer he kept in the refrigerator. The jar of red-skinned peanuts he emptied and refilled at least once a week. The *Sports Illustrated* schedule he'd tacked up on the side of a kitchen cabinet so he could tell in a glance if there was a game he wanted to watch.

There were touches of her in the apartment, a tuft of color here and there, a dab of yellow, a mix of greens and blues, a multi-colored suncatcher outside the window, a calendar of dance-related events, plus other little mementos that meant something to her, but no one else.

Most of the pictures were hers. She was a photo addict. All her friends teased her about it, but she didn't care. She loved the idea of holding onto a moment, that instant of catching a friend unawares or a scenic view that captured an entire story with the click of a camera lens in a tiny fragment of a second. She loved thinking about how that moment could be held in the reverse image of a negative, could be printed in color, framed and set into an empty space on the bedside table, or in a nook, or on a shelf, or on the kitchen counter. She loved seeing the pictures she'd hung on the wall, loved the idea that a gallery of her favorite moments waited to greet anyone who happened by, loved the thought that *Remember This?* was there at a glance to remind her that life was made up of one moment, one heartbeat at a time. No more, but no less.

She'd take the pictures when she left. She'd take the suncatcher, a few of the throw pillows, all of the yarn tassels, the funny little statue she'd bought in Aruba, the plastic lei she'd worn when she took hula lessons, and whatever other bits of herself she'd put into these rooms. She'd take herself out of this picture and leave Jack with what he'd had before she moved in. A luxury condo. A great room with a view, two bedrooms, two baths, a large kitchen, some nice furniture and one expensive piece of art per wall. As impersonal as a hotel room. A classy hotel room, to be sure. But still just a room where anyone might spend a night.

Mattie set the mail aside with a sigh.

A sigh that caught in her throat when she heard the faint gasp of air as one of the bathroom doors opened, releasing a puff of humidity and steam, which preceded the pad of footfalls coming down the hall toward her. Holding her breath, she stepped into the great room and saw him. Jack. Fresh from the shower, toweling his seal-sleek hair, his skin golden damp, bare, and boldly beautiful. Unaware of her presence until he'd taken one too many steps into the room to allow for a dignified retreat.

"Mattie." His eyes widened and his brows arched. His whole body tensed with shock and she knew he was even more startled to see her than she was to see him. "I, uh . . ." He had to grapple for his usual savoir-faire. "What a pleasant surprise."

"Do you think so? It's more of a nasty little shock to me."

Jack stood in the archway, the thick white towel drooping in his hands, contrasting against his year-round tan, covering him in a terry swath from navel to ankle. He looked distinctly uncomfortable and for a moment, Mattie thought Meredith might be in the apartment, too, that she'd stumbled, most unluckily, into the midst of their tryst. Except there was no longer a need for trysts and secret rendezvous. Their affair was out in the open. If Meredith was here, she'd just have to come out and join the party.

"Is my sister here?" Mattie asked, because she did not want to be startled by a face-to-face encounter with Meredith. "Is she with you?"

"Of course not," he said, as if it offended him to be asked, as if it was beneath his dignity to bring his new love to his home at The Crest before he'd cleaned away all traces of the old love. "She's in Washington. Washington state. At the Seattle house. With my mother."

"How cozy. So what are you doing in Dallas?"

"Business. An investment opportunity. I delayed the trip for a couple of days, but finally had to come." He gestured, causing the towel to shift positions, drape lower than before.

He was so comfortable in his body, so unconsciously proud of his athletic build, so sure of its effect on her, of the power his sexuality gave him over any woman he chose. She felt a subtle but sweet irony in noting his body had no effect on her at all. Except for wishing he had a bit more modesty and a lot less arrogance. And perhaps a little less chest hair. The thought curved at the corners of her lips and he saw it, took it as an affront to his manhood.

"You can't think I wanted to run into you here," he said sharply. "Like this."

"No, certainly not like this. I imagine you thought there wasn't much chance of my showing up here at all."

"Not true. I figured you'd have already been here and gone. I thought you were probably pretty mad and wanted to pack up and get out as soon as possible."

"I am mad," she said. "But there was a snowstorm and icy roads at the start of the week. And it took a few days to get Mother situated."

"What? The mayor couldn't handle her?"

His sarcasm riled her, salted the wounds he'd inflicted, made her want to scream at him, grab his towel and lash him with it until he understood how much he'd hurt her. But she knew he would never understand, and that even if he did, it wouldn't make her feel better. So she contented herself with the knowledge that he, like the emperor who wore no clothes, was a fool for his own vanity, and that gave her the advantage.

"If you'll get out of my way, Jack, I'll get my things and get out of here."

The faintest tinge of guilt crossed his face. "Look, I'm sorry about all this, but it's not like I meant for it to happen."

As if he'd been an innocent bystander hit by a stray bullet. "I didn't honestly expect an apology, even though you owe me one. But do not stand there and play the victim with me. You knew exactly what you were doing."

"Oh, come on, Mattie. You're the one who introduced us. You knew I'd be tempted. You knew the risk involved."

"So it's my fault you're screwing around with my sister?"

The towel twitched in his hand. "I'm not blaming you. I'm just pointing out what you knew about me from the start. You were the one who was so insecure about having me meet your family. You were the one who talked about how special Meredith is. Forgive me for discovering I agreed with you. I'm not a saint. I never pretended I was. I'm a man. I was tempted. I probably should have resisted, but I didn't. So, sue me."

"And win what? A judge's ruling that you're a horse's ass?"

"There's no need to get ugly. It happened. I fell

in love with your sister. She fell in love with me. I'm sorry, but that's just the way it is."

"That's just the way it is," Mattie repeated softly, amazed at how easily he justified his actions. "Well, how will it be from now on, Jack? Is she going to divorce Collier? Are you going to marry her?"

He lifted his shoulder in a careless shrug. "We haven't talked about that. I'm not sure what the future will hold for us."

"She has a baby, you know. You've talked about him, haven't you? What it would mean to him if his mother abandoned him?"

"I *know* she has a kid, Mattie. I'm not the insensitive jerk you seem determined to paint me. It's not like I ever asked Meredith to leave her baby. I never asked her to leave her husband either. That was her idea. Not mine. She's the one who wanted to escape. Maybe if His Honor, the mayor, had worked a little harder at appreciating what a fantastic woman he had, none of this would have happened."

"Don't call him that."

"Why not? He got himself elected mayor. That is his title."

"And you stole his wife. But he's not calling you a bastard."

Jack smiled. "I know you're angry with me, but don't get too carried away defending Collier. He's as much to blame for this as anyone. It's certainly not my fault he couldn't satisfy his wife."

She could see it brought him pleasure to say that aloud, knew he'd enjoyed playing with that idea for quite some time. She'd been an idiot not to see how shallow Jack really was. "I don't want to talk about this, Jack. I just want to get my stuff and leave."

"Where are you going?"

It was her turn to shrug. "I don't know. What do you care? I'll find a hotel. Or maybe I'll stay with Andrea for a few days."

His expression softened with a vague regret. "Stay here. I'll sleep on the sofa."

A noble gesture. In his mind, anyway. "I'm not comfortable being under the same roof with you, Jack. I might not be able to resist the urge to murder you in your sleep."

He laughed. "I do love you, Mattie. You probably don't believe that now, but it's true. If I hadn't met Meredith, I like to think you and I would have made out okay."

Mattie just looked at him, still handsome enough to take her breath away, still without a clue that he'd never again have that power over her. Even if he dropped the towel. "I don't deserve you, Jack," she said, tasting the truth she should have recognized a long time ago. She deserved an honorable man, a good man. A man who was rich in principles and honor. A man who understood the value of self-respect. "I'm not sure any woman does."

He took it as a compliment, the idiot. She could see that in the softening of his expression, the sexy hitch of the towel. "You can stay here," he said, ego spilling out in generosity. "Hell, I'll give you the place. I've never liked it all that much, anyway."

She stared at him, fighting an urge to giggle at his absurdity. "You'll *give* me the condo? What? As some sort of consolation prize?"

"No," he said, caught up in the idea that he could leave here with her heart in his pocket. "It's close to the studio. It has good security. You're comfortable here. So you can have it. I'll even pay the maintenance fees for you for the first year. What do you think of that?"

She thought he'd regret the offer in about five seconds. She thought she didn't want to take anything from him, least of all this apartment. She thought he ought to have to sweat for a while, thinking she'd accept his guilt-gift. "You want to give me your condominium."

"Sure. Why not?"

She figured he'd come up with enough why nots on his own. No reason for her to answer that. "You're *giving* me your condo. No strings attached."

"No strings attached."

There were always strings. In Jack's world, there were always strings. "Okay," she said. "I accept. Now get the hell out of my condo."

He nearly dropped the towel. "What? Now?"

"I can't really think of a better time. Of course now."

"I just gave you a very valuable piece of real estate, Mattie. A little gratitude is in order, I think."

"I'm grateful, Jack. Truly. Grateful that I can throw you out."

He jerked the towel up, giving her a glimpse of penis as well as ass, before wrapping it around his waist, concealing his treasures from accidental view, trying to show her in a gesture what she could no longer have.

Had he always been such a prick?

"I was going to forgive the loan on your school, but I suddenly don't feel that generous."

"I was going to let you get your clothes, but I suddenly don't feel very generous, either." She motioned toward the door. "Get out, Jack. Go."

"You're not tall enough to back up a threat like that."

"Try me. I'd like nothing better than to phone down to Nelson and have him come up here and help me throw you out . . . in all your glory."

"Nelson isn't going to throw me out. I'm the best tipper in the building."

"You're right. He probably won't throw you out. But the report will make for great reading at the next tenants' meeting, don't yZou think?"

Jack's eyes narrowed, he dismissed her in a glance, turned, and strolled casually into the bedroom.

But she heard him slam a few drawers, heard the twang of hangers as he jerked clothes from the closet.

She'd made him mad. There was some justice in the world, after all.

When he came out of the bedroom, handsomely dressed and carrying his latest Louis Vuitton, his face was flushed with anger, his expression set in an irritated frown. His voice, when he spoke, was threaded with a no-more-Mr.-Nice-Guy anger. "My attorney will be in touch. I'll expect repayment on the school loan in thirty days."

She expected to deliver it before that, but didn't want to spoil the surprise.

He was undoubtedly feeling a little sorry for himself and doubly sorry he'd made the magnanimous gesture of offering her the apartment. A little regret over a lost condominium would be good for him. It might make him feel worse when he found out she didn't want it. She just wanted him out.

Out of the condo tonight.

Out of her life forever.

He moved past her into the entryway, set down his suitcase. "You know, Mat, I thought you and your sister had a lot in common. You're both beautiful, sexy, smart women. But I was wrong. Compared to Meredith, you're not that beautiful. You're definitely not that sexy. And you've just proven you're not that smart. Your sister is more woman than you can ever be."

That should have hurt. It probably would hurt later, when the words came back to taunt her. But at the moment, they only strengthened her resolve to get rid of him. "You were damn lucky to win my heart once, Jack, and I know, even if you don't, that you're going to regret losing me a million times over. Go. Get out. Go back to her. Live happily ever after until the next distraction comes along."

"There won't be a next distraction, Mattie. Meredith will fascinate me for the rest of my life."

"I wasn't really thinking about you, Jack. I was thinking about the next guy who'll distract Meredith. She will leave you, you know. She will. It's only a question of when."

"Wishful thinking, Mattie. I know how to keep a woman satisfied. I won her away from Collier, didn't I? She chose me over him."

"She chose you because you were mine." The truth of that curled around Mattie's heart, squeezed tight, and sent an echo of recognition through her whole body. "The only reason she wanted you was because she couldn't figure out why you were with me."

He shook his head, pitying her such a silly illusion, confident he was going back to the good sister.

"I'll expect you to return the engagement ring. You can give it to my attorney. He'll get it back to me."

"Oh, I'll just give it to you now. I've got it right here." She turned, and picking up her keys from the credenza, she toggled the diamond off the key ring where she'd put it last Saturday and held it out to him.

He reached for it, but she pulled it back. "It's a trade. The ring for your door key."

His eyes narrowed, but his hand went into his pants pocket and came out with his key ring. He unhooked a solitary key, dangled it from the curl of his fingertip. He taunted her with it for a moment before enveloping it in a fist that aimed for her cheek. She didn't flinch and he didn't strike her, simply brushed his knuckles across her skin. A feather stroke of arrogance. A claim that he could win her back. If he wanted.

A claim she would never let him exercise.

As crazy as it seemed, Mattie felt he had given her a true gift. Better than a condo in the best part of town. Better than a diamond set in platinum. Better even than Miss Mattie's School of Dance and Drama.

He'd betrayed her trust and stomped on her heart, but—despite the pain—he'd given her the knowledge that she was a survivor.

She didn't have to forgive him the sin to be grateful for that lesson.

"Your ring," she said, taking the door key as he opened his fingers, dropping the ring in its place. "Good-bye, Jack."

"Good-bye, Mattie. Enjoy the condominium."

For a moment, she thought he might lean down

and kiss her, so she took hold of the doorknob, opened the door, and stepped safely out of his way.

He looked at her while another second imploded, his expressive eyes full of sympathy for all she'd lost, then he stepped out into the hall.

She closed the door.

Locked it.

And started taking her pictures off the wall.

CHAPTER
THIRTEEN

Mattie hurried down the hospital corridor, looking to her left for the waiting room the charge nurse had indicated she'd find at the end of the hall. She passed a row of interior windows on her way to the door and glimpsed Collier, seated in a corner, leafing through a magazine, as she pushed open the door.

"I got here as soon as I could," she said, sinking into a chair beside him, letting her bag slide from her shoulder and slump to the floor. "I don't know how many more family emergencies I can handle this month. How is she?"

"Still in surgery. You made the trip in good time."

"It felt like it took forever. Not even a week in assisted living and already she's broken her hip." Mattie leaned back in the chair, weary from the drive and the worry. "I should have taken her with me. I should have put her in a round-the-clock care nursing home even if she is too high-functioning for that."

"She could have fallen anywhere. In a nursing home, in Dallas, or while walking across the kitchen in my house. You did what you thought was best. Don't blame yourself."

"It comes with the territory," she said with a sigh, unable to keep from wondering if it would have happened if Meredith hadn't left, if life hadn't turned everything topsy-turvy. "Did you get any more information? About how it happened? The supervisor didn't know when she called me, and I was too panicked at the time to ask many questions. I just hung up talking to her and called you. I'm really sorry I interrupted your meeting."

He shrugged, dismissing her concern. "It wasn't important."

She knew it had been, though. She'd heard it in his voice over the phone. He'd only been back in the office a few days, less than a full week, and, of course, it was important. But she hadn't known what else to do. Meredith wasn't in Reyes City anymore. There had been no one other than Collier to call, no other family she could ask to go to the hospital and be with her mother until she could get there.

"I don't know much more than what you told me," he continued. "She was in the activity room playing Bingo until two o'clock and on the floor in her bathroom at five-thirty when the aide went in to see if she wanted any dinner."

"She could have been there for hours."

"Or fifteen minutes. The Gardens staff nurse said she didn't think it had been very long. Even if it was, the important thing is that they found her and got her to the hospital. She'll be okay."

Mattie couldn't see past the worry and work ahead. She was tired. She felt guilty. She felt sure Meredith would have handled everything so much better. "She'll probably have months of rehab."

"But she'll be okay."

It was what Mattie needed to hear, the comfort she craved, and she was grateful Collier offered it. Even if he was using his politician's voice. "Thanks," she said. "For being here."

"Where else would I be? Alice is my mother-in-law. I care what happens to her."

"I could understand if you weren't crazy about handling another crisis so soon after the last one. I could even understand if you needed to get a little distance from the Owens family. We've caused you a lot of grief lately."

"Meredith's caused me a lot of grief lately." His eyes held hers for a moment, settling any leftover question about who was to blame. And who wasn't.

She liked him, at that moment, in the same way she'd liked him when they first met. Collier was someone she'd choose to have as a friend. Someone she instinctively knew she could trust. Meredith was a fool to have risked losing him, an idiot for choosing an affair with Jack over the future she could have had with this man. And regardless of what the future held for the Montgomery marriage, Meredith had lost her place of honor in it. Even if Collier forgave her completely and fell in love with her all over again, he'd never look at her in quite the same way again. Mattie knew that, even if her sister didn't. But then, hadn't that always been Meredith's way? She didn't value the gifts she had, didn't treasure what came so easily to her?

"Who's with Blake?" Mattie asked because she couldn't invest any more energy in Meredith's issues. "Nurse Ratchet?"

"Mrs. Oliver agreed to stay overnight," he said, the warmth receding in his eyes. "But I'm sure you'll be happy to know my mother's coming from Knoxville to help. I called to let her know about Alice, and she decided she needed to be here. I couldn't talk her out of coming."

Mattie felt relief just knowing Linda was on her way. "Are they driving?"

"Dad's not coming this time. He's working on a class-action suit and can't get away. So Mom's flying in tomorrow. She was planning to come the week after next, so she could be here when Blake has his surgery. I don't know if she can stay until then or if she'll leave and come back."

Blake's surgery. With all the stress of the last few days, she'd forgotten the scheduled operation on Blake's hand was drawing nearer. "I forgot," she said, feeling yet another layer of worry tamp down over her spirit. "What's the day?"

"The tenth." Collier rolled the magazine in his hands one way and then another, tapped it against his leg. "Doesn't seem possible. When the doctors first told us about the operation on his hands, February seemed like a million years away."

"Which hand will they do first?"

"Left. They'll do the right one pretty soon after he gets the left cast removed. The doctors think he'll make a quicker adjustment that way. Thank God it'll be a couple more years before they do the open-heart surgery. I'm not sure I could deal with that at the moment."

Mattie didn't even like thinking about Blake in surgery, his little body all still under the anesthetic. How did Collier stand it? And with a sudden, unexpected and almost offensive fervor, Mattie wished for her sister. She wanted Meredith to be here. Now. Alice was having surgery. She had two daughters and both of them should be here. Mattie shouldn't have to face this alone. Collier shouldn't have to be a single parent when it came time to hand Blake over to the surgeons who'd give him thumbs. Meredith ought to be here. Mattie wanted her here. She wanted the old Meredith, the Meredith of before. She wanted Meredith to make the decisions, Meredith to bear the responsibility. It was selfish and self-centered and immature. But it was the way she felt. Now.

"I found a place for Mom," she said, because she didn't like knowing she was still capable of such childish thoughts. Especially now. "In Dallas. Well, in Garland. I found another place, a new concept facility in Plano that I'd actually prefer, but they have a waiting list. The one in Garland has an immediate opening, so they can take her right away."

"She's not going to be in any shape to travel for awhile," Collier pointed out. "Will they hold the bed for her?"

"I hope so. I'll give them a call tomorrow."

He nodded. "Is it nice?"

"As nice as those places get. It's a nursing home, with an assisted living section." Which pretty much described all the places she'd looked at. Except the one in Plano. "The other one, the one I'd like to get her into, is more appealing. They have a better staff-to-patient ratio, bigger rooms, nicer amenities. And they offer something they call 'on-call care.' It's something of a transition between true assisted living and full nursing home care. I put Mom's name on the waiting list, but there's no way to know when they'll have an opening."

The door opened inward and both Collier and Mattie looked up, expectantly. As did every other person sequestered in the waiting room.

"Phyllis Gilbert?" The name was called—sent out to find who in the waiting room was awaiting news of Phyllis Gilbert—by a gray-haired woman in casual clothing, who held a clipboard efficiently in her hand and made a checkmark on it as a haggard-looking man and a teenager stood and made their way to the doorway. The woman spoke to them in low tones for a moment, and then the two followed her from the room, shuffled past the glass and disappeared from view.

Tension strummed across Mattie's arms and over her shoulders, twigged the weary ache between her shoulder blades. She'd had a long day even before she'd started the long drive to Reyes City. But somehow the waiting was harder, sitting still felt very nearly unbearable. "When did you go back to work?" She put the question to Collier, diverting her thoughts from her own discomforts to his. "What happens when a mayor has to take a leave of absence, anyway?"

"Protocol," he said. "In elected offices, there's always protocol to handle the unexpected. In some cities, there's a deputy mayor who steps in if the mayor's incapacitated for some reason. In others, it's the head of the city council. In Reyes City, believe it or not, it's the fire chief."

She leaned her head back against the wall behind her. "You're kidding."

"No, apparently that particular bylaw was inserted into our city code forty years ago, after a lengthy feud over bylaws between the mayor at the time and the council chairman. The mayor didn't want the council getting too much power and vice versa and the end result was that the fire chief finally stepped into broker a peaceful compromise. Either they all agreed to designate his office as the next-in-command or he manipulated the situation to further his own agenda, but since then it's been the fire chief's duty to step in and take charge if the mayor is unable to carry out his responsibilities." He smiled and Mattie could see why he won elections. Why he'd most likely win a lot more. Collier's smile made you want to be on his team, made you feel like a winner too. "So for the two weeks I was preoccupied with family matters, Skip Billingsley was running the city."

"Skip?" Mattie remembered him as a burly tree of a man, with the demeanor of a redneck and arms the size of telephone poles. He'd been the designated spokesman for the fire department, appearing at school functions and civic clubs to promote fire safety. Mattie had thought he was scarier than any fire could possibly be. "I haven't seen him in years, but I would have thought he'd be a little rough around the edges for the mayor's office."

"He's a good delegator. What happened is that my staff did their job as usual and Skip signed off on pretty much whatever they asked him to. Fortunately, not much happened while I was out. January, it turns out, is a fairly slow month for Reyes City government."

"That was lucky. For Skip, anyway. Do you think the city council will change that section of the city code now and make the council chairman the acting mayor?"

"I imagine they'll try to get it on the agenda sometime in the next few months. But when an ordinance has been on the books for more than forty years, even if something else makes more sense, it's nearly impossible to get it changed. You know how it is in small towns. If it falls into the we've-always-done-it-this-way category, there'll always be some people who see no reason to change it."

"Are you sure you like public service? Seems to me having to deal with petty power plays would make the job very frustrating."

"I've never given it much thought, I guess. There are more challenging problems on my agenda."

"What's happening with your governor? I heard about it on the radio on the drive up."

"He's probably going to resign, which has both political parties frantically trying to spin gold out of dross. If he does step down, that'll turn what looked like a yawn of an election into a real horse race."

"Will you be one of the horses?"

The merest flicker of excitement, of desire, cross-cut his politician's bland expression. If she hadn't been watching for it, she wouldn't have seen it at all.

"One day. Not this time." Resignation wove like the thinnest thread through his voice, and if she hadn't been listening for it, she wouldn't have heard that, either. "I have a long-term plan in place that'll

get me to Oklahoma City and eventually to D.C.
Right now, that plan is to be the best mayor I can."

"I'm sure you're a good mayor."

He grinned. "You're prejudiced. But you're also
right. I'm a damn good mayor. That's why they pay
me the big bucks."

"Oh, right. Meredith told me you could make
three times your salary as a junior associate in your
dad's law firm."

The camaraderie faltered for a moment at the
mention of the name. But Collier didn't let it slip
completely away. "True," he said. "But that would
be Tennessee dollars, not real money."

She smiled at his teasing, glad he was there with
her, that she didn't have to face down tonight's
worry alone. Glad he knew, as she did, that Meredith would have hated Tennessee on any salary.
Meredith wanted to be upwardly mobile, always
moving toward the prize, and she had nixed any
idea Collier might have had of practicing law with
his father's small firm early on.

"Sorry I even mentioned her name." Mattie
shifted in the uncomfortable chair. "Do you think
it'll be much longer? How long does it take to
repair a broken hip?" But even as she said it, she re-
tracted the query. "I guess it depends on how badly
it's broken."

"She's going to be fine, Mattie. This wasn't your
fault."

"It feels like my fault."

"It's not. If you need to blame someone, blame
Meredith. She's got plenty to answer for as it is.
One more thing won't make much difference."

"Have you heard from her again?" Mattie asked,

because she didn't understand how her sister could stay away and not even call. "She must realize Blake's surgery is coming up. She must be worried about that, if nothing else."

He unrolled the magazine, rolled it back. Tighter, this time. "I doubt it. I'd like to think it's on her mind, but I don't. And I don't expect to hear from her until after the tenth."

"Do you think she'd come back if she knew about Mom's accident?"

He looked past her at the green-and-blue-striped curtains that covered a bank of windows. Mattie figured they were drawn to keep the darkness out and to keep worried eyes from dwelling on too much night. "No, I don't think anything would bring her home. I don't want her here. And I don't see how I can ever forgive her for bailing out on Blake."

"That makes two of us."

Collier's eyes turned to hers then, seeking solace maybe. Or to share a little of the hurt. Mattie held his gaze. Held it with the knowledge that she shared his disappointment in her sister. Held it with the shared understanding that Blake was both the reason Meredith had fallen from grace and the reason she'd return. Held it in reluctant acknowledgment that, eventually, forgiveness would be the only acceptable option either of them could choose. Blake's future depended on it.

Mattie's heart went out to him in that moment, and she leaned forward to clasp his hand and let him know she cared. A quick squeeze. A small comfort. She meant it for nothing more. But with that touch, emotion arched between them, struck out of the blue, struck him as well as her, twined around the two of them faster than a lightning strike. Awareness vibrated in the air between them, pulled her breath into her throat and let it flutter there. It was a mere moment. No longer than it took for a camera lens to open . . . and close.

Mattie pulled her hand away, trying to act as if she'd noticed nothing, felt nothing unusual, as if she hadn't seen that corresponding spark flash in his eyes as she knew he had seen in hers.

He leaned over, picked up the magazine from the floor, laid it on the table next to his chair, tried to smooth away the curl his worrying had created. He looked tired. And she wondered how much simple exhaustion had to do with that unexpected moment of attraction. A lot, she decided. They were each emotionally and physically drained, branded by their separate and mutual rejections, vulnerable to any touch, any breathless possibility that made them feel alive. The moment had been nothing, meant nothing. Nothing that circumstances couldn't readily explain away. "You don't have to stay, you know," she said. "Why don't you go home? Get some sleep. Give Mrs. Oliver a break."

"Blake is fine. He's in good hands, whether you like Mrs. Oliver or not. And if anyone needs to go home and get some sleep, it's you."

"I just got here."

"After driving up from Dallas. Go to the house, Mattie. I'll wait until Alice's surgery is over and she's in recovery."

"It surely can't be much longer." Mattie had no intention of leaving the hospital now. No more than he did. "But you really don't have to stay if you'd prefer to go."

"I know. Thanks for the offer, but I'll stay." He waited a moment, then spread his hands in a gesture of half apology, half curiosity before he asked, "So, since we've talked a little about Meredith, I may as well ask. Have you spoken to Jack?"

"In person, no less."

"You're kidding."

"No, surprised me, too. He was in the apartment when I got there. The jackass."

"An understatement," Collier said. "I'm surprised Meredith let him leave her long enough to make the trip. Was he there to see you?"

"He said it was business and he seemed pretty startled, so that part was probably true. He did say she was in Seattle. With his mother. That's really all he said about Meredith. Mostly he was just interested in finding some way to feel better about being a bastard. I did my best to wipe that happy thought out of his head." She paused, sighed. "He tried to give me the condo."

"The bastard."

She smiled, a little. "It's not as magnanimous as it sounds. He'd have found a loophole and had my butt evicted within a matter of twenty-four hours."

"You didn't take it?"

"Oh, I took it. But only long enough to get my stuff packed up and moved out of there. Just long enough for him to regret his generosity. At least, I hope he regretted it the minute I kicked him out of his own condo."

Collier laughed. Softly. Without much humor. But still he laughed.

And Mattie felt better about the whole humiliating

incident, even though she could think of no good reason why she should.

"Alice Owens?"

She hadn't realized the volunteer had reentered the waiting area, hadn't felt the whoosh of air as the door opened, hadn't noticed that the sounds in the room had stirred and refocused. But there the gray-haired woman stood, clipboard in hand, waiting for Alice's family to step forward.

Mattie reached for her bag, but found Collier already had it. His hand brushed across the hollow of her back as she stepped forward and he followed. A gesture of manners. Probably as unconscious as her response should have been. But Mattie felt the touch, a further awakening of awareness, another turn in the slow spool of attraction. The feeling seemed to be lying in wait for her. Ready to tip her off balance, unsettle, and unnerve her. Ready to take advantage of her vulnerability, her need for a friend. It had been a long day and it wasn't over. Tomorrow she'd have a better grip on reality.

Stepping ahead of Collier, she reached the nurse first. "My mother?" she asked.

"She's in recovery," the woman said. "They just called down. She'll spend a few days in the intensive care unit and then she'll be moved to a private room. As you requested earlier, Mayor Montgomery."

"Thank you," Collier said. "When will we be able to see her?"

"I'll take you to another waiting area now and the doctor will be in shortly to talk with you. He'll tell you about the surgery and give you a better idea of what you can expect over the next several days." She moved briskly down the hall. Collier and

Mattie followed and were shown into an alcove with only a half-dozen chairs. Mattie settled into one, nervous now as she hadn't been before. Collier stood just inside the doorway.

"May I get you some coffee?" the woman asked.

"No," Mattie answered, and was startled to hear her voice break on the word, hear the worry and fear tripping over her tongue in a single syllable. Tears pushed roughly at the backs of her eyes, thickened in her throat. All the tears she hadn't cried. All the tears she'd held in the privacy of her heart. Until now . . . when she could hold them back no longer.

The woman moved her clipboard to her other hand and stooped down in front of Mattie. "It's all right, dear," she said. "The worst is behind you. I've worked this shift and this watch for seventeen years and I wouldn't say this if it wasn't true. The worst is over now. All that's ahead is recovery."

One teardrop broke the dam and a thousand more followed, coursing down her cheeks in a silvery, slick fall.

The woman pushed to her feet, reached around Mattie to the low coffee table where a full box of Kleenex held center stage. Pulling out the top two, she tucked them into Mattie's hand and, with a comforting pat, returned her clipboard to the crook of her left arm. She nodded knowingly at Collier. "You let me know if there's anything else you and Mrs. Montgomery need. Anything at all. I'll help in any way I can."

She left them with the tiny squeak of rubber soled shoes on polished tile. A clean sound. An efficient sound. The sound of someone trying to be unobtrusive. The sound of someone who didn't know she'd made a mistake.

She'd made them a couple, labeled them Mister and Missus instead of in-laws. A simple mistake that Mattie wouldn't even have noticed a week ago. Would have laughed at, even an hour ago.

But suddenly she couldn't seem to do anything but cry.

By the time the doctor arrived and explained the operation, how long he expected Alice to remain in the hospital, and how long she'd likely stay in rehabilitation, Mattie's tears were drying up. By the time she was allowed in to see Alice for a scant few minutes, the tears were gone completely and she felt better for the release of emotion.

Even if her eyes were now red and puffy.

Even if she had a huge wad of used Kleenex stuffed into her coat pockets.

When there was finally nothing more to be gained by waiting at the hospital, Collier walked her to her car. He made no comment about her crying. Gentleman that he was, he didn't even try to soothe it over, fix her distress with meaningless conversation. He didn't talk about how cold the air was, how clear the starry sky. He didn't talk about the crusts of leftover snow from last week's storm or the predictions for tomorrow's weather. He didn't talk about Alice. He didn't talk about what the doctor had told them. He didn't talk at all.

Instead, he took comfort in the quiet and allowed her to feel comfortable in it, too.

At the car, she fumbled for her keys and he took her purse, found them, and unlocked the driver's side door.

"Thank you," she said.

"I'll see you at the house," he replied.

Meredith's house.

"Maybe I should stay here tonight. With Mom."

"You won't even be allowed in to see her again until tomorrow morning."

"I know, but . . ."

"I'll see you at the house," he repeated.

Going to his house seemed like a bad idea. What if people got the wrong idea? Her sister wasn't there. Lots of people in town knew why, knew where Meredith was and with whom. Mattie felt somehow tainted by Meredith's and Jack's guilt. As if she and Collier were guilty too. "I should get a hotel room," she said, impulsively blurting out the culmination of her thoughts. "Since Mom's in the hospital."

Collier frowned. "What?"

"A hotel room," she repeated as if that's what he'd misunderstood. "I should probably go to a hotel tonight."

"Because?"

"Because . . . well, because I shouldn't stay at the house. It might look . . . I should get a hotel room." She felt stupid for having said it, ridiculous for having thought it.

But he didn't look at her as if she'd said something stupid or ridiculous or outlandish or impossible. He looked at her and understood things she couldn't say, didn't know how to put into words.

However vague her thoughts, her reasoning was valid.

She knew it. And so did he.

"Mattie," he said, his breath a vapor under the

parking lot lights. "Don't worry about that, okay? I'll see you at the house."

She'd been foolish to raise the question, she realized. She should have let it lie, ignored the impulse, and let it slink away.

Before tonight, the idea of staying in her sister's house with her brother-in-law wouldn't have seemed laden with potential rumors. That anyone would think it was fodder for the tabloids would have been ludicrous and laughable. To Collier and to her. Getting a hotel room so no one could later question them about being alone together in a house simply wouldn't have crossed her mind. Or his.

Mrs. Oliver notwithstanding.

Something had changed tonight. In that brief moment of sharing in the waiting room, something had changed.

Mattie wished she could take back the words, make them moot again. But the very reason that it had occurred to her to say them was the reason they couldn't be taken back. They had life now, power.

They had possibility.

That was the name of the something that had changed.

Possibility.

CHAPTER
FOURTEEN

The wind whipped Meredith's hair into a raging halo, pressed the scent of ocean and pines against her face. The cold rouged her cheeks and made her want to laugh. The air off the water, saturated with moisture as thick as a rain-forest dew, had her holding her breath as long as possible before she released it and allowed the wind to send its replacement in a tart chill down her throat and into her lungs. Beneath her feet, the ferry churned a spool of spumy dark water and thrummed with a loud, cacophonous beat. If anyone had told her she'd have become so quickly acclimated to the coastal northwest, she'd have laughed and said, "Really? You think so?"

She'd always believed she would be happier forever landlocked. Give her the foothills and plains, the interior rivers with their green valleys and trees like leafy anchors between earth and sky. Cliffs and rocky shores were her idea of a place to visit for a

week once every ten years. Beaches were sandy,
southern and warm, free for the most part of capri-
cious winds and frequent rains. But here in the
Washington peninsula, she'd found a different
kind of landscape, a beautiful, misty place of shelter. If anyone had told her she'd fall so quickly in
love with a place so different from her roots, she
never would have believed them.

"Are you sure you don't want to go inside?" Jack's
voice whispered, soft as down in her ear. "It would
be much warmer."

But she hugged the mink—one of his mother's
many coats—and shook her head. "I want to watch
the lights," she said, more to herself than to him.
And the shore was dotted with them. Lights fading
in one direction, going brighter in another. She
tried to pinpoint the lights from the house where
they'd attended the party tonight. A pointless exercise as she had no idea where the house was in
relation to where they'd boarded the ferry. Looking
for it was just another way to hold the glow of the
evening wrapped around her, bundled under the
fur, warming her with satisfaction. Tonight, she was
lusciously, profusely satisfied.

The place could be incidental to the feeling, of
course. She might have loved anywhere that wasn't
home. Or she might love being where she was because she was with the man beside her. Jack. Darkly
handsome, a certain what-difference-does-it-make
disregard for the rules, a definitive *joie de vivre*. All
of that appealed to her, but it was his attitude of
privilege that tied it all into a nice, neat package.
Here, in the place he said he most despised and
avoided as much as possible, he cruised on his

family's name and fortune. She liked that. At the moment, she liked going along for the ride.

Meredith leaned against him now, angling her shoulder into the curve of his body, welcoming his arms as they slid around her from behind.

"Have I mentioned how beautiful you look tonight?" His breath, gliding warm across her cheek, sent a languid desire spilling like a slow, sweet poison through her body. His words, the sea-spray and the open air combined to make her shiver where she stood. "You look incredible. I was the envy of every man at the party."

She laughed. Because it was true. Jack brought out the best in her, did for her what Collier hadn't done in ages, if ever. Jack focused all of his consid-erable attention on her, made sure others knew he was with her, made sure other men understood that, for tonight at least, she belonged to him. Jack loved her totally, a bit obsessively, and she liked that. After eight years of marriage, of feeling herself slide into the role of Collier's wife, of realizing she was slip-ping into his growing shadow, it felt good to have a man want her so desperately. With Jack, she was the beloved, the one desired. She held the power. And she liked that, too, found it as thrilling as the free-dom she enjoyed here so far, far away from home. So far from responsibility. So far removed from reality.

"I loved everything about this evening," she said, although the wind caught the words and tossed them playfully away. She didn't expect he'd heard, but he leaned in closer, puller her tighter against him, nuzzled the curve of her neck.

"The evening isn't over."

It was a lover's promise and she decided the sex
tonight would be hot, frequent, and as luxurious as
her mood. The kind of sex married couples seldom
had. The kind of sex reserved for fantasy getaways
and vacations. The simple everydayness of life bred
familiarity, which in turn spawned repetition and
boredom. She and Collier had long since misplaced their first breathless passions, traded them
instead for the convenience of planned couplings.
Meredith hated the unexciting contours of her
marriage, and the last time Collier had approached
her, she'd done her best to pretend he was Jack, to
imagine that the kisses were electrifying, that the response of her body was spontaneous and not
preconditioned. But it hadn't worked. Collier had
left her dissatisfied and still aching with a name-
less hunger. She imagined he hadn't been satisfied
either, but with him, it was hard to tell. He moved
from one task to another, leaving whatever problem
he couldn't solve for one he could. For the last few
years, she'd felt like she was a task he had to accomplish, an item on his list, one more appointment on
his agenda. He'd be horrified if he knew and if
she'd told him, he'd have made every effort to be
more attentive, to make her know she was a valued
partner on his journey.

But that was the point, wasn't it?

If she had to tell him, it diminished both of them.
The attention he gave would always be suspect, the
pleasure she took in it less than she deserved.

She'd believed she could do it, be the wife, the
political partner. It wasn't her fault, really, that
she'd found the marriage so confining. She'd
thought his career path would be smoother, that it

wouldn't be such a slow climb. She'd imagined more parties, more social standing, more money, more power. Definitely more power.

Not that Jack exercised the power he could. He took it for granted and. consequently, squandered it.

She could change that. She could help him. If she chose.

That's what she liked most about being with him, about being free of marriage and of motherhood. She got to choose. No one else. What happened next was entirely up to her.

His lips nibbled along the curl of her ear and his tongue made fiery little caresses inside the delicate shell. He whispered to her of kisses he meant to deliver, of touches so intimate they made her quiver, of the darkness they'd need to hide the luscious, nasty acts he meant to do to her tonight.

He held her like a lover, tasted her pleasures as if she were the one forbidden fruit in the garden, and she liked to be treated with such reverence. She deserved this. She deserved this attention. She deserved to feel this treasured. She deserved more. And here, on this rugged ferry, in the middle of Puget Sound, on their way back to the mansion he called home, she meant to have it. Turning in his arms, she looped her hands at the back of his neck, smiled into his handsome eyes, and said, "The ladies' room is small, but there's room enough for the two of us. I'd have to take this dress off, but you could make it worth the effort."

"Let me," he said and trailed kisses along the curve of her neck until he reached her lips. He was aflame with desire for her, eager to worship her, body and soul.

As she was eager to let him.

He had been wasted on Mattie.

The baby kept crying and Meredith awoke with a pounding heart. Awoke to the strange, rhythmic quiet of the bedroom and the bed she shared with Jack. Jack, who slept beside her, sprawled and splayed beneath the tangled sheet, one leg cocked across the top in an angled vee, breathing in long, low puffs that weren't quite a sound, only the forerunners of soft snores.

There was the hum of ocean, a muffled whisper of rain, the chug of a boat's motor somewhere far out on the water. There was the rumble of heat filtering through the house, the creak of a stair, the drip from a faucet.

But there was no baby crying. No baby in the room. No baby in the whole house.

She'd heard Blake in her dreams. He cried for her in the dreams, connected with her across miles and miles, across day and night. In the beginning she'd missed him with a sad, vague loneliness that only subsided in sleep. She'd been so tired, so completely worn out with worry. But now that she was rested, now that life had begun to make sense to her again, Blake cried for her at night and, in the bedroom where she'd found a measure of peace, he ruined her sleep. Midnight after midnight.

Sliding her legs off the edge of the bed, she sat up. Strands of silvery light melted down the walls and pooled on the carpet. The light came from low-wattage bulbs tucked into recessed alcoves, hidden behind wooden moldings as thick as a man's hand.

It was the effect she'd wanted in Blake's nursery, but the Trummell House was too old and even new wiring wouldn't have allowed for this luxury of lighting. Even had the budget permitted it.

She hated Collier's budgets.

How would she ever stand to go back to that? Live like that again . . . after this?

Jack turned in his sleep, rousing just enough to realize she wasn't in her place. "Mer?" He rolled closer and lifted his arm until his hand could reach her, pat her, ask in a sleepy touch if she needed him to get up with her. She leaned into his palm, felt the solid width and warmth of him, turned to watch him as, question answered, he sank greedily back into deep slumber.

And for no apparent reason, that made her think of Blake again.

Blake, who had called her out of a perfectly good dream.

Her arms ached a little, but she wouldn't allow it to be from longing. She missed him. Of course, she did. And, at moments, she longed to hold him again. Longed to in the way she longed now to sleep. Longed to like she wanted to wrap herself in Evelyn Youngblood's long fur coat. A distant sort of wish. A vague desire for something she thought about only now and then. When she needed rest. When she needed the sumptuous comfort of mink.

She thought sometimes about calling Collier again, asking about the baby, asking about her mother. She missed Blake and Alice and her house. But she didn't want to know if her mother or her son missed her. She didn't want to know if there was dust on the beautiful wood floors. She didn't want to be needed again. Not yet. Not until she could sleep deeply and long and awaken knowing it was time for her to go home.

Her eyelids drifted down, elusive sleep beckoning to her again. She slid back onto the bed, let her legs glide beneath the linens, pulled the sheets over her shoulder, and laid her head on the pillow, so soft it breathed out a sigh beneath her. Jack's hand lay curved in her line of sight, relaxed across the wrinkles he'd made in his pillow when he bunched it under his cheek.

His hand.

Large. Fine. A work of living art, designed of flesh and sinew and bone. She could admire its strength, its perfect shape, remember with pleasure its fiery touch on her skin, and still begrudge him such a beautiful hand. If Blake had been born perfect, she wouldn't be here now, looking at the hand of her lover, mourning the imperfection of her son.

She wouldn't go home, she decided, until after Blake's surgery. She couldn't bear to think about the operation, to imagine the way his hand would look afterward. Her throat tightened, her heart hurt when she thought about the cast he would have to wear, the stitches beneath. She would wait until that was over. Collier would be there. Blake would never remember that she wasn't.

She would wait.

Tracing a fingertip along the curve between Jack's thumb and finger, she closed her eyes and drifted into a peaceful, dreamless sleep.

CHAPTER
FIFTEEN

"The way this is shaping up, we've got a real shot at taking November." Bill Riggs, it had been rumored, owned half of Oklahoma and a quarter-section each of Arkansas and Louisiana. He had made his money the old-fashioned way—he inherited it. While it was unlikely his holdings were as vast as the rumors reported, he wasn't the type of man to deny anything that was said about him. He wasn't the type of man to take no for an answer, either.

And Collier was about to tell him no.

Because he didn't see how he could say yes.

Yes, I'm your man. Yes, I'm ready. Yes, I'll run. Yes, I can get the job done.

"I won't say the recent publicity about your wife was a good thing, but it got your name out there." Henry Frazier, who'd earned his own fortune through savvy choices and hard work, was a no-nonsense business-man, who went to the bottom line first and stayed there. Together the two men packed a powerful punch. They were each responsible for pouring millions of philanthropic dollars into cultural and civic organizations across the state. They supplied funding for good deeds, good causes, and the public good as they envisioned it. They also financed their own political agendas, separately if those agendas differed, as a team when they dovetailed.

Tonight, the men were in complete agreement. The governor's office was up for grabs come November. They meant to back the winning candidate. That was the reason Collier had been invited to have dinner with them. He'd made it onto their political agenda.

The conversation up until the coffee was served had been general, more about college football and the recent bowl games and college basketball and the Sweet Sixteen playoffs than about the governor's scandal and impending resignation. Collier's stomach was one big knot of good food, good wine, college sports, and nervous tension by the time Henry Frazier leaned back in his chair and called the hovering waiter over with no more than a lift of his eyebrows. The dishes were removed, coffee brought to the table, and just that quickly the conversation turned to weightier matters. "Right now, Collier, your name recognition is higher than the governor's."

Riggs laughed as he sweetened and creamed his coffee. "That's saying something since Lucman couldn't have done a better job of setting up this election for us if I'd personally told him how to do it."

"That's why Bill and I are here," Henry continued. "It's your moment. If you want it."

Collier wanted it.

He wanted it so badly his hand shook under the table and he clenched the napkin in his lap to gain control, to keep from seizing the thing he knew he could not have, to hell with the consequences. It would be better not to let these men see how desperately he wanted this moment. "You know the governorship is in my long-term plans," he stalled, raising the linen to pat his mouth.

Bill Riggs stirred his diluted coffee, set the spoon with a clink on the saucer. Henry Frazier sipped his coffee, hot and black. Both men kept their eyes on Collier, gave him no cues as to their expectations. Except their expectations were shining like gold on the table. Their support. Their checkbooks. Their influence. If they didn't expect an affirmative answer, they'd have invited someone else to dinner. "My son is scheduled for hand surgery next week. I can't look beyond that at the moment." Collier said.

Both men nodded a sympathetic understanding.

"Dave Keith's a fine surgeon," Bill said. "Good man."

Henry nodded agreement. "Damn good golfer, too. We've been paired in a couple of charity tournaments."

These two men probably knew as much about Blake's prognosis as Collier himself did. They weren't men who overlooked any detail, no matter how small.

"The surgery's on the tenth," Collier said, pausing to sip his own coffee, letting the heat of it burn past the bitter taste on his tongue. "I'll breathe easier after that."

Another nod from Bill. A comment from Henry.

"Hell of a thing when a man has to face a situation like yours."

Then, the men settled back in their chairs, fully aware of the public and private details of Collier's situation and the true reason for his hesitation. The reason might just as well have steamed up from the china cups and spelled out an unmistakable *Meredith* in wispy letters.

"No reason you have to commit tonight." Bill looked around for the waiter and the check. "Take a few days. Think about what we've said. Let us know your decision."

"She's got to be back and on board by March," Henry said bluntly. "If you don't think that's possible, then we'll want to look elsewhere."

Disappointment seared Collier's throat, roiled in his gut. He wanted this race. He wanted it more than he'd ever wanted anything. The opportunity dangled in front of him like the string of a balloon. All he had to do was reach out, grab it, and he'd be on his way to the ride of his life. These men would get him where he'd dreamed of going. Sooner than he'd dared to hope. Sooner than he'd believed possible. This moment was his. He felt it from the soles of his feet to the center of his soul. He'd dreamed of it, planned and prepared for it.

And now that it was here, he couldn't lift a finger to claim it.

Meredith had tied his hands, presented him an impossible, unacceptable choice.

In all the times he'd imagined this moment, his answer had never been, *I can't do it.*

The three men walked out of the restaurant together, talking about the recent Super Bowl. As they reached the parking lot and Frazier headed for his big Escalade, Riggs fell into step with Collier. "There are some folks who'll tell you politics is about integrity," he said in his soft Oklahoma drawl, the words pointed and precise. "I'm gonna tell you it's *Let's Make a Deal*. This is politics, son. Make a deal."

Collier got the message. It was no secret that these two political brokers had the money and the power to turn negative into positive, a bad situation into a bump in the road. They were masters of behind-the-scenes maneuvers. They knew the system and they knew how to implement it to advantage. The straw of Meredith's disappearance would be spun into raw gold, Blake's battle to be a normal little boy would snag the sympathy vote, Collier's willingness to save his marriage would win over the family values block. Those were personal, fixable problems. Bill Riggs and Henry Frazier were offering the benefit of their knowledge, their contacts, their personal and financial backing, and their considerable influence across the state to fix those problems. They weren't backing the dark horse to show, they were betting he would win.

But, without Meredith, all bets were off.

They knew it. And so did he.

Make a deal.

Even if he could bring himself to ask Meredith to come home and play the part, even if he honestly believed there was a chance to save the marriage, any deal he made with her would be the devil's bargain.

He could say to hell with self-respect, offer the deal, and give her the power to make or break his career. Also, a devil's bargain.

Either way, he lost.
Make a deal.
Personal politics were never that simple.

Collier heard the music as he came through the breezeway and braced himself to find Mattie in his kitchen. His mother's rental car was missing, so he knew she'd thought of something she needed to do after the baby went down for the night, some errand that couldn't wait until morning. The Mercedes was parked in the garage, where it had sat since being returned from Colorado. Linda refused to drive it, preferring to rent a vehicle of her own because, in some misguided form of maternal support, she felt driving the car Meredith had driven would somehow condone her daughter-in-law's offense. Her illogical reasoning aside, he'd been very glad to see his mother this time, glad for her unfailing energy and unflagging encouragement. She fussed over him, fussed over Blake, and gave every cleanable surface a rosy glow of fresh perspective. No wonder her second-grade classroom blossomed with bright-eyed students who, along with their parents, lavished untold love and adoration on their Mrs. Montgomery year after year after year.

Collier knew her absence from her classroom was a sacrifice, both personally and financially, for his parents, but he had never appreciated their generosity more or been more grateful for his family's support. At this particular moment, though, he was glad it would be Mattie who met him on the other side of the kitchen door and not his mother.

The music dropped, centering its passion in a

hum of stringed instruments, as he opened the door and found the kitchen dark and deserted. He was surprised to feel a punch of disappointment at the emptiness, and stripping off his gloves as he walked, he followed the music toward the front of the house. On the drive home, he'd wished for solitude, but now that he was here, he suddenly found himself wanting company, needing conversation.

Mattie's company. Mattie's conversation.

The music felt familiar, as classical music often did with its ageless rhythms and evocative passages, and as he moved down the dark hallway he realized that in the past month, he'd formed a mental association between it and Mattie. A memory that bound the two together. Mattie and music. The bows and curtseys of her body as she exercised to the rush or hush of a classic tempo. The disciplines of dance and the disciplines of music that made both seem effortlessly easy.

Meredith had sometimes listened to classical music, tuning the radio to a public station that catered to that niche audience. Occasionally she used it as background at a dinner party. Once in a while, she would have it on in the mornings, would move around the kitchen with a meditative grace. He had never once seen her dance. Or do the stretching exercises Mattie did. At one time or another in her life, Meredith had taken ballet. And tap and modern dance. Right after they were married, she'd even spent a couple of years doing Jazzercise with a class at the Y. But she didn't take it seriously.

He wondered what Meredith had taken seriously. Not dance, although Alice had often commented about her talent. Not exercise, although Meredith herself often said she enjoyed it. Not marriage vows or motherhood. Not family or self-respect or a dozen other values he would have said were important to her.

Before she disappeared.

Before he discovered she wasn't who he'd believed she was.

He began unbuttoning his coat, but his fingers stilled on the buttons as he caught his first glimpse of Mattie. Staying one step back from the doorway, he observed her with a surge of voyeuristic pleasure.

With André sprawled like a long shadow beside her, Mattie sat on the rug in the foyer, her upper body stretched parallel across her legs, her fingers touching her upturned toes, head bent so that she formed a flexible double line of female. Her hair was wrapped and tucked and tamed into a knot on top of her head and his gaze followed the gentle curvature of her neck. A beautiful thing, a woman's neck. Graceful, streamlined, and sexy. Collier couldn't recall the last time he'd paid any attention to the arch of a woman's neck.

Unless it was the last time he'd watched Mattie stretching.

"Do you know," he said, taking a single step forward, moving into the light, "I've seen you doing these exercises morning and night, but I've never seen you put a single toe out to dance."

André lifted his head and his tail gave an idle thump of welcome, but he didn't get up. Neither did Mattie. She held her stretch, apparently not startled or surprised by his entrance, so either she was lost in her own agile thoughts or she'd known all along he was there, watching. She must have heard him come in. The house was old and full of coordinating sounds. When one door opened or closed, that knowledge was carried in a rush of air to another part of the house, as if the whole structure knew when any part of it was disturbed.

"This house has no room for dancing." She unfolded like a flower and with a supple twist from the waist, she turned to look back at him. "It's a great house, but cut up into too many rooms. Call me finicky, but I don't like to bump into the furniture."

His spirits lifted for a heartbeat, perhaps all of two. "I noticed Mom's rental car is missing. Don't tell me we're already low on cleaning supplies."

"She decided to visit my mom this evening. She called me earlier at the hospital, I came home, and she took off. You just missed seeing Blake. He went out like a lightbulb about eight-thirty." Leaning to the side, she draped her arm across the dog and stretched in that direction, giving his ear a gentle rubbing before she straightened again. "I'm not sure your mother knows what to do with herself in the evenings once Blake goes to bed. She's been here three days and I think she's already replaced every piece of shelf paper in the kitchen and reconfigured the pantry and the linen closet."

"Relaxing is a problem for her. I tell her she needs to take her batteries out and let them recharge, but she's just got too much extra energy. How's your mom today?"

Mattie curled her legs under her and bounced easily to her feet. Collier had never seen anyone who made moving look so easy. Her body was flexible grace, a willowy miracle of genetics and hard work. Just watching her made him think seriously about increasing his exercise program from a weekly hand-ball game to a daily workout. With weights.

"About the same," she answered, stepping over the sleeping dog. "Maybe slightly less confused than she was in ICU, but still not clear about where she is or why she's there. No word yet on when they'll move her to the rehab center. I don't think she's recovering from the surgery as quickly as the doctor had hoped."

He moved from the doorway and hung his coat in the hall closet. When he turned, Mattie had moved to the bottom stair and was now balanced on her insteps, toes pointing down, legs elongated in yet another stretch. Pulling off his suit jacket, he tossed it over the bannister rail and dropped onto the stairstep behind her. "I've just come from an interesting dinner," he said, tugging at the knot of his power-red tie.

"I'm jealous." She did a slow turn and dropped her heels over the stair edge, reversing the stretch. "I ate at the hospital grill and had a very uninteresting cheeseburger. You'd think a hospital would offer a few healthy choices, but the grill menu is pretty much fried, deep-fried, and covered in cheese. Comfort food all the way. It was served with lettuce and tomato, though."

"What? No pickles?"

"And pickles. Lest we forget the salt."

He pulled the tie through the fold of the collar and unbuttoned the neck of his shirt. "Maybe the next governor will promote a healthier lifestyle."

"The next governor will need to . . ." The sentence trailed off and she dropped onto the stair beside him. "Is that what you meant by an interesting dinner? Was this a meeting about your campaign? And here, I thought you were talking about the food."

"The food was good." He stalled, unsure how much he wanted to tell, how much he'd prefer not to hear himself say aloud. "What I remember about it."

"So. . . ." She leaned forward so she could look at him, eager to hear whatever he had to say. "Give me the scoop, Gov."

He felt the pull of a smile, even though he didn't feel like smiling at all. Drawing the silk tie across his palm, he tried to tell himself what an honor it was to be asked, that he was young and had years in which to build a career, run for governor, and win. And that could happen down the road. In eight years. Or twelve. Or twenty. It was also possible that the opportunity wouldn't come his way again. This could be his one and only moment to stand in this particular sun.

"Not much to tell. I was taken to dinner by a couple of men who want me to run for governor."

"Collier!" Her smile lit up the room, made him glad for another heartbeat, proud that Bill Riggs and Henry Frazier thought he could win. "That's wonderful! That's what you've always wanted, isn't it?"

"Yes." How sweet the word tasted. He tried to savor that moment, too. "I never thought the opportunity would come along this soon."

"But it did," she said with a satisfaction he'd like to be able to feel, with a confidence he couldn't replicate. "Wow. You're going to be the governor of Oklahoma."

Again, in spite of his very real frustration, she

almost made him smile. "I can't run, Mattie. I want to, but it's not going to be possible."

"You don't have to be modest with me. I know you've been planning a campaign like this ever since you were a kid. Of course, you can run. Of course, you will win."

"A month ago, I would have agreed with you. But the timing's wrong now. I can't do it."

Her eyes met his, but reality quickly had her looking away, her enthusiasm chased off by a sigh. "I could kill Meredith for this."

"Get in line." Those words turned to ash in his mouth, a sentiment he felt vindicated in expressing, but not one that made him feel a bit better. "On the other hand, it's her disappearance that pushed my name to the top of several lists. Name recognition. How's that for irony?"

"You should run anyway. Show her what you're made of. Show her what she gave up."

How did he tell Mattie that he couldn't show anyone what he was made of without Meredith at his side. However estranged. However strained their relationship. To campaign without her would be to open up all avenues of gossip about her disappearance and invite certain defeat. Family values had strict rules. Rules that could be bent, but not broken.

"A candidate in the midst of a separation or divorce isn't going to win."

Mattie didn't say anything for a minute. She reached up and pulled a pin from her hair. A scraggly curl bounced down past her ear. "Are you going to get a divorce?"

He looped the tie between his hands, watched the fabric droop across his fingers. "My wife had an affair. She left me to be with her lover. I have no reason to think she intends to come back. I have no reason to want her back. Divorce is the only obvious ending I see."

"But your career."

"I'll recover. Other politicians have. It just knocks me out of contention this time around."

"That's not fair."

He found her indignance sweet, her belief in him soothing. "Politics isn't about fairness. It's about the art of the deal." The word caught on the cusp of his voice. *Make a deal.* Bill's words, Henry's bottom line. *Make a deal.* Get your wife home, get her on board with the party line, patch over what's wrong in the marriage, and the election is yours. They had offered it to him on a silver platter.

At a price.

"This isn't my time." He summed up his options in that one sentence and declared the price too high. "Blake needs me now. He has to come first."

"Of course, he comes first. But are you sure about the election? I mean, these men must know about Meredith." She pulled another pin and a few more chestnut strands curled around her face. "You didn't have to tell them, did you? About her . . . and Jack?"

"No, I didn't have to tell them. They're aware of the circumstances."

"Well, then. They must think it would be all right for you to run. They must believe you'll win, even under the circumstances. It isn't your fault, you know. No one's going to blame you for what Meredith did." She leaned over, bumped his arm with hers. "Don't be so quick to think the worst, Gov."

It was a pep talk based on enthusiasm rather than

reality, but it gave his sagging spirit a needed boost. "I should appoint you my campaign manager."

She pulled out the rest of the pins and her hair fell in a red-gold tangle to her shoulders. "I'd be good at it," she said. "Although I should tell you that tap dancing has never been my greatest talent."

Collier laughed. He surprised himself, but he laughed. Aloud.

He wasn't going to be the next governor but for a moment, Mattie had made him feel that would be all right. On a night when he mainly wanted just to wallow in his misery, she had made him laugh.

"Thanks, Mattie. I owe you." And he leaned over to emphasize his appreciation with an impromptu kiss on the cheek.

But she shook back her hair at the instant he leaned in, her head swivelled toward him, and his lips landed at the corner of hers. The kiss, a butterfly impulse on his part, slid into an intimacy he hadn't anticipated, and that lingered too long before they each drew quickly apart, like boxers withdrawing after a one-two punch. Not a knockout, but if she'd turned a quarter-inch more in his direction, it would have been. His breathing rasped as it grew suddenly rapid, as he became fully aware that he wanted to kiss her. On the lips. Hard and long and deep.

The feeling should have been alarming, should have appalled him, disgusted him, embarrassed him, but it simply lingered, tempting and curious, as he watched a tint of peachy awareness creep into her cheeks. Her breathing, too, was faster than it should have been and he wondered what she was thinking, if she wanted to kiss him, too. Or if he had inadvertently ruined their budding friendship.

"Mattie . . ." He started to offer an excuse, a reason, but for the life of him, he couldn't think of one. So he left her name hanging there, an incomplete thought, the birth of a question.

She wouldn't look at him, but instead covered her embarrassment by bending her head, running her hands through her hair.

And he was left to look at the supple curve of her neck.

Standing abruptly, he reached for his jacket, and thankfully, heard the house give a whoosh of welcome as the back door opened and closed.

"Your mom's home," Mattie said brightly, her hair a cloud of awareness around her flushed face.

Collier slid his jacket over his arm, turned to go upstairs, then decided that would feel too much like retreat. And he had already retreated one too many times this evening.

"I'm back." Linda bustled through the doorway, cheeks red from the cold, unbuttoning her coat as she entered. "I stopped at the store on the way home. Who's up for popcorn and a game of poker?"

"I'm in." Mattie hopped up, taking the two steps to the foyer floor in one graceful gambol—one that looked suspiciously like retreat to Collier. "I'll start the popcorn. Collier has news."

And she left him to tell it.

Then, even though he had intended to go to bed and brood over his misfortune, he stayed up and soundly defeated the two women at Five Card Draw, ending the night with a whopping forty-seven pennies, six matchsticks, and a fortune cookie.

It wasn't the campaign he wanted, but it wasn't a bad haul for one of the worst nights of his life.

"Morning, Mattie."

Mattie glanced at the kitchen clock: 7:40. Bright as a button, Linda Montgomery moved from refrigerator to table like she was spring-loaded. A happy energy followed her like a sunbeam as she finished setting the table for breakfast. Four places. A mother, a son, a grandson, and an extra. Mattie, the extra.

But who could mind when the tablecloth was a sunny yellow and there were flowers—fresh flowers—at the center of a variety of jellies, jams, a sugar bowl and creamer? There was one half of a grapefruit, cut and sectioned, at three of the four places, awaiting a spoon and an appetite. On the stove, a quart-size pan steamed uncovered with cooked oatmeal. Toast, cinnamon-raisin and plain, had been cut into triangles and arranged on a plate. A full pot of coffee brewed with a bubbly, rousing aroma. Collier's mother was apparently cooking for an army.

"I hope you eat breakfast," Linda said as she wiped down the high chair. "I tell my students that it's the most important meal of the day and people who skip it might as well crawl right back into bed because they won't have enough energy to make it until ten o'clock, much less noon."

"I eat breakfast every day," Mattie said, feeling a little like a student in Linda's classroom, wanting to please the teacher. "Breakfast is my favorite meal."

"Excellent," Linda said with her second-grade teacher smile. "Take a seat. This is almost ready."

"Is there anything I can do to help?"

"I don't think so. You do like oatmeal, don't you?"

As if she'd say no. "Absolutely."

"Good. We won't wait for Collier. I just fed the baby and he's going to need a bath before his daddy brings him back downstairs to join us." She spooned oatmeal into two bowls and set one in front of Mattie. "There you go. Coffee?"

"Please." Mattie loved the bustle and homeyness in the kitchen—qualities noticeably lacking on other occasions in Meredith's pristine kitchen—and attributed both to Collier's energetic bunny of a mom. Linda might be a little on the frenetic side, but she cleaned and cooked as a labor of love. Growing up in her house must have been like being snuggled in safety. And clean towels. Lots of clean towels. "This looks wonderful," Mattie said sincerely. "You must have gotten out of bed at the crack of dawn if you've already fed Blake, too."

"I want to spend as much time with my grandson as possible. Babies grow up so quickly, plus I thought Collier could use an extra hour of rest this morning. I told him last night on my way to bed that I'd get up with Blake this morning and let him sleep."

"That was thoughtful."

"Protective. He may be thirty-seven, but he's still my baby and I still worry about him. Especially when I know last night was particularly hard for him."

"I don't think beating us at poker was that hard."

Linda smiled and pulled out a chair for herself. "It's this election. I know he wants to be governor. I know how much he wants to run. To have to watch him sacrifice what he's worked so hard to earn . . . well, it's difficult for a mother to see that and not try to do something to make her kid feel better."

Mattie paused with her grapefruit spoon in the air, poised to dig into the glistening fruit. "He's not going to run?"

Linda placed her palms on either side of her plate, ready to explain the basics of math or English. Or maybe, give out an assignment. "Mattie," she said. "Collier could be a candidate without Meredith, but he'd be putting his personal life on trial, and it's unlikely he would win. This is the buckle of the Bible Belt. A man is expected to keep his own house in order. Even when it is clearly his wife who put his house out of order."

"That wouldn't stop me from voting for him."

Linda sprinkled sugar across the top of her grapefruit half and across the top of her oatmeal. She added butter to her bowl of oats and a spiral of cream, all the while with her lips pursed, her disapproval shouting out in all the words she didn't say. "It will alter the tone of the campaign and that will make the difference. Appearances are what matter these days. If Meredith came home this morning ready to mend her fences, and *if* he agreed to take her back, then he could run and probably win. But with her out larking around, he's a man whose marriage is in trouble, and if he ran he'd lose."

He had said as much to Mattie last night, but she, naively, hadn't wanted to believe that Meredith's infidelity could cost Collier an election. Especially *this* election. One more crime it would be difficult to forgive. One more cost of cheating.

Except it wasn't Meredith who had to pay.

"How could she do this to him?" The question

sprang from Mattie's thoughts and into the air. "She's always talked about his career as if it belonged to her too. She's always seemed so proud of him, so confident of his success and supportive of him. That's always been important to her. At least, she always said it was. I don't understand how could she run off like she did, knowing how it would hurt his career."

Linda's spoon dived into the grapefruit and juice squirted across the bright tablecloth in a pattern of dark splatters. "Meredith doesn't think about anyone but herself."

Mattie watched as Collier's mother patted the splotches, half-expecting her to jerk the tablecloth out from under the dishes and head for the wash with it.

But Linda only patted the spots, then, with slightly more care, she dipped her spoon in the grapefruit again. "Meredith is self-centered and selfish and I've never known her to be considerate of anyone except her mother." Biting into the fruit, she focused on Mattie without apology. "That can't be any big secret to you. You grew up with her."

It had been a secret though. Alice's secret. *Meredith is so talented. Meredith is so intelligent. Meredith is so good.* How had Mattie not seen that as the excuse it was? Alice, living vicariously through her beautiful daughter, saw Meredith as perfect and so, unwilling to allow any flaw, molded imperfection into her character. And Mattie, watching, saw what her mother directed her to see. *Meredith. Talented, intelligent, good.*

"I thought Meredith was perfect," she told Linda. "I wanted to be like her. I wanted to *be* her. But I understood I couldn't be, so I frequently ran away."

"Disappearing Mattie. Meredith said that you caused your mother a lot of grief."

"She did? She said that?"

Linda reached over, patted Mattie's hand. "I am very angry with your sister right now, and I will admit that in the beginning I tried too hard to be her friend. She was marrying my son. I wanted to like her and I wanted her to like me. So I listened to her stories and always gave her the benefit of any doubt. But I don't have to do that anymore. She lied to me about a lot of unimportant things, so it's not a huge shock to find out she lied about some important ones too. Now that I've gotten to spend a little time with you, I can see that she lied about you too."

It was the kindest thing anyone had ever said to Mattie in this kitchen, in this house, even if it didn't feel entirely true. "She wasn't lying about me. I did disappear. On numerous occasions. And I did cause my mother grief."

"She lied about you, Mattie. Maybe she did it because she couldn't stand for you to get any positive attention. Maybe she was jealous because you're a good person. Maybe it was just habit. I don't know her reasons, but I've spent thirty years in a classroom. I can spot a brat at forty paces. She is. You're not. Jack may be the latest and the most hurtful, but I'm certain he's not the first thing she's ever stolen from you."

Mattie would like to believe that Meredith had stolen her chance to belong, to be wanted and loved, to be someone special in her own right.

But she couldn't blame Meredith for her own poor choices. She had conceded her identity and taken on the role she'd been assigned, disappearing in impotent fits of rebellion instead of standing and fighting for what she needed, what she deserved.

"Look," Linda continued. "She's your sister and I've got no business saying these things to you. You'd think I'd have learned to keep my opinions to myself. But when someone hurts one of mine, I forget. I just wanted you to know I've enjoyed getting to know you during all this trauma and I like you. Even if you are a lousy poker player."

Mattie smiled because she liked Linda too. Later, perhaps, she would weigh Linda's opinions, consider what she'd said about Meredith. But for now, she felt free to like the fierce way Linda threw her considerable support behind her son. She liked the schoolteacher matter-of-factness in her attitude. She liked her directness. She liked the breakfast. She liked that there were four places set at the table, even though two of them were still vacant. She liked the homey quality Linda had stamped into Meredith's kitchen. And she liked how simply and naturally, Linda changed the subject.

"Drink your juice, Mattie. And tell me what you're going to do about your mother once she's out of the hospital. I know she'll stay in the rehabilitation clinic for several weeks, but after that, have you made any plans? I hate to say it, but I'm concerned about her recovery. Last night, she wasn't very responsive."

"I know." Mattie worried about that, too. The hip seemed to be mending, but the surgery—or maybe the fall itself—had seemed to make the dementia worse. "I've found a place in Dallas that offers a bridge service between true assisted living and nursing home care. But after this, I may have no

choice but to put her in a full-care home. I won't
try to move her until she's completed the rehab
here though. Then, well, we'll see."

"That'll mean a lot of commutes for you." Linda
finished the last of her grapefruit and set the bowl
to one side. "There are daily flights between Dallas
and Reyes City, though, right?"

"Not anything direct. And adding up check-in
times, boarding and departures at the airport, it actually takes less time to drive. I'll manage. She is my
mother. I let Meredith take over too much of the
responsibility for her care up until now. Mother's
condition was too much for one person to handle
alone. No matter what Meredith told me."

"Don't make excuses for her, Mattie. Meredith
didn't disappear because of Alice's stroke. She . . ."
Linda picked up her cup and sipped the coffee.
When she set the cup back in the saucer, she had
her opinion firmly in check. "Let's talk about something else." She leaned toward Mattie. "Tell me
what you think of Nurse Oliver."

Feeling like a co-conspirator, Mattie leaned in,
too. "I think there's something strange about her.
Did you know that she—"

"Do not sit there plotting revenge over breakfast." Collier walked into the kitchen carrying
Blake, who was newly scrubbed and baby powder
fresh. "I will consider a rematch tonight, but the
fortune cookie is not going into the ante. It is off
the table."

Linda bobbed up to take the baby and put him in
his high chair. Collier poured himself a cup of
coffee and took his place at the table. He looked
chipper and excessively handsome, dressed for the

office in three-toned blue. Blue suit, blue shirt, blue tie. He looked very mayoral. Handsome enough to become a very popular governor.

"There will be a rematch tonight," Linda said. "But that's not what we were talking about."

He glanced from his mother to Mattie, clearly hoping she wouldn't tell him what it was they had been talking about.

Mattie looked down at her grapefruit, almost untouched in the bowl. She picked up her spoon.

"We were discussing Nurse Oliver." Linda handed Blake a ring of plastic keys, which he promptly tossed to the floor. André promptly got up to see if any food was involved. Linda promptly shooed him back to his rug and handed Blake a spoon. Which he promptly tossed to the floor. "There's something not right about that woman, Collier. Mattie thinks so, too."

This time he was the one to lean down and retrieve the spoon and the toy keys, shoo the dog back to the rug, and toss the discarded items onto the table. "I didn't hire her for her personality," he said in a let's-not-discuss-this tone of voice.

"*You* didn't hire her." Linda, being his mother, stuck with her own agenda. "Meredith did."

Mattie concentrated on digging out a segment of the grapefruit without squirting juice into her eye.

"We've talked about this before, Mom. I'm not going to fire Mrs. Oliver just because you've never seen her smile."

"Mattie doesn't like her, either."

Collier turned to Mattie. "Have you seen Mrs. Oliver smile?"

Mattie wished she'd sprinkled sugar on the

grapefruit. At least a little. "No," she said. "But she doesn't like me. I interrupt Blake's schedule."

"Did she say that to you?" Linda shook her head, not waiting for an answer. "You see, Collier, I was right. She's too concerned with time tables and routines."

Collier began eating his oatmeal. "Which is why Meredith chose her. She felt—we both felt—Blake needed a competent nurse. You can't say Mrs. Oliver isn't competent or that she hasn't done exactly what we asked. She put Blake on a schedule and she's kept him on it."

Linda made faces at the baby, kept handing him toys and spoons and a plastic cup, which he folded into his funny grasp and then dropped on the floor. "Meredith chose the woman because she didn't want anyone who would form a loving attachment with him. We don't have to tiptoe around this anymore, Collier. Meredith isn't here and, even if she was, she'd deny it, but you and I both know Blake needs someone who feels some genuine affection for him, not a strict schedule in thick-soled shoes."

Setting down his spoon, Collier lifted his cup and sipped his coffee. "Is that what you think too, Mattie? That Mrs. Oliver has no affection for Blake?"

Mattie didn't like the woman and she didn't want her around the baby. But she felt badly about asking, straight-out, to have her fired. "She seems like a very unhappy woman. I'm sorry for that, but Blake has enough troubles of his own. I think someone else would be a better influence."

His gaze held hers for a moment. "Do you think Meredith hired her because she didn't want Blake to like his nanny better than he liked her?"

"I don't know." And she didn't. It sounded possible to her, exactly the sort of thing Meredith would do. But Mattie was learning how very little she actually knew about her sister.

"If I tell Mrs. Oliver not to come back after Blake's surgery, then I have a bigger problem. Once you go home, Mom, he'll be left alone with a new hire who isn't familiar with him, his schedule, or the house. That seems like one too many changes to make just as he's recovering from the operation and adjusting to wearing a cast."

"If you get someone right after he comes home from the hospital, I'd have a few days to train her." Linda clicked her tongue at her grandson, won a grin in return.

"I could do it," Mattie said, the thought spilling straight out of her mouth, bypassing the chance for doubts. "I'd love to do it."

Linda looked at her. Collier looked at her. Even Blake grinned at her across the table.

"I thought you had to go back to Dallas."

"But you've got your mother to deal with. And your school."

And a life there that felt less real to her, less important to her, than the one she'd found here. "Mother is my responsibility now and I want to be able to keep a close eye on her while she recuperates. That means I'll be traveling back and forth at least twice a week, possibly more often. I work with some very talented instructors, who are doing as good a job of running the school as I could, and I'm going to have to rely on them, whether I'm there or here. In some ways, it would probably make things easier for them if I'm not popping in and out every day, disrupting their schedules." She shot Collier a pointed look. "I do understand the importance of schedules, and I do know how to maintain one. Plus, I love Blake. I'd love to spend time with him."

"And your mother? You'll want to spend time with her."

"I'll be right here. I can take Blake with me to visit her or we could bring in someone from the agency on a part-time basis. And I can go back to be with her in the evenings, after you come home." The more she thought about it, the better she liked the idea. "I could do it. I think this would work out well for everyone."

Collier pushed up from the table, carried his dishes to the sink.

"Well?" His mother prodded.

He leaned against the counter, sipped his coffee. "I'll think about it," he said.

"Good." Linda made a show of picking up the plastic cup and shooing the dog back to his rug— again. "Look at this big boy smile. You think that's a great idea, don't you, Blakey? You know your Aunt Mattie will smile at you all the time, don't you? You know your Aunt Mattie will take good care of you. You know your Aunt Mattie is fun. Fun, fun, fun, fun . . ."

The baby laughed, a throaty gurgle, a contagious joy that not one person in the kitchen could resist.

Collier smiled. He hadn't said yes, but they all knew that the bargain was struck.

Mattie would stay.

CHAPTER
SIXTEEN

Collier stood in the dark, one more sleepy shadow in the twilight nursery. He'd tossed and turned, but sleep was out of the question so he had pulled on a T-shirt and sweats and come into the room to be near his son. In a few more hours, he'd wrap Blake in layers of blankets and carry him out to the car. By this time tomorrow, Blake would be sleeping in the hospital crib, his new thumb set in a plaster cast, the first surgery over, the first bad day behind them.

With a jab of his finger, Collier set the rocking chair in motion, wondered how it could move without making a sound, except for the slightest stirring of air, which wasn't a sound at all. He wanted noise. Not enough to wake the baby, but enough to distract his own clamorous thoughts. He yearned for noise, listened for it, but heard only the quiet of a sleeping house in return. A settling creak, the shush of heat coming through the vents. Blake's occas-

ional sigh. That's the reason he had left his own
bedroom—the need to hear his son breathe, the ne-
cessity of knowing he wasn't alone in this long night.
This long, endless night that was still slipping away
too fast. On this night, Collier needed the company
of whatever noise he could find in the dark.

Turning his back on the rocker, he walked to the
window and looked down at the yard below. A
patchwork quilt of light and dark, of leftover fall
leaves and bare, brown grass, accented by a clump
of summer weeds that were still a defiant green.
He'd put in a swing set in the spring. Blake would
like that. In a year, two at most, he'd be climbing on
the bars, scrambling into all sorts of tight places
and challenging angles. In the blink of an eye, he'd
turn into a curious monkey of a little boy, wiry and
strong, grasping whatever crossed his path and
caught his attention, not even aware that he'd ever
had hands that would have made such actions difficult, if not impossible.

Letting the curtain fall back into place, he turned
again to the room, seeing it clearly in the dusky
glow, knowing the shapes in it and the shape of it
by heart. Restless. Wary of the minutes ticking past,
wishing he could call the whole thing off, knowing
worry came with the territory and that once the
surgery was over, it would slip into that vast well of
forgetfulness called relief and survival. The next
hand surgery would come and go as well. Even the
open heart surgery would fall away into the past,
become little more than a memory.

But tonight, it all lay ahead. Something he had to
get through. Alone.

He missed Meredith. Or rather he missed the

idea of her. He missed having a companion, a friend, a wife who would share this sleepless night, share the worry and the what ifs that seemed so much more frightening in the dark. Blake deserved to have two parents watching over him tonight.

Collier's chest tightened with anger because Meredith had deemed that duty unimportant. He didn't know when he would ever get over being angry with her. The anger revived and died inside him with little warning, catching him by surprise in the midst of a moment when he wasn't thinking about her at all. Or dissipating into thin air at a moment when he felt justified in clinging to his outrage and no one else even occupied his thoughts. She had left him, walked out on the life he'd believed they had. She'd done it cruelly and intentionally. She had left him, she had left their son. He wanted to think he'd had no warning, but he knew she had given him plenty of clues. Clues he'd chosen not to see, lies he'd believed because he'd wanted to believe them. She had blown a hole in the fabric of life, but he was coming to see how thin the fabric had been to begin with. He had moments when he could accept that he shared some of the responsibility, that a measure of guilt was his, that he, too, had earned the shame of a broken marriage.

But tonight he was only angry because she wasn't here for Blake, because she wouldn't be here for Blake tomorrow. Or the next day. Or the next. The marriage, the feelings he'd had for her . . . those were background noise in his head, like a fading dream he wouldn't even remember in the morning.

He retraced his silent steps to the rocking chair, intending to sit in the stillness and wait for morning, but as his hand slipped over the smooth wooden slats, the nursery floor creaked with expectancy and the door opened with a noise as welcome as sunlight. Quietly, Mattie tiptoed in on bare feet, her movements a furtive, secretive dance, her steps muffled in a slap-pad, slap-pad rhythm. Focused on her objective, she didn't see Collier as she made her way to the crib. She stood looking down at the baby for a long time before she leaned over and adjusted his blankets. She smoothed a wisp of his wispy hair, stroked a fingertip across his cheek, folded her hand over his.

Doing for him what his mother wasn't here to do, choosing to be with him when his mother had chosen to be somewhere else.

And Collier felt only gratitude that she was here. Since Blake's birth, since the doctors had outlined the course of his treatment, Collier had thought a few times about what this night would be like, tried to prepare himself for its coming. But in those rehearsals, he'd never dreamed that the woman standing here in the nursery with him would be Mattie.

It took awhile, but eventually she felt his presence. He saw the awareness ripple through her and settle in the curve of her neck. He knew she sensed his presence even before she pulled her hand back from the baby, let her fingers curl over the crib rail, and turned toward him in the golden-gray light.

From this distance, he couldn't make out the green of her eyes or the worry, but he knew both were there and as she moved soundlessly closer, he could see the heaviness in the way she moved, the uneasy twist of her hands. "I couldn't sleep," she said softly. "You, either?"

He shook his head. "I tossed and turned for awhile, but I feel better being in here with him."

She nodded, glancing back at the crib. "At least, he's snoozing the night away. Like a bear cub in winter."

"He won't remember this." Collier heard the words and believed them. Even though they offered only a hollow comfort. "He won't remember any of this."

Mattie sighed and looked over her shoulder at the crib. "Do you swear? Because if you swear, maybe I can relax. A little."

"I swear," he said, setting the rocking chair in vacant motion again, feeling the sough of air it stirred.

"How long have you been in here?"

"I don't know. Feels like a long time."

"You should go back to bed." Although she had to know he wouldn't. "At least, rest."

"You should, too. Tomorrow will be a long day."

She nodded. "Is it okay with you if I stay for awhile?"

In answer, he put a hand on the rocker, stopped it. "You can have the rocker."

"Where will you sit?"

"I'll just pace the floor."

"I could pace with you."

"Or we can take turns."

She smiled then. Just a slight upturn at the corners of her mouth. "Wait." And she turned, stepped back, moved away, and his heart sank with unreasoning disappointment. She wasn't going to sit. She wasn't going to stay.

"Mattie." His voice was suddenly too loud, and the whole room paused with a startled hush.

"Shhh," she said, stopping halfway across the floor, where a stream of moonlight found her, spilled across her legs, pooled around her feet. Her loose-fitting pants were made of some sort of silky fabric that glistened in the slice of silver light. Coffee cups and words he couldn't make out at this distance were splashed in every direction across the material. Her T-shirt, thin and not loose enough to conceal her shape even in this darkened room, was a pale color that turned a pearly gray in the glow of the night lights. One narrow strap angled across her bare shoulder, heading for her upper arm. She tugged it back into place without any self-consciousness. "If we're going to stay in here, we'll have to whisper."

Moving on, she bypassed the exit and reached the closet door. Putting a finger to her lips for his benefit—or maybe her own—she turned the knob with exaggerated caution as if she were trying to hear the tumblers in a lock. When the latch clicked, she pulled the door open. The hinges gave a low screech, and Blake's even breathing stopped, then resumed with a soft, cooing sigh.

Collier stood by the rocking chair, waiting as he'd been instructed to do, waiting for Mattie to come out of that closet with . . . well, with whatever she had gone in there to get.

When she came out, her arms were full of blankets and baby quilts, which she carried in a stack across the room to the wall behind the rocker, where she unfolded each one and smoothed it out until she had made them into a thick padded square against the wall. She bent at the waist and smoothed the wrinkles from the pallet and then with a neat turn she crossed her ankles and plopped down, motioning, with a toss of her curly head, for him to join her.

He started toward her, but stopped and walked first to the crib, where he checked on Blake again. It was a pretense because he knew Blake was fine, but he needed that extra look, that once more of reassurance, the comfort he found in seeing the curled and sleeping body of his son. When he slid down onto the cushion of blankets Mattie had made, he felt calmer, as if everything would be fine, as if he could stop worrying that it wouldn't. His shoulder bumped hers in the dark, but he didn't move away. He might feel like all kinds of a coward tonight, but he wouldn't deny his desire for human contact. He needed to feel the warmth of a woman's body, even if the only part of her body he touched was her shoulder.

"A year from now," she said into the moment, "Blake will be running all over the place and he'll be using his new thumbs to help him grab who knows what kind of mischief. He won't even have a memory of tonight, or tomorrow, or what it was like to be any different."

"I know," Collier said, because he did. "I still want to call the doctor right now and tell him to forget it."

"I'll dial the number," she offered, drawing her knees up to her chest, scooting her heels up close against her hips. "But if we do that, the surgery will only have to be rescheduled, and we'll have to go through another awful night just like this one."

"I know," he said, because he did. "It's the best thing for him. Having his hands fixed."

"Of course it is. And in a couple of days, you won't even remember you were worried about it."

"Oh, I think I'll remember this."

Her eyes cut toward him in the darkness. He felt, rather than saw her glance, sensed the understanding she cast in his direction. "Yea, me, too. I don't imagine this is the kind of feeling you ever forget." Looping her arms around her calves, she leaned in and rested her chin on her knees. "Do you think you'll be as scared when they operate on the other hand?"

"No," he said, although it was bravado and not belief. "Next time we'll know what to expect. It'll be the heart surgery that will drive us insane with worry."

We. Us. How easy it had become to include Mattie, to think of her as family and friend, to extend her presence into his future. Before, he'd kept her at a distance, based his opinion completely on the things Meredith had told him about her sister. *She's irresponsible. She's jealous. She's never cared about Mother. She's never around when you need her. She's trouble.* Meredith had filtered the information he had about Mattie, colored his judgment, influenced his feelings. He should never have allowed that to happen. Because no matter what Meredith had said about her, it was Mattie who couldn't sleep for worrying about Blake. Mattie, who was willing to make sacrifices to stay with Blake so his adjustments might be easier. Mattie, who was here.

They sat for awhile in silence and slowly the fear in his chest eased and he could breathe easier. His heart, too, felt unaccountably lighter. He was no less anxious, no less fearful about the surgery, but for tonight it helped a great deal to have Mattie beside him, concerned about what tomorrow would bring, finding comfort—as he was—in listening to the rhythmic quiet of the baby's sighs. "I'm glad you couldn't sleep," he said. "This is a difficult night to face alone."

"I'm surprised your mother isn't in here with us."

"She's got Dad. It's good he was able to come for a few days. I don't know how well either of them are sleeping tonight, but they have each other. They won't be joining us. Besides, I think she exhausted her worry by cleaning out my closets today."

"I wish she lived in Dallas. I'd hire her to organize my studio."

"I doubt she'd give up her second-graders for you. Although, if you asked, she'd probably be delighted to give you a weekend or a few days over the summer holidays."

"It must have been nice growing up in your family. Having your mother for a mother."

"I was cleaner than any little boy should have to be, that's for sure. Believe it or not, she's actually better about that than she used to be. Growing up, I didn't appreciate her at all. I'd have traded her in a heartbeat for my best friend's mom. There were several occasions when I'd have traded her for any one of my friends' moms, even the ones I didn't like all that much."

"Boy, did I ever wish I could trade my mother. Probably not half as much as she wished she could trade me, though. If she had liked dogs even a little, she'd probably have traded me for a puppy." A quiet bubble of laughter escaped her. "What am I saying? If Meredith had wanted a puppy, I'd have been gone like that." And she gave a snap of her fingers.

"Mom used to tell me she wouldn't trade me for a pirate's treasure, but then when I was in trouble, she'd say she should have traded me for a girl when she had the chance." He drew his right leg up, rested his forearm on it. "I was always a little scared to ask what she meant by that."

"Don't lie. You were never in trouble. I don't believe that for a second."

"Believe it. I was a handful at thirteen. So full of my own importance, it's a wonder my dad didn't stuff me into a barrel and nail the lid shut until I got a little sense."

Mattie turned her head, so that her right cheek was cradled on her folded hands, her hair catching the light in its copper strands, falling like a fuzzy halo around her shoulders. "So what happened after thirteen? Did you become the model child overnight?"

"My grandfather came to visit. He took me on a weekend camping trip and set me straight."

"Where'd he take you? Mount Arafat?"

"The Smoky Mountains. Gave me a lesson about what a man takes with him into a beautiful place and the things he leaves behind." Collier hadn't thought about that in years. "My grandfather was a wise man and he had the perspective my parents didn't at the time. He didn't criticize or tell me all the things I was doing wrong, but by the time I got home I had a new outlook and a different attitude. I never got off track again after that."

"Lucky you," she said softly. "Having so many people who love you."

He felt lucky then. Despite tomorrow. Despite the breakup of his marriage. Despite his disappointment about the election. He had family. He had friends. He had Mattie to help him get through this night.

She continued to look at him, eyes sea green and sleepy in the soft light.

And seductive.

The impulse to kiss her suffused him.

He didn't plan it, was barely aware of thinking it, and if she hadn't drawn a quick breath of awareness, hadn't lifted her head, her eyes widening at that exact instant, he might not have leaned in, cupped her head in his hand and lowered his lips to hers.

The kiss was immediately hungry and wet. Needy, passionate, and searching. It should have ended as abruptly as it had begun. But instead it turned into a slow burn, a fire struck from a single spark, a blaze that would not be quenched.

She shifted her body, came up and into his arms, and he pulled her more fully into the embrace. The pressure grew heavy in his groin and he was on his knees, her breasts pushing against his chest, her hands clutching his arms. The pallet slid and his elbow bumped the floor with a whack as they went down, lips and bodies and hearts all tangled up in each other, all mixed up in the dark.

The baby cried out a tiny bleat of alarm, an instant of distress. Undisturbed by their whispered conversation, he had been awakened by something in their muffled passion. The cry ebbed, hardly a sound at all. But it was enough and they pulled guiltily apart, the kiss ending in a segue of trip-hammer heartbeats and uneven breaths. Collier pushed to his feet, going automatically toward the crib in a fog of confusing feelings, a veil of desire and need and doubt.

Already, Blake was settling back into his nest of blankets, yawning, a small stretch, not even fully awake. His cry had been nothing, a momentary reaction to something in his dreams. He wasn't passing judgment on that kiss. He wasn't even aware they were here, so soundly had he been sleeping. With a pat, Collier tucked the blankets back around him and lightly rubbed his back until his breath slowed again into a quick but regular rhythm.

Only then did he turn to Mattie.

Mattie. Who was no longer on the pallet. No longer in the room.

But she could not have left the nursery without his hearing.

Unless she had gone through his bedroom.

He crossed the patches of light and dark on the nursery floor, felt his way through the connecting bath and entered the darker bedroom. The master bedroom, where the bedside lamp cast a pale shadow across the ceiling and tossed a triangle of warm light across the edge of the bed. The edge where Mattie was sitting, her hands curled over the edge of the mattress, her toes nosing down into the nap of the carpet.

She looked up as he came closer, her skin pale, almost luminescent in the contrasting light. A question lingered, seductively, in her wide eyes. The answer settled, reluctantly, in the wistful but resolute line of her lips.

He wouldn't try to dissuade her from her decision. He wanted to, but he wouldn't. She wanted him to, or she wouldn't be here. In his bedroom. On his bed.

This was the moment. They both knew it. Knew how simple the choice could be, how complicated it could become. Knew a move in either direction could alter not just the night, but all the nights to come. Knew this moment held the opportunity for lasting love or everlasting regret. Maybe both.

Collier knew all the reasons that this was as far as that surprising kiss should take them.

And he knew it would take a stronger will than he had at this moment to stop it.

So he took the last few steps and sat on the bed beside her, as close as a lover, the width of her hand curling over the edge of the mattress the only thing that separated them, just enough distance between them to allow a move in either direction. By either of them.

If they chose.

He looked at her. And waited.

She looked at the pink tips of her toes. And sighed. "I'd be lying, you know, if I said I didn't want this."

"I'd be telling the truth if I said it's the only thing I do want."

The softest part of a smile wisped across her lips, touching the corner of her mouth he could see and probably the one he couldn't see, as well. "It wouldn't be right."

"Doing what's right seems to be out of fashion."

This time the smile curved fully, lasted a heartbeat longer. "Not for you, Collier. It's never going to be out of fashion for you."

"Give me a reason to prove you wrong."

Her gaze came to his then, the arc of the lamp-light falling away across her cheek, leaving a tantalizing shadow of desire in the green of her eyes. "I could give you a dozen reasons right here, right now. But I'd have to live with that. Knowing I'd asked you to cross a line we both know we should not cross."

Disappointment, desire, worry, anger, and even a touch of relief rolled into a fist and punched him in the gut. She was right. No matter how much he wanted her to be wrong. With a heavy sigh, he fell back across the bed, weary from one end of his soul to the other. "Because I'm married. Because she's your sister. Even though she no longer deserves consideration on either account."

With a sigh equal to his own, Mattie dropped back beside him and they stared, together, at the ceiling overhead. "This has nothing to do with Meredith," she said quietly.

He rolled his head toward her. "It has everything to do with her."

"If it were that simple, we wouldn't be talking. We'd be . . . doing other things. Using each other to punish her for what she's done to us. Trying to hurt her in the same way she hurt us. Trying to punish Jack for being a worthless prick."

"You think this, the kiss we shared, these feelings are all about punishment?"

"No, I think this has been building between us for weeks. Tonight, we were vulnerable and it caught us. Not because of Meredith. Not because of Jack."

"But because—?" He wanted to know her answer. He needed to know.

"Because we've shared an experience that turned everything in our lives upside down and wound up putting us right side up . . . together." She turned her head toward him and a strip of fabric, a curl of rumpled sheets bowed up into a bridge from the top of his head to the top of hers. "I don't know why it happened that way. Or exactly how. But here we are."

"Yes, here we are."

"Doing what's right, because it's the right thing to do."

"Speak for yourself. I'm still debating the value of regret."

She smiled. "Exhausting, isn't it?"

"Come to think of it, yes."

"See? This isn't the right time. This isn't our moment."

A question stirred inside him. "Are we going to have a moment, Mattie?"

He didn't expect an answer. She didn't offer one. The quiet stretched like a blanket across them, two people, one fleecy silence.

"I almost think I could fall asleep now," she said after a long time. "Right here. Just like this. If I only closed my eyes for a second. . . ."

A second ticked past and then a dozen more. "Close your eyes," he whispered. "Sleep. Just like this."

"You should sleep, too." Her voice drooped with drowsiness.

"I don't think I can."

"Try."

"Sleep, Mattie. Rest."

Within a moment or two, she was asleep.

He thought about turning off the lamp, but that

might wake her, and even if it didn't, moving seemed too great an effort to make. So he watched Mattie sleep. For a long time, he just watched her sleep.

Her breathing, deep and even, was comforting and a comfortable presence there in his bed.

The way the light struck gold in her hair intrigued him.

The soft parting between her lips deserved a lengthy contemplation.

The way her fingers curved, relaxed and tender, over the pink delicacy of her palm made him believe that tomorrow would come and go and Blake would be all right.

Somehow, Mattie had him believing that everything would be all right.

Better than all right.

And somewhere between that thought and morning, he fell asleep.

CHAPTER
SEVENTEEN

The surgery lasted an hour and a half. Give or take a couple of years.

Mattie, Collier, Linda and Harry waited alone together. No one said much. There wasn't much to say. A baby in surgery was a terrifying thought, no matter how necessary the operation, no matter how logical it was to believe he would be fine. Better than fine. When it was over.

Harry read the newspaper, although Mattie noted he picked up the same section several times and went through it, front to back, as if he hadn't just looked through it.

Linda worked crosswords with a pencil, pausing every once in awhile to vigorously erase a word or two or ten that she had written down.

Collier stood, stone-faced and pale, by the window, sometimes looking down at the parking lot below, sometimes leaning back against the wall and staring at empty space.

Mattie called the rehab center a couple of times to check on her mother, then spent the rest of the time pretending to read a magazine someone had left behind. She riffled the pages and looked at the pictures, but gathered no memory of anything she saw.

And when, finally, the doctor came out, told them the surgery went well, that Blake was waking up and would be taken to his room momentarily, the family's collective relief was a palpable thing. On a piece of white paper, the doctor sketched out for them the tendons and bone he'd moved to shape a thumb, reiterated that he believed Blake would have all the range of movement he would have had if the hand had been normal from the beginning. "When that cast comes off," the doctor said, "watch out. It won't be long at all before your boy has a hearty grip on whatever he can reach."

Linda laughed a little and cried real tears and hugged her son and her husband and Mattie. Harry did the same, although his eyes only shone misty with relief. When Collier turned to Mattie, she went into his arms with a wobbly smile and they hugged like survivors of a shipwreck, shaky but saved. If the hug lasted a little longer, was a little tighter, perhaps, than a hug meant strictly for comfort, well . . . it had been a long night, a longer morning, and what they shared felt necessary and appropriate.

The relief turned sober when they gathered around the hospital crib and looked down at the thick plaster cast on Blake's arm. It started at the tips of his fingers and ended above his elbow. He lay on his back, sleeping, his breath audible and quick, his flushed, round cheeks moving in and out as he sucked fiercely on a pacifier, its red plastic unnaturally bright against his baby skin.

"Let's sign it," Harry said.

"We are not writing on that cast, Harry Montgomery." Linda frowned at her husband, unimpressed by his suggestion. "That is the most hare-brained idea you've had so far this year. Write on his cast. As if it won't be hard enough to keep clean as it is."

Mattie looked across the crib at Collier, shared the undercurrent of a smile, the cusp of an insider's joke. "He looks good," she said softly, reaching down to smooth a wisp of Blake's fairy blond hair. "And so small."

It was amazing how tiny he looked, so little and helpless and sweet, lying there with a cast that seemed to be the biggest thing about him.

"I'm going for breakfast," Harry announced with a nod. "Anyone else?"

"I'm staying," Collier said. "You can bring me a muffin and some coffee, though, when you come back. Mattie? Do you want Dad to bring something back for you?"

As if there was no question that she would stay right where she was. Beside Blake's crib. Beside Collier.

"Coffee would be nice."

"I'll go with Dad." Linda reached over the crib, stroked her grandson's cheek. "Help him carry everything."

A nurse bustled through the door, passing Harry and Linda on their way out. "How's our little man doing?" Her name tag read, Cali Snyder, R.N., and she looked about twelve, but was undoubtedly older. Mattie thought she looked familiar and watched as she did a quick check of Blake.

"Is he okay?" Mattie couldn't help but ask.

"He's doing great." Cali turned to reassure Collier and Mattie with a smile, but her button blue eyes widened suddenly with recognition. "Mattie? Mattie Owens? Oh my gosh, I remember you."

Mattie tried to place her, tried to recall why the other woman seemed familiar, too. "Cali?" she said, figuring the name tag was a good place to begin.

"That's right!" Cali seemed enormously pleased at that response. "Gee, it seems like a million years ago that we were taking tap and ballet at Miss Victoria's, doesn't it? You showed me how to tie my shoes and I thought you were the best dancer in the class. Miss Victoria was always on you, though, about something you were doing wrong. She was really mean. Do you remember that?"

"Well . . ." But Cali didn't give her time to answer. "I can't believe it's you. I think we were a grade apart in school, but I remember you mostly from those dance lessons. Remember that program we did first or second year? We wore yellow leotards and ruffles of net around our faces and painted-on whiskers and our dance number was called, The Dandy Lions." Her laughter bubbled out, hospital hushed, but still contagious. "I thought I was the cutest thing in tap shoes."

Mattie remembered their lion costumes. She remembered wanting to be in Meredith's group, wishing she could wear pink and be a Rambling Rose. "I teach dance now," she said. "I have a school. In Dallas."

Cali's eyes were blue and round, and with the

blush of excitement in her cheeks, and the blue-and-pink-print uniform she had on, she resembled a life-size Raggedy Ann. Still a little floppy around the edges. "You do? That's great. I have a little girl who's turning four this year and I want so much for her to take dance. Wouldn't you know, she's not the slightest bit interested in it. She wants to play soccer. And softball. And field hockey. She is definitely her daddy's girl. Such a tomboy already."

"It would be a dull world if everyone wanted to be a Dandy Lion," Mattie said with a smile.

Cali glanced again at the baby, seemed to realize she was ignoring Collier. "Mayor Montgomery," she said with a grown-up sort of giggle, pulling on a petite professionalism. "Your son's doing great. He'll sleep most of today. I'll be in to check on him in another fifteen minutes or so, but if you need anything, just press the call button"—she indicated its location—"and someone will be here right away. You've got a dandy right there," she said. "I'll see you both later. So good to run into you, Mattie."

She swooshed from the room and the door closed behind her, muffling the sounds outside, closing them into a sterile silence.

"You obviously made a big impression on her." Collier reached down and touched the pacifier that hung half in, half out of Blake's cupid bow lips, and the baby drew it back into his mouth, sucking once, twice, three times, before it popped half out again.

"I barely remember her," Mattie admitted. Maybe because too much of Mattie's time had been spent watching Meredith, wanting to be in Meredith's group, wanting to be a Rambling Rose instead of a Dandy Lion.

The door opened again and Harry backed into the room, carrying a cardboard carton of cups. Linda was right behind him, four Styrofoam containers stacked in her arms. "We've brought breakfast," she said. "The muffins were all prepackaged, so we just ordered up the real thing. We all need protein instead of those empty calories anyway."

Harry raised his eyebrows at Mattie. "I tried for the muffins, Mattie, I really did. But she insisted on eggs and fruit and toast." He leaned in to whisper. "What she doesn't know is I've got a muffin in my pocket. I'll split it with you if you promise not to tell."

"My lips are zipped." Mattie stood aside as Collier and his parents quibbled affectionately over the distribution of the food.

"Come on, Mattie." Linda motioned her over. "Don't be shy. You're family, and you know what that means. These two won't leave you so much as a crumb if you don't elbow your way in here."

For a hospital room, it felt very much like the kind of home Mattie had always imagined, the kind she'd always wished could be hers.

The kind of family in which a Dandy Lion belonged.

"He's sawing logs like a champion. Doesn't even seem to realize he's got a cast on." Harry walked into the kitchen, pulled out the vacant chair, and straddled it, so as not to disturb André who was curled up underneath the table. "Big day for our little guy, coming home from the hospital and all. Whose turn is it?"

"You're the last man standing, Dad. Mom and I

have folded and Mattie's raised the ante to you by four pennies and a chopstick." Collier rounded the edges of the pile before picking up one of the cardboard pagodas and poking around inside it with his fork. "I think she's bluffing, but it's your call."

Harry shuffled through his cards, making a show out of keeping them away from Linda, who was trying to peek round to see what he was holding. He narrowed his eyes over his hand, then waggled his brows at Mattie. "A chopstick, huh? All right then." He counted out four pennies, tossed them and a chopstick onto the pile, then added the coup de grâce. "I'll see your chopstick and raise you one fortune cookie."

Collier stopped eating Seschuan Beef.

Linda shook her head.

Mattie tapped her cards, face down on the table. "Oh, you are going to be so sorry you did that." She topped his fortune cookie with hers. "Let's see what you've got, Harry."

He spread his cards. Three Jacks.

With a flourish, Mattie fanned her cards in a flush. "Winner takes all." She pulled her winnings toward her, ignored the pennies, and unwrapped one of the cookies. Snapping it in two, she pulled out the fortune. " 'You will be lucky in love and games of chance,' " she read.

Collier went back to eating out of the takeout carton. "Well, one out of two isn't bad," he said.

"See what the other one says," Linda leaned back in her chair, her arms folded beneath her ample bosom.

Mattie pulled the cellophane wrapper from the

second cookie, cracked out the strip of paper and read, " 'Do not give up the things you love.' "

"There you go, Harry," Linda advised him. "You shouldn't have bet the cookie."

"It's okay. I already ate mine. That one was yours. I stole it when you weren't looking."

"You stole my fortune."

He winked at her. "You wouldn't have liked it, anyway."

"Why not? What did it say?"

" 'Beware of the intentions of someone close to you.' See? I told you."

"You'd better beware the intentions of someone close to you, Harry Montgomery."

"Fun as this has been, it's my intention to go upstairs now and get to bed." Harry stood, disturbing André who snuffled his way around the table for the umpteenth time, looking for snacks. "We've got an early flight in the morning, and I haven't done my packing yet." He pointed at his wife. "Neither, my dear, have you."

Linda began gathering up the take-out cartons, but Collier stopped her. "Leave it, Mom. I'll clean up tonight."

She came around the corner of the table and kissed him on the cheek. "I think I'll let you. It's been a long day."

"A long week," Collier said and returned her kiss. "But Blake's home and all's well."

"All's well." Harry reached into the pocket of his Mr. Rogers sweater and pulled out a fourth fortune cookie. "Here, Coll. This is yours."

"Geez, Dad, you stole mine, too?"

"All's fair in love and poker, son. Your mother taught me that."

Linda shook her head. "I'm sorry, Mattie. I've been trying to reform him for years with no success."

"Why are you apologizing to her?" Collier wanted to know. "He didn't steal her fortune cookie."

But Linda answered with only a smile and a wave of her hand as she followed Harry out of the room.

Mattie picked up a piece of broken cookie and held it under the table for André. "I'm going to miss them."

Collier traded pagodas and ate a few bites of Sesame Chicken, then set that carton on the table with a satisfied sigh. "How was your mom today? I didn't get a chance to ask you earlier."

"Better today, I think. She hates the therapy, but we actually had a fairly nice conversation just before lunch. She didn't ask me one time when Meredith was coming to take her home. That's a first. Probably a fluke. She probably thought I *was* Meredith."

"I don't think she even realizes Meredith is gone. When I've been to see her, Alice talks as if we're all here at the house and Meredith just walked out of the room for a sec."

"I hate that she's lost so much of her ability to remember things and understand what's happened to her. Other times I find myself feeling grateful because she can't remember and doesn't understand all the abilities she's lost."

He commiserated with her in a shared glance, pushed himself up from the table. "I'd better get this cleaned up. I'll give my mother ten minutes, at the outside, before she'll be back down here on one pretext or another, making sure I didn't leave the kitchen in a mess."

Mattie pushed up from the table, too. "I'll take the cartons out to the trash, if you'll wipe down the table and sweep the floor."

"Deal," he agreed with a grin. "André's already swept the floor, so my part's half-done. And Mom will mop the floor again before she leaves, anyway. She never did that sort of thing when Meredith was here. I think it practically drove her crazy, but she never did it. She's more comfortable being herself around you."

Mattie wrapped that compliment in a smile and put it away to remember another day. "Tomorrow it'll be just me and Blake. I'm a little nervous."

"No, you're not." He called her on the feeling. "You can't wait for us all to leave you alone with the boy. Admit it."

She paused in stacking up the cardboard boxes, gathering up the leftovers of their takeout meal. "Are you sure about this, Collier?"

"As sure as you are," he said simply.

Which meant he felt the uncertainty too. Knew the risk they were taking, knew they would have to be vigilant and strong. There would be no more kisses. Nothing to regret later. He understood, just as she did, that the attraction between them wasn't going to be negotiated away, excused as a vulnerable moment. It still pulsed beneath the surface, flared with the brush of a hand, the touch of a glance. The past few days, at the hospital, at the house, with her mother, Mattie had had lots of time to think about the kiss they'd shared, about sleeping in platonic peace beside him on the bed. She could find a dozen reasonable explanations for the bond that had formed between them. They were each the odd angle of Meredith's and Jack's triangle. They had that in common. They had a shared concern for Blake in common. They had Alice in common. They had more in common than she had thought possible.

They were friends. A little more than friends, maybe. If they'd met under other circumstances, if Meredith wasn't the shadow that always stood between them, Mattie thought she and Collier might have been much more than friends. If she thought ahead, a year or two down the road, well . . . who knew what lay down that path. This wasn't the time. Or the moment.

So she carried the Chinese take-out cartons outside, André cavorting at her heels hoping for a spill, an unexpected bonus.

Outside, in the crisp February air, she dumped the trash, looked up at the night sky, and wished on the only star she saw.

She wished that Meredith would never come back.

CHAPTER
EIGHTEEN

Blake loved his bath. He began jumping with excitement the minute she carried him into the bathroom and, once in the water, he splashed like a happy duckling. The cast didn't seem to bother him in the least. If anything, Mattie thought he liked the thunk of the hard plaster on the edge of the tub and against his safety seat. He didn't like it when she put the plastic bag over the cast, but that could have had more to do with the delay in getting into the water than the nuisance of having it put on. The bath was the highlight of his day, never lasted long enough, and he always cried when she finally lifted him out of the tub and wrapped him in a snuggly towel.

Today was no different. The minute she picked up the towel, his grins and gurgles faded and he kicked the water vigorously in protest. Mattie tried to make it a game, putting the towel up and playing peek-a-boo, but he knew what was coming and wanted no part of it. "You little monkey," she said as the last of the water spiraled down the drain and his lower lip popped out in a stubborn pout. "The water is all gone and your toes have shriveled into raisins you've been in there so long already."

He kicked and babbled—a string of emphatic baby language she had learned to understand all too well. Her nephew could display considerable temper, when things didn't go his way. And he was winding up for a good long run today. As if the baby wasn't making noise enough, downstairs, André began barking like a fool, a signal that the mailman was approaching or that the neighbor's cat was strolling across the front porch.

"Blake," she said over his unintelligible shouting. "It's time to get out of the tub."

But the minute she reached for him, he squealed like a whole litter of piglets and fought hard to stay where he was. Wet, cold, and strapped into his safety seat. When she eventually got him wrapped in the towel, he stiffened with eighteen plus pounds of outrage, screaming for all he was worth.

"I see he still loves his bath."

Mattie grabbed the baby hard and protectively against her body and spun around to see who had spoken.

Even though she knew the voice as well as her own.

Meredith.

Blake knew the voice, too, and he abruptly stopped screaming. He gave Mattie's jaw a painful thump with the awkward cast as he struggled to turn in her arms and peer out from beneath the hooded towel.

And there she stood, in the doorway of the bath,

dressed for an afternoon luncheon or a walk on the beach, cream-colored slacks, a pale blue sweater set that turned her eyes a deep blue violet, a solitary diamond pendant strung on a chain around her neck and glinting in the light, hair styled casually chic, and on her lips, she wore a soft rose lipstick and a Madonna's smile. "Hello, Sweetpea," she said, holding out her hands to the baby. "Mommy's home."

Blake practically broke the sound barrier with the leap he made out of Mattie's arms and into Meredith's. The towel billowed behind him like Superman's cape, waiting to be snuggled around him again. Too young to voice his pleasure, his expression conveyed the joy words never could. This was his mother. He knew her. He wanted her. He was in heaven just being back in her arms.

That broke Mattie's heart.

She pushed to her feet, aware she was splotched with bath water, that the hair around her face was frazzled and curled from the humid, steamy air inside the bathroom, that her clothes were rumpled and wrinkled from playing with Blake, that her chin bore the red sting from being bumped by his cast. Wiping her hands on a second towel, she tried to watch the mother and child reunion without showing how angry she was, without revealing how much in that instant, she hated her sister.

"I expected to find Mrs. Oliver with him," Meredith said, rubbing the terrycloth cape over the baby's back, drawing it in and tucking it around his chubby legs. "Even though this isn't the time she usually gives him a bath."

"Mrs. Oliver left," Mattie said.

"For lunch?"

"Forever. She hasn't been here for about three weeks. Nearly four."

"Really." Meredith smiled at her son, pressed a kiss to his forehead, then used the tip of the towel to erase the smudge of lipstick. "Why did she leave?"

"Collier told her not to come back."

That surprised her. Mattie could tell, even though Meredith tried not to let it show. "Really," was all she said. A bland, unconcerned *really*. "Where's Mother? I didn't run across her downstairs and she's not in her bedroom."

How could she act as if she'd been away for the morning and not on an extended leave of absence? "Mother's not here."

Meredith's eyebrows climbed. "Did you get rid of her, too?"

Mattie used her foot to push the mat across the floor, mopping up some of the leftover splashes. "She's in the Fleming Rehab Clinic. Before that, she was in the hospital. She broke her hip."

"She did what?"

"You heard me. She broke her hip."

"How?"

"She fell."

"*How* did she fall?"

Mattie didn't care for this game of twenty questions. If Meredith cared so much, she should have been here. "What are you doing here, Meredith? What do you want?"

Meredith blinked, taken aback by Mattie's challenge. "I would think that's obvious. This is my house. My baby. I've come home. Maybe the question I should be asking is what *you're* doing here, Mattie. In my house. With my baby."

"I'm taking care of him. The house, too. And your dog." She looked past Meredith to the hall. "What happened? Did Andy forget who you are?"

"*André* is trying to extract the smells from my suitcase, I imagine. Jack's mother has a cat, you know."

No, she didn't know. Mattie had never met Jack's mother, never had occasion to learn what pet she had or what she was like.

"You wouldn't like her," Meredith said. "She made me twitch . . . and that's not easy to do."

Fury ran its fingernail down Mattie's back. "You should stay away from cats then," she said, proud her voice stayed steady, sounded calm. "It could turn your dog against you."

Meredith ignored the jab, but Mattie knew she'd felt it.

"For your information, André was very happy to see me. He looks like he's gained a few pounds. What have you been feeding him?"

Mattie wished now she'd fed the poodle as much Chinese takeout as he would eat. But again, that would be misplaced punishment. Meredith might get mad, but Andy would be the one to pay the price.

"He may have picked up a few new habits since you left," she said.

Meredith's lips parted with a retort, but she snapped them closed and they pursed in a thin line. Still a beautiful lip line. Why, Mattie wondered, couldn't the ugliness of her actions show in her face? Why hadn't the pain she'd caused others carved a few wrinkles into her flawless complexion, turned her satin hair a lackluster blond? Why hadn't betrayal left any mark on her at all?

"This boy needs a diaper, don't you, Sweetie?"

Meredith, still snuggling with her son, offering him smiles and kisses and who knew how many whispered lies, turned from the doorway and carried him away.

As if she had every right. And the awful truth was . . . she did have the right. No matter what she'd done. Legally, she had every right.

Mattie dropped the towel she held to the floor and followed her sister into the nursery. "Does Collier know you're here?" she asked, even though she knew he didn't.

"I doubt it."

"Shouldn't you let him know?"

Meredith's answer came with a short laugh. "I don't need his permission, Mat. But feel free to run downstairs and call him if you think you should."

Only Meredith would turn this into a challenge between sisters, a *go-ahead, tell on me, see if I care* threat.

"He needs to know you're here, in his house."

"My house," Meredith said softly. But maybe her voice had dropped because she'd leaned in to smile at Blake, newly diapered on his changing table. He kicked his bare feet and waved his free hand and gurgled at his mother, as if he were telling her everything that had happened in her absence, his eyes following her every move. She ignored the clothes Mattie had laid out for Blake before his bath, pulled a different outfit from the drawers under the changing table, and began to dress him. Even though the shirt she'd selected was never going to fit over his cast. "Tell me what happened with Mother. If she fell, it could be a problem with her medication."

"What do you mean, *if* she fell. She fell. She broke her hip."

"Yes, so you said. How, though? How did it happen? Did she lose her balance? Make a misstep? How?"

"We don't know exactly because—"

"We?"

"She was at the Gardens," Mattie said bluntly. "I put her in the home so—"

"So you wouldn't have to deal with her," Meredith filled in the blank before Mattie could. "Very responsible, Mat."

"I happen to think it was responsible," Mattie snapped, words tumbling and tangling on her tongue vying to be said. *As opposed to the way you walked out on responsibility? As responsible as the things you've done?* But she would not be baited into defending herself. She hadn't done anything wrong. "Believe it or not, I had a life in Dallas to sort out. A few details that had to be cleared up before I could take her there with me."

"What details? Getting the money to repay Jack? He doesn't want the money. You know he has always considered that a gift, not a loan. No matter what he may have said in anger that night at the condo."

The idea that Jack had told Meredith about that, discussed it with her, set the outrage fanning through Mattie's body, left her trembling with outrage. And a helpless embarrassment. And a cold, cold anger. "You and I will not be talking about Jack," she said in a voice she had never used with her sister, never in her memory, used with anyone. "You will never speak his name in my presence again. Got that?"

Meredith had the grace to pale, the sense to

change the subject. "You were explaining how Mother fell," she said.

"She was in respite care while I was gone. That's where she fell. No one is sure how it happened."

"Did they run tests? Does Dr. Roberts believe she had another stroke?"

"He doesn't know. None of her doctors will say anything except that a stroke is one possibility. Nothing showed up on the MRI, so if it was a stroke, it was a small one."

"Well, that's something to be grateful for, I guess. How is she now?"

"She's been more confused since the surgery, but that may be a temporary reaction to the trauma and not a permanent loss."

"Mother doesn't do well in strange places. She gets disoriented and upset when she's out of familiar surroundings. You should have found some way to keep her here while you were gone."

That was rich. Coming from her. "What did you expect would happen to her when you left, Meredith? Did you think she wouldn't notice? That your disappearance wouldn't upset her, leave her disoriented and confused?"

Meredith gave up trying to pull on Blake's little shirt, tossed it aside and reached for the one Mattie had set out. "I wasn't thinking clearly. I wasn't capable of thinking clearly."

"I don't believe you."

"What does that mean?"

"It means I don't believe you."

"You think I'm lying?"

"Yes."

The beautiful lip line returned, a pout reminiscent

of Blake's, but lacking innocence. "I didn't come here to quarrel with you. I wanted to see my son. I want to see my mother. I didn't expect to find you here."

"Well, what did you expect to find? Everything just the way you left it? Everyone waiting with bated breath for you to return? Because that's not the way it works."

"How does it work then, since you seem to have all the answers? Do you want to hear me say I'm sorry? See me cry real tears?"

That would have been a start. Something, at least, to indicate remorse. But Meredith, perfect to the end, couldn't acknowledge a flaw, would never admit to Mattie that she'd made a grievous mistake. If she believed she had.

"Don't bother. I'm not interested in your apology. Save it for Collier. Save it for Blake."

The Madonna smile returned, a good imitation of triumph. "I don't believe Blake requires an apology, do you, Sweetheart? He's just happy to have his mommy home, aren't you, darling boy?"

"This isn't your home. Not anymore."

"Fortunately for me, you don't get to vote on that. That's between me and Collier." She lifted Blake into her arms, held him like a trophy. "It's really none of your business." She took a step away from the changing table, toward the center of the room, toward Mattie. "Although—"

The word hung there, an accusation, a question, a challenge.

"Although?"

"You seem to have become very comfortable in

my house, with my baby. Maybe you've become very comfortable with my husband too."

That struck Mattie hard, and the anger, both righteous and guilty, ignited like a firecracker. "It would serve you right if I had. You don't deserve him. You don't deserve any of this. You had everything, Meredith, and you threw it away." The passion shook her voice, gave too much away, but it was too late to take it back. Even if she could. "You threw it all away."

Meredith regarded her with raised eyebrows, a glint of surprise in her eyes. "I'll take that as a yes."

"Take it however you like," she said. "You can't just walk back in and expect to have everything the way it was. Collier will divorce you."

The surprise flickered with a moment's fear, switched back to impervious confidence again with the mere lift of her chin. "Really. Do you know that for a fact? Or is it only wishful thinking on your part?"

"You cost him the chance to run for governor, Meredith. Do you think he should just forgive you for that, too, along with everything else?"

"Governor Lucman has the governor's seat locked up tight for another term. Collier isn't interested in a race he has no chance of winning."

"Governor Lucman resigned. He got caught in a sex scandal and resigned. You must have heard about it. It was all over the news. Jack's mother does have television access, doesn't she? Gets a newspaper?"

"I haven't been focused on the news, Mattie. I've been busy sorting out my own problems. I told you that." Turning, she set the baby in his crib and he began an immediate protest with short, sharp cries, precursors of a full-out tantrum. She ignored him and walked toward Mattie. "Mother's at the Fleming Center, you said? The rehab clinic?"

"Yes."

Meredith swept past without so much as a backward glance for Blake. "I'm going to see her now. You can tell Collier that I was here. You can tell him I'll be back."

Then her footsteps faded down the hall, she said something loving to the dog, and in another minute or so the downstairs door opened. And closed.

Blake wailed, a lonely, sad sound that broke Mattie's heart all over again.

"There, Sweetie." Mattie picked him up, carried him to the rocker and began to rock him, patting his back, kissing the fingers she could reach. "Everything will be all right. I promise, Blake. Everything is going to be all right."

But she knew she shouldn't have said it.

She had no right to make a promise it wasn't in her power to keep.

"Do you want a drink?"

Meredith turned from the window to face her husband. She'd known when he came into the study, of course, but she'd waited for him to speak to her. Mainly, because she didn't want to speak first. She wanted to read his mood, take her cues from him.

He looked thinner, sterner, slightly older. Which was actually a good look for him. Stripped off a bit of that star athlete glow. Gave him a hint of battle-scarred honesty, a touch of war-weary valor. It was the kind of look that made voters feel confident. The kind of look that turned a candidate from just another handsome face into a powerful contender. Maybe she'd unintentionally given him a gift for which he would someday thank her.

"Glenfiddich, please," she said. "Neat."

"I remember how you like your scotch." He poured the drink, three fingers, straight, poured himself a glass of wine, red as blood. He carried the wine with him to his desk, left hers on the bar.

A lesson to her, she supposed, as she retrieved it. But probably the best way to keep his distance and not allow himself to get too close. Afraid perhaps he might give in to the temptation to strangle her. If he was the kind of man to give in to a destructive impulse. Which he wasn't. No matter the provocation.

Crossing to the sofa, she sank into the corner pocket, where he would have a straight-on view of her profile and she retained the option of turning her head to look at him. Or not.

She stared down into the amber serenity in her hand, thought about Jack and the dinner party she knew he was attending tonight. She thought of him in his blue-striped shirt and black trousers. Or maybe he'd worn the navy. And the yellow shirt she liked so much. She imagined he missed her tonight in the same way she missed him. Like a wristwatch. Or a bracelet worn several days in a row and then forgotten. It was the accustomed weight, the feel of the thing that was missed, not the thing itself. Not irreplaceable or even important. Simply missing from the place where it had been the day before.

She lifted the glass and took a long sip. Then another. Whatever Jack was doing it would lead nowhere she wanted to go. He had money. He had sex appeal. He had issues with his mother. He was

a cad and a charmer. He was a nice dresser and he
liked nice things. He was a generous man, tender,
but he would not age well or die happy. She hadn't
been able to figure out what had drawn him to
Mattie or held him with her so long and she'd wondered, at moments, if some of the attraction she felt
for him rose from a big-sister protectiveness . . . the
idea that she had to show Mattie who he really was
before it was too late.

There were better ways.

Much better ways, of course. But she hadn't been
thinking clearly, no matter what Mattie believed.
And Mattie would forgive her. Eventually. She had
to. They were sisters, weren't they?

But even if she didn't . . . well, Meredith didn't
regret Jack. How could she? At the worst time in her
life he had given her a gift of time. He had offered
the admiration she was starving for, a hope she
couldn't find on her own, distraction when she
needed it, and peace. She had been dying inside
when Jack came along, and he had saved her. She
would love him forever for that. And for a glimpse
inside the life she might have had. If she chose.

She had had her glimpse and knew what she'd
left behind was better. In the long run, with Collier,
she would have it all.

Looking at him now as he stood behind his desk,
holding his glass of wine, she wondered if she
should cry first. Or hold that tactic in reserve. Tears
were a powerful weapon. She didn't want to use
them before it was time.

His very stillness bothered her. She'd expected the
quiet would prickle his anger, create a tension she
could use to her advantage. But whatever tension lay

between them seemed to be all on her side and if he felt it, he gave her no clue.

Okay. It was time to begin.

She took a sip of the scotch, let it burn any doubt out of her voice. She didn't have any doubts. Not really. She and Collier would weather this, their marriage would be better for it. She believed that. Now it was time to convince him.

"I doubt this is what you want to hear, but I am sorry, Collier. I am very, very sorry."

He had remained standing and now, glass in hand, he came to the front of the desk and leaned against it, eyes steady and unrevealing. Which was revealing in itself.

She fought the urge to swallow more of the scotch.

"I don't expect you to forgive me," she went on. "I will understand if that's beyond your ability."

The grandfather clock chimed the half hour, the resonant bong muffled on the far side of the closed door.

"Is it beyond my ability to forgive you," he repeated slowly, giving the words a cynical twist, giving the blood red wine a swirl. "A challenge. On the heels of your apology. Impressive, Meredith. You must have worked on that delivery a long time."

He knew her. That was a problem. But she knew him too. That would have to be the antidote. "I've practiced, yes. The same way you practice before giving an important speech." She wished she'd asked for ice in the scotch. The clink would have added an emphasis the liquor alone couldn't, despite its lush golden glow. "I imagine this is the most important speech I will ever need to give."

"Oh, I'd say that depends on your next husband and what you do to him."

She almost expected him to lift his glass in a farewell salute, but he only raised it and drank. Well, she had known going in that he would not make this easy. "You are my husband and I know that what I've done is inexcusable. That doesn't mean I don't have a reason to offer you."

"A reason? Don't you mean you have an excuse to offer me? And as we are in agreement that what you did is inexcusable, I don't see much point in continuing this." He finished his wine in a long swallow and set the glass aside. "Let's talk about Blake."

"All right." She set her glass on the side table, although it was a sacrifice she'd rather not have made. But she had to look as strong as he did. She had to be as strong as she had ever been. Before. Before Jack. Before Blake. Before everything went wrong for her. "Blake is the reason I had to leave, Collier. He's also the reason I had to come back."

"No." The word was spoken softly, but it turned her blood to ice. "Don't use him as your excuse. Don't do it."

"You'd prefer a lie, I know. In some ways, so would I. But lies are what brought us to tonight. I think it's time we began telling the truth, don't you?"

"Would that be the truth about your affair? Or the truth about your getting in the car and disappearing without a word? Tell me, Meredith, how many lies add up to the truth?"

"I don't know."

"And which lie is the one that put you over the top? Which lie made you decide to abandon your child?"

"I didn't abandon him."

"Yes, you did. You did the worst thing you could have done. The worst."

"Worse than passing on a defective gene?" She gave the crime the weightiness it deserved, making sure he heard the awful, very honest guilt in her words. "I don't think I saw it that way." She crossed her legs, smoothed the fabric of her slacks. "I left because I couldn't stay, because I was depressed and afraid and struggling to make sense of my life. I left because I couldn't bear to look at my baby. I left because I had to. Because of what I'd already done to my son. I ruined his life, Collier. Ruined it even before it began."

"And you thought running away would make it better?"

"I didn't intend to run away. I didn't plan it. All I remember clearly is that one minute I was driving up to the window at the dry cleaners and the next I was passing a sign that welcomed me to Colorado."

"And since you'd made it that far, what the hell, might as well go all the way, right? Too late to turn around. Too late to pick up the phone and tell me there was a problem."

"If I'd been able to tell you, Collier, I would never have gone. If I'd been able to talk to you about Blake, about how I felt about his . . . his situation, about how scared I was, how guilty I felt, we wouldn't be here now. I'd be upstairs, rocking him to sleep, instead of in here trying to explain to you why I had to leave, why I felt I had no other choice."

"You never rocked him to sleep before you left. What happened? Did you locate some maternal feelings while the rest of us were searching the state for you?"

At least he was angry. That was a positive sign. Staring at the closed door, she wondered if Mattie was upstairs in the nursery, if she was rocking Blake to sleep. She thought about his sweet baby face, the powdery smell of him. She thought about this house and how much she loved it, how glad she was to be back in it. Despite the unpleasantness she was experiencing inside this room.

"I never meant to hurt you, Collier. I never meant to hurt Blake. That was the last thing I meant to do when I walked into that airport and bought a ticket."

"Bought a ticket to the west coast with a credit card. *Jack's* credit card, unless I'm mistaken. That sounds like premeditation. Considerable premeditation."

Keeping her face in profile, her head slightly bent so that Collier could not see her eyes, she took a deep breath. "I don't know how to explain what I did other than to say it's like I've been sleepwalking for months. Since Blake was born. Since before that. Since Mother had the stroke. I didn't realize I was running away that day. Honestly, I didn't. Jack made all the plans. He talked about it all the time. How I could drive the car to Denver or St. Louis or Kansas City and park it in one of those off-site lots. How I could get a flight to L.A. and we could meet at the airport there. He gave me the credit card, stuck it in my purse . . . just in case. I never intended to use it. I meant to cut it up and throw it away, but that day . . . Well, there it was when I reached into my wallet to pay for your dry cleaning. And something snapped."

"You make it sound so easy, Meredith. Something snapped. You couldn't help it. It wasn't your fault."

"Jack did make it easy. He made everything easy. You, on the other hand, made everything difficult. I couldn't talk to you. You wouldn't talk to me. You ignored the problems, Collier, so I ignored them too. At least I tried. Until they ate a hole through my heart."

"Are you saying this is my fault?"

She had to pause, regroup. Think. She looked longingly at her drink. But she would not reach for it. She would not show that weakness. "I never said it was your fault. I'm trying to explain as best I can what happened."

He said nothing to encourage or discourage her. In her brief glances, she could see no sign of softening in him. She had a long way to go. A long way yet to go.

"I drove to Denver, I bought the ticket and I got on the plane and I went to Seattle with Jack. I slept for a week. Maybe longer. I didn't know about the search, Collier. I wasn't aware of what was happening here. Please believe me. Jack said he'd taken care of letting people know I was all right. I shouldn't have left it to him, but I was . . ." She let the words trail away dramatically. "I was . . ."

"Sleepwalking," he supplied. "I believe you said you were sleepwalking."

She uncrossed her legs, rose, picked up her drink and took it to the bar, where she added another inch of courage to what was still left in the glass. "Piety doesn't suit you, Collier. It's easy to condemn me now, but if it had been you who carried the defective gene, you who looked at your son and knew it was your fault he was born imperfect, you might see this differently."

He considered that. At least, finally, he was considering something she'd said. "I might see it differently," he admitted. "But I wouldn't have had an affair to ease my guilt. You were with Jack as far back as a year ago. You didn't sleepwalk into that relationship. You went into it with your eyes wide open."

"Do you honestly need me to explain that, Collier? Not excuse it, but explain it. Are we going to pretend you had absolutely no idea—even as far back as a year ago—that there were any problems in our marriage?"

"Whatever my faults as a husband, they don't add up to permission for you to have an affair. I'm not going down that road, Meredith. You chose. That responsibility is yours and yours alone."

"I understand I made a poor choice. I understand you're angry with me. I understand you feel I should be punished for what I did." She turned to fully face him. "But don't you see? I have been punished. I am being punished. Nothing you can say to me will make me feel worse. Can you possibly understand that?"

The anger snapped in his eyes, and she was glad to see it. The sooner he let loose with that anger, got it out into the open, the sooner they could move past this. "Let me be sure I've got this. You feel you've been punished? And that further punishment is unnecessary. Is that what you think?"

"What I think is that there is nothing I can do except apologize and beg your forgiveness. You can punish me from now until November and it will still come down to the same thing. You'll either forgive me or you won't."

"Believe it or not, Meredith, I have no desire to see you punished. I'm not interested in making you pay. But I'm not interested in forgiveness either. There are consequences to your actions. We both have to deal with that. Forgiveness won't change the path you've put us on."

"It would be a place to start."

"I can't see a happy ending for us. You've already caused me too much pain, cost me too much."

Pain. He felt pain. That meant he still felt something. He still loved her. Beneath that pain, he had to still love her. "I'm especially sorry about the governor's race. If I'd known . . ."

"If you'd known. Then none of this would have happened, is that what you're saying?" The lift at the corner of his mouth held both skepticism and regret.

Regret. There. That could be the wedge she needed.

"I am sorry, Collier. I'd do anything if I could fix this, if you would let me try. I want to fix it. Please, give me a chance. We can save our marriage. We can make it work. You can still enter the governor's race. It's not too late."

"The governor's mansion appeals to you, doesn't it, Meredith? Well, here's a tip. Kiss that fantasy good-bye. It's not gonna happen."

"That's your choice to make, Collier. But Bill Riggs believes you'll sweep the primaries and have so much momentum going by late summer that you can win the election in an easy walk."

"When did you talk to Bill Riggs?"

A slip. She hadn't meant to tell him that. Not tonight, anyway. "This afternoon. Mattie told me about the Lucman scandal. She said I'd cost you the chance to run. I wanted to hear that for myself. So I called Bill."

"You called Bill," he said with a shake of his head.

She brought up her chin. "He didn't sound that surprised to hear from me. And he told me he was glad I'd decided to get 'on board.' He seemed very happy that I'd called."

"Forget it, Meredith. I'm not running."

"But you've always wanted to make that race."

"Oh, I will make that race, Meredith. Just not this time. And not with you. One of those unanticipated consequences I mentioned."

"Don't be stupid, Collier. There may not be a next time. I've heard you say it yourself a million times. Timing is everything, and this is the luckiest piece of timing you're ever likely to get. You know as well as I do that you're being handed a straight shot at the career you've always meant to have. With a successful term in the governor's office, you can run for a Senate seat. Or shoot straight for the Presidency. From the governor's office, you can choose to do anything you want. Eight years from now you might not have Bill behind you. Twelve years from now you might not be able to get the backing you have right now. This is the time, Collier. Don't let it slip away."

"You've very eager to be the First Lady of Oklahoma. That's why you're here, isn't it? That's why you came back."

She dampened her eagerness. "That isn't fair. I'm here because I love you. I came back because I love you. I came back because this is where I belong."

"A minute ago you said you came back because of Blake."

"One reason doesn't preclude the other. You are my husband. Blake is my son. You can give up the election if you want, but that won't change the way I feel about you or my belief that our marriage is worth saving."

"Being the governor's wife would be a nice bonus to that, though, wouldn't it?"

She wouldn't get sucked into agreeing. Or disagreeing. Too many protests now would not serve her purpose. "I don't care about the election. I care about trying to get my life back. I care about making amends for the wrong I've done. I care about what happens to my son."

"So much that you couldn't be here for his first surgery."

"I'm here now, Collier. Isn't that what really counts? Doesn't that matter?"

"Maybe you should ask Mattie."

This was new. Meredith raised an eyebrow, a show of unconcern she didn't feel. Didn't feel at all. "Since when does my sister get a vote in this family?"

"She's shouldered your responsibilities since the day after you left. I think that entitles her to offer an opinion."

"Her opinion seems to be that the moment I crossed the county line, I forfeited any claim to my mother's affection, Blake, this house, the dog, and probably you, as well. She was eager to offer me that opinion just this afternoon. I'm sure if you ask, she'll be glad to repeat it for you. Or has she already told you how she feels?"

An odd look came into his eyes. A look he turned away from her, almost as if . . . as if he wanted to hide it from her. Meredith felt the sudden chill of a complication she hadn't anticipated. One for which she had not prepared an answer. Or a question.

She disguised her quick calculations by walking, casually, to the bay window, looking out at the street-lights, the traffic passing by. She sipped her drink and went over the conversations she'd had in this house today. Earlier with Mattie. Now with Collier. Something in both had tweaked her suspicions, but try as she might, she couldn't come up with a concrete threat.

Mattie, the good little sister, had obviously been busy. Playing house. Playing Mommy. Pretending she could fit into Meredith's life. Even pretending, maybe, she could take Meredith's place.

But on her best day, Mattie posed no real threat. Even if she had tempted Collier to do with her what Meredith had done with Jack, he wouldn't have succumbed. That was the thing about Collier. There was no reason to doubt him. No reason to believe he would ever be interested in Mattie. Not in any way that mattered.

"You owe Mattie more than you can ever repay," he said quietly. "She's been a good sister to you. A better friend than you've ever been to her."

Much as she hated it, Meredith knew she had to be gracious, act grateful. "She obviously loves Blake."

"As much as if he were hers. Oddly, the shape of his hands hasn't bothered her at all."

Meredith had to get out of this quagmire now, or drown in the attempt. "We have to talk about him, Collier. About what's best for our son."

He crossed his arms at his chest, waited for her to tell him.

"If you're serious about this . . . this separation—"

"I believe divorce is the word you're searching for."

"I will ask for custody," she said.

"As will I. May the best parent win."

"He's seven months old. He needs his mother."

"He's eight months old and he needed his mother the day she walked out the door and didn't come back. He needed his mother the day they operated on his hand. He needed his mother the very first day we brought him into this house and handed him over to a baby nurse. This has never been about what *he* needs, Meredith. It's always been about you and what you want. I'm ashamed to think about all the things I should have done to protect him from what you wanted, what you convinced me he needed. It took Mattie to show me how to make him a real part of this family, not keep him in the nursery like some shameful secret."

Meredith didn't have to call for the tears. They came of their own accord. A deep, true sadness, welling up in her throat, burning behind her eyes, spilling out in a silent, cloying acknowledgment of all the ways she had failed. All she had risked for such a meaningless escape. "I'm sorry, Collier," she whispered. "I'm so very sorry."

The glass in her hand slipped and he was there to catch it, take it from her, set it aside. He was there to help her back to the sofa, to sit beside her. She didn't ask for comfort. He didn't offer it. But eventually, his arm slid around her and she put her face against his shoulder and cried. She cried until she had no more tears, until her nose and throat were thick with mucous, until her mouth was dry, and it hurt to breathe. She cried because Blake wasn't perfect. She cried because his imperfection caused her pain. She cried because she had come so close to losing everything that mattered.

And in the crying, she soaked Collier's shirt and tried to reach his heart.

She thought she had, as tender as he was with her afterward. Getting her Kleenex. Getting her a glass of water. Talking to her in a voice pitched low and gentle. But when she put her arms around him, raised up to press her lips to his in a conciliatory kiss, he pulled away as if she'd struck him, moved away as if she might try to do it again.

"Meredith," he said. And that was all.

She straightened up, revived her pride, presented him with a half-smile. "I'm sorry," she said, but promised herself that was the last time she would give him those words free of charge. "I'm feeling a little vulnerable just now. My mother raised me to believe I couldn't do anything wrong, but it turns out I'm not perfect, after all."

"I never asked you to be perfect."

"Yes, you did, Collier. You married me because I was the perfect candidate to become your wife. You had me in mind a long time before we met. None of the other women you dated measured up. You held out for perfection. You needed a wife who was beautiful and smart and ambitious to help you get where you meant to go. I'm still that someone. Imperfect as I've turned out to be, you still need me. I made a terrible mistake in leaving you, I admit that. I've told you why as best I can. I've apologized. I've offered to do whatever it takes to make amends. You can die on this hill, Collier, but you have to know that divorce is not your best option. It's not best for Blake.

It's not best for me. It's not best for you. It's certainly not the best way to get where you want to go. Stick with your pride and we all lose. Give up a little of that self-righteous honor and we can all win."

"You failed to mention self-respect."

She looked him square in the eye. "Grow up. Life and politics are full of little sacrifices." Turning on her heel, she headed for the door. "I'm staying with Ross and Claire. Don't look so surprised. They're my friends, too. Not everyone is as unforgiving as you." Opening the door, she bent to pet André, who had waited patiently for her to come out, looked at her adoringly now that she had. "You can reach me there, but I will be coming here every day to spend time with my son."

"I'll let Mattie know."

The way he said it burned through her. *Mattie.* The good sister.

One day soon, she intended to set Mattie straight about a number of things. Beginning, and possibly ending, with the suggestion that she try living her own life for a change.

"Think about what I've said, Collier."

"I will. You should think about what I've said too. You should also get yourself a lawyer."

It was an empty threat. He'd come around. He just wanted her to pay first. Well, she would. She had no trouble swallowing her pride in order to get what she wanted.

"Goodnight, Collier. For the record, I know what I did is inexcusable, but I don't believe it is unforgivable. I deserve another chance. *We* deserve a second chance."

She walked out before he could say anything else,

picked up her bag and walked out the front door into the crisp night air.

Leaving Collier and Blake—and Mattie—safe and snug inside.

Inside *her* house.

Little sacrifices.

Meredith kept her chin up, her pride intact, as she walked down the sidewalk to her rental car. Tomorrow, she'd get the Mercedes back. The day after, she'd take back her house. The day after that, Collier would have had time to think, to look ahead, to understand what was on the line. Then she'd take back her life.

She deserved to get it back.

After all, she had cried real tears.

CHAPTER
NINETEEN

Lying on his rug, Andy gnawed contentedly on a plastic toy. Blake's toy. The rubber duck in the purple hat. The toy thrown on the floor and snatched by the dog only moments before.

Sitting in his high chair, Blake happily tossed more toys, plastic measuring cups, and the occasional Cheerio onto the floor. Then he looked expectantly at his aunt, waiting for her to pick them up so he could do it again.

Standing by the sink, Mattie made a face at both boy and poodle, tried to ignore the accumulating clutter long enough to pull her body into one long, slow bend. But the minute she reached for the ankle she'd propped on the counter, she felt the strain. She'd been neglecting her barre work, neglecting her daily stretches. And the neglect pulled taut up and down her legs, in her arms, and across her shoulders. There was no good reason for her negligence. She could get up earlier, go to bed later. She could work out while Blake napped. Morning or afternoon. She had the same amount of time in each day that she'd had before. Other than Meredith's daily drop-by visits, nothing had changed.

Except that in the three days since Meredith's return, Mattie had obsessed a bit about the house, become more conscious of keeping it neater, nicer, more clutter free. Childish as she knew it was, she wanted her sister to see how well she was doing. She wanted Meredith to know the good job she'd done. Even though she shouldn't give Meredith's opinion a thought, she was determined her sister would find nothing negative to say to her about the house. About Blake. Even about the poodle.

It was stupid. She was ashamed of herself for caring one way or the other. But old habits died hard and she knew Meredith noticed. Even if she pretended she didn't.

A cramp seized Mattie's thigh, bit in and held on, a good reminder that thinking about her sister was a painful waste of time. Pulling her knee toward her chest, she hopped around the kitchen on one foot, tried to get the cramp to let go. The dog looked up. Blake stopped trying to get a whole fistful of Cheerios into his mouth. His cast scraped across the high chair tray in his excitement and cereal scattered across the floor.

That was the moment Meredith breezed into the kitchen through the back door.

"Cramp?" Meredith diagnosed the problem in a glance as she shrugged out of her coat.

A new coat, Mattie noticed. A very nice, expensive-looking new coat. It must have been cold in Seattle.

"You've been neglecting your stretches," Meredith said, leaning down to take the duck away from André. "Think how appalled Miss Victoria would be if she knew."

Mattie stared at the cool, brisk way her sister walked into the pantry to throw away the mangled toy, walked back out and over to the sink, where she washed her hands. And dried them. And never stepped on a single Cheerio. How did she do that? Walk in and own the place. No glance around to orient herself. No hesitation. No apology. No explanations. She just walked in as if she'd never walked out.

Mattie would have been consumed—*consumed*—with guilt. But then, she would never have done what Meredith did. She would never have left her husband, much less her child. She would never have left her life as if it didn't matter.

"I see you've had your morning snack." Meredith's smiles were all for Blake, who took them with an answering grin as she unfastened the safety strap that kept him in the high chair, took off the Cheerio-cluttered tray, and lifted him up and out. "Is it time for his bath now?"

Mattie put her foot down and rubbed her palm hard across her thigh, taking the question as the courtesy Meredith meant for it to be. The minute she walked in, Meredith sucked up the power like a vacuum cleaner. This was her house, no matter what she had done, regardless of her disgrace, and she consistently reminded Mattie in little ways. But if she got her kicks that way, who cared? Mattie lived in the house now. She got Blake up in the morning and got to kiss him goodnight. She could wander upstairs and down as she chose. She spent time talk-ing to Collier, learning about him, letting their friendship grow.

Meredith could be as courteous as she wanted for the few hours she was here each day. And welcome.

"You can give him a bath or just clean him up and get him ready for his nap. Either way is fine." It was a cheap shot, tacking on that *oh-thanks-for-doing-that-for-me sentence.* Giving it in an offhand tone. But her leg hurt and she thought Meredith deserved a few cheap shots.

She'd like to mention the conversations she and Collier had had about her. But that would tip a little too far toward retaliation and Mattie wasn't going to do that. Besides, their conversations were less about Meredith than about the fallout from her betrayal, more about Blake and his needs, more about what the future might hold for all of them. After that one closed-door session with Collier, there had been no more exchanges between Meredith and Collier. At least, none that Mattie knew about. And she be-lieved Collier would have told her.

They shared many sweet moments, even though there would be no more kisses, not so much as the brush of hands, not even a whisper that wasn't platonic.

Except that nothing between them felt platonic at all.

Mattie didn't know what lay ahead for them, didn't even want to project out that far. For now, the moment they had was enough. It was safe, it was sweet, and it was enough.

For all she knew, these moments might be all she and Collier ever had. She meant to enjoy them for what they were, not hold them hostage to what might be.

"Um, Mattie?" Meredith had carried Blake as far as the doorway, but stopped there and turned back. "Don't you think it's time to hire another nurse? Someone more sociable, maybe, than Mrs. Oliver, but someone who could help with his therapy once the cast comes off. Even with me being close by, Collier's going to need someone when you leave."

Mattie didn't know why that caught her by surprise. Of course, she would be leaving. Once Alice was released from the Fleming Center. Once Blake's cast came off. She'd be back often, of course, but still Collier would have to hire help.

Or let Meredith take over the full care of her son.

"I'll talk to Collier about it," she said, thinking she could postpone that a little while. Another week. Or two. Or three or four.

"When are you going back?" Meredith asked, somewhat pointedly. "To Dallas?"

"I don't know. Do you have a timetable in mind for me?"

Meredith looked surprised, but Mattie knew her too well to think she was. She had an agenda. Always had. Always would. All Mattie had to do now was figure out what it was.

"Oh, no. Collier has made it very clear to me that you're in charge here and I'm doing my best to respect his wishes. I don't like it, but I am trying."

That much was true. In her way, she was trying.

"But it did occur to me what an intrusion this is on your time. You were enrolled in your last semester of classes. And I know you must be anxious to get back to teaching."

Mattie hadn't thought about school. Or about teaching. Well, of course, she'd thought about it. She'd dropped her grad courses for the semester, postponed her graduation. But she'd pick that up again next fall. And she did miss the school and her students. But all that was *there*. Blake needed her here. Collier needed her here. And Mattie liked being needed. She liked feeling that she belonged. "Amazingly enough the dance studio is doing fine without me."

"Hmm." Meredith shifted Blake's weight on her hip. "The more amazing thing to me is that you seem to be doing fine without the dance studio."

She shouldn't ask. She knew she should not ask. "What does that mean?"

"Nothing," Meredith said too quickly, with too much innocence in the lift of her brow. "Dance has always been so important to you. It's just interesting to me that you could leave it behind so easily."

"I didn't leave it behind. And it hasn't been easy." Mattie knew she sounded defensive, but she couldn't help it. "In case you forgot, there was a family emergency. Several of them in a row. I needed to be here."

"I'm not criticizing you, Mat. I just thought you'd be anxious to get back to Miss Mattie's School of Dance."

"And Drama," she tacked on out of habit. The school did feel very far away lately. Like a part of another life. Like something she had left behind. She should never have taken Jack's money to open it. Even as a loan. That financial burden had tainted her joy in it. A few days ago she'd even thought she might ask Cynthia if she wanted to take over the school. But Meredith didn't need to know that. "I'll go back when I feel Mother is well enough to go with me."

"Oh." Again, the shift of baby weight, the subtle air of surprise. "I thought you'd go sooner than that. She's got another ten days to two weeks in rehab and then Dr. Roberts wants her to spend another two months at a nursing home here, so he can keep an eye on her. I don't think he's happy with her progress. She might have to stay at the Fleming Center even longer. That's a long time for you to be away from your business, Mattie."

Meredith was after information. Not about the school. She'd never been very interested in that. She was after something much closer to her own heart.

"I don't know," Mattie said. "Maybe I'll decide to close Miss Mattie's and open a school here."

"Here?" This time the surprise was genuine. "You're thinking about moving back here? Why?"

But before Mattie could open her mouth, Meredith supplied the answer. Everything about her, expression, manner, tone of voice, changed. Even her eyes glinted with warning. "This isn't going to last, Mattie. You have to know it cannot last."

"I don't know what you're talking about."

"Don't you? Isn't this"—she gestured widely with her free hand—"everything you always wanted? My life. My house. My baby. Even my husband?"

"How can you say that to me? After what—"

"After what I've done. I know. I say it because it's obvious you're in love with Collier. I can see it in your eyes. You don't even try to hide it. But the worst part about it—the *worst* part, Mattie—is that I'm very much afraid he thinks he's in love with you, too."

Love. Such a small word for such a huge emotion. Did she love Collier? Did he love her? Yes. And no. Those were questions for the future. For a year from now. Not for today. Not for here. Not open for discussion with Meredith.

"That would be terrible for you, wouldn't it, Meredith? To lose Collier's love? You've always taken love for granted, believed anyone you wanted to love you, would. You thought nothing could change the way Collier felt about you, that he would love you forever. No matter what you did. Love is a gift. A precious, wonderful gift. And you handed it off like it meant nothing."

"I didn't. I lost my bearings. I disappeared because he was taking me for granted. He no longer saw me. He no longer talked to me. He—"

"He wasn't paying enough attention to you."

"You don't understand. I wouldn't expect you to." She paused, visibly regained control over that tiny tremor in her voice. Or maybe the pause was strictly for effect and she'd had control all along. "I was confused, mixed up and I made an awful mistake. A terrible mistake and I'm paying for it. But I'm telling you, Mattie, I won't cede my life over to you without a fight. And I won't let you cost Collier the chance of a lifetime."

"Me? You think *I* cost him his chance?"

"You will cost him his career if you don't get out of this house. Politicians are public figures and every reporter in this state has his eye on Collier right now. I don't know what he was thinking when he let you stay here."

"Maybe he was thinking that Blake's more important than public opinion. Maybe he was thinking about what would be best for his son."

"You don't belong here, Mattie."

"It's you who no longer belongs, Meredith. Not me."

She might have said more. Meredith certainly would have.

If the phone hadn't rung out a shrill interruption, demanded a time-out.

It rang. And rang again.

Mattie wasn't going to meet the challenge she saw in her sister's eyes and answer.

Meredith made no move to do so, either.

So they stood, not saying a word, but the dare bristled like a static charge between them. As if the phone call was a test. Who had the right to answer? Who didn't? If Meredith picked it up and had to hand the phone off to Mattie . . . well, that would be a loss. If Mattie wanted to pick up, she'd have to get past Meredith to do it. So when the answering machine clicked on, there was only the hum of a hangup. And a tense, angry silence everywhere else.

Then, as if she'd won the round, Meredith smiled, turned on her heel and carried Blake upstairs.

It wasn't until Collier slapped open the back door fifteen minutes later and Mattie saw his face that she remembered the phone call, knew it had been important, the message too raw and painful to leave on the machine.

Alice had had another stroke.

She was gone before her daughters had a chance to say good-bye.

* * *

They held the funeral at the Presbyterian Church. The church where Alice had played the organ on alternating Sundays for much of her adult life. The church where Meredith had married Collier in an elaborate ceremony befitting a retiring Miss Oklahoma and a bright, rising-star young attorney. The church where, as a child, Mattie had discovered a great hiding place and stayed in it for an entire afternoon before the choir director found her and returned her to her mother.

After the service, people streamed through the house, paying their respects to the family, expressing sympathy and support. If anyone thought about the time, a few weeks back, when this house had played host to some of these same people, under similar, but much more uncertain, circumstances, it wasn't apparent. No one mentioned it. Meredith's absence was already filed away under curiosities, a topic of interest for when the weather turned mild and the grass began to grow and there wasn't much else to ponder. By summer, it wouldn't even rate very high as gossip. Unless it became an issue in the upcoming election.

Mattie didn't know why the election was still a question mark in her mind. Collier had said he didn't intend to run, and she believed him. Why wouldn't she? But no one else seemed to think he meant what he said. The deadline was drawing near, but the conventional wisdom predicted a last minute registration and then a campaign that would leave all other candidates in the shade. It seemed clear from snatches of overheard conversation that after the scandal in Oklahoma City, the comings and goings of the mayor's wife was small potatoes. Whatever Meredith had done, whatever her reasons for leaving, it all paled beside the idea that Collier would be the next governor.

It was strange. No one said anything directly. Collier had stated he did not mean to run. Yet everyone seemed to consider it a settled thing that he would.

And today, on the day of her mother's funeral, Mattie didn't hear a word about the governor or the election and yet she felt it in the air all around her. People were talking. They just weren't talking to her.

For which she was grateful. Losing her mother had been an unexpected blow, so much harder than she would have believed possible. As a daughter, her feelings had always been complicated and seldom positive, but Alice's death had left her with an immense sadness and an empty, yearning sense of great loss. Having a full house helped. She was glad so many had come. There were people Mattie hadn't seen since childhood, school friends and friends of her mother's. Cali Snyder came, sat with Mattie for a long while, reminiscing about their time with Miss Victoria, asking about Miss Mattie's School of Dance and Drama, wondering if Mattie had any advice on how to interest a tomboy in ballet classes.

Mattie was glad to talk about other things, lighter matters. And eventually she gravitated onto the landing and sat with Linda on the upper steps, out of the way, a barrier to any guest wandering upstairs who might disturb the baby. Meredith, always a step ahead of the details, had hired another baby nurse. She'd interviewed several candidates and presented the top three to Collier, who chose Jenny, a quiet, pretty, young woman with a sweet smile. Linda had approved her. Mattie liked her. Blake had taken to her immediately. But then his emerging personality was much like his father's.

Even now, Collier was in his study, people going in and out, seeking him out, wanting him to know they were there to honor his family's loss, to offer him support. In whatever context he might need it.

Long after Cali left and Linda went to the kitchen to begin putting away the leftover food, Mattie stayed on the steps. From her vantage point, she could see most of the foyer and a good-sized section of the study. She could see the living room, too, but she was only interested in watching Collier. Observing the way he worked the crowd. She couldn't hear him from here, but she didn't need to know what he was saying to know it was well-received and always the right thing to say. From one person to the next, from handshake to a grip of the forearm to a full-out hug, he responded to each person in a manner that left an impression. A good, sincere impression.

No wonder the house was full.

Alice, certainly, had had her own social circle. At least before the first stroke. But the majority were here because of Collier. He drew them. And they left feeling he knew them and valued them as a close, personal friend.

He just had that effect on people.

Meredith walked through the foyer below, stopped to speak to an older woman—Diana Rawlins, who'd been in Alice's bridge club—asked her about her daughter, Julie, who had recently moved across the country to marry a man she'd met over the Internet. Mrs. Rawlins left with Meredith's promise to drop by and give a few quick lessons on navigating the Web. Mattie watched her sister turn to the next person, another woman, another member of the bridge club. Meredith kept her movements and voice subdued, pitched low for the occasion, kept everything about her manner gracious and grateful, asked questions, gave answer, made promises she would, undoubtedly, keep. In some form or another. If she wasn't sincere, no one would ever know. Meredith knew how to make a good impression too. She knew how to maintain the image of perfection. She always had. She belonged to this house, in this life. She was perfect for it.

And yet she'd so recently proved she was far from perfect.

That was Alice's legacy. Two daughters flawed by their mother's choice to see one as perfect, one as a mistake. Mattie had always thought not belonging, being the unwanted, was the bigger burden to carry into life. But now she wondered. The pressure of too many expectations had to have been a heavy burden, too. Alice had pinned on Meredith every hope, every dream, every flight of fancy she nurtured, had tried in so many ways to live vicariously through her. Just as Mattie had struggled to get Alice's attention, maybe Meredith had struggled to escape it.

Meredith glanced up, aware of Mattie's observation. She didn't smile. Sadness wreathed her eyes, trembled across her lips. A reflection of the sorrow Mattie felt. Their mother was gone. They were all she'd left behind. Their lives, going forward, were all that would be left of hers. They were now each other's only connection to childhood, and for better or worse, Mattie didn't want to lose that, too. A few days ago, she had hated her sister. She was still angry with her. Maybe she would stay angry for a very long time. But in that moment, in that glance between sisters, she knew forgiveness was the right choice.

She had spent too much of her life sitting on the sidelines, watching Meredith dance the parts she wanted, wanting to trade places, wishing she could be as beautiful, as talented, as *good* as her sister. And all the time, she had let her own gifts languish. She had chosen to be less.

It was suddenly as clear as glass to her. She had chosen to live in her sister's shadow, chosen to see Meredith as the star, chosen to put herself in the audience instead of on the stage. Meredith hadn't stolen anything from Mattie. Not her childhood dreams. Not her mother's attention. Not even Jack.

Mattie had given it away. Handed it over because in her heart she believed that she didn't deserve it and that Meredith did. She had traded off her own talent and potential because she'd believed it wasn't as grand, as dazzling as it was supposed to be. She had stood back instead of stepping out.

But this was an end of it.

She could choose the life she wanted. This life. Meredith's life.

Or a life Mattie had yet to imagine.

This was her moment.

And, now that it was here, she knew exactly what choice to make.

CHAPTER
TWENTY

"What is this?" Collier asked quietly from the doorway. "The famous disappearing act of Mattie Owens?"

Mattie looked up, smiled at him over Blake's sleeping head. She kept rocking, patting her nephew's warm back, loving the feel of his cheek pressed against her shoulder. She would miss these times. Soon he'd be walking and talking and not as amenable to being rocked by his aunt.

Collier came closer. "You disappeared from the gathering downstairs a long time ago. I figured you'd been captured by my mother and forced to wash dishes and clean up the mess, but she said she hadn't seen you for a couple of hours. Have you been up here with him all this time?"

She nodded, kept rocking. This was going to be harder than she'd thought. "I came up to say goodnight to him. But he held up his arms and the next thing I knew I was in the rocker and he was fast asleep."

"You could have put him back into bed."

"I know."

"It's been a hard day."

"Yes. Mother would have liked the turnout."

"I'm sure she would have liked to be here in the big middle of it."

"I miss her. Isn't that crazy? I didn't like her very much. I don't think she ever liked me, but I miss her."

He knelt beside the rocking chair, laid his hand over hers. "I think she liked you, Mattie. She just wasn't good at showing it."

"That's a diplomatic way of putting it."

"You want to hear something that will make you smile? Meredith is downstairs right now, trying to bring my mother around. As if that's ever going to happen."

"It will, you know. Eventually."

His forehead creased in an expression half-skeptical, half-curious. She loved the way that happened. She was going to miss that too. All the different expressions that crossed his face in the course of a day. Or an hour. She'd miss those hours. And the moments they spent together here in the nightlight glow of the nursery.

"I don't see that happening."

Mattie met his eyes then, gave him a glimpse of what she was thinking. "You'll make it happen."

"I definitely don't see that happening."

"She is Blake's mother. In one way or another, she will always be in your life. Not on the edges of it. In it. Because you love him, you have to forgive her."

He didn't contradict her. He couldn't. That was the kind of man he was.

"I'm going back to Dallas in the morning. It's time I got back to my own life."

"But I thought . . . ?" His words trailed off. They both knew he'd thought she would stay. Indefinitely. And forever.

"I know. I thought so too. The idea of us, of you and me and Blake together as far as we can see into the future . . . that's lovely. It's the most beautiful idea I've ever had." She lifted her hand from Blake and stroked the back of it across Collier's cheek. "But it's just an idea. It's not reality. And if we try to make it real . . . well, I don't know that we can. I don't know that we should."

"I love you, Mattie. I know we're only at the beginning of this, but I wouldn't say it if I didn't know in my heart it was true. If I wasn't sure we have the potential to be more than just a lovely idea."

"I love you too. I love Blake. In another place, another time, maybe he would be our baby, this would be our house, we would be man and wife. But that place isn't here and that time isn't now. You have a plan for your life, Collier. I'd only interfere with that."

"I don't see how you could."

She smiled and loved him all the more for saying it with such conviction. "Oh, I could. I'm not cut out for the life you want. You had the right sister for that life all along."

"I think that has to be my call."

"It is. You made it a long time ago. Meredith can help you go where you want to go, Collier."

"I don't need her to get there. I don't want her."

"How about this? She needs you and Blake needs

her. That's a triangle you can't get out of. She made a mistake. A big, honking, hairy mistake. A huge one. Actually, more than one. She made several. Maybe she's been building up to it all her life, I don't know. But that doesn't matter. What matters is that you're going to forgive her, Collier. If not today, tomorrow. If not this week, then the next. You will give her another chance, because that's the kind of person you are. You ought to give your marriage a second chance, because you love your son. I wish I could go on believing she deserves to lose everything, but I can't. Talk to her. Go to counseling. Do what you can to save the marriage. Maybe it will work. Maybe it won't. But you should try. And you should make this campaign. Swallow your pride and do now what you're going to do sometime later, anyway. Forgive her and get on with your life."

"You're an unlikely champion for her cause, Mattie. What brought about your change of heart?"

"I buried my mother today. Forgiving my sister is surprisingly easy after that."

"So you vote to set aside what we want in favor of doing what Meredith wants."

"This isn't a sweet deal for her, Collier. She's lost more than she can ever regain. Your love. Your respect. Your trust. My admiration. My respect. My envy. She's really going to miss that last one, you know. She loves being envied. Meredith isn't getting what she wants. She may not realize that for awhile, but ultimately she will."

The rocking chair moved in silence for a moment. Blake slept on. Collier's hand stayed, warm and dear, on Mattie's.

"What about you?" he asked. "You're walking away from this empty-handed."

That was the beauty of it, she thought, although she wasn't sure he would understand. "But not empty-hearted. I have you and Blake in my life now. I don't mean to give up our friendship or the close relationship I mean to continue with my one and only nephew. Maybe there'll even come a time when I can have a meaningful relationship with my sister. That doesn't seem very likely, but none of us can know what the future may hold. For now, I need to step outside her shadow, see what it feels like to stand in my own light for a change."

"You're going to need a good pair of sunglasses."

That made her smile. "I think you're right."

Blake sighed in her arms. "Before I leave in the morning, I want to sign his cast. That way, when he's in kindergarten, he can take it to Show and Tell and talk about how he had surgery when he was eight months old and his Aunt Mattie was there and his Nana and Grandad, too."

"My mother would rather eat worms than put ink on that plaster."

"She'll sign."

Collier's fingers tightened over hers, then he rose and took Blake from her. He patted him softly as he walked to the crib, laid him down in it, covered him with a blanket.

It was a sweet memory to add to her collection, to take with her. This night. This nursery. This man and his son.

Mattie knew she could stay, could choose to belong here.

She could take her sister's life and make it her own. She had the power to choose that course.

But she deserved a life that was finally, really, just hers.

She would leave here tomorrow morning, empty-handed. Free of envy. Free of guilt. Free of wanting to be someone she wasn't. Free to return to the life she had left behind. Free to finally allow herself to have joy in it.

She would leave her mother and her mother's disapproval buried here, where it belonged.

She would leave Collier to follow his own path, to make the race for governor if that's what he truly wanted, to figure out for himself whether to renew his marriage or end it.

She would leave Meredith with the chance to fix what she had broken. A second chance to be the mother Blake deserved, a new opportunity to be the wife Collier needed.

No, leaving empty-handed wasn't a bad thing at all.

It would, Mattie decided, be the start of something very good.

By Best-selling Author
Fern Michaels

Weekend Warriors	0-8217-7589-8	$6.99US/$9.99CAN
Listen to Your Heart	0-8217-7463-8	$6.99US/$9.99CAN
The Future Scrolls	0-8217-7586-3	$6.99US/$9.99CAN
About Face	0-8217-7020-9	$7.99US/$10.99CAN
Kentucky Sunrise	0-8217-7462-X	$7.99US/$10.99CAN
Kentucky Rich	0-8217-7234-1	$7.99US/$10.99CAN
Kentucky Heat	0-8217-7368-2	$7.99US/$10.99CAN
Plain Jane	0-8217-6927-8	$7.99US/$10.99CAN
Wish List	0-8217-7363-1	$7.50US/$10.50CAN
Yesterday	0-8217-6785-2	$7.50US/$10.50CAN
The Guest List	0-8217-6657-0	$7.50US/$10.50CAN
Finders Keepers	0-8217-7364-X	$7.50US/$10.50CAN
Annie's Rainbow	0-8217-7366-6	$7.50US/$10.50CAN
Dear Emily	0-8217-7316-X	$7.50US/$10.50CAN
Sara's Song	0-8217-7480-8	$7.50US/$10.50CAN
Celebration	0-8217-7434-4	$7.50US/$10.50CAN
Vegas Heat	0-8217-7207-4	$7.50US/$10.50CAN
Vegas Rich	0-8217-7206-6	$7.50US/$10.50CAN
Vegas Sunrise	0-8217-7208-2	$7.50US/$10.50CAN
What You Wish For	0-8217-6828-X	$7.99US/$10.99CAN
Charming Lily	0-8217-7019-5	$7.99US/$10.99CAN

Available Wherever Books Are Sold!